"EYE-POPPING."
—*The Washington Post Book World*

"BONE-CHILLING."
—*The New York Times Book Review*

"NAIL-BITING."
—*The Denver Post*

"FILLED WITH FAST ACTION."
—*The Times-Picayune*

"A SUPERIOR THRILLER."
—*Milwaukee Journal Sentinel*

"A superior thriller. But that isn't the only thing that attracts new readers to the series or keeps faithful fans coming back for more. It's Barr's ability to plumb the hidden depths of even a well-known character like Anna; and it's the quality of Barr's writing, her seemingly off-the-cuff observations on human nature and life in general." —*Milwaukee Journal Sentinel*

"*High Country* is filled with energy, especially during a long sequence in which an injured Anna literally runs for her life through the forests of the Sierra Nevada mountains. After writing eleven Pigeon books, Barr obviously hasn't lost her zest for this series or her enthusiasm for Anna."
—*St. Paul Pioneer Press*

"The serene snow country suddenly turns deadly for Anna Pigeon in Barr's riveting twelfth novel . . . an ordeal that will keep readers eagerly turning the pages . . . nail-biting . . . Barr has a true gift for outdoor writing, using the lush snow as natural cover for the violent life in the wild as well as among the park's human custodians. Anyone contemplating a nice winter hike will think twice after entering the wilderness with Anna, but her fans always come back for more." —*Publishers Weekly*

"Nevada Barr at her best . . . She puts Anna in grave danger and takes readers through the chase—both mentally and physically, pitting the woman against nature with only her wits to get her through." —*Green Bay Press-Gazette*

"Barr's even pace and deft characterizations will please series fans while winning her new readers." —*Library Journal*

"Anna finally takes to the high-country trails to meet dangers Barr's eager fans will welcome. Even more appealing than the carefully clued mystery and the exhilarating survey of Yosemite is Barr's matchless control of fictional space, from wide-open to grave-narrow." —*Kirkus Reviews*

TITLES BY NEVADA BARR

HIGH COUNTRY

NEVADA BARR

BERKLEY BOOKS, NEW YORK

THE BERKLEY PUBLISHING GROUP
Published by the Penguin Group
Penguin Group (USA) Inc.
375 Hudson Street, New York, New York 10014, USA
Penguin Group (Canada), 10 Alcorn Avenue, Toronto, Ontario M4V 3B2, Canada
(a division of Pearson Penguin Canada Inc.)
Penguin Books Ltd., 80 Strand, London WC2R 0RL, England
Penguin Group Ireland, 25 St. Stephen's Green, Dublin 2, Ireland (a division of Penguin Books Ltd.)
Penguin Group (Australia), 250 Camberwell Road, Camberwell, Victoria 3124, Australia
(a division of Pearson Australia Group Pty. Ltd.)
Penguin Books India Pvt. Ltd., 11 Community Centre, Panchsheel Park, New Delhi—110 017, India
Penguin Group (NZ), Cnr. Airborne and Rosedale Roads, Albany, Auckland 1310, New Zealand
(a division of Pearson New Zealand Ltd.)
Penguin Books (South Africa) (Pty.) Ltd., 24 Sturdee Avenue, Rosebank, Johannesburg 2196,
South Africa

Penguin Books Ltd., Registered Offices: 80 Strand, London WC2R 0RL, England

This is a work of fiction. Names, characters, places, and incidents either are the product of the author's imagination or are used fictitiously, and any resemblance to actual persons, living or dead, business establishments, events, or locales is entirely coincidental.

HIGH COUNTRY

A Berkley Book / published by arrangement with the author

PRINTING HISTORY
G. P. Putnam's Sons hardcover edition / February 2004
Berkley mass-market edition / February 2005

Copyright © 2004 by Nevada Barr.
Cover art and design by Rob Wood / Wood Ronsaville Harlin.

ISBN: 0-425-19956-8

BERKLEY®
Berkley Books are published by The Berkley Publishing Group,
a division of Penguin Group (USA) Inc.,
375 Hudson Street, New York, New York 10014.
BERKLEY is a registered trademark of Penguin Group (USA) Inc.
The "B" design is a trademark belonging to Penguin Group (USA) Inc.

PRINTED IN THE UNITED STATES OF AMERICA

10 9 8 7 6 5 4 3 2 1

Special thanks to Don and Mary Coelho, John Dill, Letty DeLoatch and, most especially, the woman I want to be when I grow up, Ranger Laurel Boyers.

HIGH
COUNTRY

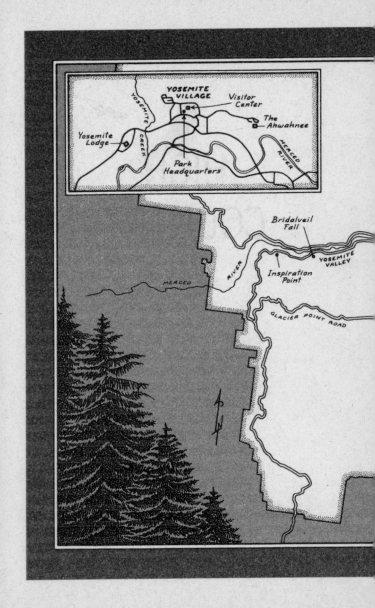

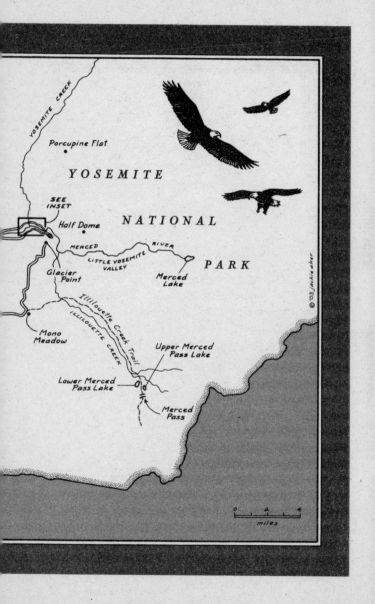

YOSEMITE CREEK

Porcupine Flat

YOSEMITE

SEE INSET

Half Dome

MERCED

LITTLE YOSEMITE VALLEY

RIVER

NATIONAL

PARK

Glacier Point

Merced Lake

Illilouette Creek Trail

ILLILOUETTE CREEK

Mono Meadow

Upper Merced Pass Lake

Lower Merced Pass Lake

Merced Pass

© '03 Jackie aker

0   2   4
miles

CHAPTER

1

"Would you like baked potato or pommes frites with that?" Anna asked politely.

"Can't I get French fries?"

"You bet." Anna wrote: "NY strip w/PF—well done," on the pad.

As the mom and dad at table twenty-nine coaxed suitable orders from a five- and a nine-year-old with hearts set on pizza, Anna let her eyes drift up to the two-story windows enclosing the end of the dining room. Beyond their comforting reflections of safety and warmth stood granite boulders the size of houses. They in turn were dwarfed by ponderosa pines with trunks eight, ten, twelve feet in diameter and these made toylike by the sheer and towering cliff that served as a backdrop. The bones of Sierra Nevada, glistening with half-melted ice, held Yosemite Valley in the rockbound embrace of a ruined Shangri-la, a place where only the youth of the mountains was immortal and people grew old at an alarming rate. On a misty December afternoon the evergreens showed black against the streaked gray of rock: forbidding, dangerous, and, to Anna, utterly seductive. It was as if, should she leave the warm gold and russet of the grand Ahwahnee Hotel and cross the parking lot into the rocks and trees, she, too, would be leached of color, would walk in the world as a ghost, a mountain breeze, the whistle of a hawk's wing.

"Do you have hot dogs?" The reality of Mom's voice cut through Anna's ghost dance with the sharp laser light of a red microfleece-clad arm.

"No hot dogs."

"You oughta have a children's menu with hot dogs," the mother complained.

"I'll suggest it to the chef," Anna lied easily. The chef, a veteran of many four-star establishments, was fanatical in his hatred of hot dogs and only slightly more sanguine on the subject of children.

A turkey quesadilla was settled on, and Anna left the table to walk down the long gallery from the alcove. She'd always wanted to work in Yosemite National Park, but even in her dreams it never crossed her mind she would be there as a waitress.

A waitress coming up on fifty might be an oddity in another establishment, but at the historic Ahwahnee Hotel in Yosemite Valley, built of the very granite and pine it sheltered beneath, carved beams and great stone fireplaces warming the bones of park visitors for over seventy-five years, much of the waitstaff was wrinkled and sere. It was a plum job. Tips were fabulous, openings were rare. As with some of the more venerable clubs, one practically had to be grandfathered in.

Anna had washed in on a tsunami of lies and half-truths: her cover story. The phrase amused her; it was so deliciously cloak-and-dagger. A spy, Anna was a spy. According to Lorraine Knight, Yosemite's chief ranger, it was a necessary bit of drama.

Parks, even the big ones like Yosemite, Yellowstone or the Grand Canyon, were, at least socially, very small towns. Yosemite concessions workers in both the hotel and her less picturesque and pricey sister, Yosemite Lodge, along with the people minding the stores, delis and shops, numbered around twelve hundred. Nearly six hundred NPS people overwintered. In a society of less than two thousand souls, everybody knew everybody at least by sight, if not by name. On the rare occasions when an undercover law enforcement person was called for, a ranger from another park, an unknown face and name, had to be brought in.

Anna was unsure whether it was her law enforcement status or the fact that she'd worked her way through college waiting tables at Pepe Delgado's in San Luis Obispo that inspired her own chief ranger, John Brown, to offer her the assignment when the call went out.

She was pleasantly surprised at how fast her skills came back. She had been wearing a dead—maybe dead, probably dead—woman's clothes both literally and figuratively for less than a week, and already her short-term memory had risen to the challenge. Crawling into trousers of the deceased hadn't been Anna's heart's desire, but a new uniform order would have taken a week or more to arrive. So far the hardest part of the job had been turning her tips over to the Mountain Safety Fund. As long as she was pulling in her pay as a GS-11 District Ranger, she wasn't allowed to keep them. A shame: they dwarfed her salary.

A quick check of the order and she put it up for the chef. Waitstaff desiring to keep the peace double-checked orders. James Wither, a man so lean his large hazel eyes bulged from nearly fleshless sockets and whose jet black hair hung over a forehead lined by at least fifty years of slaving over hot stoves, saw waiters and waitresses as either flawed delivery systems or malicious art vandals bent on destroying his creative visions. Anna had never seen him actually throw knives at busboys or fling trays at salad chefs, but she'd heard the stories and chose to tread lightly.

Several of the longtime servers could talk intelligently about food. These educated few Wither could see and hear. Anna, who shied away from meat but otherwise ate what was easy, cheap or put in front of her, was beneath his notice. This was good. Despite what they said in the movies, a spy needed to be unremarkable. Anna was finding this and the rest of the spying business harder than she'd anticipated. Chatting, drawing people out—being downright likable—was work for her at the best of times. Doing so with ulterior motives was an absolute grind.

When tempted to give it up as a nonstarter—the unapologetic opinion of Leo Johnson, the deputy superintendent—and go home to her dog, her cat and her fiancé, Anna viewed in her mind's eye the photographs Lorraine Knight had shown her.

Before donning her apron and sensible shoes, Anna had met with the chief ranger and the deputy superintendent. Lorraine had shown her pictures of Dixon Crofter, Patrick Waters, Trish Spencer and Caitlin Bates. These four were typical of the marvelously atypical young people who worked in parks.

Dixon Crofter, what parkies referred to as a "climber dude," lived in Camp 4, a mecca for rock climbers from all over the world. He'd been in Yosemite three seasons. He climbed for fun. If he could get on a funded expedition to Greenland or Austria or Patagonia, he climbed for fun and money. When the park Search and Rescue team needed a climber, they hired Dixon or several other of the "SAR-siters" living in the camp. Then Dixon climbed for fun, money and the good of his fellow man. Dixon was twenty-four years old, six foot three, one hundred thirty-five pounds. From the picture Anna guessed his body was a powerful con-struction of cable and bone. He had long curling black hair, a smile that could melt ice and a nose a Bedouin chief would be proud of.

Pat Waters worked trail crew. He was two years younger than Dixon. Where the climber was narrow Pat was broad: shoulders, jaw, chest. He looked strong—not with gym-honed, bench-press muscles, but the kind that can move rocks and stumps all day and still have the energy to tell jokes over din-ner. He sported a bleached-blond Mohawk and a grin that, despite the dusty rigors of his chosen occupation, spoke of expensive orthodonture. On his right biceps was a tattoo of Bill the Cat in one of his more schizophrenic poses.

Trish Spencer and Caitlin Bates were photographed to-gether, their arms around each other's waists, their heads close, long hair twining together. Trish's was sleek and brown, Caitlin's bleached and permed with black roots. Trish had buck teeth a shade whiter than nature intended and dark eyes that nearly disappeared with the onslaught of her smile. Caitlin wore a bandanna pirate- or—to Anna's memory—hippie-style around her head and looked all of twelve years old. Neither girl would ever make a living modeling or win a swimsuit contest, but they were beautiful nonetheless. Even in the flat, dead medium of a photograph they exuded youth and high spirits and, in Caitlin at least, an innocent wickedness that Anna found irresistible.

Trish was in her third season as a waitress at the Ahwahnee. Caitlin was one of the NPS's own. She was a summer intern finishing her first season working in Little Yosemite Valley campground, a heavy-use area a four-mile hike, most of it straight up, behind Half Dome.

Thirteen days before Anna arrived, a vicious thunderstorm dropped eight inches of snow on the park amid high winds, followed by a cold snap that had yet to let up. Ten days later the high country was blanketed in another foot of snow. In between these two meteorological events these four kids had gone missing.

They hadn't been seen leaving the park together. None of them had filed backcountry permits. They'd told no one of their plans. It was only assumed they were together because they'd all disappeared on the same day.

Patrick Waters left trail camp on the Illilouette Trail to come to the valley for his weekend. Dixon Crofter was spotted by a maintenance worker about five A.M. that same day, hitchhiking west out of the valley with a backpack and climbing ropes. Caitlin Bates had left Little Yosemite Valley camp the afternoon before, also on her weekend, headed for the apartment she shared with three other park interns near the old graveyard in the valley. Her supervisor said she'd carried nothing but an empty pack and water. He had assumed she'd hiked out the Mist Trail past Nevada and Vernal Falls. It was steep—the upper half little more than a shattered granite staircase—but only a little over four miles long. Fit and agile with knees not yet forced to bend too often to the vicissitudes of life, the young intern could reach the valley floor in an hour. Trish, pleading headache, had stayed home while her two roommates left for work that morning. When they'd returned she was gone, as were her pack and boots. Later it was discovered that the fire ax had been taken from its niche in the hall.

For Anna's edification Lorraine Knight had drawn the

containment area of the search, the area in which, based on time, distance, physical ability, terrain and weather, the missing persons had a ninety-five percent chance of being found. Outside this perimeter, Anna was amused to discover, was referred to as the ROW, the Rest of the World. To indicate even the zillionth percentile of possibility beyond that, Lorraine sketched a tiny flying saucer.

After eight days the search had been suspended—not abandoned, since in spirit, at least, the NPS never gave up looking. Wet snow, ice, three weeks: if the four were lost or injured in the backcountry, they were most likely dead. Unless—and this was the deputy superintendent's pet theory— the four of them had hitched out of the park to find warmer adventures in Mexico or South America.

Anna had not been brought in as an addendum to the search-and-rescue effort. Yosemite had one of the finest SAR operations in the country, if not the world. The park was harsh enough to provide endless challenges, and the visitors were foolish enough to provide the rangers with endless practice.

Lorraine Knight had brought Anna in because she was convinced the incident was far from over. She had stated her view succinctly: "I suspect foul play," she'd said, and smiled at the drama of the words.

With that smile, Lorraine won Anna over. They were of an age, more or less, and seemed to have like interests. Knight was a big woman, five-ten or -eleven, and powerful looking without being masculine in the least. Anna put her age at around fifty, though it was hard to tell. Sun and wind had done more to her skin than the mere passage of years. Her hair was undimmed by either time or the elements. A braid as thick as Anna's wrist and of a rich red-gold hung down past her waist. The tail of it rested on the butt of her gun like a squirrel on a branch. Out of doors, when Lorraine was armed, the braid went up with a flick of practiced fingers to be secured in place by pins that appeared to come from nowhere.

This instantaneous affection put Anna on her guard. There were those who swore by first impressions. Anna was not one of them. First impressions could be manipulated. Anybody could suck it up and play hale-fellow-well-met long enough to impress. Few could sustain a convincing façade over time. Sooner or later cracks began to show. Anna was a big proponent of last impressions.

"Something besides the disappearances is upping the collective blood pressure of the park," Lorraine finished. Anna had felt it. A poison dripped into the small, isolated community, an unspecified drift of unease that seemed to animate or enervate, warp that indefinable buzz of the human hive till it whined and grated in the mind.

Leo Johnson, the deputy superintendent, grunted at these feminine intuitions of disease. Johnson was in his thirties and as steely-eyed and lantern-jawed as a comic book character. The heroic effect was spoiled by receding brown hair with a tendency to curl over the ears, and a small mouth that, on a young and comely lass, might be compared to a rosebud. On Leo's broad face the comparison was more apt to be to one of the body's other natural apertures.

Before this interruption he'd had little to do today, so little Anna suspected he'd been pressured from above into going along with Lorraine's undercover investigation.

"It's a holdover from the Sunsocy killings," the deputy superintendent said dismissively.

Like the rest of the country, Anna had followed those grim events on the news.

People managed all sorts of ways to damage or extinguish themselves in Yosemite. They fell off the magnificent cliffs, got lost, suffered from exposure, broken ankles and bee stings. The brave or crazy died in base jumps from El Capitan. They crashed hang gliders and fell out of trees, committed suicide off Half Dome, overdosed, brawled. Search, rescue and even the occasional death were daily fare in a park as wild and yet as heavily visited as Yosemite. Even the odd happenstance of four park people going AWOL would not have shaken the social foundations as recently as two years ago.

That was before a psychopath working in the nearby town of El Portal had sexually assaulted and murdered four women, one of whom lived in an inholding surrounded by NPS lands.

Though the man had been caught, his evil had not stopped. The sense of safety many had enjoyed in the glorious stone heart of the Sierras died along with the women. The monster had graphically illustrated the fact that there is no place beyond evil's reach. Because of this, the disappearance of the park people raised fear levels in the valley till there were times when the small hairs on the back of Anna's neck fairly prickled with it.

Talk would have it that the Sunsocy murders were happening again, that a copycat had taken up residence in Yosemite Valley.

Chief Ranger Knight had brought Anna to Yosemite because she, too, feared the killings had just begun.

CHAPTER
2

In five days the only toxins Anna had sniffed came from the head waitress, Tiny Bigalo, a dried-up wisp of a woman with the energy of a hundred monkeys, all of which, if put in a barrel, would be no fun. According to her staff, Tiny, autocratic by habit and inclination, had "a bee up her ass," "a burr under her saddle" or "been on a tear for weeks." As a consequence everyone associated with the dining room scurried about in tight-lipped resentment expressing their frustrations by clashing dishes and slopping coffee.

Trish Spencer had been an intimate of Tiny's, which was one of the reasons Anna had been placed in the dining room. So far her efforts at sucking up to the fierce little woman had failed to bear fruit.

As much as being gregarious and ingratiating went against her grain, Anna managed to become friends with two others on the Ahwahnee staff. Anna Pigeon the waitress, the spy, was pleased with these human acquisitions. Anna Pigeon the ranger looked upon both relationships with a jaundiced eye.

The first contact caused Anna's conscience the fewest qualms: Scott Wooldrich, the assistant chef. At thirty-seven he was old enough and at six foot four and two hundred twenty pounds he was big enough to take care of himself. Whether or not he would prove a font of information as she wormed her way into his affections, Anna couldn't say. Even without that professional perk, he was a worthwhile ally. Bluff, good-natured, fun-loving—all those Iowa farm-boy clichés—Scott ran interference between offending waitpersons and the wrath of Jim Wither. The febrile and brilliant chef could hear Scott's baritone when his ears were closed to other voices of reason. Such were Wooldrich's charms, Anna'd even seen him tease a smile out of Tiny a time or two.

What roused Anna's radar regarding the ease with which she'd become friends with Scott had little to do with the assistant chef and much to do with human nature—hers. Whenever she became bosom buddies with a blond, blue-eyed hunk that made her little heart go pitty-pat, she questioned her motives.

The second connection was more likely to prove useful, but despite her attempts to justify it as necessary, it caused Anna the occasional stab of guilt.

Mary Bates, an exquisite, naturally blond, seventeen-year-old hotel maid, was a concessions brat. Her parents had worked at the Ahwahnee, and she'd grown up in the valley. This year Mom and Dad had moved on to better jobs at the lodge in Yellowstone. Out of love for Yosemite, Mary opted to stay behind and work for a year before going to college. It was the first time she'd been separated from family. She was a sitting duck for Anna's "hip mother" or, God forbid, "hip grandmother" routine.

Anna had intentionally adopted her to use as bait. Being a woman of a certain age there were natural barriers when it came to cuddling up to the men on trail crew who'd worked with Patrick or the eclectic and unpredictable community of climbers inhabiting Camp 4. A nubile blond opened more doors than a gold badge.

Revulsion at this subtle form of pimping might have outweighed expedience had Mary been made of lesser stuff. Having grown up in the park, despite her youth and fairy-princess good looks, she was accustomed to the dangers of bears, hypothermia, falling rocks and climber dudes.

"Hey, Anna, over here," was hissed as Anna passed the hostess's station with an armful of heavily-laden plates.

The very child she contemplated using for her own ends stuck her towhead from behind the fronds of a plant tired with winter and dropping leaves onto the stained and polished cement floor. Employees were discouraged from hanging about where they did not belong, one of the many niceties that marked the Ahwahnee as a grand hotel.

"Yeah?" Anna whispered back, stealth being contagious.

"When does your shift end?"

"Three thirty."

"Want to go for a walk? I've been making beds all day and feel like an old wadded-up piece of tinfoil."

"A walk would be good."

The blond slipped into the underbrush.

At three thirty-five Anna clocked out and left the hotel by way of a utility entrance that let out through the Dumpsters at the back. There was something Disneylike about the Ah-wahnee, about Yosemite Valley. Natural features were too big, too perfect: domes of granite sliced neatly into aesthetically appealing halves, rocks and trees juxtaposed to delight the

eye. The Merced River, clear and emerald by turns, chuckled
through in glittering communion with wind in the pines.

And, like Disneyland, Yosemite required machinery to run
smoothly; law to regulate too many people, too many cars
and buses; walls to hide the ugliness of Dumpsters, bone-
yards, toilets. Like H. G. Wells's future, parklands must have
the Morlocks to keep Eden beautiful for the Eloi. Periodically, when this stage-set unreality struck, Anna was nearly
overpowered with a need to flee into the high country, the
ninety-five percent of the park that was wilderness. She'd yet
to make it more than a mile from the main road. As with all
true evil, whatever had set off Lorraine Knight's alarms centered round the human element.

Besides, Anna consoled herself as she scuttled through
the garbage and mud-spattered vehicles, *it's cold.* Camping,
hiking and communing with the gods seemed less appealing
when temperatures dropped below fifty degrees.

In deference to her age and status as a year-round waitress, Anna had been offered one of the hotel's employee
houses—a single-room tent frame to which walls and a bathroom had been added. The dorms were reserved for seasonal
workers and those significantly lower on the food chain than
the main dining room waitstaff. Tempted as she was to snatch
at this scrap of solitude, she had requested dormitory housing in the room where Trish Spencer had lived.

In communal housing it was more likely she would hear
the kinds of rumors that never make it to the ears of law enforcement, and, by being placed in a living situation "below
her station in life," she had a built-in reason to be one of the
valley's disaffected, should she choose. All the better to be
part of the whining and plotting of others on the fringes.

The room she shared with the two busgirls, both securely

under thirty, was dark and dank due to the weather without and the décor within. Her roommates had yet to reach the age where visual order was necessary to the psyche. The place resembled the inside of a laundry hamper. Dirty clothes and female accoutrements were heaped on unmade beds and vomited out of open dresser drawers. Anna's first task on arriving in her new persona had been to pack up Trish's things while Nicky and Cricket—the roommates she'd inherited along with the missing woman's apron, shirt and pants—looked on with the thrilled misery of those half playing at tragedy.

During the search the NPS had gone through Spencer's belongings, hoping for a clue that could tell them where she'd gone. In the normal course of events it would have been Yosemite rangers who packed up the missing woman's goods for shipping or storage. Lorraine Knight left the task to Anna, hoping it would serve as a bridge to the missing woman and a way of breaking the ice with the roommates. It had been successful on both counts.

Anna waded through to her wee tidy space to peel off her uniform. White shirt, black polyester pants and black many-pocketed apron: these Anna had borrowed from the late— very late—Trish Spencer, and everything was a couple of sizes too big. Not only was Anna an imposter, but a poorly dressed imposter at that. Walking a mile in someone else's shoes was a tad creepy when done literally.

M ary was dressed and waiting. She wore Levi's, running shoes and a red hooded pullover that made her look like every wolf's dream of Little Red Riding Hood.

Perfect, Anna thought and suffered a pang of remorse for being bloodlessly pragmatic. "Ready?"

"Want to go to the village?" Mary asked as she fell into step beside Anna. "I've got to get some things."

"Sure." En route Anna would come up with a plausible excuse to get her living lure to Camp 4, see if they could coax anything interesting from the climbers. Though active and seemingly anxious to help with the rigors of the search, they'd been characteristically close-mouthed with law enforcement.

While Mary made her purchases in the grocery department, Anna poked around the souvenirs section. Depending on one's point of view, Yosemite Village with its deli, pizzeria and full-service grocery store was either a tremendous convenience or proof the park was going to hell.

Making conversation, Lorraine Knight had told her how the local public school, some forty-five miles away, had held a children's symposium on the nation's parks, asking the children what they would do with Yosemite Valley. The park's rangers sat back complacently waiting for their enlightened offspring to lead the way. The consensus of the kids from Yosemite was that a Costco and an orthodontist should be added to the village's repertoire. The three-hour round-trip drive to these necessities was a very real burden to them.

During her college days Anna and others had contemplated monkey-wrenching the village infrastructure in hopes of driving out the urban blight. Thirty years later and now, at least temporarily, a resident, she was sympathetic with the children; she was glad she didn't have to drive eighty miles every time she ran out of shampoo.

Civilization was *comfortable*.

Anna dearly hoped she'd never reach the point where the love of comfort outweighed her love of the natural world, but she wasn't about to make any rash promises even in the privacy of her own skull.

As they left the store, passing the statuesque twin pines which graced the entrance, Anna decided to nudge.

"Let's go down toward Yosemite Lodge. I'll buy you a drink." Mary would have hot chocolate, but the alcoholic phrasing flattered the girl's youth and fit with Anna's assumed role. Since Anna had picked Mary up she'd kept herself open, warm, fun and funny, winning the girl's trust. This was the first time she would use it.

Set the hook before you reel her in, Anna thought sourly as Mary bobbed charmingly along at her elbow. *Too good a catch to throw back,* she told herself philosophically and began:

"That Dixon guy, the one that got himself lost with those others, didn't he live in a camp somewhere down here?"

"Yup. Camp 4. It's really famous. Climbers come from all over. They're a wild bunch. Sort of a force unto themselves. Wanna go see it? It's just past the lodge."

Candy from a baby. "Sure. Did you know him? Dixon? That would be pretty creepy."

"Not *know* know him," Mary admitted reluctantly. Like most people, she wanted to be in the center of the excitement even if only by association. She was a longtime park-dweller, and Anna ostensibly in Yosemite for the first time. It would be tempting to anyone to embroider the truth to such a willing believer. Anna admired her for resisting.

"I've seen him around to talk to," she went on quickly lest Anna be disappointed. "You pretty much see everybody around if you live here.

"Dixon was cool. The other guys call him Spiderman. Once he climbed Half Dome in the morning—an unassisted climb, you know, just fingers and toes and a belay—then he ran down and over to El Cap and climbed it in the afternoon.

Nobody'd ever done that before. He always looked kind of wild with all that hair and that smile. Kind of like Lawrence of Arabia but not so pale and faggoty. More like that other guy, the black-robed guy."

"Omar Sharif?"

"I guess. But taller. Oh, I'm screwing it up but Dix was a rock: real and hard and unfathomable."

Dixon Crofter had been a resident on and off for three years. He would have come on the scene when Mary was fourteen. A good time for a man to steal a girl's heart without even being aware of it. At fourteen it was still acceptable to love pure and chaste from afar. Anna suspected Mary had yet to let go of this girlish habit where the lean and romantic climber dude was concerned.

"Dix was always scruffy but backpacker scruffy. You know—fine."

Anna knew. Even at her age there remained an attraction to scruffy young men, though in recent years, she'd been content to merely admire them from a distance, the way she did mountain lions and grizzly bear cubs.

"This is it," Mary announced.

They had passed the lodge and arrived at the notorious Camp 4. It was set in a field of boulders that dwarfed the tents and trees. Despite the inclement weather, men were out climbing. A new breed of climber had sprung up since Anna first visited Yosemite Valley back in college: sport climbers, people who eschewed the long dangerous climbs, preferring short speedy pitches up boulder faces which they pocked with anchors in what seemed to be an attempt to re-create indoor climbing walls on living rock. Sport climbers dotted the rain-streaked granite with brightly colored ropes and more brightly colored spandex and fleece.

"They're not real," Mary said with unself-conscious snobbery. "They're more like climbing groupies. They like to talk the talk and swagger around the campfires with the big boys."

"Dixon was one of the big boys?"

"Oh yeah. He owns a tent cabin. They're hard to come by. These guys guard their cabin rights like you wouldn't believe. Somebody's practically got to die before they change hands." Her words caught in her throat. Mary'd lived too long in a wilderness park not to know that was probably what had happened to Dixon. Her climber was most likely dead.

Maybe not, Anna reminded herself. People lost in the mountains, fallen down gullies to break femurs, off cliffs to shatter hips, had been known to live weeks under conditions and weather as severe as any the Sierra had dished up so far. Humans were tenacious and unbelievably tough for animals without claws, who were unable to run fast or jump high, blind in the dark, without any real sense of smell to speak of and no pelt to ward off the cold. That was why SAR units hated to quit looking. When the time came, they stopped spending NPS resources and talking about it, but over a few scotches the stories came out. An unsolved disappearance from ten, twelve or thirty years before would still be on their minds.

Mary shook her pale yellow hair to banish the vision of the fine and scruffy Mr. Crofter dead in a ditch. "Dix—Dixon Crofter—bought the cabin a few years back off a French climber who lost his feet to frostbite."

"Had to quit climbing?"

"Oh no. He got wooden prosthetic feet. He had 'em made smaller than his old feet so he could wedge them better, and of real hardwood because it worked better for him than plastic. I guess he's still climbing, but we haven't seem him around here for a couple years."

Anna made a mental note to ask the chief ranger how one went about "buying" a tent cabin on NPS land and whether the owning of one was worth killing for.

Camp 4 was well populated for so late in the year. The unusually cold but dry weather had lengthened the climbing season significantly. Red, orange, green and blue tents sprouted between the boulders like poisonous mushrooms. Climbers—the real and the unreal—hunkered around picnic tables dark with moisture saying little and nursing their beverages of choice from battered Melmac cups and thermos caps.

The paved path Anna and Mary followed wended through the campsites. For all the notice Anna got she might have been invisible, but in Mary's wake there stirred a hormonal breeze that brought heads up and enlivened faces.

On a small rise at the east end of the campground, forming a skeletal village, perched the tent cabins of climber royalty. Dirty gray-brown canvas houses, a door at one end and a stovepipe sticking out the other, were splattered down at odd angles as if they'd fallen from a low-flying plane. Unprepossessing in and of themselves, they looked a picture of cozy comfort next to their nylon neighbors on this gloomy, cold November afternoon.

Taking in the scene of Dixon Crofter's last known address, Anna enjoyed the scent of pine mixed with wood smoke, a perfume that captured the essence of mountains and adventure. It tickled a place in her brain that was untouched but by train whistles and engendered a need to sing sad songs and wander the globe. Maybe the smell had a like effect on Crofter, Spencer, Bates and Waters. Maybe one day they'd simply turned left toward the Rest of the World instead of right toward the containment of civilization.

"Which one belonged to Dixon?" she asked.

"The one with the porch." Mary pointed to a short narrow deck crowded with a hibachi and bicycle. Two forlorn beach towels, their gay colors muted from wear and precipitation, hung across the railing, relics from better weather. Smoke poured out of the stovepipe. Given the information Mary had shared regarding real-estate transactions in Camp 4, Anna had expected Crofter's cabin to stand empty. If it took death or something very like it for these tents to change hands, the next tenants had not stood on ceremony.

"Looks like squatters moved in. Probably sport climbers not wanting to get their spiffy new gear wet." Mary's voice, usually softened by the blurring of natural shyness, had an edge to it. Her face was set in hard lines—no easy feat with flesh firm and unmarred by time and trauma. "That just plain sucks," she said. "Dix might be coming back. We don't know anything for sure."

For a heartbeat or more Anna watched Mary from the corner of her eye. The girl was park born and bred. Her sense of pride and the proprietary pleasure park people take in gifted eccentrics attracted to "their" park had been outraged.

"Dix *owns* that cabin. They can't just move in. Makes me want to go in there and chew somebody's head off."

Anna wanted to get a look in the cabin as well, but for less exalted reasons. "Why don't you?" she tempted the girl. "The bastards have it coming."

"I just should." Now that opportunity had knocked in the form of adult approbation, Mary's courage wavered. So did Anna's. Without gun, pepper spray, baton or color of law to hide behind, she questioned the wisdom of goading the girl into a confrontation with whoever had taken Crofter's space. Still and all there were plenty of tents nearby and, out of uniform, Anna had no compunction about screaming for help at the top of her lungs should things go awry.

"They are probably even using his gear," Anna said, picking the most heinous crime she could think of.

"Will you go with me?" Pleading and fierce, righteousness ignited Mary's usually pacific blue eyes.

"You bet." Though she felt unpleasantly powerless without the weight that went with a badge—regardless of the size of the individual it was pinned to—Anna's blood ran faster and warmer at the thought of real work. Standing straighter to take full advantage of all sixty-four inches of her imposing frame, she pushed the graying hair back from where her hood had fringed it around her face and reminded herself she was yet possessed of a formidable weapon. Odds were good these squatters were in their twenties. With luck, those who did not respect their mothers feared them. If they had any buttons, Anna intended to push them the way only a woman of a certain age can.

It wasn't her style, but Anna let Mary go first. They weren't serving a warrant on known felons; they were visiting a tent in the peaceful splendor of a national park. Besides, Mary's face was more likely to get them invited in than Anna's was. The poor girl, blissfully unaware of it and never to be enlightened by Anna, was adorable when she was mad.

Anna trailed Mary up the short, well-worn path from pavement to cabin. Vehicles were not allowed in camp, but there were tire tracks frozen in the soil. Big tires, and new. The tread was crisp, cutting deep. Probably a truck or an SUV. Anna could see gouges where the vehicle had been backed up to the railing as if to load or unload something. Given the length of time and the weather since Dixon Crofter quit his quarters, the tracks had been made after he'd disappeared.

Unless Dixon kept a secret treasure in his little cloth house, there shouldn't have been much worth stealing. Climbing gear was expensive but didn't have much resale value, and it looked as if the new guys not only had their own stuff but enough to be cavalier with it. Four brand-new but filthy backpacks leaned against the railing on the narrow porch. No attempt had been made to protect them from the elements.

Mary rapped smartly on the screen door. Anna hurried up the steps to be near when whatever was going to happen happened. As she squeezed past the hibachi and the packs she was hit with a familiar smell. It was so out of place it took her a moment to place it. Diesel fuel; something nearby was soaked with either diesel or gasoline and oil.

The door opened and they were greeted by a gust of cigarette smoke and a boyish voice saying: "Well, did you get your . . ." It broke off when its owner saw them instead of whomever he was expecting. "Yeah. Hey. Um, can I do something for you?"

Anna looked over Mary's shoulder. The door's screen added its veil to the smoke nearly obscuring their intended host. Dark-haired, short in stature, confused and mildly alarmed were the only impressions she could glean.

"May we come in?" she asked before Mary could begin her tirade. From a sudden slump of the girl's shoulders, Anna suspected she'd chickened out anyway. All the better. Mary was there to get them inside. A scene on the doorstep that got them banned would be of little use.

For a second Anna's request was met with silence, then: "Hey, man . . . I don't know . . ." and the shadowy face turned as he looked inside for guidance. Anna poked Mary gently in the ribs.

"Please, sir," she said like a child accustomed to being nudged into good manners by her elders.

The plea put Anna in mind of little Oliver Twist with his empty porridge bowl, and she smiled.

"Yeah. Sure. I guess," the doorkeep managed, and the screen was opened. Anna pushed Mary into the stifling darkness. Inside it was eighty degrees or better, the woodstove crackling and smoking with too much wet wood.

"Uh, sit down if you can find a spot," their host said uncertainly.

The place looked as if frat boys had been having a three-day orgy in an REI warehouse. Equipment, new by the look of it, and backcountry apparel were scattered and heaped so thickly not even a footpath remained across the plank floor. Dixon's storage boxes and cook area had been looted. Opened cans of food, dirty dishes and socks were mixed haphazardly. Whoever these people were, they clearly knew nothing about housekeeping in bear country. No grizzlies were left in Yosemite, but the black bear population was thriving and had long ago learned the delights of people food. With this largesse, Anna was surprised bears hadn't already torn out the side of the tent.

As her eyes adjusted she realized part of the piled debris was in human form. Amid the flotsam on the cot to the left of the stove were two men. One leaned against the wooden frame of the cabin, legs splayed, one foot on the floor, one on the cot. Between a beer and a cigarette both hands were spoken for. Hunkered at the cot's foot was another man with a bottle of bourbon held by the neck. No glass. He, too, had a cigarette, but his lay forgotten on a saucer at his feet, a long white ash highlighting a burn mark on the plate.

Masked by beard stubble, smoke and the paucity of light, Anna couldn't guess their ages. They felt older than most climbers. Thirties. Maybe forties. The habitual ease with which they embraced their various dissipations spoke of long practice. Neither of them looked like athletes. "Beer" was significantly overweight and "Whiskey's" bare and dirty feet had been inexpertly bandaged in the wake of serious blistering. Despite the haze of their chosen painkillers, both looked miserable.

"Is this okay?" Anna heard Mary ask as she gingerly lifted a box of gym socks, still in their wrappers, from the cabin's only chair.

"Yeah. Sure," said the man who'd admitted them, the only one yet to speak.

Mary sat. Anna studied the doorman. At five-ten or so and maybe one-sixty, he was younger and fitter than his tent-mates. His weight was muscle. In the heat he'd stripped down to slacks and a tank-top—slacks, not jeans or sweats but much-abused pleated-front pants in charcoal gray. From the waist up he was ripped and carved with washboard stomach muscles hinted at through the thin undershirt. A poster boy for Gold's Gym. Though his legs were encased in gabardine, Anna guessed the glamour stopped at his belt. Men who buffed for show rather than practical application tended to give short shrift to areas not readily apparent in the bathroom mirror.

His face was surprisingly pleasant, so Anna forgave him the action-figure body. He was younger than his companions, not much more than twenty-one or so. A nice smile lit up a baby face roughened by a blue-black beard shadow. The kid probably had to shave twice a day.

To cover the awkwardness he took a swig from a beer camouflaged among its fallen comrades on the countertop. Even with a drink in his hand he didn't look as dissolute as the men on the cot. Several years in their company would fix that. At a loss for what to do, he fell back on early training. Gesturing at the fat man slumped in the corner he began: "This is Kurt Cl—"

"This isn't a fucking garden party," the fat one, the one Anna'd been thinking of as "Beer," snarled before his last name could be completed. Either these slimeballs were hiding or secrecy had become a way of life. Probably the former. The signs were there and writ large.

Parks, like tropical islands, were out of the way, distanced from the "mainland." Like islands, they attracted men and women who wanted to be anonymous, needed to remove themselves from the real world with its demands that one's metaphorical and literal papers be in order.

Had they not been encamped in the missing Dixon Crofter's cabin posing as climbers or hikers or whatever the hell they were trying to be, Anna wouldn't have thought to connect them with wilderness. They reeked of the city, right down to the fuel smell that permeated the place.

"You want to diddle this mother and daughter act you take it elsewhere," Beer—Kurt Cl—finished.

Anna was deciding whether anger or tears would best suit the situation insofar as finding out what these bozos were doing in Dixon's place when Mary took the decision away from her.

"We came here to find out what you guys think you're doing in Dix's tent," she said hotly. "You've just about trashed it as far as I can see. You've got no business—"

Cloaked in nothing but youthful innocence and righteous wrath, Mary had leapt in over her head. The doorman was taking the tongue-lashing and managing to look sheepish, but his two brothers in squalor were shifting in a way Anna didn't like. Faces hardened under the boozy blur, that instant sobriety hard drinkers can affect after enough years at it. Limbs stiffened and moved to positions of greater mobility.

The door banged open and a man of middling height and delicate bone structure pushed in.

"If that bitch's cunt were as hot as the shower I might be tempted to like this shithole." The words were barely out when he noticed they had company. Already Anna detested him. He'd used her least favorite word in the English language. The next few minutes did nothing to change her mind.

Vulgar jocularity vanished. He took in first Anna, then Mary, exposed in the gray wash of light from the fading day. His eyes were dark and sharp. They were also long-lashed and almond-shaped, and Anna might have found them pretty had his vocabulary not already established him as a truly ugly individual.

Mary's Goldilocks good looks didn't soften his demeanor. With no immediate use for her, she was just another object. "Get them out of here," he said. He didn't snap out the words or raise his voice, yet it was a command. There was no question that he was the leader of the strange little wolf pack.

Not wolves, Anna thought as she took hold of Mary's hand. Hyenas. There was more of the vicious scavenger about them than the clean-kill predator.

"Let's go," Anna said.

Looking close to tears, Mary rose and followed Anna toward the door.

As Anna passed the dark-eyed man, he grabbed her arm. Her whole body flinched with the effort of not driving her elbow into his larynx.

"What're you two doing here?" he asked in his even boardroom voice.

The lies that sprang to mind—Dix's aunt, mother's friend used to live here—couldn't be voiced. Mary would know she was lying and, being a bright girl, would begin to wonder why.

This close to freedom, Mary's courage returned. "We wanted to see who was squatting in Dix's house," she said.

The black karma of the place had robbed her voice of righteousness and the words came out sounding like an apology.

His hand on her arm, Anna could smell the man's aftershave and the scent of the hapless girl, probably a maid at Yosemite Lodge, whom he used for showering and other bodily needs, and though the short winter dusk was nearly spent, she could see his face clearly. Eyes and skin and an abundance of beautifully barbered hair lifted an unremarkable face to where it might be called handsome. In the instant Anna studied it, it underwent a startling transformation. Ice, crudeness and steel vanished as if they'd never been. In their place his eyes sparkled with warmth and his mouth curved in a smile so nice his lips seemed to grow fuller.

"You're friends of Dixon's? Why didn't you say so? Did any of you jerks offer the ladies a drink?" Still holding on to Anna but not so tightly now, he turned his attention to the young doorman. "Bro, get out a couple more beers."

But for the salon hair, all at once he looked and sounded genuine, welcoming. Anna was not impressed. The "C" word was lodged firmly in her craw. He would have to rescue a gaggle of little girls from burning buildings for her to soften toward him. And then there was the "Bro." Intuition told her it was not short for *brother* but a way of covering the fact that he didn't want names bandied about.

"Where do you know old Dix from?" he was asking as he cordially turned Anna to bring the party back indoors. "Fellas, shake a leg!"

The others looked baffled but shuffled around in oafish domesticity, clearing places to sit, moving piles of gear and clothes from one place to another, getting in one another's way and generally accomplishing nothing.

In the span of a few sentences the new man had turned a

viper's nest into something resembling *The Country Bears* meet *I Love Lucy*.

Anna felt plucking at her jacket sleeve. "We should go, Anna. It's getting late." Being nobody's fool, Mary wasn't ready to forget a whole lot of nasty because a teaspoon of honey had just been forced down her throat.

Anna needed to stay, see if anything rose to the surface from the muddy depths of these guys, but she didn't want to risk losing Mary's respect or friendship. She might need it again. Turning to the man still holding her right biceps captive, she sought his help.

"It really is kind of late," she said in that oddly porous voice women adopt when they want to be talked into an indiscretion yet maintain plausible deniability.

He laughed. It was a charming laugh, not at all the laugh of a man who had recently used, then verbally abused a hotel maid. "It's not even six o'clock. One beer." This he directed at Mary, pretending he believed her to be a woman of drinking age. "Any friend of Dix's got to be a friend of ours."

Mary was immune to the double flattery of being assumed older and friends with a man she admired.

"You want to stay, Anna?"

"Okay. One beer," Anna capitulated gracefully. The doorman and the slimeballs were introduced respectively as Bobby, Billy and Ben. Billy, to clear up old issues, amended it to Billy Kurt to cover the earlier lapse. Like the well-brought-up girl that she was, Mary was careful to remember their names and use them often in conversation.

Anna didn't bother. If she mentally squinted she could almost see the a.k.a. followed by "Turk," "Mojo" and "Junior." The leader gave his name as Mark. He seemed comfortable with it; if it wasn't his real name it was one he'd used before.

An hour passed amiably enough. Mary charmed by her mere existence, Mark by his art. Mark let them know he was a dear old friend of Dix's. Unwittingly Mary fed Mark his answers by embedding them in her questions.

Did you meet Dix climbing?

He'd met Dix climbing.

Was it on that expedition to Patagonia?

Yes, it was on that expedition to Patagonia.

From there, Mark managed without help, building on general human experiences. Dix had offered the use of his cabin should Mark ever come to Yosemite. He'd arrived to find the tent cabin empty and was hanging out, climbing, waiting for Dix to return. Without coming out and saying so, he managed to get across that Billy Kurt, Bobby and Ben were recent acquaintances who'd horned in on his quarters when the weather turned cold.

Anna listened and watched. By the end of the beer she might have believed Mark's version of events. He was that good. But she noticed Mark gave out very little information, yet deftly managed to get everything Mary knew about Dixon Crofter, his disappearance and the subsequent search.

And she remembered the man he'd been when he'd first opened the door, before he knew they were there.

CHAPTER

3

Anna and Mary skipped cocoa at Yosemite Lodge. The atmosphere of Dix's invaded tent had left its stench, both physical and metaphysical. Anna needed to be alone, Mary needed to call her mom. Both wanted to get to a hot shower and shampoo the reek of cigarette smoke out of their hair.

These were luxuries Anna was to be denied. When she entered her room her dorm mates were in a flutter. The two of them were young, just out of high school, and had fled California's central valley agricultural towns seeking adventure and romance in the high Sierra. Except for housekeeping habits that rivaled those of the Billy/Ben/Bobbsey triplets in Crofter's cabin, they were pleasant enough. Anna considered them dandelion fluff: lovely lighthearted, light-headed girls whose lives and thoughts were dispersed by any wind that blew their way.

During the first few days, she'd surreptitiously questioned them about Trish Spencer and learned only that she was "cool" and "fun." Anna suspected Trish, older by nearly ten years, was one of the winds that affected the two, blowing them into parties and introducing them to cute boys.

"Boy, it's a good thing you showed up," the plump one, Nicky, said as she pulled on her black uniform trousers. "Tiny's doing her Gestapo-waitress bit." The effort of standing on one leg while threading the other through a polyester tube proved too great and Nicky fell over sideways onto her bed. Further communication was lost to wild gales of laughter from Nicky and her partner in inanity, Cricket. It went on. And on. Anna guessed their natural good cheer had been chemically enhanced.

Drugs in the National Parks wasn't new. In Yosemite it was an old story, dating from the classic drug days of the sixties and seventies, complete with hippies, "pigs" and altered states. Since the early seventies, when the drug culture centered in San Francisco had decided to make Yosemite its summer playground, illegal substances had become part of the park's law enforcement history. The jail, a bleak modern set of cells walled into an historic stone building above the fire station, was kept busy housing the perpetrators of assaults, batteries and disturbers of the peace whose uncivil interactions were fueled by consumable evils imported from cities.

"What's Tiny on about?" Anna asked when the giggling finally subsided. The toking of busgirls was not her problem.

"They got this last-minute reservation for thirty-two. A wedding party or something. We got to take another shift. You too. We're to wait tables. Big promotion. She said if you didn't show she would fire your sorry ass."

The gale began again. While it rippled and guffawed at full blow, Anna took off her reeking clothes, stuffed them into the laundry bag, then began to dress for work.

Cricket—the girl's given name was Charlotte but she was such a bouncy, chirpy individual she'd been called Cricket since grade school—recovered first.

"She did *not* say 'fire your sorry ass.'"

This set them off again. Anna finished dressing.

"What did she say?" she asked mildly when they subsided.

"'Find other work,'" Nicky admitted. This was too banal to elicit laughter even from those primed for it, and the girls began stuffing themselves into the rest of their clothes.

Anna stopped at the door before she left. They were good girls, if silly.

"Straighten up," she warned. "A blind woman can see you're high. Keep a lid on it or *you'll* be looking for other work." Leaving them, it occurred to her how forgiving some occupations were. She could overlook coworkers loaded on this job. Worst case, a plate might get broken, a meal delivered cold. A stoned busgirl wasn't a threat to life.

Anna smiled. Not being a hard-ass was actually quite restful to the human spirit.

The dining room was quiet, most of the regular diners gone or finishing up. Tiny was waiting as Anna came in through the employees' entrance by the kitchens. In a building as old and fine as the Ahwahnee, even the regions behind the metaphorical baize doors had a sense of grandeur: hallways were spacious, ceilings high.

"The girls said you'd gone AWOL," Tiny said in a voice that managed to make an accusation out of every statement. "If you hadn't showed you would have been looking for another job."

Anna hated being lectured for doing right simply because another person had gotten their dander up thinking she might do wrong.

"I'm here," she said as she tied on Trish Spencer's short black apron with its many pockets. "Nicky and Cricket are right behind me," she added to save herself from a spirited recitation of what would be done to her roommates should they fail to report for duty. "A wedding party?" she asked to distract Tiny from fussing further.

"That's right. Thirty-two. Last minute. The bride must be eight and half months along to be doing this kind of thing at the last minute. Hah!" Tiny finished, the one word serving as personal shorthand to save her the bother of actually laughing.

She came and stood too close for Anna's comfort. Tiny was always infringing on one's personal space, standing so close it was hard to focus on her pointy little face.

"You smell like an ashtray," she snapped. "If you want to kill yourself with cigarettes have the decency to shower before you show up where people are trying to eat. If Chef Wither gets a whiff of you, you'll be—"

"Looking for another job," Anna finished for her.

"Don't be impertinent. You're not paid to be impertinent. You're paid to serve food and not stink up the place."

Tiny couldn't have been more than ten years Anna's senior, and some of her waitstaff were older than that, but she spoke to them all as if they were slightly retarded preteens.

"Where do you want to put them?" Anna asked. "The wedding party?"

Tiny strode away without replying. At least on a larger woman it would have been striding. Having too much energy for such a small frame Tiny Bigalo moved from place to place at a dogtrot.

Dutifully Anna followed and dutifully she stopped while the headwaitress surveyed the dining room with the air of a general planning troop deployments before battle.

"The alcove," she decreed. "They don't deserve it but it's

dark, so they won't see much anyway. They'll be out of the way there."

Since the vast room had nearly emptied and the alcove was a significant hike from the kitchens, Anna could have wished she'd put the party closer, but it would have been more than her life was worth to suggest the change.

"Yes ma'am."

"Put tables together for thirty-two. Set up chairs. Count them. I don't want it turning out there's only thirty or thirty-one and us looking like idiots. Put out the cloths—clean, mind you. I don't care if the bride's the whore of Babylon, in my dining room she gets *white*. Then do the place settings and come get me to check it."

Anna survived the condescending list of details and began shoving tables together. The usual night shift was cleaning up. She wondered why none of them had opted to stay for the extra money. At least a fifteen percent tip was guaranteed. Big parties—oddly enough this included wedding parties, which one would think to be the cheeriest and most generous of customers—were notorious for stiffing waitresses. Like most other restaurants, the Ahwahnee automatically added the gratuity to the bill. Enlightened self-interest: it reduced the odds a hostile waitress would punch out a stingy bride in the parking lot.

Nicky and Cricket arrived. They were so stoned Anna had to redo their place settings more often than not. Periodically, fits of giggles dragged them into a far corner of the alcove where they could recover without attracting the wrath of the headwaitress. Anna considered killing them herself or at least knocking their empty heads together but, remembering her own misspent youth, satisfied herself with huffing and rolling her eyes.

Finally, the table was set. Tiny trotted down the long room to check it.

"Straighten it. God! It looks like it was laid by Hottentots," she declared, and trotted away.

"Must be some bigwig," Nicky whispered as they set about straightening the already straight and tidying the already tidy.

"Probably a movie star. Tiny's got major hots for Johnny Depp. Maybe she hopes he'll take one look at how beautifully the table is laid and get a stiffy for her."

"Oh gross," Nicky cried. Giggles descended once more.

"Get a grip," Anna snarled. There wasn't much use in yelling at the stoned, but she hoped to at least frighten them into being less irritating.

Mercifully, the giggling stopped. Anna turned her back to keep from thinking evil thoughts about their dewy little sheep's faces and soggy little sheep's brains.

An exaggerated gasp of horror-movie quality grated across her nerves. To calm herself she straightened two steak knives. Nicky laughed, then squeaked.

"Cricket's having a heart attack."

Anna gritted her teeth, moved the dish of butter pats a fraction of an inch.

"She's not breathing. Oh God."

"For Chrissake," Anna turned on them. Cricket was on the floor, her face slack and already turning pale around the mouth. Nicky, her mouth a perfect "O," was staring at Anna with desperately wide eyes.

"Holy shit," Anna muttered. Kneeling, she gently nudged Nicky aside. "Nicky, you call nine-one-one," she said firmly.

The girl nodded but didn't move.

"What are you going to do?" Anna asked.

"Call nine-one-one?"

"That's right. Go now. Call nine-one-one and come right back here to me. Go."

Nicky stumbled to her feet and began to run.

Ear positioned above Cricket's nose so she might hear or feel any stirring of breath, Anna slid her fingers onto the girl's carotid artery. She'd forgotten how soft the skin of the young could be. Cricket was a girl encased in supple velvet.

A heartbeat: weak and too fast. No breath.

Anna began rescue breathing. In all her years as an emergency medical technician she'd never seen a case of respiratory arrest caused by anything other than drugs or choking. As she counted twelve even breaths blown into Cricket's lungs and watched the reassuring rise and fall of her chest, she wracked her brain for causes. All she came up with was either the girl suffered a bizarre allergy or she'd been poisoned.

Lest in her zealousness she actually occlude the flow of blood to the brain, Anna moved her fingers from the carotid in Cricket's neck to her wrist. As oxygen was forced into the girl's lungs her pulse slowed, grew stronger.

"Hallelujah," Anna whispered.

After what seemed an excessively long time but, by breath counts, was under two minutes, there came the sound of people running the length of the dining room. With waitstaff in rubber-soled shoes and floors of polished concrete, there was no clatter, just the hushed pad-padding as of a horde of ghosts.

"The rangers are coming. The rangers are coming," Nicky shouted like a modern-day Paul Revere. Anna didn't look up.

"Good." Anna breathed for Cricket. *Two. Three. Four. Five.*

"What's the matter with her?" Tiny Bigalo. *Breathe.*

"Respiratory arrest." *Three. Four. Five. Breathe.*

"Oh," Tiny said as if that meant anything.

Others had come. They crowded too close, began to babble. "Back to work," Tiny ordered sharply. But for Nicky, the horde shuffled away.

"Let me stay," Anna heard her beg.

Tiny didn't reply. Apparently that was as close as she could bring herself to giving a "yes" answer to an employee request.

Nicky knelt on Cricket's other side and took her friend's hand in hers. "Is this okay?" she asked. Her voice had become that of a very little girl; she was abdicating responsibility for herself to the nearest adult. Anna hoped she wasn't going to require something in the way of care anytime soon.

"Okay." *Breathe. Two. Three.*

"Can I do anything?" Nicky asked.

"No." Anna kept breathing, counting, feeling the pulse.

"Is she going to die?" The voice had lost a few more years, edging toward baby talk.

Shock, maybe, Anna thought, but there was nothing she could do about it.

The reassuring sound of boots and ranger voices finally came down the vast hall. *'Bout damn time,* Anna thought uncharitably. Eighty-four times she'd breathed for Cricket. Seven minutes. Not a bad response time.

Three rangers Anna didn't know by sight edged her to one side. Cricket was efficiently intubated, and one of the EMTs began squeezing the football-shaped plastic bellows that pumped air into her lungs. The other two lifted her onto a gurney, asking Anna questions as they worked. They were wheeling Cricket out when the chief ranger walked into the dining room.

"Who helped her?" she asked, looking at Anna.

"She did. The older lady," replied an EMT whom Anna had liked till that moment.

"Could you come to the clinic with us?" Lorraine Knight asked.

Anna looked to Tiny. Amazingly the head waitress nodded assent.

"Please," Nicky whispered, catching Anna's hand as she turned to go. "You've got to take me with you." Her face had lost color, and though her friend was in good hands, none of the terror had left her eyes.

"See if Tiny will let you go home. You need to lie down, get something hot to drink. Do you know Mary Bates? She's just down the hall. Tell her I said she was to keep you company, make you tea."

"No. Please. I've got to see the doctor."

Anna looked at her more closely. She didn't appear to be having trouble breathing. If anything, she was in danger of hyperventilating.

"Ah." Anna got it then. Whatever Cricket was on, Nicky'd taken, smoked, dropped or shot up the same stuff.

"Anna!" Lorraine called.

"In a minute," Anna said curtly then turned her attention to Nicky. "Where did you get it?"

"I don't know."

"Anna Pigeon. Come on." Lorraine again.

Anna would get no more from Nicky. Anyway, she was pretty sure the girl was telling the truth, part of it anyway.

"Let's go," she said.

"Pretty impressive."

The voice, so close, startled her. Scott Wooldrich, the assistant chef, stood in the shadows not six feet from them. With half his face catching the light, he looked different, menacing.

"You're a real take-charge kind of gal, aren't you?" The

menace had leeched into his voice. Then he smiled and was himself again. "I like that in a woman. You seemed to have everything under control. I just hung around in case you needed any heavy lifting."

"Thanks," Anna said and meant it. Having him close was both comforting and exhilarating. Maybe because he ran interference for her when Wither was on a rampage. Maybe because of the sheer unremitting maleness of him.

"Hey! Get a move on," the chief ranger called again, and Anna was rescued from having to think about it.

"Ranger Knight, Nicky's having a little respiratory distress as well," she said to keep the girl near her.

"Bring her." Lorraine left the dining room.

Anna and Nicky looked to Tiny. Lorraine might be chief ranger but Tiny Bigalo was empress of the dining hall.

In the second miracle of the evening, she said: "Go, then." Anna thought Tiny would have expected employees to die on the job out of loyalty to the company.

"Respiratory problems," Lorraine said to the waiting EMTs. One of the rangers dropped back to look at Nicky. "We'll put you in the ambulance. Do you . . . ?" Before she could ask any of the diagnostic questions, Nicky was backing away.

"No. No. I'll come in my own car. I'm okay. I just . . . I might . . . I might need to see a doctor."

"You want me to come with you?" Anna asked, remembering the panic in Nicky's eyes.

"No. You go. Please. Please. I'll get my car. I'll be right behind you." This last was delivered over her shoulder as she hurried from the dining room.

Since the busgirl wasn't to be carried out feet first after all, Anna thought Tiny might make her finish out her shift, but the headwaitress had already retreated into the kitchen, no doubt calling back the shift that had just clocked out. Anna glanced at her watch. The wedding party was late. Tiny hated that. Anna was glad she wasn't going to be around to collect the fallout.

"She going to be okay?" the EMT asked of Nicky.

Anna had seen no signs of difficulty breathing, disorientation, sweating or any other symptoms. "I guess so," she said. "I think she's mostly scared. Still, she'll need to be checked out."

"Yeah. They do that at the clinic."

Anna heard the huff in the ranger's voice and wondered at it till she realized she'd spoken not like a middle-aged, divorced, down-and-out waitress but as if she were the woman's district ranger. America's caste system was not immutable or state sanctioned, but one did exist. Waitresses were frowned upon if they spoke with force or confidence regarding anything but the daily special. Inadvertently Anna had behaved as an equal, and the ranger was offended.

"Let's go," Lorraine ordered. "It'll be tight in the ambulance. You ride with me," she said to Anna. This time conscious of her place in the pecking order, Anna humbly followed the chief ranger, walking a half step behind as befitted her reduced circumstances. There was some satisfaction in knowing she'd earned this lesson in humility. Unthinkingly, she'd perpetrated the same subtle form of snobbery more times than she was comfortable remembering.

The clinic was small but well equipped. The staff was comprised of men and women who'd chosen this remote outpost in which to practice medicine not because they couldn't compete for jobs in the open market but because they preferred the glories of Yosemite to the monetary rewards of the cities. Cricket was put on oxygen and the doctor was called from his home. By the time he arrived, Cricket was resting more easily and seemed out of immediate danger.

The rangers who'd responded to the 911 call told the doctor what they could of the incident. Anna once again chafed on the sidelines. When she could stand it no more, she bulled her way into the conversation to tell them she believed Cricket had been using an inhalant, probably marijuana or crack, and had suffered an adverse reaction either to the drug or to some additive of the drug. Her news was listened to politely but only taken seriously by Lorraine Knight.

Because of the life-threatening nature of any ailment that compromised breathing, it was decided Cricket would be transported to the hospital in Merced, an hour and a half southwest of the park.

What with one thing and another, forty-five minutes passed before Anna noticed Nicky had never arrived at the clinic.

CHAPTER

4

There were plenty of reasons Nicky might have stayed at the dorm: sloth, addiction, aversion to doctors. The only one that concerned Anna was collapse from respiratory arrest. She looked around for Lorraine. Through the windowed half-wall between the waiting area and the "No Unauthorized Persons Allowed" zone of the clinic, Anna saw her talking with the doctor.

In her present guise Anna couldn't very well barge in and report. One of Lorraine's law enforcement rangers chose that moment to walk past. Anna grabbed her.

"Nicky, my roommate, never showed up. She said she was coming. Whatever Cricket was into, Nicky did the same stuff."

For the briefest instant the ranger looked blank, and Anna feared the NPS was going downhill. The information jelled, the woman's eyes focused and she said, "I'll give you a lift."

It wasn't waitresses whom emergency-response people looked down on; it was anybody who wasn't them and/or wasn't in need of them, tunnel vision born of seven parts necessity and three parts arrogance. One on one, the caste differences disappeared.

The ranger's name was Diane, but that was all Anna learned during their short ride to the employee dorms. She talked a blue streak. A listener by training and inclination, Anna was uncomfortable doing all the talking. An indefinable power was lost. When one opened one's mouth, learning, seeing—the kind of seeing Anna was good at, seeing behind faces to the gears within that drive human emotion and action—was lost. Still, she persevered, telling Diane of the out-of-control hilarity, loss of balance, confused spatial relations, the sudden wedding party—every detail she could remember. It was her hope the ranger would repeat the information to Lorraine. What good it would do, she didn't know. There was nothing in it relating to the four missing kids, but it might help in diagnosing Cricket or, if they were unbelievably lucky, in finding the source of whatever it was Cricket and Nicky were using.

The door to the room she shared with Cricket and Nicky was closed. To Diane it meant nothing. In Anna tiny alarms went off. To her unending annoyance, the girls never closed the door. They were party animals who craved the incessant noise and constant comings and goings of their fellows.

Anna pushed the door open. The lights were off.

"Nicky?"

A squeak came from the darkness on Cricket and Nicky's side of the room. Nicky—or something—was alive and awake.

"It's Anna. I'm going to turn on the light, okay?" Without waiting for an answer, she flipped the switch by the door. For reasons she'd never been able to fathom, institutional light came in only two forms: dim and creepy like the leavings of a brownout, or harsh and glaring. The overhead lighting in the Ahwahnee dorm was of the former variety. The dirty wash of feeble illumination gave the room the look of a tenement building in a Eugene O'Neill play.

Nicky was on her bed in her waitress uniform, down to the small black apron she'd apparently forgotten to take off. The ticket book was sticking out of the pocket. She leaned against the wall, hands loose at her sides like a broken doll, face simultaneously blank and afraid. Anna wondered if she'd slipped into a drug nightmare and couldn't tell whether the demons she battled were from within or without.

Followed by Diane, Anna entered the room but didn't crowd too close to Nicky. "It's me, Anna," she said again soothingly. "This is Diane. She's one of the EMTs who came when you called. You never showed up at the clinic and we got worried."

"Is Cricket okay?" Nicky asked.

Anna relaxed, shoulders she'd not realized she'd tensed dropping, the small bones in her neck cracking softly. Nicky was in and of this world and able to think of someone beside herself. Good indicators of health and sanity.

Diane took over. Anna let her. While she asked Nicky the standard EMT questions and the pale, clearly shaken girl answered, "I'm fine, I'm good," in an unvarying monotone, Anna looked around the room. Nothing was amiss. Clothes were hung neatly in closets or folded away in drawers. Shoes were in regimental lines, books and magazines squared up in tidy stacks, cosmetics tucked in plastic carry-all baskets. Having left the place not two hours earlier looking like a pigsty populated by a herd of teenage clotheshorses, Anna found the pristine order unsettling.

"The place looks nice," she said guardedly.

Nicky shot her a frightened look and clamped her lips shut so tightly their childish plumpness was reduced to a thin line of white. Until Diane, with her badge, gun and uniform, was gone, Nicky wasn't talking. Maybe not even then.

Blissfully unaware of the currents of unease, the ranger satisfied herself that Nicky was in good health and left. Moving for the first time since Anna had returned, Nicky sprang from the bed with an energy startling after so prolonged a stillness. She closed the door behind the ranger. She didn't slam it as if angry, but closed it softly and firmly as if attempting to muffle the click of the latch lest some evil being hear and come to investigate.

Anna sat on her bed and kicked off her shoes. "What gives?" she asked.

To Anna's annoyance Nicky flopped down on the bed next to her and began to cry. Uncomfortable with weeping women, even when it was she herself doing the weeping, Anna sat rigid with her shoe in her hand. The nonsense nursery rhyme "diddle diddle dumpling, my son John . . . one shoe off and one shoe on," rattled through her head.

She removed her other shoe to quell the rhyme. Since Nicky was still sobbing and gulping on the mattress next to her, Anna patted her head as if she were a dog and muttered, "It's okay, it's okay," wondering what "it" was and sincerely doubting it was okay.

Minutes passed. Rather than subsiding, the crying grew more breathy, more shrill. Nicky was working herself into a fit.

"Stop it," Anna commanded. "My nerves are getting frayed." Nicky cried harder. "Stop it now," Anna ordered and gave the girl a whack on the shoulder, not enough to hurt her, just enough to get her attention.

Nicky flinched and cried out as if Anna had struck her with a tire iron.

"Shit," Anna hissed. With great gentleness, she moved the prostrate girl's long hair, exposing Nicky's neck. A bruise, so new it had yet to lose its angry red color, was forming there. The shape and placement indicated the heel of a hand and a thumb. On the front of the shoulder Anna knew she would find the corresponding finger marks.

In the brief time she'd been gone, an hour and fifteen minutes at most, someone had come into the room and forcibly held Nicky facedown.

"Jesus fucking Christ," Anna muttered. "That does it. Sit up. There you go." She helped Nicky up and saw that her feet were planted firmly on the floor, lest she flop over in defeat again. "Look at me now. Here. Let me." Using the tail of the girl's shirt, Anna dried her face, then pushed her hair back over her shoulders. "Three deep breaths. No more weeping and wailing tonight. The son-of-a-bitch doesn't deserve it. What's needed here is a lust for revenge."

Nicky smiled at that.

"Good girl." For no reason except that it felt right, Anna got a brush from the dresser and started brushing Nicky's straight brown hair, gently working out the tangles. The sobs subsided to an occasional outbreak.

Having set aside the brush, Anna again tucked Nicky's hair behind her ears so she could see her face, and said: "Do you want a drink of water, blow your nose?"

Nicky nodded. Anna fetched a box of Kleenex and a plastic bottle of the newly fashionable Yosemite Water that stood half empty on a night stand.

"Can I go wash my face?" Nicky asked in the voice of a three-year-old.

"In a minute." Anna didn't want her washing anything till she'd satisfied herself there would be no evidence going down the drain with the soap and water. She turned on the bedside lamps and switched off the overhead light, making the room feel homier, less bleak and transient. Sitting in the desk chair, she rocked back, propping her feet on the bed next to Nicky, consciously staying close but not too close, and choosing a pose that was both relaxed and unofficial.

"Now why don't you tell me what happened. Start at the beginning when you left the Ahwahnee and tell it till you get to the part where Diane and I came in."

Nicky heaved a big sigh, then winced as the attendant shoulder-shrugging inflamed her bruised muscles. Pushing her hair back with both hands she tied it out of the way with a soft band that she'd had around her wrist. Eyes red and puffy but focused, she looked at Anna, confusion clear on her face.

"Who are you?" she asked.

For half a beat Anna thought the girl had slipped a cog. When she realized the question was actually astute and perceptive, she felt a stab of alarm, wondering where she'd failed in her cover persona.

"Just a lady who's been around the block often enough to smell a rat, especially when the rat leaves a paw print the size of the one you've got on your shoulder," Anna replied. With intonation and expression, she suggested she'd been on the receiving end of physical abuse a time or two herself.

Nicky looked at her suspiciously, then chose to accept things at face value. The moment of insight passed. Her eyes lost the sharp look. "Okay," she said.

"Tell me," Anna said, taking pains to sound kind rather than curious.

A number of emotions could be read on the girl's open countenance: fear, hesitation, need. Need won out after an exceedingly brief struggle. Anna doubted Nicky had ever kept a secret for more than ten seconds in all of her short life.

"You've got to promise not to tell anybody," Nicky said earnestly. "Especially not like rangers or cops or anything, okay? They said they'd kill me if I told anybody."

"I promise," Anna said. Lying was getting easier and easier. After the big lie of who she was and why she was waiting tables, the little ones rolled off her tongue effortlessly. Of course she would tell law enforcement. Villains thrived on fear and secrecy. The ones who would really kill a victim for telling were those who never would have left a victim alive to tattle in the first place. "Your secret is safe with me," she added for good measure.

"When I came back I was going to—to clean up some stuff—before I went to the clinic." She looked at Anna to see how the story was going.

Anna nodded reassuringly. "You came back to get rid of the dope you and Cricket were smoking before we went on shift," she said matter-of-factly and without a hint of judgment or condemnation.

"Yeah!" Nicky showed the pleased surprise of a teacher getting an unexpectedly correct answer from a dull student.

Anna stopped herself from smiling. The last thing she wanted was for Nicky to regain that spark of insight that suggested Anna was not who she pretended to be.

"Did you get rid of all of it?" she asked neutrally.

"All of it, I even flushed the baggie."

Again Anna nodded. This time to hide her disappointment. When analyzed, a sample of the marijuana might have given them a clue as to where it had come from and what might have been added that had nearly proved fatal for Cricket.

She wanted to ask who Nicky had bought the stuff from but didn't dare. The instant she sounded like a cop—or disapproving parent—she sensed Nicky would clam up, retreat into that place youth suffer with such painful pride: that imaginary world where they are so unique, their experiences so rarified, that adults cannot possibly understand them. Instead she asked: "What then? After you'd gotten rid of it?"

Nicky's face screwed up but she didn't give in to the urge to dissolve into tears again. Anna thought better of her for this small act of courage.

"Afterward I came to the room—"

Anna made a mental note: the girls' cache was not hidden within these four walls. They were cleverer than she'd given them credit for.

Battling another attack of emotion, Nicky stalled out. Patiently, Anna waited till she recovered in her own time. Telling was, in a very real sense, reliving.

"I came to the room and the door was shut. I didn't think anything. I mean, me and Cricket might even have shut it for all I know. We were pretty high when we left."

She looked up at Anna through strings of hair fallen again in front of her face. There was that about her that put Anna in mind of a caged and cowering puppy. A desire to inflict great bodily harm on whoever had abused her hit hard. The emotional tidal wave evidently changed the open, interested expression she'd adopted. Nicky's chin dropped and her hair closed over her face in a curtain.

Anna wasn't ready for the show to be over. "Sorry," she said. "I wasn't listening. I got to thinking about killing whoever put that bruise on your shoulder."

As Anna hoped it would, the hard edge of truth in her brutal confession reassured the battered girl that she was not the one in trouble. Nicky found the courage to continue.

"So I came on in, not thinking anything, you know. Just walked in like always. The light was off and there were these guys with flashlights, two of them I think, and they'd torn the room apart."

Anna's first thought was *how could you tell*, but she kept it to herself.

"One of them said, 'fuck,' then a big one—not fat, big but tall big—grabbed me and pushed me down on Cricket's bed. He mashed my face into the pillow and I couldn't breathe." Here she stopped and looked at Anna, expecting something.

"Bastard," Anna murmured sympathetically.

"He sat on me and the other guy kept on. I could hear him throwing things around."

Nicky stopped. Anna waited. When it became clear the girl wasn't going to continue on her own, Anna asked: "What then?"

"The one on top of me got funny."

In her years in law enforcement Anna'd heard her share of rape stories. It was one form of violence she'd never become inured to. There was something about the using of a person's body as if it were a thing, an object to be exploited, played with, degraded then left as one would leave a dirty diaper or soiled Kleenex that shriveled her soul.

"Did he rape you?" she asked bluntly.

"No . . . It wasn't anything like that or anything. You know how you can feel guys when they start heating up toward something crude? Well these guys had no heat. Like it was business. I was part of a job. Like a glitch, you know. This one that held me down, keeping my face in the pillow so I couldn't see or anything, he's sitting on me, his knees on my arms and he starts pulling my head back. I thought my neck was going to snap but this other one says: 'We don't need that kinda shit.'"

Anna was surprised to find herself relieved. It hadn't been

attempted rape, God forbid, but merely attempted murder. Why that seemed cleaner, more decent, she wasn't sure. Certainly a woman had a much better shot at recovering from rape than from death. Anna realized her gut reaction was based not on her feelings for the victim but on her feelings toward the crime, the criminal. Murder wasn't usually about dehumanizing, making an "it" of a living, thinking person. Murder was most often about removal, revenge or perceived gain. The victim lost his life but not his personhood.

"Then they left."

Nicky wanted to be done.

Anna sympathized but had a few more questions. "They left right away?"

"Not right away. Maybe five minutes after."

"Did they say anything else?"

"No. Yes. Wait." Nicky thought a moment. "One said 'Nothing.' Then the guy on me said: 'He should've figured that.' And the other guy said: 'No. It was left.' Then they told me they'd kill me if I ever told anybody and they went."

For a while the two of them sat in shared silence, each alone with her thoughts. Without the chatter of speech, the small sounds of the dormitory crept in to fill the void: the bathroom door opening, footsteps of someone returning late, the faint broken hum of conversation from another room.

"Did they take anything?" Anna asked at last.

"Not even our tip money."

For anybody looking for quick cash in small unmarked bills, robbing the room of three waitresses would be a dream come true. Though they were encouraged to deposit their money regularly, because of the inherent lack of security that comes with communal living, between the three of them there was usually a lot of cash lying around. Whoever these men were, they hadn't bothered to pick up such small change, not even to try to make the break-in appear to be a simple theft.

"Anything else?"

"I didn't notice anything."

"They didn't say anything more? Do anything? Did you see them to recognize them again?"

"God no!" Nicky said believing that to recognize the bad guy meant he would kill you.

"This sucks, but do it anyway," Anna said. "Close your eyes." Nicky obeyed unquestioningly. Guilt at using innocent young women to her own ends had been spent earlier in the evening when she'd dragged Mary to Camp 4. Anna felt nary a qualm about the discomfort she was about to cause Nicky.

"Let your mind go. We're going to do a memory exercise. It'll help find these guys. Anyway, it won't hurt," Anna added a dash of honesty from old habit. "You've flushed the dope. You're standing outside in the hall about to come in the room. Be there now. Feel the floor under your feet, your hand on the knob. Now push open the door. Okay. Is it open?" Nicky nodded an affirmative. "Now we stop time. What do you see?"

Nicky proved a good subject for this sort of game and recovered information she'd not known she had. The knee pressing down on her right elbow was clad in what looked and felt like slacks from a man's suit. She'd seen one of her assailant's feet. The shoe was a black dress shoe, out of place on a sleeting winter day in a wilderness park. The man who'd contemplated snapping her neck had smooth cool hands that smelled faintly of lotion. Both men "sounded" white. They'd spoken no extraneous words. There'd been no unnecessary touching or violence. That, coupled with the cash left behind, was too professional for the simple tossing of a girls' dorm room. Somebody in Yosemite was into something way over their head.

The memory exercise had been so productive—and apparently cathartic—when they finished Nicky said, "Let's do it again. I bet I'll remember a bunch more."

Anna declined. A second run-through and creative memory had a habit of filling in pesky blanks. "One more question," she said. "You told me the man who held you down smelled of lotion."

"Yeah. You know, like Jergens or something. Hand lotion."

"Any other smells?"

Nicky closed her eyes, back in the game Anna had not wished to reprise.

"Maybe cologne, but faint."

"Any bad smells?"

Nicky squeezed her eyes more tightly shut to aid recall. Finally she said: "He didn't fart or anything if that's what you mean."

Anna laughed and the girl opened her eyes looking offended. To make up for her lapse, Anna became extra serious. "I was thinking more along the lines of gasoline, smoke, skunk, things like that."

Nicky sniffed the air as if she wanted to be able to smell something for Anna. "Nope," she said disappointedly. "He smelled okay." Then: "You're not really a waitress are you," she asked shrewdly. Anna had forgotten her role; like a bad actor she'd dropped out of character. Mentally she cursed herself for carelessness and stupidity. Mistakes the magnitude of the one she'd just made could get a person killed under the wrong circumstances. Maybe she was the one in over her head.

"Not exactly," Anna admitted. "I was a school psychologist in my former life."

"Why did you quit?"

"Personal reasons. I needed to get away from the town I lived in for a while."

"Messy divorce?"

"Something like that."

"He beat you?"

Anna said nothing. Lies were getting so easy she could tell them without saying a word. The wicked web's weft and warp was getting complex. Lies take on a life of their own.

"He stalking you?" Nicky asked with an odd mixture of sympathy and hope. She was a child of TV movies and in love with domestic drama.

"I just need to stay away awhile," Anna said in such a way it was clear further questions would be rebuffed. To crowbar the subject back onto the track she wanted to follow, she stood, turned in place, hands on her hips and said: "Then you cleaned up?"

Nicky nodded. "I didn't want anybody to know. They said they'd kill me."

Nicky cleaning was as suspicious as it got, but Anna said nothing. The girl hadn't been thinking clearly. Who could blame her?

Anna got her a cup of hot tea with plenty of sugar. The Brits had it right: good strong tea made everything more bearable. The next half hour was spent convincing Nicky to report the break-in and the assault. In the end a compromise was struck. Anna would report it, but only if the rangers would first promise not to make a "big deal" out of it. Anna reassured her the chief ranger would probably be circumspect, sending a ranger over in street clothes so the villains would be none the wiser.

Knowing the girl would feel safer that way, Anna sat up with the light on, pretending to read till her roommate's breathing evened out in sleep.

When Nicky first began telling her story, Anna had jumped toward the conclusion that it had been the men she and Mary had spoken with in Dixon's tent cabin. As the tale unfolded and Nicky told of the man who'd restrained her—smooth-handed and sweet smelling, the slacks, the dress shoes—she'd become less sure. Anybody who'd spent time in the tent cabin inherited by the erstwhile climbers would have reeked of tobacco and probably whiskey.

Still, there was such a thing as showers.

Maybe they suspected Anna wasn't who she pretended to be and came to find out if their suspicions were well founded. If so, they'd discovered nothing. She'd been careful not to drag along a single scrap of her past: not a badge, not a gun, nothing.

Anna doubted Bobby, Billy and Ben, the pseudonymous stooges, would have been able to behave with the professional coldness Nicky described, particularly not after consuming the amount of booze they'd downed two hours before the break-in. Mark, the leader, struck her as a man with sufficient control, but who was working with him? He wasn't the one sitting on Nicky's back. He was slight of build and, when Anna met him, he'd just showered. Unless he'd showered again he had been in the tent cabin long enough that his clothes, hair and skin would have recovered their ashtray stink.

However unlikely, these thoughts triggered sudden fear for Mary, Anna's unwitting accomplice. Careful to make no noise, Anna crept out of the room and down the hall to peek into the girl's room. Mary and her roommate slept the sleep of the innocent.

Relieved, Anna returned to her room. For her, the sleep of
the innocent had ended many years before. Lying in bed,
grateful to the marauders for not harming her roommate and
for being the inspiration for cleaning the place, Anna planned
her morning. As soon as it was decent for a citizen to go calling, she would return to Camp 4.

CHAPTER

5

Long before sunup Anna was awake. Longitudinally Yosemite National Park wasn't much farther north than Mississippi, but the deep narrow valley that bore the brunt of visitation—referred to by the park employees as The Ditch—didn't receive day's blessing for an hour or more after the sun gilded the tops of the Sierra. Rising early was a perk of middle age and a boon to law enforcement. Anna had never seen any statistics on it, but she was willing to bet four A.M. to eight A.M. were the safest hours of the day. In many ways criminals were a lazy bunch.

Taking advantage of this diurnal edge, she left her room-mate sleeping soundly, bundled up for a December morning in the mountains and slipped out of the dorm.

As often happened, the valley lay under a small tailor-made inversion layer imposed by the surrounding peaks. Air was trapped in The Ditch and, though campers were few this time of year, the cold damp air was redolent with the smell of campfire smoke.

Anna had reached an age where sleeping on the ground with the bugs and the sticks no longer held the appeal it once had. Still, the smell of woodsmoke on a winter morning called forth a strange nostalgia, an ache that vacillated between a yearning for home and hearth and a need to carve an adventure out of untrammeled land.

Enjoying the sweet sting of this dichotomy, she buried her hands in the pockets of her parka and lengthened her stride.

The path away from the Ahwahnee led through a field of boulders a story and a half high. Beneath an overcast and as yet lightless sky, rocks and trees loomed black and close. Anna remembered one of Yosemite's unsolved mysteries. On a sunny afternoon in the mid-eighties, a young woman had walked into this rocky defile. A hundred yards behind her was a family of four. Ahead about the same distance were two newlyweds honeymooning in the park. The woman had walked from sight into this granite alley. Two screams were heard. By the time the family ran to see what the problem was, the woman was dead, stabbed thirty-nine times. Her killer was never found.

Remembering this gruesome history some might have walked faster. Anna stopped, let the darkness cease swirling in her wake and opened herself to any sinister vibrations that might remain in the ether. There were none; all was peace. The natural world lived and died by tooth and claw, without malice and without regret. Ghosts, it seemed, could only be bound to the earth by man-made walls.

As befit her rank and status, Lorraine Knight had one of the better homes in the park. Built of wood with a deck overlooking a creek, quiet now with winter but a frothing orchestra of liquid sound in spring, it was tucked up on a gentle rise beneath the southern cliffs. In the nineties the Merced River flooded, wiping out much of the park's housing. Some had yet to be rebuilt, making what was left even more precious.

Despite the early hour, a light burned in the kitchen and Anna was relieved. Where there was light there might be coffee.

Lorraine was still in her pajamas, but she was conscious and had the coffee on so Anna adored her. The thick braid in which her glorious hair was incarcerated for duty was unbound. A cascade of red-gold floated around the ranger to well below her waist. With a face sculpted by laughter and weather for half a century, Lorraine looked to Anna like a wise woman of fiction. Or a white witch.

Over coffee—Folgers with two percent milk in place of cream, but being in the beggar's category, Anna was not choosy—she told Lorraine of the situation that had awaited her when she'd returned home from the clinic the previous night.

The chief ranger listened without interrupting, an occurrence rare and welcome enough that Anna noted it in Knight's credit column.

When she was done they sat a moment in silence. Then Lorraine asked: "What do you make of it?"

A good part of the night Anna had lain awake trying to answer just that question. She shared the pitifully few thoughts she'd come up with. The intruders were accustomed to and proficient at their chosen career. They smacked of city-dwellers in the park for nonrecreational reasons. It was not random. They'd chosen Anna, Cricket and Nicky's room for a reason. They'd known where it was and that the three women would be out that night. That spoke of a connection inside the dormitory.

"Do you think these men might have had something to do with the girl—this Cricket's—collapse? Poisoned her to guarantee you'd all be out?"

Anna thought of that. It might work for Nicky and Cricket—Nicky's poisoning not taking—but it didn't account for her.

"I think it's linked to the disappearance," Anna said. "These guys were searching for something specific—something they didn't find. Something one of them at least thought worth snapping a young woman's neck for. Maybe Cricket or Nicky possesses this desirable object. We'll have to talk to Cricket when we get a chance. Nicky seemed genuinely baffled."

"Maybe it's about you," Lorraine said. "If so, we'd better pull you out of this job." The chief ranger looked genuinely concerned for Anna's safety and Anna was flattered. "These guys are not your average dog-off-leash, campfire-out-of-bounds park criminals. If you're right and it is connected with the four missing persons it could get ugly. Uglier." Lorraine licked a drip of coffee off the side of her mug with an amazingly pointed tongue.

A dog, an unimpressive heap of breeds with warm and soulful eyes, pushed its head into Anna's hand and she scratched its ears as much for her comfort as for the dog's. "Wendy," the chief ranger said fondly. "She's a keen judge of character, a kind of doggie sixth sense that helps her nose out people who are likely to drop food. She especially loves children."

For the briefest of moments, Wendy's soft ears put her in mind of her dog, Taco, the cozy kitchen reminding her of home and, so, of Paul, with whom she would soon share a life. Anna considered pretending she believed the night searchers were about her, about her undercover identity. Just for a second she indulged in a fantasy of going home.

"It's not about me," she said before fantasy could mature into temptation. "At first I thought maybe that it was, it coming so soon on the heels of a visit I made to those bozos in Dixon's tent cabin. I'll check it out but I'm sure it wasn't them. At least I'm pretty sure it wasn't." Anna explained her logic of following Nicky's nose in the matter.

"They didn't smell right," she concluded.

Lorraine smiled at the literal application of the old law enforcement saw but otherwise seemed to accept Anna's reasoning.

She went on: "If it wasn't me and—I know we've got to check this out—it wasn't Nicky or Cricket who inspired our visitors, then it had to be Trish. Something she'd cached. According to Nicky, the man searching said he'd found, 'nothing' and the man holding Nicky down said, 'He should have figured that.'

"I know there's a slew of reasons for that remark, but the obvious one is Trish Spencer. She's gone missing. I've taken her place in not only the Ahwahnee dining room but in the dorm. It makes sense that the 'he' who directed this search should have realized Trish's stuff would have been packed up and moved."

"Ah," Lorraine said, and: "Let me get dressed."

Alone with Wendy, Anna wondered what "Ah" meant. "Ah yes, you clever thing," or "Ah, so, you're in therapy for this?"

Lorraine emerged looking official: Rapunzel hair in a tasteful knot at the nape of her neck, Scooby-Doo pajamas replaced with the green and gray. "I'd give you a lift but I expect folks are stirring by now. When it looks like a good time, drop by the medical clinic. I'll leave the key to the old fire cache. For lack of a better place, Ms. Spencer's stuff was stored there. We couldn't track down her parents. None of the

people at the Ahwahnee seemed to even know if they were
living or dead. Nobody else appeared asking after Trish or
her things. I'll see if we can turn anything up on two city
men entering or staying in the park last night."

Anna left first, feeling pleased and reassured. Despite the
silly pajamas, Lorraine was a woman of business. A good
boss was a blessing indeed. With a boss as clear-thinking and
action-oriented as Lorraine Knight, Anna felt half inclined
to obey orders.

Having returned to the dorm, breakfasted, checked on
Nicky and seen the tragic erosion of the so briefly clean
room, Anna decided it was late enough to wander down to
Camp 4 and nose around. Given her age and civilian status,
unless she could come up with a believable reason for
metaphorically ringing their doorbell, a direct assault on the
denizens of Dixon's cabin would be out of character and
most likely unproductive. Anna didn't know precisely what
they were up to in Yosemite but, judging from the soiree the
previous afternoon, it had Secret Squirrel written all over it.
What she needed to figure out was whether theirs was a secret she need worry about or if she could leave them to their
nefarious activities without compromising her own quest for
the missing people.

The sun, watery and white with winter, had crawled
above the cliff tops and poured light if not heat into the valley. Camp 4 was astir. Men were hanging clothes on the trees
trying to dry them from yesterday's sleeting rains. Men huddled around fires and crouched over camp stoves. Men stared
at each other over morning coffee. In the entire village of
eleven tents Anna didn't see a single female. Climbing was
mostly a boy's sport, though women were uniquely suited to
excel at it.

Not finding an amiable woman with whom she might

strike up a conversation based on gender or age, she approached three men in their late thirties or early forties who had pitched their tents fairly close to Dixon's cabin.

"Excuse me," she said pleasantly, "but is that North Face's newest tent? I've been thinking about getting one. Are they any good?"

Outdoorsmen dearly love to talk about gear. Before the wonders of the high-tech tent were halfway extolled, Anna was seated at their picnic table sipping their coffee. When she'd listened to the virtues and shortcomings of various pieces of equipment long enough to establish her credit, she shifted the conversation.

Gesturing at Dix's cabin with her tin mug she said: "Now that's the way to go: standing room, plank floor, woodstove."

To her surprise, the second her meager line hit the water, fish began virtually leaping into the boat. Her coffee klatch had a great deal to say about Dix's tent cabin.

A party had raged within its walls long after these sober fellows had wanted to go to sleep. Along with apparently every climber in Camp 4 and a generous sprinkling of concession employees from nearby Yosemite Lodge, they'd gotten wind of the gathering by the usual osmosis. They'd attended the first three hours readily enough, but when they'd called it a night the others were just warming up. The racket had gone on till three A.M.

"The rangers should've done something," one man groused.

"Did you report it?" Anna asked. He hadn't. Given that the park was fairly deserted this time of the year, probably no one had been patrolling within earshot of the festivities.

By careful questioning—controlling the direction of flow rather than trying to keep it going—Anna found out what she wanted to know. From around eight-thirty till the men she talked with pooped out at midnight, all four of the tent cabin's occupants were in attendance. At midnight the "slobby guy"—Anna guessed him to be the heavyset man she'd first dubbed "Beer" and who was later introduced as Billy Kurt—took the others, booted, bundled and backpacked, off in a red Ford Excursion.

"Big into winter camping," the man opposite Anna at the picnic table said.

"At night?" Anna asked.

"They like to hike in by moonlight," the fellow at her right elbow said. "They see more game that way." After this contribution he and his buddy exchanged an odd glance. Anna guessed this rationale had made a lot more sense the night before after a couple of six-packs.

"Thinking the party's over, the three of us turned in," said the first speaker. "Then Slob and the boy-faced prick come back, park that big damn gas-guzzling piece of shit in front of the tent like we were in a Wal-Mart parking lot, and the party starts up again."

"You can't park your vehicle in a campground. The rangers should've done something."

This time Anna didn't bother to ask if they'd reported it. These three had joined that majority who believe an all-seeing, all-powerful government owed them safety, comfort and a living whether they lifted a finger to help themselves or not.

A couple more nudges and she discovered they didn't know where the men had gone on their moonlight hiking and camping adventure. She stayed long enough to finish her coffee, then left with what she'd come for: none of the squatters could have been in on the search of the room and the assault on Nicky. She'd also gotten a bonus: the truck tracks she'd wanted to trace belonged to a red Ford Excursion. Instead of doubling back, Anna continued on past the tiny cluster of tent cabins at the east end of the campground.

Billy, or the boy-faced prick, was home, that or a black bear was napping on somebody's cot. Wet growling snores came through the tent's sides with such gale force Anna was surprised the canvas walls didn't puff out and in the way they did in cartoons.

Fairly confident that the owners of the Excursion were either gone or comatose, she headed back through the grounds of Camp 4 toward the parking lot that girded its western side. Campers had begun emerging from their brightly colored cocoons. There was an edge of excitement that she wouldn't have expected on a cold and hungover morning at the bedraggled tail end of the climbing season. Nights got below freezing and, with the previous night's drizzle, Anna would have thought the rock faces too icy to climb before ten o'clock.

The bustle and low-grade buzz kept company with her through the camp. Groups of guys were dragging out packs and boots. Climbers were mostly obsessed by the climb. Many never set foot more than a mile into the park, at least not horizontally.

Anna guessed the unusual combination of ice on the granite walls and dry conditions in the high country had inspired them to try their hand at winter camping. But for the single snowfall that had effectively sabotaged the search effort, there'd been no precipitation to speak of. Even at eighty-five hundred feet there was only a foot or so of frozen crusty snow. If the pattern didn't break, Yosemite was going to have one hell of a fire season come summer.

The coffee she'd cadged from various generous parties was completing its morning rounds, and she stopped at the camp's restroom.

Above her chosen commode near the outer wall was a small high ventilation window. Through this came the desultory morning conversation of a group camped just outside.

"What a bash."

"That fat guy was off his head."

Anna's ears pricked at that with such interest, had she been a terrier, the tips would have been quivering. She climbed on the commode seat to get her ears nearer the window, and began to eavesdrop.

"You think it's like he said?"

"Shit, even if you figure sixty percent was just hot air, it's worth going after."

"He swore he'd been there."

"Lot of people there last night. It's going to be a fucking gold rush."

"The guy'd been somewhere. Did you see the dude's feet? Hamburger."

"Yeah but I'm not dragging my butt all over hell and gone in the snow trying to figure out where."

"He said a low lake. How many can there be?"

"A shitload."

"That's what I want. A load of shit."

This scatological sally was met with much laughter. The voices trailed off as the climbers walked away from their site. Anna sat back down for some serious thinking.

Deep thought having availed her nothing, she zipped her trousers and rejoined the world of men. Slob or Billy "Beer" Kurt or whatever his name was wasn't the type to stray too far from an easy form of transportation. Taking an educated guess, she thought she'd find the SUV in the closest parking lot.

As luck would have it, one group of backpackers had their vehicle parked next to the only red Ford Excursion in the lot. She didn't dare get too snoopy—she'd look fishy as hell. Wandering past slowly she was amazed—as she always was—at how damn *big* SUVs were. Unless she was pulling a six-horse trailer fully loaded she'd have been embarrassed to be seen in the thing. Oversized SUVs were conspicuous consumerism taken to such lengths she marveled that people willingly participated in cruel caricatures of themselves by driving them.

Mentally she noted the Excursion was brand-new—or nearly so—and hard-used by the look of the frozen mud caked on its underside. The plates were from Mendocino County outside of San Francisco. Anna memorized the tag number and moved on. Vehicle information and perhaps a closer look would be done by Yose's law enforcement rangers.

Being undercover, even such a benign undercover as a waitress in a fine restaurant with nary a mob boss or biker ring in evidence, was a pain in the ass. Divested of power, clout, radios, backup, cell phones, All Points Bulletins and computers that could talk to the DMV, NCIC, the FBI and, if one knew the e-mail address, probably God, she felt as if she was working half blind and mostly deaf.

Though remaining successfully undercover in a small isolated community was considerably more difficult than in larger operations, Anna felt slightly silly picking up the key Lorraine had promised her at the clinic. She gave no explanation as to why the chief ranger had left it for her—indeed Lorraine would probably have sent it with someone with a much lower profile than herself—and the nurse receptionist asked for none.

The key was not to the main fire cache that held the newer equipment—that was to the back of the Search and Rescue building resting its rustic beporched self between the barn and the old graveyard. Fortunately for Anna—otherwise she'd have had to tell too many lies to people too clever to believe her—Trish Spencer's belongings were stored in the old fire cache, a junk room more or less, in one of the snowplow garages up the hill. The garage doors were aligned with the SAR building and sat cheek-by-jowl with the great stone building that housed fire trucks, jail and law enforcement offices.

Looking as boring and unremarkable as possible, Anna fought briefly with the padlock, raised the door in an alarming clamor, then pulled it shut behind her. The odds of her fellow concessionaires smelling her for the rat she was were small. The odds of a ranger getting curious and chatting about it to the ruination of the investigation were much higher. Hiding from her peers was an unpleasant sensation. She shook it off with a twitch of her shoulders.

Locking herself in a grimy old garage piled with boxes undoubtedly providing winter homes for black widow spiders didn't add to her comfort or self-esteem. Batting at an eyeball-high string, she caught it and pulled. A hundred dusty watts from a bulb suspended from the eight-foot ceiling clarified matters.

Spencer's boxes were easily located. Last in, they were freest of dust and closest to the door. When Anna had packed them, she'd marked them with Trish's name, last known address and the date packed. There were four. Squatting on her heels, she cut the first one open with her pocketknife, which she had remembered to stuff in her checked luggage at the last minute. Confiscating Swiss army knives was an affront to that sovereign nation's neutrality, but she doubted that argument would have impressed airport security on her flight out of Jackson, Mississippi.

Using the unopened boxes as tables, she began to methodically sift through Trish Spencer's things. Over the years she'd had cause to rifle through people's belongings a number of times: the domestic detritus of the living, the dead or, like Ms. Spencer, those whose status was as yet undetermined. It wasn't a task she particularly liked or disliked but—and this she would confess to no one but her sister, Molly—it never failed to fascinate her. Other people's stuff. Being civilized to a certain extent, she wouldn't dream of going through her host's medicine cabinets or peeking in drawers. Being as curious as the doomed cat and of a sleuthy disposition, when the task was forced upon her she couldn't deny a certain thrill. When poking through another person's papers, underwear or computer files, there lurked that prurient and delicious possibility that one might come across a secret, the dirtier and more horrifying the better.

Secrets—if one could glorify them with such a titillating appellation—whispered or hinted at by most people's belongings tended to be little and boring: Grecian Formula, Viagra, pornographic magazines, bad poetry. But reality wasn't where the voyeur's excitement lay. It was the *possible*.

Ignoring this ignoble part of her psyche, Anna combed through the boxes with clinical dispassion. Trish's collected estate was run-of-the-mill. Perhaps better suited to a girl of nineteen or twenty than a woman of twenty-seven, but the seminomadic lifestyle of a concessions worker could account for it. Two of the boxes were crammed with clothes; a sparse wardrobe when spread out. Anna was reminded that Trish had a taste for gaudy finery and real short skirts, and the money for a couple of designer pieces: a Ralph Lauren leather vest and red Gucci stiletto heels. Underneath the clothing was a black leather satchel, a sort of soft-sided briefcase. Either Trish had found it or she'd had it for most of her life. The leather was scarred and stiff from at least one drenching. The handle was torn off and the stitching along one side ripped open. Anna looked inside. Nothing. The bag was out of place, but having no idea where it would be in place, she moved on.

The third box was full—completely and totally full—of cosmetics and hair-care items.

Working so long in the parks, makeup hadn't been much of a factor in Anna's life. Since moving to Mississippi she'd begun to notice it. Southern women wore a lot of makeup, expertly applied. On any given day on the Natchez Trace Parkway, Anna would stop speeders wearing more makeup than her husband, Zach, had applied when, at the age of twenty-six, he'd been cast as King Lear in an off-off-Broadway production where Shakespeare's characters were portrayed as lizardlike creatures in a post–nuclear holocaust setting.

Mississippi had not sold her on makeup, but she didn't sneer as she might have done a year or two earlier. Since moving to Dixie she'd developed a bit of a taste for true red lipstick and once, when feeling wild and crazy, had painted her toenails to match.

A nine-cubic-foot box filled with paints and powders, hairpins and curling irons wasn't standard for wilderness use, but then Yosemite Valley was not wilderness. In an unavoidable and unsettling way it and its adjacent areas were urban. Not in the good sense of art, culture and cinema, but in the vaguely creepy sense of . . . well, of lizards in a postapocalyptic world.

Anna went through the items one at a time. Trish liked earth tones and metallics and put a lot of goop in her hair. With the care she always took of the belongings of those whose privacy she invaded in her professional capacity, Anna neatly replaced the cosmetics in their box.

The last box was the most promising, though it was less than a quarter full. It held books and papers. Trish had only two books, romances—a Nora Roberts and a LaVyrle Spencer. Both were dog-eared and rumpled, as if much read.

Anna leafed through a checkbook. Entries ratified the suspected vanity; most were to department stores, the notations reading clothes, makeup and miscellaneous. Trish used a bank in Merced, the largest town within a two-hour radius, and did most of her shopping there. Regular deposits had been made for her tips, deposits considerably larger than those Anna reluctantly set aside each week to be plowed back into the park's budget. Either Trish was an excellent waitress or she had some other source of income.

The rest of the papers consisted of a pile of "dear occupant" correspondence and one unfinished letter. The salacious glee of the village snoop flicked the edges of Anna's brain as she picked up the most personal of human flotsam; writing, the only place other than conversation where a human being's actual thoughts could be discovered, a direct peek into the brain of another creature.

"Dear Dickie," she read. "Your gym is closer than you might think. I've become a miner. There's gold in them thar hills . . ."

That was it. The letter had never been finished. Since there weren't any missives from "Dickie," Anna guessed the correspondence—and possibly any relationship—was one-sided.

She replaced the books and papers, closed the boxes and sat on the cold concrete, her breath visible in the still air.

Miner, mining.

Having so recently stolen, via eavesdropping from the ladies' john, the thoughts of another group who spoke of a gold rush, the words reverberated. Maybe this Lost Dutchman's Mine theme connected the events of Dix's squatters, Camp 4 and the disappearance of Trish Spencer. Gold, actual honest-to-God gold, in the foothills of the Sierra had populated

California in the rush of '49, but Anna had never heard of it being found in this glacier-carved granite country.

Whether metal ore or another form, the letter fragment suggested Trish had found a way to get money, quite a bit of it. "Your gym is closer than you think." Either she'd found a convenient way for Dickie to buff up or Dickie had the dream of owning a gym or gym franchise. Anna'd worked with enough down-and-out young people to recognize a standard fantasy: girls wanted to own their own clothing boutiques, boys wanted to own their own gym. Taxi drivers and waitresses wanted to be stars of stage and screen.

Profiling—so severely frowned upon that Anna, a middle-aged white lady from Mississippi, had been searched three times on a two-plane flight on the off chance it was she and not a male of Middle Eastern descent between eighteen and forty who was intent on the overthrow of America—was not only a useful tool in law enforcement, but absolutely un-avoidable. Profiling was merely using a lifetime's experience to make an educated guess.

Anna guessed Trish had stumbled on a real or virtual gold mine and intended to use the proceeds to buy Dickie his heart's desire and, if she were lucky, his heart as well.

CHAPTER

6

Prophylactically squinting against the expected glare, Anna raised the garage door a few feet to slip out. The weak December sun had given up all but the ghost. Heavy fog had settled back into the valley. Anna scrunched out and lowered the door. Gray and damp and close, the granite walls of The Ditch were getting to her. The dry weather had nothing to do with crisp sunny days and clear starlit nights. Fronts, cold and slow moving, marched in from the Pacific, offering all the delights of a nasty winter without the life-giving snows. "Fog" wasn't even the proper term. The mountains seldom suffered the fogs for which the valleys were famous. Fog suggested graveyards and London, Jack the Ripper and little cat's feet: frightening, fascinating, creeping, elusive, hidden things. This California mountain fog was freakish, lacking in romance or menace. A pewter lid, it effectively sealed off the view above three or four hundred feet and made the cold cut deeper than it might otherwise.

For a moment she stood beside the storage space's door. Being undercover had yet another drawback: there was simply no place one could be comfortable. Her room was dark and, since Nicky had probably been awake for five or ten minutes, a disaster area. Even if it had been warm and light and tidy it still would have lacked privacy. Virginia Woolf had it right: a woman needed a room of her own. That was especially true for a woman leading a double life.

Having taken time to acknowledge her disgruntlement and give crabbiness its due, Anna walked to the Ahwahnee employee dorm. Nicky didn't go on duty till ten, and Anna not till three-thirty. There was plenty of time to enjoy the squalor and visit with her roommate.

Nicky was up. Hugging a mug of coffee to her chest with one hand, she sat in bed clad in T-shirt and sweatpants, reading a comic book. Anna had grown up on the comics: Spiderman, Superman, Casper the Friendly Ghost, Donald Duck, Uncle Scrooge, Archie. Her habit had followed her into high school where Classic Comics served to assist her with book reports, then to whet her appetite to read the unillustrated and unabridged versions of *Lorna Doone, A Tale of Two Cities, The Count of Monte Cristo* and too many others to hold in a single flash of memory.

The comic book Nicky pored over resembled none of Anna's remembered favorites.

"How're you doing?" she asked as she began the time-consuming process of peeling off layers.

Nicky put down the comic. "I'm okay." The girl looked at Anna differently this morning. Cricket and Nicky's combined ages didn't add up to as many years as Anna had birthdays. Because of this, they may have observed her, but they'd never bothered to *see* her. Occasionally, when she cracked a good joke or displayed some other bit of cleverness, she had

gotten the sense that for a moment—just a second or two—
she had flickered out of the pale world of parental-aged
wraiths and been seen by them to be real, as real as themselves. These glimmers were few.

This morning Nicky was looking right at her. The previous night's events had destroyed artificial barriers of age.
Two humans in a room together. Anna hadn't realized how
much she'd missed existing in the eyes of her fellows till that
moment. It felt good to be visible again. In a very real way,
when working undercover, one ceased to exist. The old persona was buried with great care. The new one was a fraud.
The only moments of genuine reality were when reporting to
the contact in the old life regarding the goings-on in the new.

Anna had thought she would be much better at living a lie.

Before she had time to enjoy it, she regretted the passing
of her invisibility. Though lonely, it had been handy. Nothing
she said, did or asked made much of an impression. Neither
Nicky nor Cricket evinced curiosity about where she went,
what she did, who she was.

That wouldn't be true now. As if to ratify Anna's conclusion, Nicky said: "Where were you off to so early? I got up
to pee around six and you'd left."

Faint but discernable to a Catholic school–trained ear,
Anna could hear the accusation under the words. What with
one thing and another she'd gone from invisible nobody lady
to surrogate mom. Since there was no changing this and no
guaranteeing that it wouldn't shortly slide into teenage resentment, Anna decided to capitalize on it.

Nicky was listening and needing to talk: the search of
their quarters the night before provided Anna with an ideal
excuse to openly pump her about Trish Spencer.

No pumping was required. Since Anna, by virtue of "saving Cricket's life" and being "cool" about them being high,

had become one of the gang, Nicky was willing, anxious even, to talk. Trish's disappearance hadn't hit her as hard as one might expect. The realm of seasonal park workers was peopled with itinerants, the turnover considerable, often unheralded and usually sudden. Concessions employees commonly "disappeared" for reasons of their own or those of their employers.

The fact that three others had gone missing at the same time, coupled with the attendant hullabaloo of the search, had affected Nicky in a way Anna had often witnessed in young people living through tragedies peripheral to their lives, a public trying-on of grief fed mostly by the attention of adults or the media. Anna didn't hold this self-centered worldview against them. The life experience of most people under twenty was too limited to embrace great tragedy. It was one of their charms, making them appear innocent and simple to more jaded eyes.

Nicky's first tidbit of shared information was no surprise. After seeing Trish Spencer's checkbook and the large deposits written off to "tips," Anna had suspected it. It explained why the dorm residents had been tight-lipped when the rangers questioned them in hopes of gaining a direction for the search. Trish was the local drug connection. According to Nicky, she dealt only in marijuana and only in small amounts, but she admitted neither she nor Cricket ever asked for anything else.

Thinking "Dickie" might be the source of Trish's goods, Nicky and Cricket had been careful not to enlighten law enforcement about his existence. As Dickie was to be the recipient of largesse as outlined by Trish's unfinished letter, Anna doubted he was the supplier. If he was the boyfriend apparent, Nicky and Cricket's keeping him secret might have had dire consequences for Trish. If he knew where she was headed, Yosemite's SAR team might have been able to question him and perhaps locate Trish in time to save her life.

Briefly, Anna was tempted to tell Nicky this in hopes she would learn a lesson about the cost of not cooperating with rangers. In the end she decided against it. There was already too much ambient guilt in the world.

And this particular guilt might be groundless. Trish might not have died.

With these thoughts, Anna wondered if Trish had somehow engineered the fate of the others, then disappeared to throw suspicion in other directions. How she could take out three hardy people all by her little self and why she would do that to her best friend and two pals, Anna couldn't venture a guess. The obvious motive was that they knew she was dealing, but probably half the park knew she was dealing. Salesmen had to market their wares. It was one of the risks of the profession.

Anna decided not to chase this particular wild goose, at least for a while.

With a bit of creative questioning, she was able to get Nicky to recall Dickie's last name: Cauliff. She was pretty sure he lived in Mariposa, a little town fifty minutes southwest of the park. Though Nicky couldn't remember her ever having said so, she got the idea that Trish stayed with Dickie Cauliff when she was there.

Nicky left for her bussing duties. Anna bundled up again for the walk to Yosemite Lodge with its discreetly tucked-away pay phones.

Usually Anna wasn't a proponent of cell phones. Having been born to the heft of a rotary dial, when she used a cell she felt as if she were holding a bar of soap to her ear and talking to empty air. Still, she would have used one and been grateful for it in her current position. Unfortunately, satellite

phones were too costly and the other services had yet to pen-
etrate large chunks of the Sierras, including Yosemite Valley.

One nifty call to information and Anna had the phone
number for a D. Cauliff in Mariposa. The initial threw her off
briefly. Usually it was only women who listed themselves by
an initial instead of a name, mistakenly assuming it dis-
guised gender.

A man answered.

Whatever it was—if anything—Dickie Cauliff did for a
living, he didn't do it at ten-thirty A.M. on weekdays. For that
Anna was grateful. She didn't relish spending her free time at
pay phones.

"Yeah?" The voice sounded wary and Anna had yet to in-
troduce herself.

On the walk over from the dorm she'd given considerable
thought to this introduction. If Trish spent a lot of time with
this guy, Anna doubted she'd be on safe ground pretending to
be a friend. If she admitted she was a ranger she would need
to use an assumed name; she had no way of knowing whether
Cauliff was on speaking terms with anyone at the park. Should
she use an assumed name with ranger credentials, too many
people at administration would have to be let in on the secret
in case he called park offices asking for her fictitious self.

Honesty was not the best policy. She decided on the in-
trinsically uninteresting yet seductive persona of a mid-level
bookkeeper in payroll at the Ahwahnee Lodge.

"Hi," she said with moderate chipperness. "This is Angie
Dickinson at the Ahwahnee." The name had leapt from some
mental archive. An alias was the one thing she'd forgotten to
come up with. Hoping her quarry was too young to be con-
versant with Hollywood's Ms. Dickinson, Anna waited.

"Yeah?"

A man of few words.

"What relationship did you bear to Ms. Spencer?"

"I'm her . . . Hang on."

By the muffled whump that followed, Anna guessed he'd covered the mouthpiece. What seemed like an excessively long time later, at least two full minutes, he came back on the line. "She got money coming or what?" he demanded.

"Yes. But I'm going to have to ask you—"

"Hang on." Whump. Ninety seconds by the big hand on the wall behind Yosemite Lodge's hostess station and he said: "How much?"

Anna didn't have to pretend to sound miffed. She had lost control of the interview and probably not to the monosyllabic Dickie but to whomever he conferred with during the pauses.

"It's a good bit, sir, but first I'm going to have to ask you some questions."

"Wait a sec." This conference was blessedly short. Abruptly he was in her ear again. "Forget the money. Trish left some stuff up there. Her stuff. What happened to it?"

Anna was startled by the request and the unlikely order to "forget the money." Obviously she'd missed something of real or perceived importance when she went through Trish's relics.

"You mean like her clothes and stuff?" she asked stupidly.

"Yeah. Like that. What happened to it?"

"I believe it was packed up and put into storage to send to her next of kin if it comes to that."

"You got it in storage? I want it."

"I don't personally have it," Anna countered. She wasn't yet ready to turn him over to the NPS. "Ms. Spencer's belongings go to her next of kin. What is your relationship with her."

Whump. Wait.

"Her brother."

Anna didn't believe that for a minute. "You have different last names," she said sounding vague.

"Yeah. She married that asshole Jerry Spencer." Maybe Dickie was her brother; this nugget of history rolled off his tongue with the familiar contempt of a family feud.

"Then Mr. Spencer needs to be notified—"

"They're divorced. You gonna give me that stuff or not? You got no right to keep it."

The wall had been hit. Anna would get no more. Not that she'd handled things brilliantly and gotten anything of much consequence prior to the metaphorical wall.

"I don't have anything to do with the deceased's property," she said primly. "You'll have to call personnel."

Dickie hung up without even bothering to curse her for wasting his time.

Whether Mr. Cauliff was brother, paramour or drug connection, he was singularly uninterested in Trish Spencer's fate. He had not asked about the search, nor had he shown grief at her disappearance. When Anna intentionally referred to him as "next of kin" and Trish as "the deceased" he hadn't protested—at least not audibly. Chief Ranger Knight said they'd found none of Trish's relatives.

Now suddenly she had a brother who showed no surprise or sadness at her probable demise and demanded her fancy shoes, electric curlers and cosmetics be returned immediately.

Perhaps Dickie knew precisely what had happened to Trish Spencer, and had tried before to collect whatever it was he believed to be among her effects, and Trish had not survived the encounter.

Anna bought yet another cup of coffee and further jangled her nerves as she sat outside on the lodge's patio trying to figure out what she knew now that she hadn't known when she'd crawled out of bed six hours earlier.

Camp 4 had been festive late into the night. None of the men in Dix's tent had corporeally participated in tossing her dorm room and assaulting her roommate. Billy "Beer" Kurt had dropped his companions at an unknown destination for nighttime winter camping. He'd returned, rekindled the party and told tales that the climbers of Camp 4 thought could foment a gold rush. Trish wore too much makeup and wrote to Dickie of finding a gold mine. Trish was a small-time dope dealer connected to a Dickie Cauliff in Mariposa. Dickie wanted something he believed Trish had left behind.

Unable to put it together herself, Anna decided to invest a quarter and unload it on Lorraine. The chief ranger would be able to dispatch law enforcement to interview Cauliff, track down the red Ford Excursion and start an investigation into where Spencer was getting the dope.

Lorraine's secretary answered. The chief ranger was not in. She had been sent to Missoula, Montana, that morning. Leo Johnson, the deputy superintendent, was slated to teach a five-day wilderness management class there. At breakfast he'd broken a tooth trying to crack the shell of a Brazil nut with his bicuspids. The tooth had snapped above gum line, the woman insisted on sharing. He had to go to a dentist in Merced. Lorraine was to go teach in his place. Deputy Superintendent Johnson, however, would be back tomorrow.

Anna refused the woman's kind offer to take a message and hung up. Feeling abandoned and having no more leads to follow up on, she mentally turned back into a waitress without even the aid of a proper phone booth.

Life as a waitress was pretty decent, relaxing actually, until she went to work. As she passed through the kitchen and said "hi" to the chef, she didn't receive her usual noncommittal grunt. Jim Wither, occupied with chopping celery—a task beneath his dignity and customarily reserved for the salad chef—gave her a look of such black hatred it literally stopped her in her tracks. Glaring at her balefully, he chopped with greater vehemence till, with a burst of rabbit courage, she escaped his cobra stare, afraid for his fingers if not her throat.

Her first two orders were slammed on the counter with such force it was a wonder the plates didn't break. Every interaction was accompanied by a poisonous scowl. Wither had too much professional pride to screw up the food, but anything he could do to make her look a fool and screw up her tips was done: bread was late or cold, side orders were late, wrong, cold or all three. If she needed anything special or rushed he ignored her. Had Scott not been willing to step in, she would have suffered more verbal abuse from the diners than was already being heaped upon her.

Halfway through the dinner rush, desperate to get hot rolls for a table of people who'd evidently decided man could live on bread alone, Anna decided to fetch them from the kitchen herself rather than fight through the wordless malice flowing from the head chef.

The Ahwahnee's kitchen was large and, despite its age, gleaming. Wither kept it surgically clean and organized with military precision. As she entered this sanctum sanctorum, the bustling of the underchefs hiccoughed. One looked at her with the surreptitious sympathy of a fellow sufferer. The other two let their eyes slide away without recognition. Jim Wither's inexplicable animosity made her dangerous to associate with. Cooties, like mumps, were ten times worse when contracted as an adult. Only Scott behaved normally. He gave her a wink and a shrug before returning to his drizzling and chocolate curling.

An island of warmth in the cold war Jim Wither was waging, Anna felt a sudden surge of affection for the assistant chef. She winked back and was rewarded by a smile that would reassure children and make nuns go weak at the knees.

Encouraged, Anna tried to recapture that middle-aged-waitress invisibility she had so lately belied, and slunk through the counters and pots toward the warming ovens beside the oversized gas range. She was opening the oven door when Wither shouted.

"Out!"

The violent bark of sound startled her and she banged her elbow on a countertop, momentarily disorienting herself with the explosion of pain from the misnamed funny bone.

"Out!" was shouted again and: "Look out."

"Christ!"

Then she was in the air, her toes slapping cabinet doors as she whirled past.

A crash.

A scream.

She was on the ground again a couple of yards from the ovens. Scott stood between her and the gas range. Water steamed and streamed over the floor. Underchefs cowered on the far side of the kitchen's central island. Dark eyes, sunken and burning like hot coals in his pale, fleshless face, Jim Wither stood to Scott's other side. The cadaverous chef was trembling as if an emotion too great for his being raged through his wasted frame.

The abruptly fragmented world coalesced.

Wither had knocked over—or thrown—a pot of boiling water that landed where Anna had been standing. Had Scott Wooldrich not snatched her up and moved her, she would have been scalded from waist to ankle. Scott's apron and trousers were wet. Anna hoped they'd saved him from being burned. The back of his right arm was an angry red where the boiling water had splashed him when he'd stepped in to save her skin.

The sight of burns on him made her angrier than if they had been on her own body. Grateful as she was for the rescue, she now owed Scott, if not a pound of flesh, then at least an ounce or two.

The slow boil that had simmered on her mental back burner since Jim Wither had begun his vendetta went over the top.

Stepping around Scott, she faced the chef. "What in God's name is your problem? Did I run over your dog? Make a pass at your wife? Tell me for Chrissake. I'll apologize—hell, I'll grovel. What is it?"

The quiet after this brief interrogative tirade was absolute. No choppers chopped. No pans clanked. The spilled pot ceased to boil.

Tiny's sharp voice cut through the palpable silence. "What is going on here?" she demanded.

"That's what I'm trying to find out," Anna said. She did not look away from Wither. There was something wrong with the man and she wasn't sure if it was overblown prima-donna or homicidal tendencies. Another three gallons of scalding water stood at his elbow. If he so much as looked in that direction, Anna would take him down. Better an undignified brawl on a wet floor than getting burned.

"What are you doing in the kitchen?"

Tiny's voice cut at the back of Anna's neck. She ignored it.

Unblinking, Wither held her gaze. Tremors she'd noticed before traveled up from his hands till his head shook on his neck in a palsy. The flush of anger drained from his face leaving it paler than usual and covered in a sickly sheen of sweat. He broke eye contact and looked past Anna to Scott or Tiny or one of the underchefs. What, if anything, was communicated, Anna couldn't say. She'd not yet reached the place where it was safe to divide her attention.

Wither came back to life in the sense that the peculiar mix

of rigidity and trembling broke into a more ambulatory pattern.

"Get back to work," he snapped. "Clean this water up. Now. Now. Now!"

The kitchen muttered and hummed. Wither shot Anna one more hard look. This time it seemed more searching than menacing. "Rolls'll be hot," he said and turned his back on her.

Suffering a touch of palsy herself, Anna returned to her task at the oven. Scott was still near—pleasantly so—a shield for her back, a screen for her momentary weakness.

"Are you all right?" he whispered. His mouth close to her ear, she could smell mint on his breath, or maybe parsley. Whatever it was, she liked it.

"I'm okay." She was glad to have the business of loading fresh bread into baskets. "How about you? The back of your arm doesn't look too good."

"I'll live. Look, I don't know what got into Jim tonight but I . . . You want to get a drink after work? Unwind. Bad-mouth Wither?"

Anna laughed and turned, baskets in hand. "My treat," she said. "You saved my life. Let me buy you a beer."

Delivering her hard-won rolls, Anna suffered a small maelstrom of thoughts and feelings. Had mayhem been attempted? What had caused Jim Wither to take against her so suddenly and vehemently? Why did Scott wish to have a drink with her? Friendship? Boredom? A taste for older women? Professionally, it was good to get this chance to sound him out. As an affianced woman, she doubted she should be looking forward to it quite as much as she was.

Briefly, she wondered how many officers of the law were married when they went into undercover work. And how many were still married when they came out of it. When one

donned a new world, the rules, mores and traditions of the
old dropped away. Without conscious decision the unthink-
able was thought, the unacceptable became the norm. Lines
one learned never to cross shifted or vanished altogether.

Slipping off to the staff bathroom, Anna took a moment
to pull herself together. She was merely having a drink with
a potential source of information, not committing adultery
with the entire Knicks team. Her nerves, usually dependable,
had grown frayed. The high drama of the spilled or hurled
cauldron oddly enough wasn't the most wearing factor. It
was the cheek-by-jowl parade of the small and annoying: a
room searched while she was out, a surly "brother," unsettling undercurrents first in Camp 4 then the Ahwahnee's
kitchen. Of all the things Anna hated, high on the list were
secrets she was not privy to.

Since coming to Yosemite Valley she'd had a sense of a
dark river flowing below the surface, a cold current which
had swept away four young people. She credited this ambient
evil with bringing professional thugs into her dorm room;
hikers smelling of petrol, with new boots, into Dixon Crofter's
tent cabin; dope smoke that paralyzed lungs and made an obsessive culinary expert so angry he'd accidentally or in the
throes of black passion nearly scalded her half to death.

These anomalous secrets to which she was not privy
might not be connected. The metaphorical river whose un-
dertow tugged at her mind was not necessarily of a piece.
Secrets were like rabbits. If you got two in January, by year's
end you had two hundred.

Secrets corrupted. Camp 4 was tainted. The Ahwahnee,
James Wither, were part of something bigger; maybe he was
just a half-crazy cook with a grievance and the corruption
centered around the Yosemite Lodge, where Mark despoiled
maids. Maybe it was fostered by the NPS staff. Anna

couldn't begin to guess. She was severed from the society of rangers more completely than if she had, in truth, been a waitress. As a real concessions employee she would have been allowed to make friends.

Lest she grow too philosophical—or maudlin—she focused on being a good waitress for the next four hours. Wither didn't relent to the point of apologizing or commit any radical act like speaking to her, but the hostile stares were gone and her orders were served up as they should have been. Still, she felt a weight lift when at nine o'clock Wither went off duty.

At ten-thirty her last table, a party of four, two nice couples from Canada come south for a holiday, left. Anna went into the bowels of the building, to the employee locker room. Regardless of history, fresh paint or company goodwill, backstage rooms were uniformly dreary whether one worked as an elf in Macy's on Thirty-fourth Street or served pasta primavera in God's country.

She flopped on a scarred bench in a horseshoe of lockers that looked as if they'd been salvaged from an inner-city high school. Having kicked off her shoes, she rubbed her feet. The absurd but accurate cliché she presented made her laugh. Why eight hours waiting tables in a gorgeously appointed temperature-controlled restaurant should leave her more tired and footsore than the same amount of time crossing harsh terrain in heavy boots was a mystery.

"You survived."

Scott was leaning in the doorframe, his muscled arms crossed on his chest. The scald on his forearm had blistered. Anna suffered annoyance instead of gratitude. Being rescued was a burden she seldom carried gracefully.

Burned, aproned and spattered with food, Scott Wooldrich was still a good-looking man. Another stab, this time of guilt,

stirred Anna's innards. A soon-to-be-married woman, a
woman hurtling toward the half-century mark with blinding
speed, should surely be past the dangerously addictive nonsense attendant on cute boys.

"I survived," she said for lack of anything witty or erudite.

"Put on your coat and let's go get that drink. How about
our sister lodge, just for a change of scenery? A little slum-
ming is good for the soul." Anna slipped her shoes back on,
then stood to open her locker as he asked: "Shall we walk
or drive?"

Even after an eight-hour shift on concrete floors, Anna
would have chosen to walk. The air, the night, the unfettered
movement were more refreshing than sleep. Tonight for some
reason a vision of the woman stabbed thirty-nine times while
in the stony embrace of the great boulders flashed to the front
of her mind.

"Ride," she said. "My feet have had it for one day."

She pulled her jacket from the locker and swung it around
to put it on. The sleeve slapped the metal of the door and
thunked.

Thunked.

It was a down jacket with knit cuffs. There was no thunk
about it. Anna caught up the sleeve and looked inside. A hair
below cuff-line she could see a white plastic disk the size of
a dime.

"What the . . ."

"A problem?" Scott came close, looking over her shoulder.

"There's something . . ." Anna held open the sleeve and
peered in, remembering the silly childhood joke of holding
one's fist hidden in a sleeve and saying: "Want to see stars?
Look up my telescope."

"Jesus."

"What?" Scott demanded.

"Got a handkerchief?"

Scott gave her a blue cowboy bandanna. Using the hand-kerchief to protect any fingerprints, she reached carefully into the sleeve and pinched the barrel of a hypodermic syringe. The plunger—the end of it being the dime-sized disk she'd seen—was duct-taped firmly to the inside of the cuff. The barrel of the syringe was loosely affixed with the same kind of tape. Had she jammed her arm in the sleeve with the cus-tomary abandon of folks getting off work and heading into the cold, the force would have shoved the needle into her hand or wrist and depressed the plunger, injecting the sy-ringe's contents into her arm.

She pulled the barrel, plunger and needle out and held it up to the light. "Blood," she said. "The syringe looks like it's full of blood."

For a second she thought she saw recognition spark be-hind Scott's eyes.

CHAPTER
7

"Holy Toledo," Scott said. Shock blew out the spark, if it had ever been there.

Anna looked away from him to the hypodermic pinched in his handkerchief. Standard stuff. The kind doctors give out by the handful to patients with a variety of maladies. The liquid inside had the viscous clinging qualities of blood still moderately fresh—that or thinned with an anticoagulant. There was nothing remarkable about it except for the fact that someone had wanted to inject it into Anna's arm.

"Here. Let me take that." Scott reached for the needle.

"I got it." Anna held it away from where he hovered, hand outstretched, with that peculiar intensity men get when wanting to snatch a power tool or computer mouse from their female compatriots. In Anna's pack was an unopened plastic bottle of water. Retiring to the sanctity of the ladies' bathroom with coat, backpack and bloody syringe, she poured the water down the drain, dropped the hypodermic in the bottle, and screwed the cap back on. That done, she turned her jacket inside out, searching carefully for any other booby traps. She found none, nor had she expected to. Whoever had rigged the syringe was an amateur. No practiced, competent doer of harm would rely on a delivery system that depended so much on luck.

Secreting the bottle in the bottom of her pack, she rejoined her "date."

Scott had doffed his apron and changed his white uniform shirt for a black T-shirt that wasn't warm enough for a mountain winter and too tight. On him it was flattering, stylish rather than déclassé.

"Nice build," Anna said because it was true and displayed for the public's enjoyment.

"I used to spend a lot of time working out on weights," Scott said as they left the hotel.

"No more?" she asked to make conversation.

"Some. Enough not to get fat. But that's about it these days."

"What changed? Decided you were already handsome enough?"

Scott laughed. His teeth were small and straight, giving him a boyish look when he smiled. "I learned to cook. Love at first bite."

Scott drove a classic '68 Mustang, the body spotted with rust-colored patches where dents had been filled in, sanded and primed. A gentleman by upbringing or education, he held the passenger door for her. As Anna started to buckle her seat belt, good manners were overcome by fashion sense. "You gonna wear that?" he asked, sounding genuinely alarmed.

Anna looked down. In the excitement of finding a hypodermic of blood duct-taped in her sleeve she'd forgotten to take her apron off. She untied it and chucked it in the backseat along with her pack. After eight hours of seeing, smelling and serving food, she was not anxious to wear it during her free time.

On the short drive from the Ahwahnee to the Yosemite Lodge they talked about the Mustang, the ins-and-outs of what would one day be a restoration to rival the first phoenix rising from the ashes. Anna was content with this harmless chat. She'd not yet decided what she wanted from the assistant chef, though the black T-shirt and melting smile were loading that question with unprofessional possibilities. Unprofessional and unethical. For the first time in a long while she had to consciously remind herself of Paul Davidson. He, along with the rest of real life, grew ever more dim. Scott, on the other hand, showed almost superreal, the heat and energy of him nearly enough to bask in like a cat in the sun.

Anna pulled her thoughts from basking. *It's the damp,* she told herself. *The unrelenting gray. I can't get warm.* She told herself lies but it served. Her mind obediently returned to the task at hand.

Questions.

Mostly she would just be casting around hoping her line would snag information to help tie together the bits of suspicious jetsam that had washed up over the past days. As he waxed poetic about polymers, paint and Internet parts stores, she let her mind drift back over the evening shift: Jim Wither, scalding water, finding the needle, who was where and why.

The Ahwahnee's back door wasn't kept locked, nor was her locker. She never kept anything of value in it, a seven-year-old down jacket being as worthless in Yosemite as last year's computer in Silicon Valley. Anyone could have access at any time. Had they wanted privacy, they could have had that too, as long as they didn't hit the locker room at a shift change. When on duty, the staff seldom went there. Anna couldn't even factor out people unfamiliar with which locker belonged to whom. Employees' names were written in magic marker on strips of masking tape on the doors. Whoever planted the syringe had meant to harm her specifically.

Personal malice. At least she had that going for her. Anna smiled in the dark.

Scott turned the Mustang into Yosemite Lodge's parking lot. Only then did it occur to her how bizarre his conversation about automobile rehab was. In the six or so minutes door to door he'd not referred to her needle-in-a-bottle once. It was as if she'd lost a button or broken a shoelace, an event traumatic enough to gain a drop of sympathy at the time, but of no sustaining interest.

Because this respite from the clamor of the dining hall had been so welcome, Anna hadn't questioned it. Now she did. Most people would have been ababble with speculations and questions up to and including what should be done with the macabre gift. Scott hadn't said a word. Either he was one of life's coolest customers or there was a reason he didn't want to talk about it.

Anna put the syringe on the list of things she would bring up over drinks.

Mrs. Wooldrich had raised her boy right. Had Anna waited, he would have come around the car and opened the door for her. She sprang out unaided. Marriage to Zachary, a Westchester, New York, boy, born and bred to the silver spoon despite the family not having cash for anything better than stainless flatware, Anna had come to appreciate mannerly men. The car door thing, though, she could never get used to. Brought up in a rough-and-tumble county on the California-Nevada border, she always felt like an idiot queen waiting while the driver circumnavigated the car to release her.

Scott seemed happy either way. Anna stuck her wallet in

the pocket of her coat and left her pack behind, trusting mother nature to refrigerate the blood sample. The lodge, though not so grand as her older sister, was by no means a fleabag. The public rooms were high-ceilinged and gracious with glass and unpainted timber. Where the Ahwahnee had the rich feel of a turn-of-the-century spa, the Yosemite was as crisp and sharp as a modern upscale ski resort.

Scott ordered bourbon on the rocks. Anna ordered tea. Tea, hot and fresh, had a clean taste that nothing else could touch.

"So where did you learn to cook?" she asked, because Wooldrich was sufficiently polite he couldn't be trusted to focus the conversation entirely on himself without a nudge.

He took a sip of bourbon. *Playing for time,* Anna thought, though she couldn't guess why. The question wasn't loaded.

"Actually Jim taught me," he said. "I'm a little old to be a protégé, I guess, but that's it. He taught me the basics, then brought me up here as an assistant salad chef—pretty low on the totem pole. I did that for a year, then he promoted me. It's who you know. Guys who've been to chefs' school in France don't have the kind of job I've got. I'm big on gratitude these days."

He smiled and rolled the bourbon around in the glass, watching candlelight play through the amber liquid the way she remembered her father doing when she was small. The image startled, then reassured her. Her instantaneous attraction to the burly cook wasn't preadulterous. It was Freudian. Scott, though he looked nothing like her dad, reminded her strongly of him: the way he tossed his head back when he laughed, as if the merriment reached down to his toes, the blunt power in his shoulders and hands, the way he leaned in doorways with patience and good cheer, the utter maleness of him untarnished by any blight of macho.

She laughed out loud.

"What?" he asked, half smiling.

"You remind me of my father."

"Is that good or bad?"

"Good."

"Good as in you'll let me put you through college or good in the Electra sense?"

A corner of Anna's mouth twitched and Scott laughed. "Snob," he said.

The Electra reference had taken Anna off guard. He'd read her mind, something her father'd never been able to do—which accounted for the fact that she'd not been locked in a convent till she was thirty.

"Hard to say." Then she did the eye thing. A drink, a look over the rim of the cup. A smile. Anna knew she was wading down a slippery slope into deep waters, but she didn't repent. She drew energy from the sexual tension between them. She was ten years older than he and not interested—except in the knee-jerk way she felt hungry when she smelled bacon frying, she assured herself—but the power was there and she took it.

Scott ordered a plate of nachos to share. Anna remembered she was working.

"Where'd you meet Jim? Did he work in San Francisco before coming here?" Gossip, as all-pervasive as air in the National Parks, had already informed her that Jim had been at the Ahwahnee for fifteen years. She wanted to see why Scott hadn't answered the question the first time she'd put it to him.

"Shoot," he said and shook his head ruefully. "I'm going to tell you something only a handful of people know. Maybe because you remind me of your father's daughter. You sure don't remind me of my mother. You'd need higher heels and a ton more mascara for that. Okay: I lifted a lot of weights. I had plenty of time to read the Greek classics."

He waited expectantly but Anna couldn't answer the implied riddle.

"Aw, come on, you're a sharp cookie. Guess."

Anna hated guessing.

He stopped the game before it became obnoxious. "I was sent to cooking school through the generosity of the California taxpayers. I spent nine years in the state pen in Soledad. Got out three years ago. I'm off parole the end of March. Jim and Tiny know. The park superintendent and whoever he told and the hotel's general manager knows. It's all on the up and up, papers filed, prints taken. I just don't choose to spread it any further than that. It's not that I'm ashamed of being an ex-con . . . It's just that it's . . ." He smiled. "Well it's sort of like being an astronaut. As soon as you mention it everybody gets tongue-tied. All the women want you to be the father of their children. All the men want to be you—or prove they're just as tough as you."

He was poking fun at himself but there was a lot of truth in what he said. An ex-con, especially a big, good-looking, articulate ex-con, confused people. Weak men wanted to prove they were as strong, strong men that they were stronger. Contempt, curiosity, fear, prurient interest or envy at wild adventures imagined clogged people's brains. Easier just to be a cook. Just to be Scott.

"And they say crime doesn't pay," Anna said. "Jim teaching inmates. Hard to picture. He's a big-deal chef, isn't he? Educated abroad, et cetera, et cetera?"

"Jim's the best. Why? You think he's too good to bother teaching bottom feeders like me?" Scott was smiling and

Anna sensed no edge to his words. Probably because he didn't believe he was a bottom feeder and never had.

"He's sure got no time for lowly waitresses," she said. "With the exception of Tiny."

"Jim's been under a lot of pressure," Scott said repressively.

Anna would get nowhere casting aspersions on Scott's mentor. Annoying as it was at the moment, she admired him for his loyalty.

Perhaps realizing he'd been too abrupt, Scott resumed on his own. "Jim and Tiny go way back. I don't know if they knew each other before he came to the park, but I know she has a brother who's got some pull. That and Jim's reputation in cooking circles is what got him the gig at Soledad. He came twice a week for three of the years I was there."

"Why would a four-star chef want to teach cooking to cons?" Anna asked. "Not that convicted felons aren't handy with paring knives and meat cleavers but you've got to admit teaching in a prison system is not a big item on most of the haut mondes résumés."

"I wondered at first too, but it turned out to be pretty straightforward. Jim's best friend had been put away for murder. Since he wasn't coming out, Jim found a way to come in more than just visiting hours."

Deftly, Anna looped the string around her teabag and wrung it out against her spoon. "What were you in for?" As soon as she'd spoken she realized, in the world of civilians, the question would probably be considered rude. Between cops and robbers it was talk around the office water cooler.

Scott gave her the same sharp look she remembered from when Cricket had collapsed. "You're an odd duck, Anna Pigeon. Where'd you learn to wait tables?"

"You first."

"You're going to be disappointed. This is another reason I don't like to tell people."

"Now I'm all aquiver."

He smiled an unvoiced double entendre. Again the tension. Again she embraced it. "In my former life I was a book-keeper by training and inclination, a CPA. I suppose you could say I came by my present job honestly. I was sent to Soledad for cooking the books for a dot-com in San Raphael. We were making money by the bushel. At least on paper."

"A bookkeeper." Anna wasn't disappointed but she was amused. Scott was about as far from the cliché of a bean counter as a man could get.

"A good one," he said.

"But not quite good enough."

The smile left his face. He took a hefty swallow of bourbon and raised a finger to the barmaid for another round. "I guess not," he said neutrally. "Anyway, after Jim got hooked up with the system and started teaching, being a swell all-around guy and a nonviolent offender I got in on it. I took to cooking and Jim took to me. When his buddy died, he kept coming anyway.

"Luther, my cellmate, and I kept on with the lessons. Jim brought us a lot: something to do, be interested in. When the food he needed for the classes was brought in he'd always manage to sneak us chocolate or good coffee. When you're locked up little things you used to take for granted become a big deal. When I got out he got me this job. There. Me in a nutshell," Scott finished. The smile was back.

"How did his friend die?"

"Pneumonia."

Anna fiddled with her tea for a moment. Now that her first thirst had been assuaged she was getting picky. The tea had come the way it usually did in American bars and eateries: an aluminum pot of rapidly cooling water and a generic tea bag on the side. In order to get much flavor out of the leaves one had to massage the bag with the spoon.

Scott took to cooking. Jim took to him. For the first time it occurred to her that Scott's flirtation might not be completely genuine. He didn't "look gay," but then he didn't look like a bookkeeper either.

"Are you and Jim lovers?" she asked.

"That's for you to figure out." The words were an invitation but she could tell the question made him mad. Since there were a lot of reasons it might, including the fact that it was none of her business, Anna didn't attach much importance to it.

"Now it's your turn," he said.

Anna told him a short version of her psychologist–abused-wife story. He seemed to accept it, even if he didn't swallow it whole. Perhaps he was a man who knew about secrets best left untold. Perhaps he was just lulling her into a sense of complacency for reasons of his own. Anna hadn't forgotten the look on his face when she'd pulled the boobytrap from the sleeve of her coat, nor the fact that, after that initial reaction, he'd showed a stunning lack of interest in the incident.

"How about that needle in my jacket? That was totally bizarre," she said for openers. She'd hoped to jolt him with the question. She didn't.

"Maybe not as bizarre as it should be," he said. "The restaurant business is cutthroat. People defend their turf. You came in at the top of the food chain, took a plum shift in the best restaurant in the park. Big tips. There's bound to be resentment. My guess is somebody is trying to scare you off."

"Why a needle? Why blood?"

"Beats me. Easy to come by? Scary? Creepy? Besides,

you don't know for sure its blood. Could be teriyaki and maraschino cherry juice."

"Somebody wanted to marinate me?"

"Make you inedible more like," Scott said with a laugh. "Probably just a bad joke."

The needle and syringe, without whatever vile substance was inside, would have given a vicious poke. Though crude, the duct-tape rigging was cleverly thought out and executed to deliver the injection. Not a joke.

"Probably," Anna agreed.

Scott had been folding his cocktail napkin into smaller and smaller squares, each newly folded edge scored by his thumbnail. When Anna agreed with him he glanced up, startled she'd swallowed his bullshit, no doubt.

She kept her face empty and receptive. It went against common vanity not to indicate by a wink or a purse of the lips that she was being facetious. Appearing a fool frightened most people more than heights, small enclosed spaces or speaking in front of crowds. Nobody wrote magazine articles about it; probably afraid of looking stupid. It didn't bother Anna. Her stupidity—real or feigned—made others overconfident and sloppy. While undercover she'd failed singularly in this department. She'd been a clever take-charge waitress but a stupid federal law enforcement officer.

Evidently it was too late to change character. Scott didn't believe her.

"Probably," he said again and nodded as if they'd made a pact. In a way they had.

"So how 'bout those four missing kids?" she said brightly.

Like most people, Scott loved to gossip. Nothing is so fascinating to humans as the fusses and foibles of other humans. Without much effort, Anna got his take on Trish,

Caitlin and Dix Crofter. The only one of the four he didn't know was the trail crewman, Patrick Waters.

According to Scott, Trish and Caitlin had been joined at the hip. Trish often hiked up to Little Yosemite Valley on her days off and stayed in the tent cabin Caitlin used. Though the tourist season was four months long, NPS folks lived ruggedly: no showers, cold water from a single spigot, toilets several hundred yards through the woods in the visitors' campground. Because the jobs were seasonal and the living conditions harsh, LYV rangers tended to be young, strong, dedicated and independent. Caitlin met and exceeded these qualifications. At nineteen, she was the youngest ranger there. She loved all things outdoorsy and played fast and loose with NPS rules that she believed to be "bogus." "Caitlin was irresistible," Scott said wistfully. "If I had a daughter . . . no. Scratch that. I would *not* want a daughter like Caitlin. She'd worry you into an early grave. No. If I were nineteen again, she'd be the love of my life. She'd break my heart, naturally, but I'd secretly harbor a torch for her through all subsequent marriages."

For a second or two, Anna toyed with the idea that, in his mid-thirties, with a felony record, Scott had fallen in love with Caitlin, gotten his heart broken, then helped her to vanish. She had to give it up. Scott spoke so clearly she couldn't but believe he had a realistic view of life that was truly invested with the gratitude he'd professed earlier. Not the sort to pine and kill for love.

"Trish wasn't good for Caitlin, I don't think," Scott cut into Anna's thoughts. "Being—what? Nine, ten years older, she ran the friendship and Caitlin didn't even know it. Once I kind of tried to feel her out on the subject. I was reminded of myself at nineteen. I knew everything. I even knew what I didn't know so there was no sense telling me I didn't know something because I already knew that." He laughed, head tipped back, the sound big and flowing. Anna joined him because it was infectious and because, on an undoubtedly deep and psychologically fraught level, it made her feel like a little girl again, safe and free.

The instant she recognized those seductive sensations, she scotched them. Given that people were tossing her room and secreting sharp objects in her clothing, feeling safe was dangerous.

"Why don't you think Trish was good for Caitlin?"

"Nothing real specific. Trish was a small-time dealer— nickel and dime stuff, you know, just the party supply line."

Anna nodded. "Nicky told me."

"My guess is the only people who haven't been told are the park rangers—the ones in law enforcement, I mean. Cops. Jesus." Scott shook his head contemptuously.

Anna was unoffended. Often the curtain of silence between the illegal world and that of law enforcement, though thin, was stunningly opaque. Once it was torn down the cops looked like idiots but, till it was, law enforcement had no way of knowing it even existed.

"Marijuana?" Anna asked.

"Yeah. Maybe coke, but if she did, not much. There's hard drugs here, like everywhere, but mostly brought in from the outside. Drugs were never my thing. In prison you just develop a sense for who's using. Even without the petty dealing, Trish felt bent. Rotten inside. Hard to explain. Maybe I just didn't like her."

"Maybe she was rotten inside."

Scott might have amended his statement to say *illegal* drugs were not his thing. He raised his glass, his third, in a salute. He was pleased Anna hadn't blown off his gut feeling about Trish. It wasn't mere flattery. Anna respected intuition.

"I pretty much steered clear of Trish," Scott said. "Bad news. Once girls—women—who felt bent lit me up. Now they just scare me. Getting old, I guess."

"One of the perks," Anna said. Over the years she too had lost her taste for dangerous lovers and counted the loss among her blessings. She hoped this particular state of grace was not on the wane. To pay Scott in kind for the information and because she wanted to, she told the story of her visit to Dixon Crofter's tent cabin with Mary and the four unsavory men they'd found squatting there. Scott got satisfyingly hostile when she related the crude welcome they'd received before Mark returned from the shower. Having grown up underfoot, Mary Bates was a favorite around the hotel. Young, delicately pretty and surprisingly unspoiled, the staff was protective of her. Scott was no exception. Over the next few minutes Anna rode the roller coaster of his esteem. That she was Mary's friend took her up in his estimation. That she'd taken Mary to a place of vile males dropped her way down. That she'd brought Mary home safe leveled things out again.

"Now, Mary is exactly the sort of girl I'd want for a daughter," Scott finished. "But, then, I'd probably end up back in Soledad for wringing the neck of the first boy who looked at her the wrong way."

"You keep mentioning imaginary daughters," Anna noted. "Do you have any real kids?"

"Shoot," Scott said and smiled ruefully. "Three bourbons is too much on a first date. Lowers inhibitions."

"Nah," Anna said. "Just makes you forget about consequences. Kids, then. Any to speak of?"

"I might have a daughter." Scott was grinning and Anna

couldn't tell whether it blocked laughter or tears. Or simply indicated his bourbon level.

"You don't know?"

"She looks like me. The timing is right but her mom swears otherwise."

"You could maybe get a DNA test."

"No."

"Why not?"

"It was right before I got arrested. The mom married. Shea—the little girl—has a nice family. Why screw that up?"

Anna had nothing to say to that. She concurred. These after-the-fact custody battles because one parent belatedly grows a conscience—or what they believe to be one—seemed to turn out badly for the kid whom everybody professed to love so much.

When enough nachos had been consumed to let the emotional dust from this disclosure settle, Anna moved on.

"This Dix guy. Mary seemed enamored of him. Did you ever get to know him at all?"

Scott brightened perceptibly. Anna was sorry she'd never known Dixon Crofter. He'd captured the imagination of so many.

"Spiderman. Everybody knew Dix." Scott stopped there and thought for a while. "Or nobody did, come to think of it. Dix was a wildman. If it was vertical, he'd climb it. On one level he was always easygoing, a lot of laughs. The only time he'd get serious was when he talked about getting funding to climb something that sane people would be nervous flying over in a seven-forty-seven. Now that I think about it, I'd have to say no, I didn't know him. We went to the same parties, hoisted a few too many together but all we talked about was climbing. I don't know where he was from, brothers, sisters—nothing personal."

"You say 'was.' Do you think he's dead?"

"Don't you?"

"I guess," Anna said.

"Probably all of them. It's been too long. Jiminy," Scott said. "What did you slip in my drink? I don't think I've gossiped this much since I was inside. Nothing better to do there. We've pretty much chewed over everybody at the lodge but old Tiny Bigalo."

"Don't want her to feel left out," Anna said.

"Okay. So what do you want to know about Tiny?" The question was rhetorical and Anna waited as he gathered his thoughts. He'd knocked back a hefty dose of bourbon and was feeling it. Most people wouldn't notice, but the way he handled his whiskey was another thing he had in common with her dad. Anna's father had two small scotches every night. On the rare occasions he had three or four he never seemed drunk or high, but his smile would widen, his laugh deepen and he'd do silly tricks like wiggle his ears if she or Molly asked him to. Scott's smile was wider and his laugh deeper. Anna chose not to push her luck by asking him to wiggle his ears. She was already pushing her luck. And for reasons she chose not to examine, she didn't want to lose his good opinion.

"Tiny's a hard one," Scott began. Mentally Anna prepared to take notes. "I've been here, what? Three years? And I've never really gotten to know her. Jim knows her better than anyone and their relationship's kind of bizarre. Like family. They don't seem to get along all that well, and he bad-mouths her a lot, but they stick together. They've got some kind of tie. Maybe just years. All I know is she's like this hardheaded businesswoman who waits tables for some unknown reason. She's got no family—kids, I mean. She's got a brother and two nephews she's always sending money to. Kind of a surrogate mother thing. Far as I know she's never

married. So that's all I got on Tiny. Anybody else we should
dish the dirt about?"

He smiled and Anna smiled back, but she was wracking
her brain to make sure there wasn't another hotel employee
she needed the lowdown on. "Maybe later," she said.

They sipped in silence for a while. The last hangers-on in
the bar muttered softly over their drinks. Windows, blind-
black with an overcast night, put Anna in mind of cave walls
and a sudden panic of claustrophobia shuddered through her.
She rode it out.

"Tell me about working with Jim," she said to keep the
conversation going.

Telling stories of his mentor, Scott grew animated, joyful.
Listening to him extol his eccentric patron's virtues, Anna was
put in mind of David Copperfield and Oliver Twist, Dickens
characters who knew and showed gratitude untouched by resentment or shame. The picture Scott painted of Chef Wither
was very different from the man Anna saw each day, and she
wondered if something had happened to change the sensitive, funny, driven man Scott described into the obsessive
curmudgeon she knew.

"Why was he so pissed off at me tonight?" she asked.
"He's never exactly jumped over the counter to give me a
welcome hug but he usually ignores me pleasantly enough.
Tonight he was furious."

Scott fell quiet. Enthusiasm for talking about Jim Wither
drained from his face. He picked up the much-folded napkin,
spread it flat and began tearing it along the scored creases.
"Who knows," he said. "Jim's a moody guy. The price of genius, I guess. He is a genius when it comes to food. He's in-
ternationally known. Or was. He's kind of semiretired here."

Scott looked up from mutilating the napkin. Gossipy ca-
maraderie was gone. There was no trace of boyishness or

bourbon. His years in Soledad stood in his eyes like rusty nails. Voice gone hard, he said, "The reason I'm not hauling plastic pipe for some pool company in San Diego or pushing buttons at a wastewater plant for six-fifty an hour is because of Jim. I won't let anybody fuck with him."

He was warning Anna off. He might as well have waved a red flag in front of a bull.

CHAPTER

8

Veiled threats had a way of damping conversation. Anna's "date" limped quickly to a close. She doubted there'd be another tête-à-tête with Scott Wooldrich to challenge her undercover skills or tweak her affianced conscience.

They drove to the Ahwahnee in silence. This time Scott didn't open any doors for her. After he'd driven off—to park his car, presumably—Anna changed direction, walking not to the dorm but toward the hotel. Feeling conspicuous in her uniform, though black trousers and a down jacket weren't exactly dead giveaways as to profession, she used a pay phone in the lobby. Chief Ranger Knight being out of town, she called Deputy Superintendent Johnson at his home.

"I have something I need to show you," she said when he came on the phone. "I'd rather it be tonight," she told him when he tried to put her off and added, "I'd rather not tell you over the phone," when he wanted to know what it was.

Hanging up the receiver, half a dozen movies where

the protagonist uttered the fateful words "I'd rather not tell you over the phone" flashed piecemeal through her mind. Roughly translated into cinemaese those words meant: a bad thing will prevent me from telling you until the plot thickens considerably.

Pretending she didn't feel the cold hand of superstition clutching the back of her neck, she went to her dorm room to change clothes. Another minute or two wasn't going to make any difference and she was tired of feeling like the tablecloth after the feast.

The door to the room she shared with Nicky and Cricket was open, soft light falling in a bar across the mud-tracked linoleum of the hall. The sight reassured her that criminals were not ransacking within and Nicky had recovered sufficiently to return to her happy social self.

Nicky was not alone. Sitting on the edge of her bed, a glossy magazine open on her knees, she looked as if she were waiting in a dentist's office for a root canal. Slouched in Anna's desk chair was a lumpish young man in the ubiquitous winter costume of Levi's, fleece pullover and dirty running shoes. Both of them looked immensely relieved to see her. Two young persons of opposite genders alone in the dark of night thrilled to see a middle-aged lady; the news couldn't be good.

"Hey," Anna said. "What's up?"

"This is Richard Cauliff," Nicky said.

Before she could continue, the man in the chair said. "I came to get my sister's stuff."

Richard. Dick. Dickie. "Right," Anna said. She flipped the switch by the door turning on the overhead light to get a better look at him. He was in his early twenties, thick from between the ears to the hips. Not much neck to speak of and not nearly enough hair. He hadn't shaved his head—maybe not living close enough to fashion's cutting edge for that—but he'd had it clipped as close as a new boot camp recruit's.

The effect was not flattering. His ears were too big and his skull an unattractive shape, the forehead sloping back to a pointy crown, the bone over the spine ridged and protruding.

"Anna Pigeon," Anna introduced herself and thrust out her hand in a manly fashion, a habit picked up from a feminist mother and years spent in what had been, when she'd begun, a man's profession.

Without rising, Dickie leaned forward and shook it tepidly. "I came for Trish's stuff," he repeated. "I'm her brother."

It occurred to Anna that he didn't recognize her voice from the phone call earlier in the day. A good thing. It wouldn't do for a mid-level payroll clerk to be showing up in the employee dorm smelling of pepper steak and blackened catfish.

Her first impulse was to ask for identification, but it was too heavy-handed for a disinterested waitress and one who'd never even met his sister. Besides, Dickie's ID was in his DNA. If not a brother, he was a close relative. Anna recognized the dark brown eyes and buckteeth from the photograph of Trish the chief ranger had shown her. Dickie's teeth were even more prominent than his sister's. A rude comment of her dad's surfaced in the back of Anna's mind: "Looked like he could eat corn on the cob through a picket fence."

Despite the slipshod way he'd been slapped together, Dickie might have been appealing in a goofy sort of way had not acne ruined his skin. The scars were deep, pitted, the flesh ruddy and new outbreaks thrust through the damaged flesh. Treatments now existed for cases as severe as his. Anna pitied him that his parents had been too broke, indifferent or ignorant to save him the disfigurement.

"I'm the lady who took over Trish's job—just till she gets back," she said.

An emotion other than dull, carplike sullenness flickered in Dickie's eyes. Anna couldn't tell if it was in response to her stepping into his sister's shoes or to the halfhearted sop she'd tagged on the end about Trish's imaginary return. Either way, it wasn't a happy gleam. Suddenly Anna got tired. Fatigue dropped on her chest so heavily it was hard not to stagger under it. The day had been excessively long and filled with people who wanted, feared, or hated things Anna couldn't quite get a grip on. Sour peevish humanity had soaked her in spiritual brine till, had a vampire been around to sink fangs into her, he would swear he'd bitten into a pickle.

"The rangers took her packed-up belongings just after I got here," she said. "You'll have to ask them what happened to them. Now if you don't mind, I'd like to go to bed."

Nicky shot her a look of admiration, and Anna was reminded of her salad days when she thought she was tough but in reality was so very young and unsure she couldn't even get rid of Jehovah's Witnesses who came uninvited to her door or hang up on phone solicitors, let alone evict a person who'd managed to get inside.

The force of age and authority brought Dickie up from the chair but didn't move him out the door. He wanted to go; Anna could see that in the shuffle of his feet and the cant of his shoulders. It was as if his body were pulling for the door and only a stubborn mind held it back. And maybe not the mind of Richard Cauliff; he didn't look like a man determined to stand his ground to get what's rightfully his. Everything about him, the body language, his eyes shifting away from hers each time they met, the sullenness, screamed of a servant afraid to return to his master without whatever it was he'd been sent to fetch.

"I got that stuff, but stuff was missing from her stuff."

Anna wanted to give him something just to avoid having to hear the word "stuff" one more time.

"You want to search the room?" she asked. "Be our guest. Just hurry up. I'm dead on my feet."

"You got her clothes on. She said." He pointed at Nicky with a forefinger, the nail bitten till the quick was bloody in places.

Anna laughed. "Jesus. You want her *uniform*? Hell, I'll buy it from you. Twenty bucks suit you? Depreciation on polyester pants is a bitch. Not much resale value."

"They're mine. I got a right."

Though he'd yet to show any sign he suffered grief over the loss of his sister, it crossed Anna's mind that he might want the clothes because they had belonged to her, because she had worn them. She backed off.

"Sure. They're all yours. Step outside and I'll change."

He didn't move.

"I'm not changing in front of you."

He left, closing the door behind him. Nicky jumped up and turned the deadbolt. "He was probably afraid we wouldn't let him back in," she whispered.

"We won't," Anna replied. She skinned out of the shirt and trousers, pulled on a pair of Levi's and a work shirt. Zipped, tucked and buttoned, she unlocked and opened the door. "One waitress uniform."

Dickie took it, wadding it in one hand. Not a treasured relic of filial affection after all. "Is there anyplace else you guys keep stuff?"

"Lockers. You want to go through Trish's locker over at the Ahwahnee?"

"I'm her brother. I got a right," he said stubbornly.

A wee little switch was thrown in Anna's brain, the switch that controls the circuits separating the civilized from the uncivilized. "Shit yes, you got a right," she said. "Let's search it. Come on. Hell, we'll search them all. There might be a pencil stub or hairpin somebody borrowed off Trish and by God *kept*. Can't have that. You got a right. Let's move it. No time to lose. The market value of half-used order pads might be tanking as we speak."

"Anna!"

It was Nicky. She'd squeaked like a mouse.

"Sorry," Anna said, more tired than before. "Sorry," she said to a stupefied Dickie. "Come on. It'll only take a minute. I don't think you'll find much."

Anna had gone through Trish's locker, as had park rangers seeking clues prior to and during the search. She didn't recall precisely what was there, only that it was of no interest. Dickie followed her past the Dumpsters. The employee entrance was locked after midnight and they had to enter through the front of the hotel. So late, the lobby was nearly empty, just two women sitting talking quietly in front of one of the great fireplaces.

"Can I help you?" came from an alert young man behind the counter. Anna recognized the face but had to read his courtesy tag to get the name. "Hi, Josh. I'm Anna Pigeon. I work with Tiny in the dining hall. This is Richard Cauliff. He's Trish Spencer's brother."

Joshua, having better manners than Dickie, shook his hand over the counter. "Hey, man. Sorry about your sister. She was cool."

"He's come to get his sister's things from her locker," Anna said.

"Sure. Sorry, man."

The locker room was even grimmer without bustle from the kitchen to lend it life. Anna opened her locker. It was empty but for a hairbrush, a tube of Chapstick, a ticket book and a spare apron. Anna'd never worn it, she preferred the other; it had more body. This one hung like a limp rag. "The Chapstick and the brush are mine," she said.

"That apron hers?"

"Take it."

Dickie wadded the apron up with the dirty shirt and pants.

"You want the order pad?" Anna asked sourly.

He picked it up and riffled through the unused pages. "Naw. You can keep it."

"You're a prince."

Anna walked him back out through the lobby and around to the parking lot, more to make sure he was really leaving than because of any desire for his company. He left her there without a word of thanks or good-bye and hurried across the asphalt with the air of a man escaping.

Having returned to the dorm, Anna retrieved her pack. Before she could end this annoying day she had to deliver the needle and syringe into the hands of the deputy superintendent.

"Too weird," Nicky said.

"Way too weird," Anna agreed.

"Where are you going?"

"Out."

On the quiet, lonely and, so, blissful walk to Leo Johnson's quarters, Anna replayed Dickie Cauliff's visit in her mind. Of all the various weirdnesses, two stuck out in her mind. Since he'd been so desperate to collect every shred of material goods his sister had left behind, why hadn't he jumped at the chance to search the room when Anna'd offered? Had he been intimidated by her hostility and sarcasm? Or did he know it had already been searched? And when she had handed him the order book from the locker, why had he riffled through the pages before choosing not to take it? Did he merely crave a sample of his sister's handwriting or was he searching for something small enough it could be secreted between the pages of a three-by-five pad and, not finding it, rejected the item?

"Too weird," she repeated aloud.

CHAPTER
9

Leo Johnson's place was three houses down a gentle hill from Lorraine Knight's. It was slightly larger, as befitted his rank, but on a tiny scrap of land, houses pressing close to either side, and it lacked the wild glamour the creek lent to the chief ranger's home. The windows were dark. As she banged on the front door, Anna thought maybe the deputy superintendent had given up on her and gone to bed.

Time on a doorstep has little relation to time anyplace else in the universe. Anna fidgeted and scuffed and wondered where the hell he was for what seemed an age. When she could stand it no longer she knocked again. This time she got a response.

"Hold your horses," was shouted from the internal darkness.

Anna'd heard the phrase her whole life but, coming by itself into an ear accustomed to silence, it sounded absurd.

"Champing at the bit," she called back for no other reason than that she was tired and it amused her.

A bang, a muttered curse and the porch light glared to life. The door opened. Leo Johnson stared at her owlishly. He was still in uniform down to badge and brass nametag. Shoeless feet, his big toe coming through the cordovan-colored sock on his right foot, and the rumpled state of the very nearly unrumpleable fabric of the NPS uniform attested to the fact he'd been lounging in it. Or sleeping. Or rolling around on the floor. Dog hair and bits of lint stuck to the breast pockets. No dog had barked. *Maybe cat hair,* Anna thought hopefully. Petting a cat would have been good after the cold comfort of her day.

"What is it?"

Johnson had forgotten she was coming. Given that, why was he up and more or less in uniform in a dark house after one in the morning?

"I called," she said. "I have something to show you."

"Oh. Yeah. Right." He stepped back to let her in and had to steady himself with the door. One mystery solved: he'd been sitting up half the night in the dark drinking. Leaving her to shut the door he moved into the living room and switched on a lamp. Following, Anna watched him. He wasn't any good. Not careful. Unsteady on his feet. The drinking was not habitual; he hadn't yet developed the coping skills of a longtime alcoholic.

"Sit down," he said. "Sorry for the . . ." He waved vaguely at the rest of the room.

Usually when a host or hostess said "sorry for the mess" it was merely to point out how tidy a place was. Not so with Leo Johnson. There was little furniture, one La-Z-Boy recliner and two office chairs, the padded kind that swivel. Walls were devoid of pictures or decoration. The mantel above the cold maw of the fireplace held only one personal item, a brass plaque mounted on wood leaning crookedly against the

brick. Magazines were piled on the hearth and beside the recliner. By a lamp on the one end table were two glistening
rings. Her wait on the doorstep had probably been caused by
the deputy superintendent's trip to the kitchen to hide his
bottle and glass.

The place was in such disarray that at first Anna thought
he had only recently moved in. After closer study she
changed her mind. Someone else had recently moved out,
taking most of the furnishings, the family dog and undoubtedly the children, if there were any. The house looked like the
crash site after a marriage has gone down in flames. Probably this was what had fomented the drinking. Chances were
he'd not been at it long. Alcoholics didn't rise to assistant superintendent in crown-jewel parks.

Leo sat in the recliner, careful not to lean back or slouch
or crumple, sucking it up to appear in control. More from a
sense of duty than because anything would come of it—if
Johnson even remembered this interview come morning—
Anna outlined the events of the evening then produced the
blood evidence from her backpack.

"It's a water bottle," Leo said, the confusion of drink over-
coming his futile attempt to control a world out of whack.

"I put the syringe inside." Anna was pleased to note she
sounded more patient than she felt.

"Okay. Yeah." He unscrewed the bottle's cap and started to
shake the syringe out, needle first.

"Careful!" Anna snapped. "You could poke yourself." At
this point she didn't much care whether or not he inoculated
himself with whatever the needle held, but she wasn't going to
let him screw up any fingerprints that might be there. Reaching out, she took the bottle from his hands. "Cap, please."

Leo didn't relinquish it. Instead he closed the hand that
held it into a fist. The blear in his eyes was darkening, shifting

to red. Anna suppressed a sigh. Her father-in-law had been an alcoholic, a longtime guzzler of bourbon. Over countless spoiled holidays she'd seen this same metamorphosis, as soggy drunk became belligerent drunk.

"You say you think somebody stuck this in your sleeve?" Johnson asked.

Anna's father-in-law had employed this trick too, bringing up a subject of interest or a challenge just as his disgusted audience was about to walk out on him. In no mood for it, Anna stood. "That's it," she said.

"Sounds like somebody doesn't like you much."

That stopped her. Not because of the insult. When the alcohol changed his face she'd known cutting words were bound to make an appearance. Since she preferred them to flying fists, she wasn't particularly offended. What stopped her was the clumsy double entendre in his tone. Johnson had emphasized "somebody" in such a way as to suggest he knew who it was, that maybe it was somebody in this room.

"Who?" she demanded.

The harsh command in her voice sobered him momentarily and he snapped out from behind the leering mask dripping over his face. He pushed himself to his feet. "Must be somebody knows you're working at the hotel," he said.

Way to go, Dick Tracy, Anna thought. She held out her hand. "Could I have the cap to the bottle, please?" He gave her a blank stare. She pointed to the fist hanging at his side. Johnson opened his hand, surprised to find it contained a white plastic bottle cap. Wordlessly he handed it to her. Anna screwed it back on the bottle.

"That's evidence," Johnson said. He appeared to be sobering at a phenomenal rate. Drunks did that. Anna had learned not to trust it.

"It is," she said. "Of what, I don't know. The contents of

the syringe need to be analyzed. It's probably blood. We need a tox screen at the least."

The deputy superintendent plucked the bottle from her hand. Short of snatching for it and possibly ending up in a wrestling match she'd lose, Anna had to accept that it was gone.

"I'll get on it." He set the bottle on the arm of the lounge chair behind him. It toppled off onto the carpet.

"You'll want to refrigerate that," Anna said. "It's already been at room temperature for half an hour that I can account for and who knows how much longer it was in my jacket."

"I'll take care of it," he said in his sober voice. "It's late. I don't know about you, but I've got an early day tomorrow." The man's rapid changes, from stupid drunk to mean drunk to assistant superintendent, had Anna off balance.

Giving up the evening as a bad job she said, "Good night." Reluctantly leaving the message in the bottle to its fate, she turned toward the door.

"If they know who you are at the hotel, there's no point in you and Lorraine keeping on playing this game of yours. You've been made." The phrase tickled him and he laughed too long and too loud. "Cops and robbers. You girls should've signed on with the LAPD."

The booze had lowered Johnson's guard as well as his IQ. Leo was a sexist. Lorraine Knight was everything he wasn't: smart and strong, energetic and brave. And very possibly being groomed for a position he was rapidly drinking himself out of. No wonder he wanted her to fail in this endeavor. If she discovered what happened to the four missing people, even if it was too late to save their lives, it would be an enormous feather in her political cap.

Anna took a last look at the bottle and syringe and debated whether or not to tell him again to put it in the refrigerator.

She decided not to. Given his mood, the more she pushed for it, the less likely he was to comply.

"I'm for bed," she said and headed for the door. This time he didn't stop her. As she closed it she glimpsed him disappearing into the kitchen. Probably to retrieve his bottle.

The following day was the first of Anna's two days off. She celebrated by sleeping late. Once "late" had been noon. In her thirties her internal clock shifted. Now "late" was seven-thirty. The dorm's kitchen was blissfully deserted. She sat over her morning coffee unmolested, her mind turning over the scraps of information she'd gathered.

Lorraine was to take on the task of tracing the red Ford Excursion driven by the Camp 4 squatters as well as tracking down the nice-smelling city boys who'd held Nicky down and searched the room. Since Lorraine had been sent packing to Missoula, Montana, to teach Leo's class, Anna assumed these chores had been handed on to one or more of her rangers. Having no way of knowing to whom, Anna had to let that go. Short of breaking into the deputy superintendent's house and stealing back the blood and needle for analysis, that avenue was closed as well.

Since she'd had the good sense to rent a car for the duration of her stay, driving to Mariposa and paying a visit to Richard Cauliff was a possibility. With luck, she might be able to unearth the root of his peculiar greed for his sister's old clothes and used cosmetics.

"Hey," she said aloud. The sound snapped her out of the speculative life of the mind and into the gray kitchen; gray because the ceiling of clouds that had settled on Yosemite two weeks before had yet to show any sign of lifting.

The previous night Anna had suffered distractions venial,

mortal and professional. A possible connection had been missed. Richard Cauliff had been in Yosemite Valley all evening. It was not beyond the realm of possibility that he'd rigged the needle in her jacket sleeve. In the classic litany of means, motive and opportunity, he had opportunity. Motive, always a subjective thing, could have been to revenge himself on Anna because she'd taken his sister's place.

Weak, Anna thought. It was the motive of a lunatic and Dickie came across as relatively sane. And, too, it required a passion for the deceased that was markedly missing. Dickie was either indifferent to his sister's fate or a stoic of mythic abilities. Had Cauliff planted the needle, he would have known what was in Anna's locker. There'd have been no need for the midnight visit. Unless he hadn't realized Anna had taken his sister's locker along with everything else of hers. He could have searched for one marked "Trish" and failing to find it, plunked himself down in the dorm to await Anna's return.

Dickie Cauliff was directly connected to one of the missing persons Anna had been brought to Yosemite to find; that was more than she could say for the rest of the facts she'd collected. Dickie won pride of place on her "to do" list.

Glad to have an objective, she hit the road. First Mariposa, then another hour to visit Cricket in Merced. Nicky had said she would be in the hospital a couple more days for observation and testing. Since Anna had ostensibly saved her life, she hoped for a warm welcome and a cooperative spirit. Hoped. The shelf life of heroes was short.

By eight-thirty Anna's alarmingly turquoise subcompact was threading through the granite boulders that heralded the southwestern entrance to the park. The sudden narrowing of the valley with its mansions of stone and press of evergreens was at once magical and oppressive. Despite the cold and the lowering sky that held the park in grim stasis, Anna was not blind to the beauty of the place. It was easy to understand why Yosemite imprinted on the souls of so many. People spent lifetimes worshipping at her granite altars, painting and photographing her every mood, fighting to protect her waterfalls and lakes. Still, as Anna left this natural bottle-neck, she experienced a sense of release and a lifting of spirits. For her, the glory of canyons and glens was best appreciated from the crest of a nearby hill. Open empty spaces where she could see what was coming suited her best.

The road to Mariposa followed the Merced River. On the opposite bank from Highway 140 ran an old railroad bed. In the early 1990s, the flood that swept so many buildings from the park had taken out a lot of bridges, leaving derelict railroad buildings and the weathered ruins of barns, sheds and homes marooned in a time when the railroad was the main artery pumping commerce through the foothills to the mountains. Rather than slavishly attend to the rats running pointless races in her skull, Anna amused herself by imagin-ing the lives and times of the softly delineated world across the river.

Mariposa was a lovely town, coy and cute enough to trap tourists but with a life of its own coursing honestly behind the rough-cut gingerbread. At a guess, the population was un-der three thousand. Anna found Dickie's address obligingly published in the phone book and located his house without difficulty. Feeling anything but inconspicuous in a shocking blue car, she parked across the street and what would have been half a block down had this steep neighborhood been structured in an urban grid instead of narrow crooked lanes.

Mariposa snowplow drivers must be among the best in the world, she thought idly as she double-checked the num-ber on the mailbox, then settled in to get a feel of the place.

Dickie's home was down-at-the-heels but looked solid and surprisingly neat for the residence of a young unmarried man. Anna stopped herself. She knew nothing of Cauliff: whether he was married or single, owned or rented, worked or lived on unemployment.

Smoke trickled from a stovepipe above what was probably the house's main room. Someone was home. The windows were blanked with curtains of maroon with twisted parallelograms in gold, a fabric the like of which Anna had not seen in forty years. It put her in mind of *The Jetsons* with its cartoon vision of the future. The colors were still vivid, as if the curtains had not often been pulled over the years.

Nothing to be gained by sitting obtrusively in blue, she left the car and crossed the street. The short concrete walk to the front door was broken by tree roots. Three alders towered up from the tiny yard. Probably planted as saplings when the house was first built, they now rose thirty or more feet above the roof ridge. Grass, if there was any, was hidden beneath their leaves, long since fallen and never raked away.

Over the entrance was a truncated porch roof with asphalt shingles. Anna stepped onto a mat that read "Welcome!" and knocked. The door had been painted recently. The faint odor of latex enamel still lingered. A bright brass eye, at odds with the age of the house and, despite its new coat, the door, poked out from the center. A peephole had been put in. Hence the paint job.

From within this newly cloistered world, Anna felt or heard the faintest drift of shushing, a living whisper of socks on hardwood, breath on still air. For a moment she could have sworn an eye applied itself to the other side of the peephole, weighed her and found her wanting. She knocked again, but this time even the might-have-beens were gone. She felt only emptiness and imagined the ghost of stocking feet and staring eye hiding behind the divan, waiting for her to leave.

Shades of Boo Radley.

Returning to the rental car, she wondered what had tickled below the threshold of her senses: Nerves strung too tightly? Sixth sense? Human beings thought in words. Pictures were involved but words had taken over much of the brain. There were times Anna believed the senses could divine information too delicate for the essentially crude and limited tool of language to express; information which animal brains had easily made sense of before humans learned to speak and so reduce all life to words. Now, but for a lucky or insane few, that subliminal input served only to raise the hairs on the back of the neck, leave hollow pits in stomachs and unnameable dread in minds.

Driving out of the mountains and into California's central valley, known for its agricultural output, not the beauty of its landscapes, was a joy to Anna. Decades had passed since she'd attended college in San Luis Obispo. Entranced with the drama of New York City, the cold magic of Isle Royale and the wild glory of the Four Corners area, she'd forgotten how deeply she loved California's rolling hills. In spring they were a heartbreaking green and looked as soft as velvet. By August they were gold. Winter turned them a faded yellow-gray. Promising hidden meadows, mystical live oaks and other wonders beyond the rounded crest of each and every hill, they rolled away. Lichen-painted rocks scattered over the winter grass—not with the forbidding size and crushing weight of the granite Sierra, but just enough to add interest and subtle color. Oak trees, limbs twisted and complex, dotted the hillsides; trees for climbing or picnicking beneath, kinder cousins of the black-boughed evergreens constantly whispering of the Donner party and other harsh snowbound gossip.

By herself in the car Anna laughed aloud. Till these thoughts assailed her, she'd had no idea how much the close valley limned with the bones of the mountains had oppressed her.

Merced was flat and low. Not a town to inspire poetry or songs but with a good solid middle-class feel that Anna appreciated after the isolated idiosyncratic world of Yosemite National Park.

The hospital was clean, modern and well-lit. A crisp Hispanic woman wearing the classic nurse's cap perched on hair so sleek it would have made Eva Peron feel frumpy had Anna sign in, then asked for identification which she compared with the signature. "Sorry," she said, flashing a smile barred with braces and tiny rubber bands. "Security's been beefed up since 9/11. Why any self-respecting terrorist would want to blow up a hospital in Merced beats me. There's drugs and disease cultures, I guess. Anyway you're you." She directed Anna to the second floor. Room 209 was a double room but the bed near the door was unoccupied. Lying small and childlike in the glare of a window that took up most of the wall, Cricket sat propped up in the second bed reading *Cosmopolitan*. Half a dozen other magazines of similar intellectual content splashed colorfully over the baby-blue blanket.

"Hi," Anna said.

Cricket shrieked. The *Cosmo* flew into the air with a flutter and three magazines were sent slithering to the floor.

"Anna?" she said when she'd recovered.

Anna picked up the magazines and put them on the metal rolling table, then sat in an orange plastic armchair between

Cricket and the window. "Sorry to startle you," she apologized. "How are you doing?"

"I'm going home tomorrow morning."

It wasn't much of an answer but Anna could read what
she wanted to know in the girl's face. Cricket was pale. Dark
smudges showed like bruises beneath her eyes, and she'd lost
weight, noticeably so, though she'd been in the hospital only
a couple of days. Her fingers fidgeted, folding and unfolding
a corner of one of her magazines, and several times she
glanced at the door as if expecting an evil headmaster to appear and cane them for talking during quiet hours.

She was scared out of her wits.

It crossed Anna's mind that she might be dying, that her
collapse had nothing to do with whatever she and Nicky had
been smoking, that she looked to the door, not for an apoc-
ryphal headmaster but for the Grim Reaper himself.

"Did the doctors find out why you collapsed?" she asked.

The question, as harmless and mundane as any asked from
beside hospital beds over the ages, alarmed Cricket further.

"My medical records are secret! Nobody can look at
them. Secret? Is that the right word?" she asked desperately.

"Sealed? Privileged?" Anna cast about for the language
to calm her.

"Privileged. That's it. Nobody can look at them but me."

For a few heartbeats, Anna sat, her face composed in a
mild and friendly mask, while she wondered at the reaction.
Who worried whether their medical records were sealed?
Pregnant unmarried girls? Girls who'd made themselves ill
doing something illegal?

"Just making conversation," Anna said. "Nicky and I and
the folks at the hotel have been worried about you."

Cricket relaxed a little. "I don't want any trouble," she said.

"Are you in trouble?"

An ache came into Cricket's eyes. Anna'd seen it before in people yearning to unburden themselves. For an instant she thought the girl would confide in her, but Cricket glanced again at the door and the moment passed.

"Have you had lots of visitors?" Anna tried.

"No," she said quickly.

"Must've gotten pretty lonely."

"I'm okay." Cricket picked up the magazine she'd been mutilating and opened it across her knees. "Before I go home I've got to get my stuff from the dorm. Tomorrow, probably around noon. Will you tell Nicky? See if she can swap shifts or get the day off?"

"Sure," Anna said. "We'll miss you," she added because it was the polite thing to do.

"I'm going home," Cricket insisted as if Anna had threatened to drag her bodily back into the park to her old job.

Incapable of doing or saying anything that wouldn't terrify the girl, Anna just nodded and left.

Hospitals gave her the creeps: the smells, the canned voices over the public address system, the hard light, door after door open on misery after misery flashing past as she walked down the halls. Still, she didn't leave immediately but stopped in a waiting area on the second floor, opposite the elevators. Sitting in a square armchair with the ubiquitous orange upholstery, a shade seen nowhere but in institutions, Anna opened her mind to evils past, present and future to see if she could figure out what had frightened Cricket so badly that the only thing she could focus on that didn't bring on an anxiety attack was going home—a place the newly "adult" Cricket Anna had roomed with had referred to with derision on many occasions.

The hospital itself, haunted by unanswered prayers and

the clank of bedpans, would frighten anyone, but not to silence. Not a young woman like Cricket. Any normal fear would have her chattering like a magpie.

Cricket's fear was fluid, flowing easily from one horror to the next. Fear Anna would look at her medical records. Why? Anna wasn't family. Morality-based worries—pregnancy, venereal disease or AIDS—Cricket would probably have welcomed a chance to talk about with the cool-grown-up character Anna had created for this job.

The specter of illegality didn't work either. Anna already knew Cricket was using illegal drugs. Cricket knew she knew. No secrets there. Maybe. Or maybe there was something else about her illegal participation that needed to be kept quiet.

Anna shook her head. What was more likely was that whatever stopped Cricket's breath had left a scar on her mind as well. In the strange old days when LSD was heralded as a miracle drug, a drug that allowed one to see God and hadn't the unpleasant side effects of addiction or overdose, Anna had known a number of people who had returned from their trips with demon hitchhikers dwelling in the mind. Seeing God, it seemed, was a good deal more dangerous than the New Testament let on.

A hollow tone sounded. Elevator doors opened. Anna rose and walked into the box. Too long in a hospital was detrimental to one's health. Anna found herself suppressing a need to glance over her shoulder, as Cricket had, to see if she was being stalked.

This mild paranoia struck a chord. *As if she were being stalked.* One didn't stay vigilant, starting at footsteps and watching doorways, out of fear of secrets being exposed or death by a doctor's decree, but because one was afraid of some corporeal thing: a foot hitting the floor, a three-dimensional body casting a shadow.

In the short time since Cricket had fallen in the Ahwahnee dining room, someone had threatened her with something so dire the once independent and spirited young woman wanted only to run home and hide her head under the covers.

Access to hospital patients was limited. Barring the real possibility that someone had sneaked in up the fire stairs or service entrance, Cricket had either been visited through normal channels or called on the phone. Blessing the security measures she had sniffed at earlier, Anna stopped in Registration. The sleek-headed RN in braces had been replaced by a short, very fat woman in one of the bright-colored outfits styled after surgical scrubs that nurses had adopted when they'd finally won freedom from snug white uniforms and thick white hose. The new keeper of the desk was younger. Her brown hair was wadded up in a clip, ends waving free like a cockatiel's headdress.

Unobtrusively, Anna watched her. The nurse was efficient, quick. She kept an eye on everything. Anna wouldn't get a chance to study the sign-in sheets on the clipboard unnoticed on this woman's watch.

When dealing with bureaucracies, it was Anna's experience that showing interest in information immediately made the guardian of that information decide it was sacred, not to be defiled by unauthorized eyes. Insisting only convinced them one's motives were suspect. Honesty and rationality were not particularly efficacious in bureaucratic settings.

She waited till two others were in line at the desk, then walked up to the chest-high horseshoe of Formica. "Excuse me," she butted into a conversation in progress. "I just have a quick . . ." She elbowed the clipboard with the sign-in sheets onto the floor. Making much scrabble and fuss as she retrieved it, she pinched the clip and allowed the sheets to scatter. With a great show of repentance, she insisted she be allowed to clean up the mess she'd made. Taking her time, she picked up the sheets one by one.

Anna had hoped they'd go back over several days, but she was disappointed. Only today's visitors were included. She scanned the lists anyway. Had she been paying more attention when she'd first arrived, she'd have spared herself this charade. Seven lines above her signature was another slated to visit room 209. The handwriting was abysmal, a scribbled initial, a huge "C" and a trailing "f," the tail of which ran off the page. Scarcely an hour before Anna had arrived, minutes after the commencement of visiting hours, Cauliff had come calling.

Cricket lied when she said she'd had no visitors.

At last, something tangible. Delighted, Anna skipped the elevator, took the stairs two at a time, and returned to 209. Again the shriek but this time Cricket managed to hang on to her magazine. She'd moved on to *Mademoiselle*.

Once again in the plastic chair, Anna braced her forearms on her knees and looked intently into Cricket's face. This unheralded return had shaken an already crumbling foundation. Anna wouldn't have been surprised if the girl began to shiver from nose to tail like a scared Chihuahua.

"You need to tell me what's going on," Anna said. "You're scared to death; you've quit your job; you're running home. Talk to me."

"I'm not scared," Cricket said and attempted a smile that was gruesome in its parody.

"Who is threatening you?"

Cricket's face went a shade paler and she swayed as if losing this last bit of blood from her head made her dizzy. "Nobody. Don't you say that. You can't prove it. I'll sue you for . . ."

Had she ever known the words "defamation," "slander," "harassment" or whatever she sought, they'd fled her mind.

"I can prove you lied," Anna said.

Cricket clutched the baby-blue blanket in both fists and pulled it up to her chin. Feeling old and hard and evil, but not minding it all that much, Anna pressed on.

"You lied about not having visitors."

Cricket squeezed her eyes shut.

"Dickie Cauliff came to see you." Anna sat back and waited for this grand slam to bring some if not all of the players home.

Cricket's eyes opened. Her little fists unclenched. She opened her mouth and said: "Uh-unh, no sir."

Except that she knew for a fact the girl was lying, Anna would have sworn she was telling the truth.

CHAPTER

10

Depression settled like dust over Anna's mind as she followed the road up into the mountains. There'd been no sun in the San Joaquin Valley, but she'd been able to breathe in the space between the earth and the bottom of the sky. As she drove into the park, slate-colored rock and clouds closed around her in a tight box.

Frustration and a sense of failure further darkened her mood. The hectic activity of the past days had turned up everything and nothing. When she'd arrived in Yosemite there'd been one pressing question: What happened to Dixon, Patrick, Caitlin and Trish? Now there were half a dozen: Who put a needle in her sleeve and why? Who'd tossed the dorm room? What were they looking for? Were the men in Dix's tent cabin up to something illegal or just slimeballs polluting a new environment for the holidays? What was Cricket so afraid of? And why in hell had the chef at the Ahwahnee taken against her all of a sudden?

Distracted by these fruitless inquiries, Anna's foot grew heavy. A ranger stopped her for speeding and wrote her a ticket. Another reason never to go undercover: no professional courtesy.

Nicky had succeeded in turning the dorm room back into a disaster area, no mean feat without Cricket's able assistance. Anna lay on her bed and tried to read. The walls kept closing in. She fled outdoors, caught the bus to stop sixteen, disembarked and walked up the path leading to the bottom of the Mist Trail where Caitlin Bates had last been headed. In sunlight the scenery would have taken her breath away: two stunning waterfalls linked by rocks and deep pools. Beneath the settling cloud, no wind, no rain, scarcely a sound but the clatter of her feet on the paved path, it was suffocating.

Anna had to get the hell out of The Ditch. Short of going AWOL, she had but one choice: the high country.

Decision made, there came a modicum of relief. The leaden sky would be even closer above the valley floor, but the trails wouldn't be paved and there'd be no people with bourbon breath and lousy housekeeping habits.

Winter camping had never been on her list of fun things to do, but any weather was good hiking weather. Contemplating the pull of her muscles on an uphill stretch, the depth of her breath after a scramble, lightened her heart. Moving so little and always in walled spaces had left her feeling her own skin, her very sinews, were closing in.

The short day was dimming to an end. She tempered her impatience to go by pulling out a topographical map of the park. Plotting a journey was part of the fun, and Anna pored over maps with the pleasure sane women took in shopping: deciding what to pick, what to leave behind, fantasizing over treks for later, savoring the selection of the one for tomorrow. A cup of hot tea at her elbow, she ran her fingers up dotted lines marking trails and let the music of places cleanse the thoughts of her heart: May Lake, Tenaya Lake, Echo Valley, Sunrise Lake, Long Meadow, Clouds Rest. Mount Starr King, Lower Merced Pass Lake.

Lower Merced Pass Lake. The name sounded a sour note in the song of Sierra. Jarred out of her pleasant mind trip, she sat back and took up the cup of rapidly cooling tea. Lower Merced Pass Lake; it lacked euphonic charm, certainly, but it was more than that. It was almost as if she'd heard it before, though she was ninety-nine percent sure she hadn't. Maybe in the old days, thirty years back, when she'd visited Yosemite? That didn't click anything loose. Having nothing better to do, she cleared her mind, sipped her tea and waited. If she prevented herself from chasing a memory or blocking its entry with faulty guesses, it would usually surface.

This one was a long time in coming, so long, in fact, she'd completely forgotten not to think about it and had drifted off into the gray-on-gray beyond the window, fascinated by the incremental creeping of night, as if the sun never set but was slowly turned off by a cosmic dimmer switch.

Not *Lower Merced Pass Lake*—that was too idiosyncratic to forget. What she'd heard was: *a low lake.* That's what the man had said when she'd inadvertently begun eavesdropping from the ladies' bathroom in Camp 4 the morning she'd learned of the squatter's party. The climbers had been restive, a low-level fever stirring the camp. Through the window she'd overheard three men talking as they had packed. "The guy'd been somewhere . . . if you figure sixty percent was just hot air . . . a fucking gold rush . . . a low lake . . . How many can there be? A shitload . . ."

Since she and Mary had had their run-in with the men in Dixon's tent cabin and Anna's follow-up visit the next morning, so much had unraveled in her tiny world that that

particular conversation had been put out of her mind. Tea
forgotten, Anna replayed everything she'd learned. The night
of the party the city men left, new boots on their feet and
packs reeking of diesel on their backs, ostensibly for a
moonlit hike into a frozen wilderness. The heavy guy with
the worst manners and the bloodiest feet had returned to the
party. Judging by the general tenor of the camp and the conversation she'd overheard, he'd gotten drunk and spewed out
heavy-handed hints concerning a plan or project that if even
forty percent of it was true would "start a fucking gold rush"
to "a low lake."

After garnering that unilluminating fragment of gossip,
she'd repaired to the storage garage and found the letter Trish
Spencer had written to Dickie referring to having become "a
miner" and acquiring the cash to buy him a gym.

The only possibility these thoughts brought to mind was
an impossibility. Still, it gave her direction, and she grabbed
at it. With renewed energy she returned to the map. Despite
the prognostication of the climber dude, there was not a
plethora of low lakes in Yosemite National Park. As near as
she could tell there were exactly none. The only lake she
could find with anything "low" about it was Lower Merced
Pass Lake which at nearly nine thousand feet in elevation
was low only in comparison to Upper Merced Pass Lake.

There was a trail through the pass with a lake to either
side. If Anna drove up to Mono Meadow Trailhead and hiked
in from there it was twelve miles to Lower Merced with a to-
tal elevation gain of two thousand feet. Over rough terrain,
elevation gain on a map meant little; one could easily climb
three times as much as was recorded, as elevation was gained
and lost and gained again over the wrinkles in the world.

Usually, in December, trails in the high country were im-
passable but for snowshoers. Winter snows easily reached

five to eight feet. Because of the ongoing drought in the Sierra, less than a foot of snow remained in most places. On exposed rock, even that had melted away. Hiking to Lower Merced should be doable. The worst danger would be on ice over the granite shoulders pushing through Yosemite's thin mantle of soil. Slipping and shattering an elbow or knee was a real possibility.

Sunrise wasn't till after six, sunset around five—or so Anna was guessing. Since coming to California she'd seen the sun only twice and then but for an instant. To the people of Mississippi, California was all sunshine and sandy beaches. Her rangers were expecting her to return with at least a tan and possibly one or more body piercings.

Six to six if she started in the dark and returned in the dark. Twenty-four miles round trip, twelve hours, two miles an hour, half uphill. She could do it. The next day she'd probably be sore—she'd been living at sea level in a state where the highest peak was slightly above her porch roof—but she didn't report in to the Ahwahnee till three-thirty on the next day. Time enough to ease out of bed gently.

Twenty-four miles in the cold across rugged country. *Beats the hell out of sitting here,* Anna thought. Twenty-four miles. Twelve hours. She pushed back from the map and tried to think past her arrogance and enthusiasm. It would be a killer hike. Cold sapped energy as surely as altitude and distance. She needn't go all the way, just far enough to be sure there was activity in the area. That done, she could simply report, let the rangers do the heavy lifting. Report to whom? Leo? A picture of his sodden face and bleary eyes flashed before her.

Never mind, she told herself. *Burn that bridge when you come to it.* Having crammed a dozen granola bars, water, dry socks and, because one never knew, a down sleeping bag into her day pack, she set her battered hiking boots beside the bed, set her alarm for five A.M. and went to sleep with what passed these days for great good cheer.

By the time the sky began to gray with a sun that rose everywhere but where Anna was, she had hiked a ways up the Illilouette Creek Trail. Her rental car was parked at Mono Meadow Trailhead. Hiking in the dark wasn't nearly as hard as one might imagine when on an improved and wellmarked trail. Winding white between the trees, the gentle trough worn by feet and paws and hooves, held the snow longer than the surrounding earth. Her flashlight lit the trail up and it unrolled as inviting as the bride's white satin down a church aisle.

It wasn't until she'd hiked in a mile and a half that the tracks appeared.

Winter campers, that hardy breed, were alive and well in the Sierra, but Anna doubted they could account for the traffic this trail had seen. All at once the pristine snow became scuffed and muddied. Before she added her boot prints to the mix, she stopped and played her light over the churned-up snow. The flashlight's beam poked between the surrounding trees to reveal several trails across patches of snow and duff. All convened where Anna stood. A meeting place? A gathering before the trek?

"Nope," she said. In the utter silence of fog, darkness and forest, this breach of etiquette annoyed her, and she kept the rest of her thoughts inside her head. These hikers hadn't wanted the patrol rangers to notice that the trail to Lower Merced Pass Lake was getting such heavy use. They'd hiked in cross-country to meet the Illilouette.

Dry crisp snow and half-frozen mud were splendid tracking mediums. A few minutes' study and she was fairly sure she was seeing not the tracks of nine or ten men, but three men who had come repeatedly at different times. She had little doubt that, should she follow their tracks downhill, they would lead to the road somewhere in the vicinity of Mono Meadow Trailhead. Knowing she was on the right track, the pure pleasure of pursuit made her boots light and her heart strong. Had the need for stealth not made her circumspect she would have been singing.

Outside, moving, tracking, she forgot about time and distance, about the halfhearted promise she'd made herself to go only partway. She walked too far and too fast. Sweat soaked the collar of her shirt and lay damp between her breasts. Forcing herself to take a break, she dried off as best she could and sat down to rest, eat and cool down.

According to the map, her body and her watch, she'd covered close to eleven miles. Lower Merced Pass Lake was nearby, not more than a mile or two. This was where things got dicey and a person could get herself lost. The lake might or might not be visible from the trail. On a clear day she wouldn't have given a thought to wandering haphazardly into the woods. Due west was Merced Peak, at 11,728 feet. East-southeast was Buena Vista at 9,700. Orienting one's self with landmarks of soaring granite was a piece of cake. With clouds clamped down, and the sky oozing between mountains and leaking through trees, there was no place but here, a moveable feast of rock and pine. It wouldn't do to forget where "here" was at any given moment. In weather this thick even map and compass were no guarantee. The human mind and the wilderness were foxy things. They had the power to bend reality, cause blindness, make madness seem a viable path.

Food warmed her from within as her sweat-soaked shirt of microfiber dried faster than anything in the natural world had a right to. It was quarter past twelve. She'd been hiking seven hours. Four hours of daylight remained. She knew she should turn back, but she was so close. Shouldering her pack, she returned to the trail, heading uphill.

Worry over finding the lake had been pointless. At the top of a small boulder-capped knoll, not three hundred yards beyond the copse where she'd picnicked, the veritable pack of boot prints she'd followed half the day took an abrupt right turn off the trail.

Rather than thunder along this muddy highway, she drifted into the trees and walked parallel to the beaten path. Snow was heavier at this elevation. Drifts were a couple of feet deep, but there were bare patches and, in general, it wasn't more than six inches. The going was relatively easy. Around her, ponderosa pines, needles looking more black than green in the still air, vanished upward into the gloom. A granite streambed, slab on overlapping slab, black water laced along the edges with silver-white ice, ran in a westerly direction. The duff of needles on the forest floor provided the only real color; that and Anna's flame-colored fleece pullover. Mild discomfort niggled at the back of her mind for being so out of step with nature's decor. She ignored it.

The lake pierced white on white through a fringe of trees.

Approaching as quietly as crunching snow and heavy boots permitted, she surveyed this hard-won scrap of the park. Undoubtedly a jewel in the summer months, by the feeble light of the dying year it was unprepossessing in the extreme, disappointing even. Not more than ten or fifteen acres, she could see its entirety without bothering to turn her head.

Scrubby brown grasses, inundated in years with normal precipitation, spiked through crusty snow down to the water's edge. The lake itself slept under ice and snow. To the west, Lower Merced Pass Lake ended in a wall. At first Anna took it to be a berm of snow forty to sixty feet high but quickly realized it was granite shattered and tumbled over so many years the boulders formed a scree wall half as high as the shoulder of the mountain behind it. On the opposite shore from where she stood, trees reached to the water's edge, a jagged black line between gray ice and ice-gray skies.

Other than that, there was nothing. Anna didn't know what, exactly, she'd expected to find, but with the multitude of tracks, the same three or four pairs of boots trekking in and out over a period of time, the careful avoidance of the trailhead, the odd habits of the even odder men in Dixon's cabin, she'd expected something.

Damn. Staring into the colorless gloom, trying to get up the energy for the long cold walk down to the valley, she noticed a festooning of odd-shaped snow scraps in the fringe of evergreens across the lake. From ground level to about fifteen feet up, the trees were marred with what looked to be flotsam from a bygone flood. Drawn by the anomaly, she stepped out from the shore, tested the ice. It was rock-hard, a foot thick or more. Emboldened, she crossed. Twenty feet from the far shore she stopped to study the peculiar decorations these pines had acquired just before Christmas.

Chunks varied in size from several feet long and half that wide to tiny shards. Metal and tubing and what looked to be canvas, twisted and torn, was shattered and sprayed into the trees as if a large machine had been pulverized, then blasted toward the southern shore. Mystified, Anna scanned lake, trees and ice. Toward the granite scree wall was a near-perfect triangle several feet high. Perfect geometrical shapes weren't alien in nature, but they were rare enough to catch her eye and, on an otherwise flat field of ice, worth investigating. She dropped her pack to give her shoulders a rest, walked to the small white pyramid. Brushing the rime of frost away, she exposed a blue metal cone sitting neatly in the middle of the wilderness lake.

The cone made sense of the other disparate pieces. Kneeling in the snow, she cleaned it off. Thin metal, sky blue in color, rivets running up one side; it was the nose cone of an airplane, not abandoned rusting alone in the middle of nowhere, but intact and unharmed in the idiosyncratic way of disasters. Rocking back on her heels, she looked around with a new perspective. An aircraft—a fixed-wing—had crashed with tremendous force, blasting bits of metal, tubing, Plexiglas, fabric, anything that could be smashed, into the trees. The plane had crashed before the last snow, possibly during the violent storm that preceded the kids' disappearance. Looking behind her, she tried to figure the angle from which the aircraft had come down, find the main body of the plane or scars that would indicate point of impact. There were none. From the look of things, it had flown straight—or very nearly straight—into the ice-covered lake. The body of the plane broke apart on impact, the pieces blown into the trees with the resultant force. Smashing through the ice, the main fuselage along with the heavy engines would have sunk. Water closed; ice refroze; new snow re-created a virgin lake.

There would be corpses beneath her.

Standing, Anna wondered how many. A pilot. Maybe a copilot. Passengers? Why had the plane not been reported missing? California skies were painted with radar from both naval and civil installations. Pilots filed flight plans. In an area as well kept and densely populated as the great state of California, airplanes seldom went missing for long. Were any craft lost over this part of the Sierra, the park would have been notified immediately. With the hue and cry of the search the rangers would have been on hyperalert. This wreck was weeks old. There'd been no word, no hint, not even a rumor of a plane down in the mountains.

A failure of multiple systems—flight plan, radar tracking, friends and family reporting their loved ones taking to the friendly skies and never coming back—usually meant considerable effort had gone into circumventing the authorities. A pilot taking off from a noncommercial strip, filing no flight plan, flying at night in bad weather beneath the radar, those expecting him or her careful not to report failure to arrive; it had to be a drug plane up from Mexico or Baja, headed into Reno or maybe Salt Lake City.

This realization like a clarifying lens over her mind's eye, Anna saw what she'd been missing. A disappointed mind, tired eyes and light that damped rather than brought forth color, her brain had dismissed what it had deemed natural excrescences in the ice along the water's edge.

"My God there's *bales* of the stuff," she whispered. Stunned, she trotted toward the nearest. Half frozen in the ice was an eruption of black plastic three feet long and half again that wide and tall, littered with dark green sodden straw. Crouching, she pinched up the frozen hay and sniffed it. AV gas and dope. When the plane struck and ruptured, its cargo, along with much of the fuselage and probably the brains of the pilot, spewed across the ice and into the trees.

Now that she knew what she was looking at, Anna was astounded she'd not noticed before. Broken, half in ice, wrapped around trees, were fifty or sixty bales of what was undoubtedly prime Colombian or Mexican marijuana. Nearer the shore were places where the ice had been hacked away with axes to free the stuff.

The entrepreneurs who'd sent and/or purchased the weed would have known it had gone missing. Had they a brain in their head they would have had a pretty good idea where it had gone down. But an educated guess was nowhere near enough to locate something as small as an airplane in the vast rocked and wrinkled acreage of the Sierra. Either the pilot had contacted someone on the way down or the drug plane had been stumbled upon by sheer dumb luck and those who'd struck this mother lode decided getting rich was a higher calling than reporting an accident to the authorities.

The references of the ex–party boys to a gold rush were apt. Evidently the squatters in Dixon's tent had been mining this vein for some time, maybe since a few days after the crash. That accounted for greenhorns suddenly willing to hike past blisters and sore muscles, carrying double-bladed axes and backpacks reeking of fuel.

The squatters had not fortuitously stumbled upon it while on a Boy Scout campout. Anna doubted any of the four had spent a night outdoors in their lives. Therefore someone had told them, someone who'd seen it, knew the pilot was dead, the dope accessible. Someone in the park.

A detail she hadn't paid much attention to first time around flashed into her mind. About the time of Trish Spencer's disappearance the fire ax in the dorm had been taken from its place at the end of the hall.

The better to hack dope out of the ice with, my dear.

Had Trish stumbled onto the plane? No. Not Trish. Patrick Waters. Anna remembered where the punky trail crewman had last been seen: on the trail she'd just traipsed. Trail crew was rehabbing in a burned area six miles below the lake where the Illilouette had subsequently washed out. Who better to discover the crash, perhaps hiking on his day off?

So Patrick takes a sample to sell to Trish, his local connection. Trish worms the truth out of him and teams up with buddies Caitlin and Dix to become "miners" and strike it rich, buy brother Dickie his dream job.

When the local market was saturated, they must have gotten greedy, looked farther afield. Had Trish with her petty low-level drug dealing thought she could play with the big boys? Taken her wares to the nearest city and shot her mouth off? It wouldn't take long for the really big boys to decide to take over the excavation, cut out the middleman. Or in this case, woman.

A reverberating crack came on a high pitched singing sound. Anna staggered, her train of thought derailed.

Till she saw the blood she thought the ice had begun to give way.

CHAPTER

11

Another crack split the silence. White powder plumed at Anna's feet. Shots fired: she was a target, iridescent in the red pullover. Her mind snapped back to the unease she'd felt trundling this rag of color onto the ice. The tiny watchwoman in the back of her mind had been screaming of this possibility. In her preoccupation, Anna had ignored her.

Instinct overrode further thought. The snow had spewed toward the south and the wall of boulders. Guessing the shooter was at the lake's north end, Anna bolted for the eastern shore and the cover of trees. Gravity had gone mad. She fell. Rose. Fell again.

Shots rang out, two, three, fifty—Anna's mind wasn't on counting. Twice more she stumbled but managed to keep her feet. Reaching the line of trees, she dove, belly down, across the icy snow and duff.

"*Safe!*" a memory of Mr. White, her fifth-grade teacher, shouted as she slid into home on a base hit.

Crawling lizard-fashion, elbows and knees bent, she scuttled deeper into the trees. Like all of Yosemite National Park, the shores of Lower Merced Pass Lake were littered with granite boulders. Anna didn't stop till she was snuggled up to the base of a big friendly rock.

Two more shots smashed into the stillness. If they landed anywhere near her, she didn't hear them hit. Either the shooter had bad aim or was using a pistol. Regardless of the reason why, Anna was alive and grateful for it. With this new lease on life came wracking pain. Every nerve in her left leg fired till the cacophony coalesced into a bone-breaking ache that nearly paralyzed her from toes to hip. She ignored it. Pain, shock and their attendant stupidity would have to wait. Crouching small behind her rock, she skinned out of the alarmingly red pullover. Beneath, she wore a gray turtleneck. The turtleneck was next. Then she pulled the red fleece on first and stretched the turtleneck over it. Feeling somewhat less visible, she answered the clamoring of pain from her ankle. Her sock blossomed with an oddly beautiful bloom of crimson. A bullet, probably a ricochet or even a shard of ice, given she'd walked away from the scene—albeit with less grace than was wanted—had struck just above the cuff of her boot, shredding her sock and tearing away a chunk of flesh. No spurting, but plenty of blood. Nothing to bind it with and no time. The cold would help stanch the bleeding.

The cold could also kill her. Pack, water, food and down sleeping bag were stranded in the middle of her own personal killing field. *Move on.* If she were to have a future, even a short one, there were plans to be made.

Making an educated guess, Anna figured there were two men, possibly three. They had at least one firearm, probably a handgun. Judging by the ice and what she'd seen outside the tent cabin, they also had a double-bladed ax.

She had a wounded leg and a Swiss army knife.

But they were city boys and Anna was home.

"Not bad odds," she whispered, not because she believed it but because it amused her to say the words. Far better to play Clint Eastwood than Little Nell.

For a while longer, she sat, the forest's quiet reknitting around her, and dared hope they'd gone away, confident they'd scared her off and could return to their harvesting or, given the lateness of the day, packing out their loot. Maybe they would choose to shut down the whole operation, cut their losses and escape to whatever hole they'd crawled out of, leaving Anna alive to report her find.

An awful lot of dope remained entombed in the ice. Thousands of pounds, hundreds of thousands of dollars.

They weren't going to go away. Already four people had been killed to keep the secret. One more would hardly tweak their consciences.

As if to ratify her conclusion, voices cut through the still air; men calling to each other. Anna could hear the conversation so clearly her heart raced wondering how they'd crept so close without her noting their passage across the crusted snow.

She crept from the shelter of her rock, then tree to tree for the half dozen yards separating her from the lake. They were not as close as she'd feared. Sound carried well across the ice. Two men were on the lake, one closer to the shore where she was, the other in the middle. The leader, Mark, the lithe dark man from the tent cabin, carried a pistol, either a .38 or a .357. The man farther out, one of the three stooges, but not Billy "Beer" Kurt, the fattest, had the ax over his shoulder. Of a third man, she saw nothing. Either these two had come alone or one stayed with their gear.

Lower Merced Pass Lake was cupped in a hollow on the breast of a small hill footing Buena Vista Crest. The uphill side of this hollow was closed by the granite wall of scree. The lower lip was another granite outcrop, far less imposing and partially cloaked in soil and trees.

At this altitude, with its deep snows and short growing season, undergrowth was sparse. What there was grew low to the ground, not more than a foot or two high, and most of that leafless with winter, but there were plenty of rocks. Anna could try to run on a bum ankle or she could go to ground beneath a chunk of granite, squeezing herself deep into a crevice, and hope the men would not find her. The decision to run was made for her.

"There," Mark shouted. He'd seen the track where she'd entered the trees. He began jogging toward it. The pistol was held at his side, muzzle to the ground, as if he'd grown up running with guns. *His mother should have let him run with scissors,* Anna thought as she turned and fled awkwardly back the way she had come.

She should never have stopped, never have checked her wound, taken the time to switch the red for the gray, never have crawled back to see who was coming for her. After the first shots she should have run and kept running like a scared rabbit, putting as much ground between herself and these men as the laws of physics and physiology would allow. Then, maybe, she could have gone to ground.

She wished she had the leisure for a comforting bout of self-recrimination, but she'd frittered that time away as well. As she staggered and didn't curse, slammed weight on her wounded ankle and didn't scream, the topographical map unfolded in her brain. Illilouette Creek flowed out of the north end of the lake and down along the trail to the valley. On the west side of the lake, the side she'd come in from, was another creek, a smaller one, which flowed from Upper Merced Pass Lake down into Lower Merced.

For a number of reasons, Anna needed a creek. To get to
Illilouette Creek she'd have to head south, parallel to her pursuers, and run the risk of meeting the third man. If there was
a third man.

Reaching the other creek was considerably more arduous,
but it might prove less hazardous to her health.

Though the plan was half-baked, her brain blanked with
the pure animal need for flight. Panic would have had her run
flat out, heedless of the agony in her leg, of the noise she
made, the tracks she left. Training pushed panic aside. Education was one of the many reasons humans proliferated
while animals thundered into extinction.

Clinging to humanity while drawing on what animal
courage she possessed, Anna bent low and ran in rapid leaps,
hops, jogs and spurts, stepping in places the snow had melted
off, a rock lay exposed, on thick low underbrush where city-
bred eyes would not notice a foot had trod. Forcing her breath
quiet, she choked down squeaks and moans as her damaged
ankle was tried. Blood, more than she'd hoped, less than
she'd expected, drenched the remnants of the sock and her
trouser leg. Inside her boot she felt its warm slosh. Outside
there was enough it began leaving a pinkish stain on the
snow. Precious moments were wasted stopping to wipe the
boot on her sleeve to leave a less telltale trail. She had to have
a lead, had to have time. There was no way she could win a
prolonged footrace or a fair fight.

Despite these necessary maneuvers, she covered ground,
choosing to go behind any thing tall, putting as many obsta-
cles between their eyes and her fleeing backside as she could.

Halfway up the eastern edge of the scree slope, shielded
behind three stunted and twisted pines, she stopped to listen.
For a time all she heard was her heart pounding and the thin
whistle of air sucked too hard and too fast through her nostrils.

Heart rate and breathing slowed. Anna mentally patted herself on the back for the long hours she'd served on a Stairmaster in the flatlands of Mississippi. She waited. She listened. Men's voices didn't come to fill the silence. They'd not given up, of that she was fairly sure. It was too soon and the stakes were too high. She hoped they'd not suddenly developed the sense or the self-control to move stealthily. Knowing where they were was the only edge she had at present. That and keeping them from knowing where she was.

Relief came with the sound of muttered curses. They'd made it about a quarter of the way up from the lake to where she waited. Trees muffled sound and she couldn't make out their words as she had before, but a reassuringly confused tone ran through the exchanges.

Anna checked her watch. Three-fifteen. Even with the thick cloud cover it was a good hour and a half till full dark. A worshipper of Ra in his myriad forms, she never thought this close to winter solstice she'd be wishing sunset came earlier.

The voices stopped. Leaning forward as if four inches would make a difference in what she heard and what she didn't, Anna listened. Cold, windless, the temperature unvarying from shade to open space, there was no ambient noise to contend with. Faintly she heard boots moving through snow and duff, the tiny ice crystals formed from fog and subfreezing temperatures crunching.

Torn between the need to listen and the desire to run, she remained crouched behind the trees, ears so open they fairly popped with it. Luck broke her way. A man stumbled or fell and swore loudly. The other crunching never varied. One came up on the hill after her. The other headed back down toward the lake. For a moment, she dared to hope they'd split up, then a shout, louder and clearer than the others, broke through the muffle of pines.

"Got it!"

Her trail had been found. Anna had underestimated them. They'd split up to circle and find her track. She made a mental note not to underestimate them again. City boys they were, but the hunting down and killing of men was clearly on their résumés. It was impossible not to leave some trail. Even the expanses of granite left marks where her boots scraped frost from the stone. Night was her best hope. In the black dark of the wilderness, no moon or stars, a flashlight would not be enough. They'd have to give up. Again Anna checked her watch. An hour and twenty-eight minutes.

The men were working up from the lake, moving faster now, learning as they went what signs to look for. Time to run. She pushed to her feet and stepped out from her hiding place. Knife-sharp pain cut through her wounded ankle, which gave way and sent her sprawling. The partial anesthetic of shock had worn away during her brief respite and now the damage was making itself felt. From the intensity and localized nature of the pain, Anna knew the flesh wasn't the only thing broken. The force of the impact had cracked or broken a bone.

Cracked, she told herself as she pushed up from the ground. *If it was broken I couldn't walk.* Though it wasn't necessarily true, she held to that thought and began the ascent. She tried for the bare patches, the granite, the ground cover. Pain bit into her brain at every step, eating away thought. She walked and fell, crawled and scrambled. At one point she realized tears were running down her face. The image of a whimpering helpless female strengthened her spine and spirit. Far better to die quietly and peacefully of the cold beneath a rock like a wounded cat than to be gunned down by bozos.

Anna liked most things about guns: the artistry, the mechanics, the cowboy heritage, the way they felt in her hand, the soporific effect of a Colt .357 in the bed stand at night when the house made creepy noises. What she hated about them was the power of destruction they conferred upon men otherwise weak and impotent. Any pathetic fool could pick up a rifle and cause havoc. The Washington, D.C., snipers had proven that.

Dead was, presumably, dead; she didn't know why it was worse to die at the hands of a low-rent idiot, but it was. Worse than dead was helpless. They must never get their hands on her. "They'll never take me alive," she whispered, but the pain and fear were too great for the game of movie macho to boost her courage. Wild thoughts of guns and pocketknives and cyanide in hollow teeth splattered through her mind as she made her vows, scrambled, crawled and cursed.

Drenched with sweat, hot and cold at the same time, she finally won the top of the hill backing the lake. The men were closer now. She could hear them as they ranged for tracks, found them, shouted, lost them again, moving inexorably up the way she had come.

Not long. Not long. The shoulder of the hill presented good and bad news. There was a great expanse of veined granite running across the top of the upthrust forming the scree slope. Despite the frost, granite was harder to track on than snow and duff. But granite also left her exposed should her pursuers break free of the trees. Her ankle slowing her down, Anna wasn't sure how long it would take her to cross. It wouldn't do to scratch and scramble. A trail anyone could read even in fading half-light would mark her passage. Any track would lead them to her. Pondering variables wasn't a luxury she had. Again the gray turtleneck and crimson pullover came off. Upper body bare, Anna moved.

Throw the turtleneck down; step on it. Pullover down; step. Turtleneck; step. One in each hand, a swinging rhythm

built and she moved with surprising speed. The ankle
screamed. Anna didn't. The frigid air felt good on her over-
heated body. When it chilled, she would be in trouble. *Better
than bozos,* she told herself.

Two minutes, maybe three, and she was across. There'd
been no outcry, no wild pounding of boots. She'd won a bit
more time, crept closer to night. Fleece and microfiber once
again on, she looked back. Even knowing where she'd
crossed it was hard to see her trail.

"See her?"

"Not yet."

Anna saw them. Him. Mark. His dark head bare, green
parka unzipped over a black sweater, he stepped onto the
granite, silhouetting himself against the graying sky. A clear
shot. At that moment Anna would have traded five years of
her life for a rifle and a bullet to put in it.

Resisting the need to keep him in sight as if by so doing
she could in some way control him, she ducked behind her
rock and began to crawl. The first drag on her ankle brought
a tide of pain that blocked her vision at the edges and caused
the narrow tunnel of remaining sight to swim with spots. She
pushed on: one hand, one knee, one hand, one knee, dragging foot, a shriek of swallowed agony, one hand, one knee.

Behind her the voices rose, quarreled, fell. They searched
the edges of the granite looking for where she'd left the
trackless stone.

Anna crawled.

Her gloves were soaked through and pricked with needles
that jabbed her fingers and palms. Her pants from the knee
down were caked with snow that melted against her skin and
packed into her boots. Any idea of covering her trail was
abandoned. She could not stand, could not walk, until she
stabilized the ankle. Maybe not even then.

She had to reach the creek.

She headed downhill, this time to the lake's other side. Broken rock was so plentiful in places there was no way to cling to the earth, and she tumbled as best she might down stony irregular steps three and four feet high. When possible, she lowered herself with care onto her good foot, then to her knees. When she couldn't, she tucked and rolled and hoped the fall would either kill her or leave her alone.

The voices of the men grew fainter and she was heartened. Maybe they had abandoned the expanse of granite, assuming she'd headed deeper into the trees to the east or south rather than doubling back around the lake. Going toward their camp was the act of a madwoman. Anna prayed to whichever gods tend to wounded and hunted animals that her pursuers would think so.

High and muted on the crown of stone the voices changed. Like most prayers, Anna's had gone unanswered. Men or dogs, the baying when they scented blood was unmistakable. They would come quickly now, her trail as obvious as that of a loggerhead turtle crawling across smooth beach sand.

The lake was on her left. She'd made it down the hill it had cost her so much to climb no more than two hundred yards to the east. Marsh grasses poked through snow and frozen mud, thick up to the treeline. Beneath black boughs and the gloom that drifted from day to dark with no need for twilight, she was protected from eyes on higher ground.

She crawled.

The creek was close; she could smell it.

Thank God for small fucking mercies, a cramped and bitter part of her mind hissed. Unaccustomed to creeping on all fours, her arms shook with exhaustion. On the few occasions she dared to stop, her muscles had twitched and quivered. Her shoulders ached; the ball joint in one of them—heard through her skeleton rather than her ears—grated as if broken glass ground in the rotator cuff.

Soon, Anna knew, she would devolve further, from quadruped to arthropod crawling on her belly.

Worms tended to have short life spans.

Duff gave way to layered rock, slabs of stone overlapping like flagstones for a giant's patio. Her trail would not show here; the tree cover kept the frost off, at least in the so-called heat of the day. Her knees and palms complained of the hard surface and it surprised her. With the clamor of pain sounding from ankle to hip she'd thought newer, lesser pains would be drowned out. The incredible delicacy of the body's nervous system never ceased to amaze her, though at the moment she could have done with less sensation.

Running water. The sound came to her ears like a balm. The creek was right where the map had promised. Winterfull, six inches deep, clear and ice cold, it ran over granite steps fifteen feet across.

First Anna drank, sucking up the frigid water so greedily her head ached and the fillings in her teeth sparked.

Skidding.

Swearing.

They were coming. Forcing herself upright or nearly so, hands catching at trees, she made her way along the creek's edge, careful to splash water on the rock. Ten, thirty, fifty feet more she kept it up. Distance had become a single step, and had to be continually done over again. When she reached a break in the giant's paving stones where the creek left the granite to dig into the shallow skin of soil supporting the forest, she walked up and down several times as if making a decision.

That done, she sat on the rock ledge where water boiled over the lip to the deeper creekbed below and unlaced her

boots. The right boot slipped off. The left she would have
had to have removed with a prybar. Her ankle was swelling.
Once the boot was off, she'd never get it on again. Removing
the much-abused turtleneck, she wrapped it around the snow-
caked boot. One sock on, one boot swathed, she stood and,
careening from tree to boulder to tree, moved back across the
overlapped slabs of granite till she'd put three or four yards of
rock and a thin screen of pines between herself and the stream.

The closer she stayed the better it would work. It would
work. It would work. Anna was counting on the accumulated
power of thousands of books and movies about good guys
tracking bad guys, Indians tracking cowboys, convicts fleeing bloodhounds and innocents running from vigilantes.

Still so near she could hear the gentle life of the stream,
she dragged the filthy turtleneck on once again to mask the
offending red fleece. She hadn't the strength to deal with the
boot. Pain and cold and crawling had sapped her energy till
each movement was almost impossibly hard. Curling down,
she lay with her back to the creek, pulled her knees to her
chest and tucked her head in. Devolution was nearly complete. She'd adopted the defense of a pill bug. All that remained
was to slide back into the primordial seas. On a metaphysical
level, that might happen all too soon.

She would rather have remained standing or, failing that,
sitting in such a way she could watch for the approaching men,
but none of the trees were big enough to screen a body, and
hide-and-seek logic dictated that if she could see them, they
could see her. And there was the superstition that people could
feel hidden eyes upon them. Despite the fact she had watched
enough people to know that if a sixth sense attuned to eye
pressure existed it was exceedingly rare, the feeling persisted.

It rankled to curl and hide, blind and helpless. Should
trouble come she preferred to meet it head-on, though against

a pistol and a double-bladed ax she'd probably make a pretty poor showing.

"Here! She came over this way." The speaker was not the man who'd introduced himself as Mark and been a gracious host, but the Mark who'd first slammed through the cabin door. The hard-edged misogynist who used showers and women with the same utilitarian contempt. "Where you looking?" A duller voice, thicker, the breath coming in heavy labored gasps. One of the stooges. Not the youngest, not the one with a soul behind his eyes.

"Here, you stupid motherfucker. Look at the rock."

The chase across the lake, up the hill and down again hadn't improved Mark's temper or vocabulary.

They were so close it sounded as if they stood over her, trying to figure out if her gray and curled form was animal, vegetable or mineral. Unaware she did so, she squeezed her eyes shut. Had she covers, they would have been pulled over her head.

"Shit, man"—Mark again—"she's gone into the creek. Look here. No way to track her. Fuck. Take that side."

"How am I gonna get across?"

A thump. A splash. A laugh. "Walk. Keep your eyes on the ground. She's gotta come out somewhere. Jesus. Did you bring a fucking flashlight?"

"I got one back at camp."

"That's a big fucking help."

The conversation faded. They followed the creek. Or rather, followed the script where the hunted inevitably reached a creek, predictably chose to walk in it to lose the hunters. Trackers always checked the banks; ambient knowledge gleaned from America's fiction.

Without moving, Anna listened till she could no longer hear them. Silhouettes turned to shadows, shadows faded into night so black she could feel its weight on her eyes, its body as she breathed it in and out.

In a moment she would move, get up, put her boot on, figure out how to survive the night. Cold cradled her, as tight and close as a lover, comforting, almost restful. Soon she would get up, but first she must sleep. Just a little, just enough to get her wind back.

Ice and night closed around her brain and Anna felt the bliss of sinking into it.

CHAPTER

12

A perfect dream of warm sand and blue ocean was being repeatedly interrupted by a need to scrape stinging jellyfish off of her left foot. After what seemed a lifetime of fruitless washing and scratching, the irritation dragged her from the sunlight and the shore. Opening her eyes to the darkness Geppetto must have known in Monstro's belly, Anna had no idea where she was. Several times she tried to fix her mind on the problem, and several times she drifted away to the delicious heat on the white sand beach. Each time the stinging jellyfish brought her back, unfriendly fire burning her ankle. She tried to think and could not. She tried to move and could not. With a herculean effort she succeeded only in stirring up pain so sharp she heard herself whimper. *Make a noise and you die,* one part of her brain informed another. The whimpering ceased. *I'm already dying. I like it.* It's warm, the brain answered itself, and Anna smiled. It was warm.

Dying. Vaguely she remembered promising someone she wouldn't do that. Molly. It must have been her sister, Molly. With the blink of a mind's eye Anna was looking through Molly's window then and saw her seated in the tiny kitchen of her Upper West Side apartment, her husband's long legs bent out like a grasshopper's from beneath the Barbie-sized table. The two of them were sipping fancy coffee, heatedly and happily arguing politics. Molly was okay. Molly was good. Frederick was there to take care of her.

Anna turned away from that airshaft window above Manhattan's streets and wafted toward her beach. Sunlight shattered on the waves, the glitter as bright as mirror shards. She walked toward it.

Not Molly, came an intrusive voice. Paul. She'd promised Paul she would not die, not this time, not this trip, not this assignment.

Without thought or effort, she was in Mississippi. For some reason it was raining, though it hadn't been when she'd left. Paul was not in his beautiful historic home in Port Gibson with its hardwood floors and marble-tiled fireplace, stretched out on his overstuffed couch, as she might have expected. He was in her dreary Mission 66 government housing—built in the mid-sixties as part of a grand plan—in Rocky Springs campground, carport full of spiders, backyard full of Baptist Church groups and Boy Scouts.

Hovering above the cracked cement of her front walk, she watched him through the living room windows. Unlike with her sister and brother-in-law, she could not hear him, but his lips were moving and his face was animated as if he spoke to someone.

Piedmont, her old orange-striped tomcat, came out from the kitchen, his tail hooked in its customary question mark. Paul squatted down and the cat trotted over to be petted. Cats liked Paul. A sign of favor from the gods. Taco, her three-legged dog, wasn't in the scene. When she'd left, Paul had promised to look after her family. Taco, valuing real estate over personality, went to Port Gibson to live in style. Piedmont, for exactly the opposite reason, stayed home.

Anna hadn't thought to be gone long enough for it to matter.

Paul lifted the big cat and draped him over one shoulder. Having let himself out, he awkwardly locked the door behind him and carried the cat to his truck parked in the driveway.

He'd worried about her cat, come fifteen miles in the rain to take Piedmont home.

Shit, Anna thought. For a while she hovered in the nowhere of her mind between the bright beach and the black cold.

One could break promises. It was allowed.

One could not abandon one's cat. Not and retain any hope of heaven. Turning her back on the sparkling sea, she opened her eyes, or thought she did. It was too dark to tell. By dint of will, she focused her mind. Hypothermia; irrationality was a late symptom. She seemed to remember being taught that if a patient could raise his or her hands overhead and wiggle them then they weren't too far gone. Anna couldn't even find her arms.

Pain was as realistic as life got. She would start with that. Ever so slightly, she moved the foot the jellyfish had been attacking. Pain, duller than she remembered from whatever lifetime she was returning to, coursed up her shin bone.

Better than smelling salts, she thought as the fog in her brain began to clear. Broken ankle, curled in a ball, half-frozen in the backcountry, two, maybe three men trying to kill her, black as pitch: it all came back. Despite the jellyfish, the beach looked better and better.

Move, she ordered herself and kept on repeating it like a mantra till her gloved hands found down and pushed. Elbows locked, head hanging, she rested a moment.

Not resting, drifting, she reprimanded herself. *Move.* She did and kept on doing so, inch by bloody inch until she was upright, boot in hand, leaning against the rough bark of a pine tree no bigger around than her neck, but sturdy and kind.

Blind, invisible and glad of it, she performed homemade calisthenics tailored to a gimpy ankle. Had she been able to see herself, she'd have been further warmed by a good laugh. Alone in the dark she flapped and writhed and stretched, hugged herself, scrubbed her face and hair with gloved fingers, massaged, patted and pawed various parts of her anatomy till ten zillion exquisitely agonizing prickles announced returning life. Even her butt was numb. At least that was a new, if not pleasant, sensation.

Being alive pretty much sucked, she decided, but no longer harbored any desire for the shore. In memory there was a decidedly sinister aspect about that sunshine-and-warmth routine, rather like the alluring scent of cheese mixed with the slightly metallic tang of a well-used trap.

Eventually enough flapping and posturing had been executed that coordination as well as mental clarity returned. She put her hiking boot back on. Her bad foot had swelled until it was squashed into the other boot so tightly she couldn't wedge a finger between the leather and her sock.

This was good. The boot created its own pressure bandage to stop the bleeding. Working blind, she gathered materials for a splint to immobilize her leg to the knee. Technically the knee should have been splinted as well to keep the pull of muscles and tendons on the injured bone to a minimum. Anna couldn't afford to cripple herself that much, and she was fairly sure the ankle was only chipped or cracked, not broken through.

Over the years, she'd fashioned a lot of splints. With the leather boot, thick sock and trousers protecting her flesh, this one didn't need to be padded, smooth or pretty. Strong, relatively straight sticks tied around ankle and calf with strips of red fleece hacked into service by her pocketknife would have to do.

She put her weight on it. It hurt. A lot. She could stand it, but she didn't know for how long, and there was no way in hell she was going to outrun anybody.

Cloaked in utter darkness, cold but alive, she set her sluggish mind to figuring out how to stay that way. She could not survive the night injured in a damp turtleneck with no food to warm her. Her pack, if the men had not retrieved it while she slept, was somewhere on the ice. Without moon, stars or flashlight she would never find it. Crippled and without light she wouldn't be able to hike out. Mark and his buddy had the things she needed, but they weren't likely to share, at least not intentionally.

With no plan but to refrain from sleeping and so returning to death's bright and inviting sea, Anna made her way toward the creek. The complete absence of light played havoc with her sense of direction. She was reduced to following the sound of water over stone, hands in front of her, gait lurching. *Night of the Living Dead,* she thought, then pushed the image away. Too apt. Too scary.

When she heard her boots splash she knew she'd reached the water. She couldn't see her feet. She couldn't see her hand in front of her face. Her ankle would not allow her to crouch. Bending at the waist, one glove removed, she reached for where her toes should be and found the water.

This simple maneuver took the concentration of a high-wire act.

Cold as liquid ice, the creek burned over her fingers. Anna waited till she was certain of the direction of the flow, then followed it, one baby step at a time, downstream toward the lake. Twenty steps—Anna counted simply because it gave her at least an intellectual knowledge of forward progress—and the toe of her boot struck something solid. In the black world she traversed, her sense of hearing had become acute. The boot didn't knock or clack but thudded. Not suitable for anything she'd fallen over as yet.

An unpleasant shiver coursed through her at the thought she'd come across a dead body, perhaps the frozen corpse of one of the four missing kids. For reasons rooted in childhood nightmares, fear that a cold dead hand would grab her ankle rattled up her spine. To fight it, she forced herself to bend closer. Folding at the waist like an old woman picking flowers, she put both hands on the thing.

It was a body: soft but not too soft, a squared torso clad in nylon. No legs. No arms. No head. Her hands slipped over straps and buckles. Too many straps and buckles. Not a body. "Thankyoubabyjesus," she muttered. A backpack. Hoping for a flashlight, a warm coat or food, she fumbled the top open. Plastic and frozen straw. The pack was filled with dope mined from the lake of the dead.

Disappointed, she straightened then stood still till the dizziness passed. The pack probably belonged to Caitlin, Trish, Patrick or Dix. Since the dope had not been taken, she surmised whoever was carrying it had dumped it and run. Mark and his buddies must have tracked the kids down as they were trying to do with her. They must have found the owner, but not the pack. Come spring the bodies would show up, gruesome surprises for unsuspecting wilderness enthusiasts. Unless the rangers found them first.

Having moved carefully to the pack's other side lest she get turned around in the dark and lose her way, Anna continued following the creek.

Darkness, her body an invisible source of misery with no size or shape in relation to the world around her—indeed, no sense of a world being around her, no sense of anything but cold so thick it seemed as if it pressed in on her with actual weight—there was no way to anchor in reality. Thoughts, well begun, would fray out, unravel till she'd come to a standstill, her mind choked with immense amounts of nothing.

Despite the overcast night the lake's shore was not without light. Years before, deep underground in Lechuguilla Cave in New Mexico, Anna had known true darkness, darkness so intense she couldn't but feel that staring into it would blind her the way staring too long at the sun was said to. Here, out from beneath the trees, the snow-covered ice gathered to itself what tiny insignificant particles of light managed to make it through the clouds. It didn't glow as a snowfield did on a clear night. It didn't show white, or even gray, but the black of the lake's surface was less than that of sky or trees. There were now two places; an up and a down had been created. Blurred edges cut through the ink canvas, forcing the horizon away from the bridge of her nose.

Filling her lungs, she realized she'd been subsisting on small sips of air as if afraid the crushing dark would drown her.

She pulled the navy-blue watch cap she wore down to her eyebrows and the neck of the turtleneck up over her nose. She doubted the precaution was necessary, but she couldn't afford any mistakes. Without strength, speed or artillery she would be relying on stealth. If she didn't succeed on the first try she wouldn't succeed at all.

Moving more easily without the oppression of mind and eye and the worry a fearsome invisible thing would strike at her face or trip up her injured foot, she walked onto the ice. Order restored to the universe by a simple line of lighter and darker to navigate by, she knew the scree slope was to her left; the shore from whence the first bullets had come, to her right. She turned right. It had been late in the day when they'd seen her. An hour, maybe two, would have been wasted chasing her, then following her phantom trail up the creek. Dark came early. Unless they'd chosen to hike out at night— and hiking downhill wearing heavy packs over icy surfaces was far more hazardous than hiking uphill with the packs empty—they would have camped.

No light indicated this was true. Slowly, she limped over the ice. Halfway down the frozen lake the red-gold spark she'd been searching for glimmered between the trees or rocks that had shielded it from sight.

For a moment she rested, took the weight off her ankle, and stared at the fitful flames. With complete certainty, she understood the awe prehistoric man must have experienced on first discovering fire. It was the most beautiful sight she'd ever seen. Had Paul Davidson been standing beside it, an orange cat on his shoulder and a three-legged dog at his feet, she would have known the glittering shore for a trap and this red-gold shimmer the true promise of heaven. Primitive DNA lingering deep in her chromosomal helixes urged her toward it, a lame wolf hoping for something slow or small or stupid to kill for its supper.

Nearer the shoreline she began to hear the murmur of voices. By the time she was close enough to smell the smoke and feel the change beneath her feet as snow-covered ice changed to snow-covered earth she could make out words. The filthy smothering night, so recently an enemy clogging eyes and mind, switched allegiances and became her ally. If she was careful to stay beyond the campfire's seductive circle of light, they would never see her. Had her body in its innate frailty not been awkward with cold and pain, she might have felt as ephemeral and powerful as a malevolent ghost, coming to this fireside gathering to prey. Trapped in an imperfect vehicle of bone and flesh, dragging an all-but-useless leg, she just concentrated on moving without making a racket.

With the men awake and outside their tent, there was little she dared do. Ignoring the fire's siren call, she stayed back. Moving slower than any Mississippi box turtle, she eased between the trunks of two good-sized pines, close enough she could see the camp and hear the conversation.

She would have dearly loved to cuddle down between the supportive trees, hug her knees to her chest for what little warmth they offered and rest, but if she did she would fall asleep. Come morning the wretches would find Christmas had come early and a macabre Kris Kringle had brought them the gift of a frozen corpse.

Allowing herself the small luxury of leaning, she took stock of their camp. The ranger part of her brain, not quite lulled to sleep by hypothermia, was outraged. These men were as slovenly outdoors as in. Food cans were scattered over the ground along with cigarette butts, chip bags, candy wrappers and plastic eating utensils. The fire, built for security as well as warmth, wasn't in a fire ring but raged in a circle of trees the limbs of which had been chopped off to feed it. Littering and unauthorized fire; crimes that could add two to three minutes to their prison sentences should a federal judge ever find out. Sleeping bags hung like pupa from a limb, probably in hopes the fire would drive out the chill and damp before bedtime.

Set to one side was a tent, a skiff of hoarfrost glittering on its rain tarp. Chances were good the tent had been there some time, pitched when they'd first hiked in and left as a bivouac for future expeditions. Anna was relieved. She'd been hoping they would have a tent. Now she hoped they would retire into it before she froze to death.

None of the niceties required for backcountry camping were in evidence: no bear-proof canisters, gas stove, latrine shovel. These, had they been brought up the mountain, which was unlikely, had been jettisoned to make room for dope. Two backpacks lined with black garbage bags bulged with marijuana mined from the lake. Behind them, near the tent, the double-bladed ax leaned against a tree.

The bigger of the two men pulled a bottle from the pocket of his jacket, unscrewed the cap and took a swig.

"Go easy on that, Phil," Mark said. "She's still out there somewhere."

"Probably froze or bled to death by now. There was blood on the snow."

"Probably. Give me that." Mark took the whiskey bottle and drank. "Still, go easy."

"Like I always do," Phil said and laughed.

Eat drink and be merry, Anna thought and wished for a case of whiskey that they might drink themselves insensible. While she was at it, she wished it weren't winter, that the black bears weren't in hibernation and would descend like a biblical plague and rend these unbelievers.

"We gonna fiddle around trying to find her? I want to get the fuck off this rock pile. Packing this shit out forty pounds at a time we'll be here till the Fourth of July," Phil complained.

"You don't want your cut, just say so. I'm sure the boss will be understanding."

"Yeah. Right." Phil took another drink and held the bottle out to his comrade. To Anna's disappointment, Mark resisted temptation.

Hell of a time for rehab, she thought bitterly.

"We do it till we've got what we can. This is prime stuff," Mark said.

"Soaked with God knows what weird shit."

"It'll give the college kids a new kind of kick. We ought to charge extra."

They laughed and it grated on Anna's nerves. The desultory conversation continued. Soon she heard nothing but a mangle of voices. Standing, leaning, she'd fallen asleep on her feet like a horse. Weight shifted and she would have fallen but that her ankle sent a vicious wake-up call. Either she grunted or stumbled. She came awake to full silence. Phil and Mark stared in her direction.

"What was that?" Phil said.

"Shh."

"There's nothing."

"Shut the fuck up."

Anna stopped breathing. Her heart beat loud in her ears, so much so it seemed they must surely hear it.

"Snow falling off a tree or something," Phil said. "The bitch is dead or about to be. It's colder than a witch's tit up here. We got her pack. She's got nothing."

They listened a moment longer.

"I guess," Mark conceded. "Give me her pack."

Phil lumbered to his feet and retrieved Anna's backpack from a pile of debris that had accumulated at the base of a tree.

Mark took it and dumped it out. Her good down jacket was thrown on the fire. Her compass pocketed. Phil grabbed up a granola bar, ripped off the wrapper and began eating it. Till then, Anna had not realized how hungry she was. Great ravening hollow-eyed hunger thundered over her, leaving her weak, shaken and so livid that for a moment she was no longer cold. Slobby, malodorous Phil scarfing down her food made her angrier than being shot, chased and left to die of exposure.

Mark continued to go through her belongings, throwing everything into the fire after he'd looked at it, including the things that wouldn't burn. When it was empty he turned it inside out.

"Not here," he said and her pack, too, went onto the conflagration smoking and sizzling with nylon, paper and down feathers.

"Why would she have it? She's nobody. Just some old broad still waiting tables at fifty," Phil said.

"She outran your fat butt with a bullet in her."

Anna had eluded them both and Mark had been in the lead. From her place in the night, she watched this retort crawl across Phil's beefy face, followed by the probably wise decision not to say anything. Anna wished him more whiskey and less wisdom. To see one of them kill the other would almost be worth the stiff admission price she'd paid for the show.

"She was up here, wasn't she? And she's been living in that dorm. She knows something," Mark said. "I'd bet my life on it."

"She bet hers," Phil said, "and lost." He laughed. Mark merely smiled.

"Maybe." Mark stood and stomped to get circulation back into his feet. Anna, who'd continued the quiet flapping, clenching and bending that had restored life to her nether

parts after her near-fatal nap, envied him the ability to do so.
"Maybe not. We better post a watch. You first." Mark smiled
again and Anna was amazed she'd not seen the cruelty there
when she and Mary first met him despite the fact that he'd
entered Dix's tent cabin on a gust of woman-hating invec-
tive. The human disguise he'd adopted was near perfect. In
this wilderness he'd dropped his mask. Fire, usually the kind-
est of lights, bringing warmth and the illusion of youth to
the tired and old, flickering past flaws and scars, showed him
demonlike.

No flames reflected in his dark eyes, no moving shadows
suggested a horned skull beneath the skin—nothing so the-
atrical. The orange glow reflected back from his nice straight
teeth illuminating the joy he took in one more small cruelty
perpetrated upon his loutish companion. How much greater
his pleasure would be tearing the wings off flies or drowning
kittens. Or catching Anna before the cold killed her.

Lurking in the dark, unsure whether the cold or her ankle
hurt worse, she remembered an old aliens-among-us film.
Once the scaly lizardlike beings assumed human form the
only way to know them was by the little pinky of the left
hand. It didn't bend, some technical glitch in the metamorphosis.

This Mark creature undoubtedly had a stiff little finger.

He pulled down one of the sleeping bags, then stuffed it
and himself into the tent. Phil took a long pull on his bottle
and, now that Mark could no longer see him, indulged himself with a look of pure hatred.

For another twenty-two minutes, according to Anna's
watch, several hours if she listened to her internal clock, Phil
stared into the fire and drank. Bottle emptied, he hurled it
into the darkness. Having nothing better to do with his lips

now the bottle was gone he began muttering. Scraps and fragments of sentences slipped through the bitter air.

"Fucking bitch's an icicle by now . . . watch . . . for chrissake, I freeze my balls off . . . goddamn Marlon Brando *Godfather* shit . . . he's a fucking low-rider from Fresno . . . stupid fuck . . ."

Anna began to suspect, were the "F" word excised from the English language, Phil's vocabulary would be halved. He used it as noun, adjective, verb and adverb.

Finally he rose unsteadily, and while Anna was willing him to fall into the fire, he retrieved the second of the two sleeping bags, worked his boots off and threaded himself into it, coat and all. Snoring started before he'd zipped the bag. If she listened hard she could hear a faint echo of alcoholic gurgles. At least she needn't wonder whether the two were asleep. These were men whose bodily functions were scarcely more subtle than their language.

Keeping her eye on her watch face, the subtle blue glow of its nightlight oddly comforting, she waited through an eternity of fifteen minutes to let Phil sink thoroughly into sleep or stupor. Finally the big hand made it to its destination. Anna pushed away from the trees that had been holding her up this long, cold time. Unaware she did so, she gave them a pat of thanks. Not offending the woodland gods was a habit so deeply ingrained, she no longer gave it conscious thought.

Despite her efforts to keep her circulation going, she was alarmingly stiff and clumsy. Try as she might, the sole of the boot on her injured leg scraped when she lifted it and thumped when she set it down. Whatever part of the nervous system it is that informs the brain how far one's foot is from the ground had suffered from the vagaries of bullet, blood, constriction or cold.

Other than stopping her heart with each tiny explosion, the noise had little effect. Both snorers were too far under the sandman's shovel to be bothered by minutia.

Moving facilitated moving; as Anna shuffled along outside the ring of light, muscles warmed, stiffness abated. A prolonged rage of tingling and pain served to sharpen her mind. Enduring rehab-by-fire, she circled the camp, ever attuned to the tenor of the snores and the posture of the one visible enemy.

The magnet which drew her through rock- and tree-studded darkness leaned against a ponderosa pine opposite where she'd kept watch. She had no way of knowing who had the gun, but from what she'd observed, Mark and Phil had issues. Despite the fact that Phil had been left out in the night to defend against intruders, it was a good bet the handgun was inside the tent, snuggled up next to Mark's heart. The weapon available to Anna was the double-bladed ax. Hand-held weapons—axes, hatchets, baseball bats, butcher knives, lead pipes—all lacked the effective distance of a gun, but they had the edge psychologically. The damage incurred was close and wet, crunchy and dripping. Personal, vicious violence. Used improperly they could be more intimidating than a firearm. Or so she told herself as she worked her way across uneven ground knowing she would die if she couldn't find warmth and knowing her weapon of choice lay locked in the firearms safe behind the chief ranger's office.

At length, sweating and, for the moment, warmed, she stood behind the ax's leaning tree. The fifty-foot trek from one side of the camp to the other had taken ten minutes and nearly as much effort as the twelve-mile hike into Lower Merced Pass Lake. Circumstances had compromised her ability to leap tall buildings and move faster than speeding bullets. As a rule it offended her to be rescued, but this one time she would have welcomed it, been gracious even. And grateful. With staggering suddenness she felt lost, defeated, small and middle-aged, and hurt. This time she would die.

To counteract this frailty of spirit, she picked up the ax and held it in her two hands, the handle across her chest. The blade, evil-looking and running red with the light from the fire, comforted her. The wooden handle felt warm and strong, the ax head heavy and sharp.

Courage returned—or the last vestiges of reality departed. A dreamlike quality took over; a nightmare, but one experienced from the point of view of the monster. Anna was not afraid. She felt very little either internally or externally. The cold and the hurt that had invested every move, every moment of her being since the bullet had damaged her ankle, receded; still with her but muted, faded, of no real importance. Whether she limped or not as she walked toward the fire, she couldn't have said, but the move was swift, effortless.

Heat from the flames soaked through her trousers, alien against the back of her thighs. Air passed into her lungs without burning cold. The sudden warmth made her eyes and nose run. She made no effort to wipe her face. From the tent, to her right now, scarcely six feet away, came the even, intermittent growl of the sleeping Mark. She didn't look his way. He could wake at any time from intuition, a misstep on her part, a full bladder, but she knew he wouldn't. She had all the time in the world. Fleetingly, she wondered if, in just this state, reality only a dream, the dream merely a disconnect from a place of godlike loneliness and indifference, Lizzy Borden had wandered, ax in hand, from room to room.

Then she was standing over Phil. Head resting against the bole of a young tree, jaw loose, snapping half shut with each snoring inhalation, his throat was bared and white. A chicken's neck stretched over the chopping block.

Aware of every spark of firelight on the blade, of the smooth passage of metal through the frosty air, of the small pulses and throbs in the man's throat as he snorted and gurgled through his whiskey sleep, Anna swung the ax back.

She had become a thing of nightmares, the boogeyman, the midnight escapee from the lunatic asylum.

C H A P T E R

13

Silent, beautiful, cutting through the air with a faint hypnotic whistle, the ax fell. Time warped. Anna watched its graceful arc, the play of the flames on the blade, the liquid way light ran over the honed edges. Then nightmare turned on her.

Wild-eyed, spattered with blood and brain, ax dripping gore, hacking again and again, chunks of meat that had once been a human being falling away from scarred bone. Sleeping bag tethering kicking feet, blood, rendered colorless in the red light of the fire, glowing suddenly ruby as it struck snow. Her, hobbling, crooked, evil, insane, kicking embers from the fire as she waded through it to the tent and the second sleeping man. The ax falling again and again, tent collapsing, flexible plastic poles snapping, the man within screaming, terrified, fighting the nylon, the funny grotesque shapes his shroud made as he fought, bright humps and angles purple-blue against night and snow, the absurdity of it—of him—making her laugh even as the blood began to ooze through the fabric.

"Jesus," Anna whispered as the dream broke over her. Her hands turned. The blade rotated into the twelve-and-six position the instant before it struck. Flat metal struck skull bone with the sick-making sound of a watermelon hitting pavement. Phil slumped over on his side.

The snoring stopped.

Shaking as much from the vision of carnage as the actual attack, she bent and felt his carotid. He lived. She didn't know if she was relieved or disappointed.

Her shakes did not subside but grew worse. Wave on wave of shudders jellied her viscera and rattled her bones. Unable to continue standing, she sat down next to the man she might have butchered. A half-eaten granola bar lay in the dirt beside him. She ate it. Then she ate the inch of beans remaining in a tin a few feet away, then another granola bar. Between bites she gulped water from a bottle Mark or Phil had left standing on a rock nearby.

Hunkered down troll-like, she devoured the leavings of their supper, stuffing food, swallowing, scarcely taking the time to chew, washing it down with water. Finally she slowed, then stopped. Food and warmth chased the shakes away. The *Texas Chainsaw*–style massacre she'd counted on to save her own skin had been thwarted by conscience—or an overactive imagination.

Eventually Mark would wake. He'd find Phil, who might or might not wake up in this mortal coil, and he'd come after her. Remembering the cruelty of his smile, she didn't dare hope he would cut his losses, let her go and pack out. That smile would hunt her down and kill her. Sitting before his fire, having eaten his food, listening to his snoring, she tried to think how she might even the odds. The rule in law enforcement wasn't even odds but a stacked deck. No self-respecting lawman wanted a fair fight with a criminal. They wanted an edge.

Momentarily she wished she'd suffered madness just long enough to dispatch them both with the cutting edge of the ax. It passed. Those were not images she wanted to add to an already full repertoire of nightmare pictures she carried in her head. Lethargy took her and for a time she simply sat in a lump, soaking up the warmth, staring into the fire and promising herself she would start thinking real soon.

A cross between a whimper and a groan from Phil or Mark—the nature of the sound making it difficult to gauge direction—galvanized her. One man, awake with pistol in hand, and she would have bashed in Phil's skull for nothing.

Moving more adroitly for the rest, food and heat, she slipped to the tent where Mark slept. He'd zipped both tent and rain tarp, and she didn't dare try to unzip them. He'd not consumed nearly enough whiskey to render him that deaf.

Blessing the entire Swiss nation, she took out her much-used knife and opened it to the smaller blade, the sharpest, least used blade. Just above the ground she cut a horizontal slit about fourteen inches long, then a vertical slit of like length intersecting it. This done she put her hand through.

A story she'd been told years before came back to haunt her. It was of a stone mouth, the Bocca della Verità—the Mouth of Truth—in Rome, into which people giving testimony must thrust a hand. If they lied the mouth would close, bite the hand off at the wrist. Anna's skin tingled with anticipation, not of stone jaws but of a viselike grip followed by a bullet in the face.

Her fingers poked and plucked through soft places, the inside of a tent even on short trips usually resembling nothing so much as a dirty laundry hamper.

Her fingers closed on a hard round object and a needy
mind told her it was the barrel of a pistol, but it proved to be
a water bottle. Anna slid it through the cut. Either she'd take
it with her or destroy it. Oddly it took more courage to put
her hand in the second time. Rather than being emboldened
by her success, she had a bad feeling that life held only so
many chances for any given individual and she'd spent hers
with the abandon of a drunken sailor; one day, maybe this
day, she'd use up her last.

A whimper.

She jerked her fist from the hole as if she'd been scalded.
Her heart swelled till it blocked her breath. She fought the
sudden panic and won. The whimper had come from Phil.
Now that she was between the two men she could tell from
where sounds emanated. He might be close to waking. Anna
hoped not. She'd have to hit him again, and if the first blow
did enough damage, a second would kill him. Why killing
him now repulsed her when half an hour before she'd been
ready to hack his head from his shoulders with his own ax,
she wasn't sure. Maybe because now she didn't have to.

A deep breath and she plunged her hand back through the
nylon and reached. They were there, on the opposite side of
the tent flap from the cut. One by one she eased Mark's boots
out and put them on the fire. Phil was next. His boots followed Mark's. Flames licked and curled in pretty blues as the
fire found new and wondrous components to consume.

Methodically, she ferreted out everything she could that
might be of use and fed it to the blaze. Inside the tent there
would probably be a flashlight, certainly a sleeping bag and
possibly a second water bottle. These things being beyond
her reach, she didn't waste time thinking about them.

For herself, she took one of the backpacks, two pairs of
socks, a gas camp stove and matches and Phil's sleeping bag.

If any food was left it wasn't in either pack. In cold weather, fuel for the body to burn to warm itself was important. Lamed as she was, Anna wasn't sure she could hike out in less than two days. Maybe three. And that was if the weather held. Without food to cook, she considered jettisoning the stove but, should the expedition drag on, hot water would do her body more good than cold.

Throughout the rummaging, packing, pillaging and burning the big man remained comatose. Anna rolled him onto his side. A bottle of Jack Daniel's with a concussion chaser were going to make him vomit at some point and she didn't want him to choke to death on his own bile. For like reasons, she left him in his down coat. At what point he'd changed from prey to patient, she couldn't have said.

The tenor of the snores from inside the tent changed. Maybe the fierce and fitful alteration in the fire's light had penetrated to Mark's subconscious. Time had come for Anna to vanish like the thief in the night she was.

The pack wasn't heavy and she welcomed the warmth it lent her back. The ax was heavy but it served as crutch, cane and companion. It never crossed her mind to leave it behind.

"Phil?"

She'd stayed too long. One last look around the camp let her know her welcome was long worn out. Leaning heavily on the ax, she limped away, keeping to the more treacherous but less trackable granite humps where shoulders of stone broke through the thin mantle of earth.

"Phil? What the fuck?"

The words followed her into the trees. A part of her that was still young, strong and unhurt, the Huckleberry Finn soul of every woman who has dreamed of hiding in the choir loft and watching her own funeral, wanted to stay and watch the fun as Mark explored the carnage she'd left. The old cynical part of her that just wanted to stay alive kept her walking, each step slow, short and painful.

"Goddamn son-of-a-bitch motherfucker," shot over her head, an expletive missile.

Anna smiled. It was good to have one's work appreciated.

Away from the lake, again in the trees, she was forced to use the stolen flashlight. With her injured ankle, no stars or moon, her compass gone, she didn't dare try a cross-country adventure. The trail was a trough of India ink running along the floor of a lightless tunnel. Until nearer dawn it would be impossible to follow without a light.

If the gods were good, there wasn't a second flashlight tucked away in the tent. Anna doubted they were that good. She'd already strained their generosity with her raid. With gods it was a bad juju to push one's luck.

Two good legs had led Anna to remember the trail as far less rugged than it was. Patches of comparatively easy walking on dirt trails were broken by long passages over rock, sometimes smooth as ice, other times shattered into erstwhile steps of varying heights, widths and sharpness. Her geriatric shuffles through the woods seemed a breakneck pace compared with the creeping and scooting, much of it on her rear end, required to cross the granite expanses.

Traverses that had been so easy as to be forgotten in health and sunlight became treacherous and exhausting. Every misstep was punished by nauseating pain. By five A.M. her flashlight was browning out and she was so tired just breathing was a chore. Her legs shook and her knees gave way every three or four yards, forcing her to stop or fall. Without rest she wouldn't make it, not another mile, not another fifty yards. It was an hour or more till dawn.

Sitting on a fallen log at the edge of the trail, she began to cry. The only ray of sunshine in the whole miserable, cold, pain-filled universe was that there was no one to see her doing it. Tears sapped the last of her energy. She could feel herself falling asleep where she sat, but she was unable to do anything about it. On some level she knew to sleep was to die, knew in the pack she had never abandoned, though its little weight had taken on the weight of the world, was a sleeping bag that would keep her alive. She simply couldn't find the wherewithal to stand and pull it out, crawl into it.

Soon, she thought. *Just let me sit here another minute, then I'll do it.*

And she slept.

I ronically, her life was saved by the grim reaper in yet another of his many guises. A fury of pain shot up from her ankle and a rough voice growled: "You dead? You're gonna be."

Anna hated irony.

She opened her eyes and was instantly blinded by the light of a flash trained on her face. Instinctively she threw up her arm to shade her face. It was batted away by a fist of ice and bone.

Her wits coalesced quickly, adrenaline winning over cold and fatigue.

"Mark," she said. "What brings you here?"

He laughed then, standing there unshaven, looking immense in a down jacket, his feet wrapped in socks and shirts and God knew what else. "You're a freaky bitch."

He would shoot her now and hike out on his Sasquatch paws, climb in his red SUV and disappear back into whatever urban hole he'd crawled out of. In a day, maybe two, Lorraine's rangers would become suspicious about Anna's rental car parked at the trailhead. Someone would be sent up to find her corpse, frozen and bloody, sprawled on the trail. The account of her demise would be detailed in the Ranger Report and e-mailed to every National Park in the country.

"What a drag," she murmured.

"You got that right."

A second passed. Two. He didn't shoot. There must be a reason for the delay. A tiny spark of hope began to burn away the strange indifference that had clogged her mind at the sight of Mark and the pistol so close to her face.

He was hulking, feet planted wide, a few feet in front of the rock she'd fallen asleep on. He'd let the beam of his flashlight drop to her chest, and she could see his face. The cruelty she'd noted before was honed by fatigue and the shock of finding his camp trashed. She guessed he wanted to torture her before he ended the game, vent the anger he probably always carried with him and, tonight, carried for her.

Torture was good. It gave her time. The cool efficiency of an assassin's bullet to the base of the skull was hard to outsmart.

"Is Phil dead?" she asked because she needed to keep the conversation, and so herself, alive.

"He wasn't when I left," Mark replied. A half smile tugged at the corner of his mouth, and Anna knew he had finished the job she'd started before he came after her. Phil, if he could walk at all after the blow to the head, would have slowed Mark down. Left behind, there was a chance he'd be found by the rangers before the wilderness killed him. He might talk, trade information for leniency. Either way, he had become a liability. Mark had cut his losses.

In a selfish and heartless way, Anna was glad. Phil might have died eventually from brain injury. This way she was absolved to a certain extent. She could pretend he would have awakened, seen stars, staggered a few steps, then, like Wile E. Coyote, been right as rain.

"Ah," she said.

Mark sat opposite her on a matching boulder across the trail. He put the flashlight beside his thigh. Its beam now struck her in the sternum and enough was reflected back that he showed the ghoulish effect children try for when they put flashlights beneath their chins. The muzzle of the pistol remained steady, pointed at her center body mass. Without disturbing his aim, Mark fumbled a cigarette out of his jacket pocket and lit it with the dexterity of a longtime smoker.

Anna tried to see past blood and bone to the tickings of his mind. What would keep him talking? What would put him off guard? As far as she knew he believed her to be a crippled, middle-aged waitress—albeit with a homicidal streak where double-bladed axes were concerned—who had inadvertently stumbled on his salvage operation.

She had that going for her. Might as well play it.

"Why did you guys shoot at me? You scared me half to death. Did the gun go off by accident?" Innocence, stupidity, her husband, Zach, had once told her, were the hardest things for an actor to portray believably. Unlike him, Anna had never been much for being on stage. To her the lines sounded false to the point of absurdity.

Mark twitched his aborted smile once again and blew smoke through his nostrils. In the strange light and frigid air the smoke swirled into the steam of their breath connecting them like ectoplasm. In an uncharacteristic flash of superstition, Anna nearly recoiled lest his evil enter her being. Horror passed but not this sudden sense of palpable evil.

She'd arrested felons of various stripes: rapists, wife beaters, murderers, even a child molester. Several had done their damnedest to kill her. One had died by her hand. She'd sensed anger, greed, indifference, sickness of mind. Never before had she felt surpassing evil.

Mark's wasn't even a sickness of the soul so much as an indefinable soullessness; the pleasure of other people's pain not a lust nor an addiction but merely a passing entertainment. She'd never seen his eyes by the light of day, but she doubted all the sunlight in the world could illuminate the spark of the divine that cats, dogs and real people carried from cradle to grave.

It was as if he were a spider in a man's body.

This staggering gestalt jolted through her in less time than it took for him to suck in another lungful of smoke. She was left with a creepy hollow feeling.

"Yeah. An accident," he said. Her question seemed so long ago it took her an instant to figure out what he was talking about. "I'm not used to these things." He waved the gun with a degree of comfort that suggested he was as accustomed to pistol grips as Tiger Woods was to golf clubs.

"Why did you bring it? It's against park rules," Anna said in the phony bad-actor voice that had settled in her throat. He couldn't be buying her act. Evil wasn't stupid. Evil was cunning.

"Why did you run?" he countered. He tilted his cigarette and studied the growing ash.

When the cigarette was finished, he'd kill her; Anna knew it as surely as if he'd told her. She'd only been left alive to amuse him during his smoke break.

"Why did you chase me?" her own voice was back. It got his attention. His eyes locked on hers and widened slightly.

"Well hello," he said and she felt that the devil had seen her, recognized her. "What have we here?"

"I don't know what you mean . . ." Anna tried to get back into character and failed.

"Don't bore me." It was a warning. Her life span might not be as long as his smoke.

Strong and cold, a pillar of ice formed in the place womb, stomach, lungs and heart had once been. Her eyes narrowed. She leaned in toward him. In a voice Colleen Dewhurst would have found grating she said:

"You stupid fuck, you know who I am."

His face went blank. Quick as a snake Anna struck. One hand swatted the gun from her chest; the other snapped to his face. Two fingers like fangs bit into his eyes. Anna felt the jelly wetting her finger as one burst. A gunshot deafened her. Cordite stung her nostrils. Muzzle-fire seared her retinas. The shot was wild. Mark was screaming, clawing at his face.

Anna snatched his flashlight from the rock and staggered into the trees leaving him shrieking obscenities and flailing in the place that was to have been her grave.

CHAPTER

14

The chilling core of hate stayed with Anna, supporting her as she gouged through the miserable black gut of the woods beside the Illilouette Creek Trail. Tree cover was sparse and undergrowth virtually nonexistent. Stone shouldered through the earth's skin, rotting trunks fell like matchsticks. A metallic taste in her mouth, biting fear at the edges of her mind, she drove on, stepping over, limping, scooting. Where she could, she confused her trail: circled, doubled back, crossed then recrossed granite slopes. Distance wasn't as important as disappearance. Soon the ice pillar holding her up must melt and she would collapse. When this happened she must be well hidden. In an hour it would be light. If Mark were not dead or blind, he would try to find her.

She moved and she hurt and she kept on moving and she did not think. She never wanted to think again.

After forty minutes or more of tangling and obscuring her trail as best she could, she took shelter. The stolen pack with its stove and matches she eased under the low boughs of a lodgepole pine, careful to leave no drag marks and disturb none of the snow on the evergreen's skirts. A hundred yards away she entombed herself in a log rotted out by cuboidal fungus. The tree's flesh, red and shattered into thousands of cubes slightly bigger than sugar cubes, she used to bury the bits of sleeping bag that could not be fitted beneath the shell of wood that still existed. From the waist up she was sheltered, snuggled in the dead tree's dark embrace like an outsized grub. Here she would sleep and hide through the daylight hours or here she would die. Her body would not allow her to run, and Mark wouldn't hesitate a second time.

Moving, she'd believed if she could stop she could sleep, would sleep; it would force itself on her the way it had when she sat down to rest on the trail. At last supine and, if not warm, at least not freezing, sleep did not come. Her insides were sick and creepy and scared. She wasn't afraid Mark would find her hiding place and put a bullet in her brain. That fear would come later when daylight showed him her trail. The close, dark confines of her woodland sarcophagus didn't bring forth the familiar terrors of claustrophobia. The thin shell of tree trunk above her was sufficiently weakened by weather and fungus she could break her way free should she need to.

What sickened her was the encounter with Mark. She'd gouged out his eye. In the great scheme of things, that was no worse than clobbering him with the ax or shooting him—she would have welcomed either course of action—and given her size, age and weakened physical condition, it was one of the few ways left to her to disable an attacker.

Had she chosen to blind him she would have done so without regrets. But it had not been her choice. The voice she'd cursed him with had not been her voice. She'd said, "You know who I am." But somehow it was not she who spoke, and the

"I" was a black shadow within her. His evil had called forth an answering evil, a darkness she'd not known was there, a thing without any light in it, any goodness or compassion or hope.

You're overtired, she told herself. *Shock. Your head didn't spin. Green bile didn't fly out of your mouth. Leave it alone.* Still, she didn't sleep. This was something she needed to lay at Paul's feet. A woman in Mississippi once said that being engaged to a sheriff/priest must be glorious. She could sin, get caught, repent, atone and be forgiven all in the arms of one man.

Thinking of Paul Davidson's kind eyes and slow smile, Anna drifted off.

C onsciousness came in a welter of confusion. Unfocused dream images crawled through her sleeping brain leaving snail-trails of dread. A serial killer stalked her. Or she was a serial killer and, like Pilate, like Lady MacBeth, she couldn't cleanse the blood from her hands. The serpents of the id called to her in high-pitched sing-song voices:

"Come out, come out wherever you are."

"You can run but you can't hide."

It took longer than she would have liked—longer than it ever had before—to metaphorically find her feet. A crescent moon of light arced over her hips. Day had come. She was in a log, partially covered by its hollow trunk, partially by rotted wood cubed by an architecturally minded fungus. Wrists crossed on her chest in the time-honored tradition of earthly remains put out for viewing, she was able to see her watch. The darkness in her end of the log was such that she had to put on its tiny nightlight. Careful to shield the blue lest this electronic glowworm get her killed, she read the hands: ten-seventeen. She had had four or more hours of sleep and was better for it. The monsters were no longer within but without.

"I got all day."

Then: "Goddamn it where the fuck . . . Show yourself and I'll kill you quick," and the heavy thump of wood struck with tremendous force.

Anna was fully awake now. The thud was the ax blade buried in a tree. She had had to leave it behind. Mark hadn't given up. He'd not been blinded. He was here. A shock of adrenaline would have made her twitch, give herself away, but numbness saved her.

A grunt sounded. Probably Mark pulling the ax out of whatever tree he'd hacked into. Bundled feet whuffed and crunched over the crusty snow. A dragging shush. Hawking, spitting. More footsteps. Nearer. Then seemingly to the left of her hiding place. The right. Down by her feet. Snuffling. Anna listened till her ears ached with the strain. There was nothing she could do but wait and hope. Prayer had been burned away when The Presence entered her on a column of ice and saved her. *Saved me for what?* she wondered. *For himself?* "No time to get the vapors," she heard Edith, the mother-in-law she had dearly loved, say. "There's work to be done."

Anna would have welcomed physical or mental work, business for hands or mind. The work before her was of the kind she found the most trying: she must do absolutely nothing in complete silence for as long as she could.

Her clattering thoughts moved from the realm of Catholic horror stories of demon possession and soul snatching to the world of make-believe—a short trip at best. She saw herself from above, lying still and cold in the hollowed log, a near-perfect arc of wood covering her from hip to head, cubed pine like chunks of red gold heaped over her from hip to toes.

It put her in mind of the glass-topped bier in which Prince Charming laid Snow White. At least he did in the Disney version.

Snow White waited to be awakened with a kiss, Anna with an ax.

Her mother had warned her that comparing herself to the other girls would make her miserable in the end.

Noise from without began to lose meaning and direction. Thinking clearly on one's back in a hollow log was harder than Anna would have guessed. Disorienting. Mark was out there but the snuffs and shuffles and grunts seemed to come not from a man but from bears, out of their dens and around her log for a late-autumn snack before the long winter's repose.

"Damn. About fucking time." This was said so close by, Anna opened her eyes wide in order to be paying attention when she died and not miss anything. Despite the earlier threat, she believed it would be quick; not out of mercy—the devil prided himself on mercilessness—but because he, too, was cold and hungry and tired and hurt. Pure hatefulness was probably all that kept him around. That and the fear she'd report back and federal claim jumpers would take his find.

Four gunshots cracked, the sound exploding so loud Anna knew she'd been hit. Numbed from so long without moving and the shock of bullets ripping her flesh, she couldn't tell where. Stilling her breath, she waited for the agony, then the peace of life pulsing out.

Mark's footsteps stamped purposefully away. "God," he muttered. Anna found it preferable to his usual expletive. "If I ever leave San Francisco again, they can fucking shoot me." Anna was disappointed. The last thing a person heard should be Shakespeare, music or the purring of a cat.

"Goddamn it" exploded almost as loud as the gunfire, but farther away. Crashing and more cursing followed.

Anna was not shot. Anna was not found. The pack she'd stolen had probably been fatally wounded, but she was okay. A fervent prayer of thanks began to form. She quashed it, not knowing to whom or to what she owed this extra time.

Silence returned and stayed. Evil had moved on or waited motionless nearby. Anna dozed and dreamed. Listened and waited. Pins and needles tortured her. Pain throbbed from her ankle. Her bladder filled. A true mountaineer would have watered the tree rather than suffer. Childhood taboos and a vestigial training in how to be a lady would not allow her this crude comfort. The worst was thirst. Because the body could go only a short time without water even in the earliest stages of deprivation, the cravings were intense. Customarily she would have cursed herself for a fool, holing up without water. Since, at the time, she'd had a lot on her mind, she gave herself a pass.

Sleep helped. It made the time pass, and with no food and an injury, being warm and still were next best to getting out or being rescued.

Two o'clock came. Two-thirty. Three. Mark didn't return. If he ever left. He left, Anna told herself. *If he knew I was here, he'd have killed me. If he didn't know I was here he'd have left. Ergo* . . . Regardless, she didn't dare move till full dark. If he had waited, if he saw her, she had no defenses: not speed, not strength, not weaponry.

The afternoon passed in a misery of dreams and physical demands unmet, but it did pass. When the crescent of light that was her entire view of the world had completely vanished, she began to stir. Emerging from her cocoon, she struggled as mightily as any newborn butterfly. Nerves buzzed and snapped, firing off mixed messages of cold, burning and electrical shock. Finally upright, she turned on Mark's flashlight, the only thing she'd taken to bed with her, and scanned the area. He'd gone. His pack—her pack—had been dragged from its hiding place beneath the pine tree. Bullet holes pierced the nylon, and the aluminum frame was bent where he'd vented his frustration with the ax. The camping stove had been hurled against the tree. Matches lay scattered on the ground. The water bottle, half full and undamaged, was beneath the pack. Anna drank it all.

Feeling stronger, genuinely hopeful, she repacked sleeping bag, stove, matches and empty bottle. The smashed frame rested uneasily on her back but it weighed little and she didn't know how much longer she'd be in the backcountry. Already the sleeping bag had saved her life. If she were forced to go to ground it might do so again.

Lame, without compass, stars or landmarks, Anna had to find her way back to the trail. If he'd hiked out, Mark would have used the trail as well. Without a flashlight he'd have had to do it during daylight hours. The ruined eye would be hurting him, and Anna had heard, though she couldn't remember where, that after the loss of sight in one eye a person could suffer visual disturbances in the remaining eye. She hoped it was true, but not so true as to keep him from leaving. She wanted him to escape, to run as far away from her as he could. There'd be plenty of time to track him down later.

Picking her way slowly down the Illilouette, a sturdy branch for a staff and the flashlight for a guide, Anna played these rationales over and over in her mind. The logic calmed her somewhat but didn't lessen her wariness. Her ears strained against the near perfect silence of the night. Her eyes strained against the darkness. Her soul waited for a return of the stench of evil Mark had called forth from the depths of her being; practical evil that had saved her life.

Necessary evil?

She wasn't sure there was such a thing. At least not that the average pagan could afford to invest in.

Steps and minutes, steps and hours ticked past with the slowness of seconds on a wall clock. Pain and fatigue returned in force, jarred through her for timeless time, then seemed to recede. They were still there, she could still feel them. It was just she didn't mind so much. She stopped focusing on hiking out. She focused only on hiking, making that one small step into the white circle of light that was always one step ahead of her on the trail.

A waltz rhythm kept time in her head. Not a classic waltz, but one she and Zach had danced to, the Rock and Roll Waltz: one, two, three—rock; one, two, three—roll. It was in this strange auto-induced trance that she came down out of the granite-polished high country into the gentler wooded slopes where the Illilouette ceased to tumble and fall and ran placidly beneath a skin of ice. It was four thirty-five in the morning. The six-cell flashlight she'd stolen from Mark was beginning to fade. She was three miles from Mono Meadow and her rental car and, with luck, codeine or Percocet or some other kindly obliviating painkiller.

Trees closed overhead. Anna could smell the closeness of the pine. Under this cover her crunching footfalls were muffled, less alarming. The trail bed was of needles, not rocks, and her ankle wasn't viciously jarred by a misstep every few feet. She moved faster.

As she was thinking she would make it out and was considering allowing herself the distraction of a small dream of a hot bath and a hot cup of tea, the white circle of light that led her brought a horror up from the ground with a suddenness that made her scream.

One smashed, but still attached, eye cried down a cheek as ashen gray as dirty snow. The other eye was red and weeping, swollen nearly closed. Floating on the darkness—the body that it supported invisible in black down and dark-blue denim—was Mark's face. He'd been sitting, waiting, like the spider that possessed him. Knowing she must come.

As the light hit him and Anna screamed, he roared to life. A gloved fist rose from his lap, the pistol clutched in it. Anna clicked off the flashlight and stumbled off trail into the black of the swallowing night. Bellowing, he crashed after. Shots were fired. None found her. As blind as he, she ran, fell, rose, ran again, struck a tree and reeled to one side. The flashlight was lost. Direction was lost. She could as easily run to him as away. It was over after all. He would catch her. The noise of her passage could not be masked.

She had but a twenty-foot lead. Forcing down the need to flee and keep on fleeing though the exercise was doomed from the onset, she stopped, became absolutely still.

For perhaps half a minute he bashed on, coming straight toward her. The urge to run was so strong it was a tangible thing, pulling at her heart and lungs. She didn't move. He veered, crashed, cursed. He was moving away from her now. She prayed he'd gone mad.

Then the crashing stopped. Heavy breathing rasped at her ears as if he were but inches away. Cold magnified sound. A minute more and the rasping ceased. Darkness froze over the mountains, a solid thing with no chinks or breaks. It pressed against Anna, clung to her eyelids, soaked into her clothes. She breathed it in and felt her blood turn black.

She waited.

He waited.

The waiting built, an unvoiced scream, until Anna wanted to clap or laugh or stomp just to end things. She didn't.

Mark broke before she did.

"It'll be light in half an hour. I'll kill you then."

His voice was gravelly, the throat dry and raw from his night's exertions. Weariness robbed the words of drama and made them more frightening; not a threat, a mere statement of fact.

Half an hour. Anna didn't dare look at her watch, but she figured he was right. Maybe even less than that. He didn't need the full light of day to see her. A slight graying in the east, enough to separate trees from the overcast sky, would be sufficient.

Probably she had a little over a quarter of an hour to live. She wondered if she should be thinking of anything in particular, maybe sending out a spam of last-minute prayers for forgiveness to assorted deities, making mental good-byes to loved ones, savoring her last moments, seeing her life flash before her eyes.

It was too dark for the last item on her list. Even inside her skull it was night.

No other thoughts coalesced till unto her awareness came a spectral voice.

"Come and take it."

She never heard anyone say that. She'd seen it crudely stitched on a homemade flag by the women of Gonzales, Texas, a tiny town on the Texas-Mexico border. Santa Anna was marching north with two thousand men. Orders came before him. All settlements were to turn over their weaponry. The town of Gonzales had one cannon and no shot. The townspeople loaded it with scrap, wheeled it to the edge of the settlement, draped it with the embroidered flag and stood their ground.

They were, of course, slaughtered, but the flag had made Anna cry.

Mark would have to take her.

Working as quickly and quietly as she could, she slipped the ruined pack off and pulled out the sleeping bag. The sound of fabric slithering out was as of a hundred snakes loosed on the snow.

"I hear you."

Anna kept working.

"What are you doing?"

She said nothing. She could hear him as well, tentatively feeling his way toward her. Mercifully the sleeping bag was still unzipped. Awkwardly she spread it in front of the tree she kept at her back.

Crunch. Shuffle. "Fuck." He was closer now. How close, she couldn't tell.

Groping in the near-empty pack she took out the last remaining items in her improvised arsenal, the camp stove and matches. Cold had numbed her hands, and she had to pull off her gloves to unscrew the cap from the stove's tiny fuel tank.

A slap of a branch. Another curse. He couldn't be more than a few yards away, homing in on the noise from her machinations.

The cap was off. The stove slipped from her frozen fingers and fell. No matter. By feel she found it and emptied what had not already spilled over the sleeping bag. That done, she straightened, put her back to the tree, faced into the darkness and said, "Come and take me."

CHAPTER

15

Anna used the noise of his approach to cover the sounds she made moving behind the tree. Ignoring the pain pumping up her leg, she scraped the side of her boot hard against the bark, making as much racket as she could.

When she stopped, there was silence. Mark was waiting. She didn't know where. But she could see something; above her was the faintest lightening. Just a hint of day. Enough to differentiate black of pine from sky. To see her was to shoot her. Soon it would be over.

With all her strength she hurled the empty stove straight up, then covered her head with her arms. The metal made a satisfying disturbance, crashing into the boughs and loosing a cascade of snow. A thump let her know it had come again to earth nearby.

"You some kind of damn polecat?"

The voice was so close Anna jerked like a trout on a line, but she made no sound. Had the pine not been between them they would have been face to face. The evil that had called forth its namesake from within her and stalked her dreams as she lay in her hollow log poured forth into the darkness, a palpable miasma that sickened Anna body and soul. Her knees shook, her stomach heaved, her head ached and swam. From the other side of her tree she could hear the whispering of Mark's feet, wrapped in layers of fleece and wool, as he shifted them over the sleeping bag at the tree's base.

Soon. *A few seconds more,* she told herself. Having him so fiendishly close made the back of her neck tight and loosened her bowels.

"You're some kind of fucking she-devil. You can forget whatever you're planning. I'm not climbing the goddamn tree."

Four shots rang out, one after the other. Anna flinched as if the bullets had hit her. Snow cascaded down her collar. The deafening reports were disorienting. She touched the bole of the tree that she might know up from down.

She could wait no longer. Hoping osmosis had done its thing, she knelt, leaned around the tree and struck a match. It flared to robust life. She blessed the quality control people at Blue Diamond.

"What the—"

Anna touched the match to the gas-soaked sleeping bag.

Night was swept away on a voracious orange wind. The sleeping bag didn't so much catch fire as explode with a suddenness that sucked the air in at ground level and blew the flames upward. From what seemed an eternity of black, light blasted forth. Anna's eyes hurt with it and at the same time drank in the incredible blessing of sight. It was a glory simply to see color, shape and form.

This visceral celebration lasted only an instant. Then Mark began to scream. For a while—it seemed a long time but couldn't have been more than a few seconds—Anna was transfixed.

Evil became manifest in a Dantean vision. A creature in flames, face monstrous, feet outsized, danced and capered in orange and blue fire.

The creature was a man. And Anna had burned him alive.

Reality was worse than a visionary hell. Staggering, she pushed into the remaining dark. The macabre beacon from behind lit her way with singular clarity for the first fifty feet, then, like the screaming, died.

Maybe Mark had saved himself, dropped to the ground and rolled. Maybe the fire had consumed the available fuel in record time.

A rule from her wildland firefighter's training clicked on in her brain and she had the compassion to hope Mark was wearing cotton underwear. Other fibers had a nasty way of melting into burned flesh. Anna wanted him gone—dead even—but torture was not part of the plan. It moved her too close to the spidery force that had helped her to gouge out his eye.

Just as if somebody's world had not ended, the sun began to rise. A difference was born between earth and sky. She could see enough to move between the trees. She pushed in the direction where she remembered the trail was.

Anna woke in a hospital bed. Twice she'd awakened in like situations. Much as she loathed hospitals, it was a happier ending to her adventure than she'd foreseen, and she had the grace to be grateful. Sun poured in the window, real, gold, honest-to-God, bright sunlight splashing in a distorted square across her knees and feet. Having been so long in gray and black, Anna felt like rolling in the stuff. She might have done so had an IV needle not been taped into her arm. Out the window, she could see rooftops, branches of winter-bare trees and dusty green live oaks. She was in Merced.

Bits of memory led her to this moment: tumbling out of her rental car into the parking lot of the Yosemite Valley Medical Clinic. A woman ranger, the same one who'd given her a lift to the Ahwahnee dorm the night Nicky had been assaulted, sitting beside her in the back of an ambulance saying: "Don't worry, you're not dying. The doctor gave you a sedative." A nurse in funny pink scrubs with blotches of baby blue and yellow on them clucking. "My Lord, what have you been up to?"

Anna pushed herself into a sitting position. The use of her hands gave her a jolt and she looked at them. The right had a loose gauze wrap and the tips of three fingers on the left were bandaged. Fire flashed behind her eyes and she saw again the explosion of flame. Her hand had been engulfed for a moment. The left brought forth no images. A touch of frostbite maybe. She pulled at the tape and unwound the dressing. Not bad. Blisters on the heel of her hand over an area about the size of a half dollar. Painful, but it would heal quickly and leave no scars.

There was no memory of other injuries but for her ankle. She threw back the covers to assess the damage. The move elicited an unladylike grunt. Muscles ached and flesh was bruised till she felt twice her age. Her foot and calf were swathed in an Ace bandage, her toes, looking pathetic and young, peeped out the end. Assorted scratches and scrapes accessorized her bruise collection, but no one had seen fit to bandage or splint any other portion of her anatomy.

Her greatest sufferings at the moment were from light-headedness and hunger. The lightheadedness convinced her not to go scavenge. She had had her fill of falling down for one lifetime. Once one's center of gravity grew more than twenty-four inches from the ground, these gravitational visits became jarring. A clock on a metal bed stand said it was two-thirty. Way past lunch and far too long till dinner. Anna pushed the nurses' call button. Unless there was some injury she wasn't aware of—a concussion that left no headache or a mysterious fever—she'd been here for less than twenty-four hours.

Ten minutes passed before a nurse came. Anna didn't mind the wait. Little things were giving her immoderate joy: drinking the flat-tasting water from the metal pitcher on the bed stand, seeing and feeling the sun on her legs, watching airplanes as they made their pattern prior to landing at Merced's small airport.

This idyll was eroded around the edges by niggling memories of what she had done: the axing, gouging, burning. Whether because of residual drugs in her system or because these things had happened in the dead of night like the grisliest of dreams, they were mercifully unreal.

With the nurse and the food came information. As she had surmised, she'd been in the hospital half a day. Her ankle bone was cracked, but not broken, and she'd suffered a bad sprain. The doctor hadn't put a cast on it because six weeks of atrophy would do the leg more harm than the crack in the bone. The bone would heal more quickly and with less discomfort than the sprain. The bandages on her fingers were for frostbite, but it wasn't severe. She'd lose no digits, just a little skin. Mostly she'd been suffering from exhaustion and dehydration.

The nurse took the intravenous tube from her arm and Anna immediately felt better. Lying in a hospital bed, tubes and needles invading the body, felt like the precursor to a long and humiliating death.

Proving hunger really is the best sauce, she devoured the

hospital food the nurse brought. Reassured and fed, she decided to face her responsibilities.

"I need to make some calls," she said. "How do I get an outside line?"

The nurse explained the hospital's phone system and the billing system for calls. Following the lead of America's finest hotels, hefty surcharges were levied for simply lifting the receiver from its cradle.

Mostly Anna wanted to call Molly, but her sketchy memory of her less than triumphant return to the valley following her mountain sojourn didn't include her having reported to anyone. Because she was known only to a handful of people as anything other than a waitress at the Ahwahnee, the clinic wouldn't automatically inform the ranger division of her injury. Anna called information for the park number and waded through choices and button pushing before she got a live human being who could transfer her call to the superintendent's office. Experience had taught her that, when a death was involved, if the superintendent wasn't one of the first to hear, sparks would most definitely fly.

The secretary, a wonderfully efficient young woman whose only shortcoming in the eyes of her superiors was an irreverent tendency to come to work with hair dyed in neon blues and reds, told her the superintendent was still at a conference in Washington, D.C. Anna had known that but had hoped for an early return. Accepting the inevitable, she asked to be patched through to Deputy Superintendent Leo Johnson.

After what seemed an excessively long time the secretary came back on the line. "Leo's in a meeting right now. Can he call you back?"

"It's urgent," Anna said. "Did you tell him it was Anna Pigeon calling?"

"I did," the secretary replied without a hint of defensiveness. "Hang on. I'll tell him it's urgent."

Another few minutes slid down the black hole Anna held pressed to her ear.

"He'll have to call you back," the secretary said at last. "Is there a number where you can be reached?" Her tone had the balance of a top-notch secretary; enough disappointment the caller knew she was on her side and enough firmness she knew continuing to push it would get her nowhere.

Anna gave the number on the phone next to her bed and the number stenciled on the door to her room, then hung up.

Food made her sleepy. Sun soothed her. Not yet recovered from forty-eight hours of assorted trauma, she dozed off. When she woke again the sun was gone, the short winter day over. It was twenty after five and Leo hadn't returned her call. She dialed the park number again. A machine answered and a recorded voice told her the administrative offices were closed for the day and would reopen at eight A.M. the following morning. She was instructed to dial 911 in case of emergency. Within the boundaries of the park, 911 would put her through to the law enforcement dispatcher. In Merced it would get her the local police.

"Damn," Anna whispered.

Phil was dead and Mark was very probably dead. Whoever had been in the drug plane when it crashed had been dead quite a while. Dead people didn't really constitute an emergency. One could dawdle and lollygag for hours—days—and they'd still be dead when rescue finally arrived.

The drugs themselves didn't constitute an emergency either. Twelve miles in over rough trail in winter: odds were good nobody would bother them tonight. When Mark and Phil failed to reappear packing product, whoever they worked

with—or for—would send others up to find out what happened. That shouldn't happen for a day or two.

Excuses in place for abandoning the fruitless telephon-
ing, Anna threw off the thin covers and stood up gingerly.
When her brain had gyrated around in her skull and adapted
itself to this new position, she put a bit of weight on her bad
ankle. It hurt, but the pressure bandage and the rest had done
wonders. With a crutch or even a cane, she would be able to
move fairly well.

Anticipating a fuss and not wanting to go into it with her
bare bottom exposed, she moved to the narrow closet, supporting her weight on the furnishings when she could and
hopping when she couldn't. Her clothes were hung neatly inside. Shirt and pullover were distinctly disreputable-looking
and smelled vaguely like a locker room, but they were dry.
Anna put them on. That was as far as she got. Her trousers
had been cut from waist to hem when they'd removed them
to tend to her damaged ankle. The laces on her hiking boot
had been cut as well. Socks and underpants had gone missing, probably down a trash chute. Anna thought harsh things
about whichever EMT had gotten scissor happy.

There's nothing like having no pants, no transportation
and no money for making a woman feel helpless. Anna got
back in bed and called the Ahwahnee dorm.

Two hours later, with crutches and an ankle brace from
hospital stores, she was headed back up into the mountains
in Mary Bates's rusting old Chevrolet. To pay for the ride,
Anna told Mary her story, all of it.

"I knew it, I just *knew* it," Mary crowed when Anna finished. "My whole life I've been in the Ahwahnee. I've known
waitresses who dropped out of lawyering, who could've
been beauty queens, even some hiding from outstanding
warrants or abusive husbands. I knew you didn't fit in. Ha!"

Anna was offended. She'd worked hard to fit in. It hurt her pride to think a seventeen-year-old girl had seen through her cover. "You didn't know," she said.

"Yes I did."

Anna sniffed. Mary, being a well-brought-up girl and one with keen intuitions, must have sensed Anna's hurt feelings. She went on to say: "Oh, I didn't know you were a *ranger* undercover or anything. And you were a good waitress. Honest. Really and truly."

Two protestations of verisimilitude. She was lying. Anna was a lousy waitress. Depression began to settle over her sternum, stirred by a soupçon of peevishness. Even knowing it wasn't from her failure in the restaurant business but a conglomerate of the other shocks and horrors, Anna had trouble shaking it off.

"I thought maybe you were working for the hotel," Mary said. "Sometimes my dad would do that. When he felt something wasn't right and couldn't figure out what it was, he'd hire somebody to work in the hotel who would report to him. A bunch of us thought maybe you were doing that."

"A bunch?" Anna repeated. The depression thickened. No wonder she hadn't been able to get any information. The staff thought she was a stool pigeon for the bosses.

"Well, not a *bunch*," Mary admitted and Anna felt a bit better. "Just me and Scott, I think."

They rode in silence for a ways. Anna thought about Scott and the unanswered questions that had been pushed from her mind the last three days. Scott Wooldrich. Picturing him in his youth and strength sent a tingle through her tired bones. So much so, she pushed the image aside. Going through adolescence once had been more than enough.

The questions were more comfortable, if only because they were familiar. She returned to the litany. Who had put the needle in her jacket and why? Who had tossed the dorm room and why? If Trish had known about the downed plane and had been mining the frozen dope to buy a gym franchise for her brother, then had Dickie known? Was that why he'd shown no interest in the search? Had he been aware his sister was murdered and either not wanted to get involved with Mark and the gang or chosen not to alert the NPS so he could take up where Trish left off? How had Mark and his boys known of the plane's whereabouts? How had they known Trish, Caitlin, Patrick and Dix were jumping their claim?

And were the answers to these questions related?

Anna focused on the needle. A syringe full of blood; had it been a mere scare tactic meant to frighten off a person suspected of spying for the boss, it could have been left in her locker where she would see it but not be injured. The fact that it had been carefully and ingeniously rigged to inject into her arm suggested that whoever put it there wanted a surer and more permanent solution to her nosing about. The only thing that could be genuinely threatening—other than the inherent scariness of blood found outside the skin it belonged under—was if the blood were in some way poisonous.

The obvious blood-borne poison was HIV or AIDS. Scott had looked as if he recognized the syringe. He had wanted to take the syringe from her. Scott had been in prison. Scott seemed to love his job as assistant chef. Could he be infected and afraid Anna, in her mistaken role of stoolie, had been sent to ferret out the truth and so get him fired? It was illegal to fire someone because they had AIDS, but considering he was in the food-services business, fear of a miserable and lingering death sentence might outweigh fear of the law.

Anna sat with that idea as they drove through the tiny town of Mariposa. The solution fit a lot of the kinks and bends in the chain of events, but it didn't feel right. If AIDS were the secret a person was trying to hide, delivering a needle full of infected blood that could be tested for DNA and matched to the suspect made no sense. There was always the possibility of vicious revenge, a sort of *you hurt me because I'm sick, I'll make you sick so you'll know how it feels*. Anna wasn't a great judge of character, but she couldn't see that kind of petty virulence in Scott Wooldrich.

If the blood wasn't his, whose then? And if they'd wanted to keep their disease a secret, the same illogic applied. Scott knew more about the syringe than he should have. Anna remembered the sudden jarring of his facial muscles when she'd pulled it out of her jacket sleeve. Maybe it wasn't Scott's blood and he'd had no hand in the booby trap but he knew who did.

That worked.

Mariposa put Anna in mind of Trish and brother Dickie. That they were into this thing up to the eyeballs, she didn't doubt. Precisely what role each had played she wasn't sure. Trish was a dope dealer, the local connection in Yosemite Valley. From the aborted letter, Anna guessed she'd stumbled onto the news of the downed plane. Because she'd gone missing and because Anna walked into a backpack with no owner up near Lower Merced Pass Lake, Anna figured she'd been murdered for her trouble. The other three were probably brought into the scheme of quick money and high adventure by Trish and ended up dying with her.

Dickie Cauliff didn't fit into this tidy scenario except as the proposed beneficiary of his sister's benevolence. Anna thought back to her phone call to him, then meeting him in the flesh. He was young and strong—certainly capable of acting the mule and packing the stuff out. But he struck Anna as lazy, indifferent, sullen. The kind of man who waits for others to give him things, then gets angry and resentful if it's not enough. He might have been convinced to shoulder such a profitable burden if his sister told him to, but Anna didn't think she had. The unfinished letter she'd found in Trish's belongings was written shortly before she disappeared. It suggested the plan had been kept secret from him, merely hinted at.

When Anna had contacted Dickie he'd been singularly uninterested in anything but his sister's belongings. Given the impression of selfishness and sullenness she'd gotten of him, it didn't surprise her that he hadn't been suffering paroxysms of grief over Trish's disappearance. Sentiment over family keepsakes was out. Self-interest was more likely. Since in all likelihood he didn't know about the marijuana, he must believe there was something of value in the things Trish left behind in the park.

Recalling the items in Trish's storage boxes—clothes, cosmetics, paperback novels—the one that didn't fit was the battered, water-soaked leather satchel. It had come from the downed plane, Anna was suddenly sure of it. When the airplane hit the ice and shattered, the pilot's briefcase must have spewed out of the cockpit along with everything else that busted loose. Customarily a captain's briefcase would contain maps, charts and whatever personal paraphernalia were deemed necessary for comfort. A satchel in the cockpit of a drug plane might well carry cash, enough of it to make things interesting. That would account for Dickie's pressing need to recover his sister's effects.

"Damn," Anna whispered and ignored a questioning look from Mary. Her thread of reasoning had snapped. If the aborted letter was any indication, Dickie had been ignorant of the downed plane and, so, of all proceeds derived therefrom. This wads-of-cash theory also left unexplained Dickie's urgency to recover each and every little scrap belonging to his sister right down to her apron, ticket book and uniform.

Anna let Dickie slide from her mind but retained the satchel and its presumed contents. Given Trish found the bag and packed it out, who might know what it contained? The three people with her, whomever they might have told, and the folks responsible for the drug run in the first place. Any of these could have been behind the search of Anna's dorm room, but given Nicky's albeit sketchy description of the two men as strangers and city boys, Anna's money was on the drug importers.

It was a fine solution, but brought with it more questions: How had the importer known where in the great Sierra wilderness his cargo came to earth? How had he known a satchel of cash had been thrown from the cockpit? How had he known Trish Spencer found it?

The rational answer was that Trish, Dix, Caitlin or Patrick told the importer or told someone who'd passed the information on. Dix, Caitlin and Pat might have done so either intentionally or inadvertently. From what Anna had learned of them, they were adventurers, casual dope smokers and opportunists, but none of them had the record or reputation to indicate they were more deeply involved in the trade.

Trish was the dealer. She would likely have only one contact, the person who supplied her, the next bird up in the pecking order. That was the person Trish would have approached to unload the dope she couldn't sell to her park cronies, the person who would have passed the information up to the next level.

They passed through El Portal. Full darkness had come but without the crushing overcast which had oppressed eastern California for two weeks. Night was no longer the blinding dark of Lower Merced Pass Lake. Stars, looking impossibly close, were caught in the tops of the pines and flowed in a silver-white river over the highway. A thumbnail moon as perfect as any in a children's picture book—or cut in the door of an outhouse—rose above the mountains. The jagged black of the forest pressed close and, as they passed the boulders standing sentinel at the park's entrance, rock walls began to rise. Even in this faint and frosty light, the stone glowed, polished granite catching the light and reflecting it back. Though they were again in The Ditch there was no sense of claustrophobia. Narrow as this crevice in the bastion of the Sierra was, all of the great universe looked down on it.

Anna breathed a sigh so deep it was a marvel stars weren't sucked into her lungs. "I'm glad the weather's cleared," she said.

"I know. Me too," Mary replied. "The world gets way too little up here when there's no sky."

CHAPTER

16

Since Anna had awakened in the hospital—indeed, before that, about the third time she'd tumbled off a stone step in her flight from Mark and Phil—she had assumed her undercover operation was at an end. A gimp waitress wasn't much good to anyone, and in her mind at least, she'd blown her cover. In reality, she hadn't. Except for Mary Bates, she'd told no one. According to Mary, the "bunch" that suspected her of spying for the Ahwahnee higher-ups was, in truth, only herself and Scott Wooldrich.

Because she'd been attacked, threatened, hunted and shot, Anna had assumed she was back in her role as a federal law enforcement officer. She had forgotten that most violent crimes are perpetrated upon ordinary citizens. Mark hadn't struck at the arm of the law stretched out to snatch him from his felonious pursuits and slap him in the penitentiary, nor had he defended himself against the force of the legal system as personified by Anna Pigeon, National Park Ranger.

Mark had set out to butcher a waitress out hiking on her day off just because she might cost him money. With this thought a rush of anger warmed and strengthened Anna. She pulled out of the slump she'd allowed herself to collapse into. "What shits!" she exclaimed. Mary laughed, then apologized, lest it was an inappropriate response.

"What is it?" she asked.

"Those bastards thought they were killing a nice middle-aged lady who maybe had kids, a husband, a dog for Chrissake."

"Not you," Mary said carefully.

"No," Anna fumed. "Somebody innocent. Bastards!"

Mary made a noise as if suppressing a laugh. As Anna saw nothing funny, she ignored it.

Anna had intended to make Leo Johnson's house her first port of call, but it was after ten P.M. when they drove into Yosemite Village. If his bingeing ran true to form, Leo would be drunk on booze and self-pity by this hour. An interview would be pointless. Come morning he might not even remember it. Lorraine would have put one of her rangers on as acting chief, but Anna didn't know who it was. In retrospect it struck her as odd that Lorraine had left her with no interim contact. A chief like Lorraine Knight would have left behind instructions, messages, a phone number in Montana. At least that was the impression Anna had gotten of the woman. And she hadn't changed her mind.

The only thing that made sense was that the messenger hadn't bothered to deliver them. For this crime of omission Leo Johnson was Anna's prime suspect. Tomorrow, when she was stronger, braver and more patient, she would tackle him.

Mary turned toward the Ahwahnee. "Mary," Anna said. "Don't tell anyone what I told you, okay? I'd like to stay on in my waitress persona awhile, just till I can get a few more answers."

Mary was thrilled to be in on such a terrific secret. Lest the girl endanger herself by knowing only a fragment of the truth, Anna had left out none of the pain or the terror. She hadn't wanted Mary thinking of this as a game and getting in the way of evil. She'd told her everything up to the point when she'd ignited Mark. That wasn't a story she was ready to share with anyone, much less a seventeen-year-old girl who looked like a Christmas angel.

"I can help," Mary said too eagerly.

"You already have, just by letting me talk."

"No. Really. Trish tried a bunch of times to get me to smoke marijuana. If I noise it about that I'm ready, could be somebody else'll pop up to offer to sell me a baggie. Nobody'll offer it to you. You're ol— not the right age."

Anna thought about it awhile. Mary was right. If she should start asking for a supplier it would look fishy. Mary Bates wouldn't look fishy with an armload of mackerel. Because Trish was dead didn't mean the drug business wouldn't go on as usual. Either Trish's contact would step in to fill the void or another user would be recruited to keep the party circuit supplied, particularly if there was an overabundance of weed. Whoever was moving the stuff in the park would want to get rid of it. What better way than getting patsies to pay for the privilege of burning the evidence?

"Okay," Anna said. It was against her better judgment and, if Lorraine Knight found out she had enlisted the help of a civilian and a minor, Anna would be severely reprimanded, probably sent back to Mississippi in disgrace. Not only did it run counter to policy, but it created an ideal situation in which the park service could be sued for punitive damages to the tune of half the gross national product. Anna invited Mary to assist because she was ninety-nine percent sure Mary was determined to do it anyway. By the pale green light washing back from the dashboard, Anna could see the glitter in her eyes and the set of her jaw. To deny her would be to send her underground. Mary was safer if Anna kept tabs on her.

"Got to promise me three things," she said.

"Anything," Mary replied. No hesitation, no jockeying. Anna believed she would be as good as her word.

"You tell me before you do anything."

"Okay."

"You report back to me immediately after you do anything."

"Okay."

"And if I tell you not to do something, you don't do it."

There was a fraction of a pause, but not enough to be alarming. "I can live with that," Mary said.

Anna sincerely hoped she could.

"We're home."

"Home" was of course the dormitory. At forty Anna'd sworn she would never accept dormitory accommodations again. The pajama-party atmosphere she'd so enjoyed as a boarder at Mercy High School and, to a lesser degree, in college, had lost its allure. There were times when even the strong sweet presence of Paul was too much for her to bear; times when her psyche couldn't deal with the impact of any life not blessed with fur and paws. Paul seemed to understand this rather than take offense. An upstairs room in his historic house in Port Gibson, Mississippi, had been set aside for her exclusive use after they were married. He very kindly didn't offer to decorate or furnish it for her. It was hers alone to do with as she pleased. He'd promised to knock before entering.

Anna wished she were in it now, bare wood, bare walls, bare of furniture. Often as not, privacy and a hard floor beat company and a soft bed. The memory wavered, then faded. A room of her own and all that entailed belonged to another life. One that grew ever harder to hang on to. By repetition, the big lie of who she was became ever more believable.

She stopped at the door of the room she and Nicky shared. Mary continued down the hall calling a "good night" over her shoulder. The prospect of being Anna's partner in anti-crime had her jacked up.

"Before you do *anything*," Anna reminded her, "you tell me."

Mary spun around, came to an abrupt halt, heels together. Saluting smartly, she said: "Ma'am. Permission to brush my teeth, ma'am."

Even knowing it only encouraged children, Anna couldn't help but laugh. "Permission granted."

Anna opened the door and flipped on the light.

Nicky wasn't in. Anna had figured that when she'd found the door closed. Both Nicky and Cricket suffered from the fear that they were missing something when they weren't at the heart of a group of babbling people.

The room was a shambles. It seemed ironic that the only time she'd seen it tidy was after it had been tossed by professionals. She was half sorry she'd spent so much time and energy assuaging Nicky's fears. Had she stayed scared she might have continued to pick up after herself if for no other reason than to create an illusion of control over some small part of her life.

"Oh, for heaven's sake," Anna exclaimed, hearing her dead mother-in-law's voice in her own. Nicky hadn't been happy simply to trash her own side of the room, she'd trashed Anna's as well.

"Doggoned, silly-assed little nitwit," Anna cursed gently. Up near Merced Pass she'd gotten enough of the brutal sort to leave a bad taste in her mouth when it came to four-letter words. She flicked on her desk light.

"Oh dear." Where she had been merely annoyed she was now alarmed. The clutter covering her unmade bed, spilling out the open door of her narrow closet and littering her desktop did not belong to her roommate. All of it was hers: books, papers, clothes, everything dumped out and tossed into a dismaying salad of single shoes, pencils, unmarried socks, Altoid mints, paper clips and other small things she'd thought to bring along as necessary to life and human dignity.

Snapshots of Paul and Piedmont were on the floor. Snatching them up protectively, she held them to her shirt front as if she didn't want them to see the mess.

Much as she'd denigrated this cramped and crowded space, for the moment, it was all the home she had. On one level or another she'd been missing it for three days and two nights. Here she had pajamas that didn't leave her fanny out in the breeze, a pillow that had been molded to her head, blankets that didn't smell of cleanser. Her *things*.

Now somebody had messed with her things, tainted them, made them unfamiliar and scary. Still clutching the pictures, she sat down in the desk's plastic chair and fought unsuccessfully not to cry.

"You're just tired," she said to herself to excuse the childish outburst. The storm passed. She didn't make a move to clean up but sat looking at her pictures. The smiling blond man with a badge on his chest leaning on a shovel; Anna had taken it one day when business took her to the nuclear power plant west of Port Gibson. She'd come across Paul digging Mrs. Mack's pickup out of the mud. The cat was photographed asleep over the arm of her great-grandfather's couch in the pose of a lion in the Serengeti draped over a branch waiting for an unwary wildebeest to happen by; a small defiant race memory of being king of the forest.

The snap of Paul unsettled her. He looked a stranger somehow. Scott Wooldrich's warm smile superimposed itself over the sheriff's face as if Scott were real, Paul a figment of her imagination. She put the picture back in the desk drawer and closed it.

Piedmont was still Piedmont. She stared at his likeness and longed for his rattling purr in her ears.

Anna was communing with her absent family in this fashion when Nicky came in.

"Anna! Where've you been? You only had two days off. Did you know that? Tiny'll be shitting bricks. What happened to your foot? Why is your hand bandaged? My God, woman, where have you *been?*"

The frenetic energy Nicky brought with her only served to make Anna realize how tired she was.

"I went camping," she said vaguely.

Seemingly satisfied with the answer, probably because what had happened to her was of far greater interest than what Anna had been up to, Nicky plopped down on her unmade bed and began to chatter.

"Boy did you miss all the excitement. It was totally bizarre. I mean *totally.* Yesterday—no wait, the day before yesterday—Cricket comes back. Something happened to her for sure. I mean it was like she quit breathing, you know, saw the white light and came back from the dead but different. Like in *Flatliners.* She was so weird. She comes in and hardly says 'Hi Nicky' before she's going on about how she thinks you took some of her stuff. I mean she hadn't even *looked* at her stuff, hadn't started packing, nothing, so why she's on about you taking things beats me. So I say, 'Took what?' Not that I thought you'd stolen anything. What would you want with anything Cricket's got? Like you're going to sneak off with a half-used tube of lip gloss or a pair of thong panties. Cricket didn't have money except a jar of tips, which was all there. I know because I borrowed a couple bucks for pizza. Cricket and I do that all the time. Borrow from each other. So it wasn't money she was missing. And her jewelry's all junk. Anyway, where would you wear it? In this fishbowl somebody'd say, 'Hey, aren't those Cricket's earrings?' And there you'd be.

"Anyway, she doesn't tell me what she thinks you took but just starts plowing through your stuff. By now I'm getting a little pissed, back from the dead or not, and I start saying like, 'Is it bigger than a breadbox? Smaller than a postage stamp?' But she is just throwing your stuff out of drawers and crying, 'It's got to be here.' Man, what a trip," she finished.

Nicky wasn't the worse for wear, but Anna was out of breath from listening to her. For a moment she sat, eyes on the mess on her side of the room, trying to get her mind to work. "Did she find it?" she asked finally.

"Nope. Her folks showed up. They packed Cricket and all her stuff in the back of their SUV and she was gone. Bizarre. She didn't even say good-bye to me. All she says is, 'If you see her, tell her I couldn't find it.'"

"Ah." Anna's bed, torn up and littered with what worldly goods she'd brought, began to look impossibly inviting. "Who was 'her'? Me?"

"I guess. Anyway, whatever it was, she didn't find it. What was it?"

"I have no idea," Anna said.

"Oh come on."

"Really."

"Have it your way. If everybody's going to go all double-oh-seven, you might at least let your roommate in on it."

Nicky waited expectantly, but Anna hadn't the energy to protest her innocence at greater length. After a moment the girl harrumphed and slammed off to the bathroom to brush her teeth and Anna was left in peace.

Two thugs had searched the room. Dickie Cauliff had come seeking something. Cricket had looked and couldn't find it. Anna thought again of the water-and-fuel-soaked leather satchel. Were they all after the cash it had contained—presuming it had contained cash? The plane had been inward bound, probably from Mexico or the Baja, fully laden. The load had already been purchased. In a logical world the pilot would have flown out loaded with money, paid for the dope and started back. He would have had only enough to pay personal expenses on the return trip. How much walking-around money did the average drug mule need? Surely not enough to warrant three searches with the inherent risk and exposure that came with them. And the satchel hadn't been large, about the size of a briefcase. Unless stuffed full of high-denomination bills, it wouldn't contain enough money to be of serious interest to the sort of entrepreneur who imported high-grade weed by the planeload.

Anna gave up thinking. Her brain was not in good working order and she had too little information. What she needed she could not get in her persona of waitress to the rich and pampered. Lorraine Knight had been the one carrying out that end of the investigation: tracking the red Ford Excursion, checking the lodging houses for suspicious registrants, background checks, the tox screen on the blood in the syringe—the details where the devil and often the truth were rumored to live.

Johnson was worthless. Tomorrow Anna would call Montana and ask the chief ranger what the hell was going on.

Not being in the mood for another chat with Nicky, she shed her clothes, crawled into the pile on her bed and, the picture of Piedmont under her pillow in hopes of good dreams, turned her face to the wall and slept.

CHAPTER
17

Anna slept soundly, did not dream and woke refreshed. As she showered and dressed, drank her coffee and made desultory conversation with Nicky, what she had done, who she had been, those dark nights on the mountain nagged at her. Surely a decent human being would be wracked with guilt. Scenes of fire and ax should flash before her eyes, sudden terrors burn in her brain. Anna felt nothing. When she recalled the events of the past seventy-two hours it was as if she were remembering a movie or a story about something that had happened to somebody else. When time permitted, she needed to call her sister. Maybe she'd suffered a disassociation due to trauma. At present she scarcely felt there'd been a trauma. Oh, sure, she had knocked a man named Phil in the head with an ax and lit his buddy on fire, but other than that nothing much had transpired.

She should suffer—care—but she couldn't focus on it long enough to work up a good case of angst. She was grateful she wasn't being assaulted by the creeping horrors, but it concerned her all the same. It would be a relief to know she wasn't an amoral monster but merely suffering from a perfectly normal mental disorder. If not, then perhaps that icy visitation, the glacial stillness filling her, then turning to venom, was who she really was; the evil Mark called forth had not arisen from some otherwhere but resided in her.

Was in her now.

Anna didn't want that to be true, though she had to admit it had been handy at the time. It was refreshing to be able to do dastardly deeds on a Sunday and report for work on Monday none the worse for wear.

Seven-thirty and she was banging on Leo Johnson's front door. She wanted to deal with Lorraine Knight, but chain-of-command and simple self-interest persuaded Anna to try Leo first.

Johnson was awake and shaved, and because he was new to this business of drinking and not quite past redemption, looked like hell; his body hadn't adapted to the nightly poisoning. An empty bottle was rolled partway under the lounger in the living room. Anna pitied him, but not much.

"Anna," he said, sounding surprised and not entirely pleased. "What dragged you out of bed so early on a cold morning?"

The morning was freezing, crystal clear and the coldest since Anna had come to Yosemite. Till this morning, constant dreary cloud cover kept the temperatures moderated. The cold bit her ears and made her nose run. Such small inconveniences were nothing to the pleasure she felt in the blue of the sky and the bright white light of the winter sun.

"I need to talk with you," she said.

"Let's go on down to the office. I was just on my way."

"Here would be better." Leo gave her a blank stare that lasted long enough she knew he'd forgotten precisely who she was and what she was up to.

"Right. Right. Lorraine's undercover operation." That was all he said, no aspersions cast, but the tone was intentionally lighthearted and dismissive. The very worst sort of condescension, the kind that can be felt but not proved. The kind that, in the retelling, sounds paranoid on the part of the teller.

Anna ignored it. Leo crossed behind the counter that separated the entry hall and living area from the kitchen, poured her a mug of coffee and shoved it over the Formica in her direction. The very thing to win back her good opinion. "Thanks," she said. "Did I talk with you the other day when I came into the clinic?"

"No." His eyes darted around in a worried fashion. For a moment she wondered what in the hell he was up to. He settled, looked at her. *Evidence,* she realized. He was checking to see if any telltale bottles or other signs of his addiction were in the kitchen area. Finding it clean, he was able to concentrate. "I heard from the nurse practitioner there. Sharon. She said you'd come in a little banged up and had been full of wild stories she'd thought she'd better pass on to me."

"Did she?"

"What?"

"Did she pass them on?"

Leo's face hardened in annoyance, the impervious variety that higher-ups don when their subordinates become insubordinates. "Why don't you tell me what happened?" he suggested.

Marveling at the neat way he'd not only gotten out of answering a question that might pertain to his own competence
but subtly put her in the wrong, Anna pulled up a counter
stool. Admiration for good politics didn't negate her anger,
and as she sat down she took a moment to remember that she
wasn't in Yosemite to correct or improve the deputy superintendent. Due to unforeseen circumstances, Leo Johnson was
all she had at the moment. It behooved her to find a way to
work with him.

She gave a concise report of her trip to Lower Merced
Pass Lake. Speculation, deduction and emotional content she
kept to herself. When she'd finished, she waited in silence for
him to respond.

He sighed. He drummed his fingers. He looked at her.
Looked away. Sipped his coffee. Anna half expected him to
shake his head as Sister Mary Janel had been wont to do
on occasion, saying: "Anna, Anna, Anna, what *am* I to do
with you?"

Sister Janel had never had to deal with her axing one man
and igniting another, but Anna rather wished it were the nun
across the counter rather than the man. Sister Janel never suffered from muddled thinking.

"The nurse—Sharon—said something like that," Leo admitted after a while. "It was over the top. I figured you were
delirious, confused—hypothermia, a knock on the head."

Anna quashed the need to shout: "Then why didn't you
check it out, you lunkhead?" Obviously Leo hadn't wanted
to check it out. He wanted it to be delirium because then he
wouldn't have to take action. Action was risky in any bu-
reaucracy. If things went wrong the blame must be laid at
someone's door. Usually that someone was the last provable
decision maker.

"That's how it happened," she said instead. "I got the idea Phil was killed. Mark, the one who came after me, might be alive. I didn't stick around."

"What a mess," he said more to himself than her. "What a god-awful mess."

"They were staying in Dixon Crofter's tent cabin. You might want to check—"

"I'll see to it," he cut her off.

Anna closed her mouth. A tide was turning and she had the unpleasant sensation it was turning against her.

"Don't leave the park," Leo said. "You'll be wanted for questioning."

He grabbed his coat and preceded her out of his house. Just like that she'd been demoted from investigator to suspect. At least that was the way it felt. From the bullish set of the deputy superintendent's shoulders and the crimped line of his lips, Anna guessed now was not the time to pepper him with questions.

Taking the line of least resistance she said, "Yes, sir," and headed back toward the concession dorms.

By quarter after eight she was in the Ahwahnee's fine lobby armed with her credit card. Getting this particular call reimbursed by the NPS might prove tricky, but if she could get hold of Lorraine it would be worth it. After a few minutes wrangling, she browbeat a harassed-sounding fellow into pulling the chief ranger out of the class she was teaching.

Feeling a bit of a whiner and a bit of a tattletale, Anna told Lorraine of her adventures to date and Johnson's lack of support or assistance.

When she'd finished, Lorraine didn't hesitate. "Look. Stay out of Leo's way. He'll get a couple rangers up the trail and, if your story proves out—which I have no doubt it will—

he'll call in the Navy." Anna was grateful for this; she'd been with the Park Service long enough that she was not accustomed to being blown off when she reported a double homicide. "Yosemite has an understanding with them. They've been very good about lending us support—particularly air support.

"While he carries that end, you get in contact with George Kastner. He's acting chief ranger while I'm gone. He knows everything that's going on. I'd left word for you to be notified, but it must have slipped through the cracks."

The cracks were in Leo Johnson's brain—or his ego—but Lorraine hadn't risen to the position of chief ranger in one of the crown-jewel parks by venting to underlings.

They talked a while longer. Lorraine wanted Anna to give up the undercover business and turn the investigation over to Kastner. Anna argued against it. She appreciated the sentiment—it was clear Lorraine Knight was putting her health and welfare above the need to catch the bad guys. But though Anna's nights in the wilderness had apparently left her without feelings for her fellow men, they had engendered a finely honed desire to get to the bottom of things. In the end she prevailed. After talking with George Kastner, she would face Tiny Bigalo and see if she still had a job. Lorraine promised to put in a call to Dane Trapper, the Ahwanee's general manager, to make sure Tiny would be in a forgiving mood by the time the interview rolled around.

George Kastner was in his mid to late fifties. A barrel-shaped man, he carried his weight in chest and shoulders. Anna guessed he'd been devilishly strong in his youth and could still impress the new rangers when he had to.

Snowy hair topped a face as craggy as any mountain. He'd been born to fit Yosemite. That, or the Sierra had carved him in its likeness.

He ushered Anna into his office as if he'd been expecting her, which it turned out he had.

"Lorraine called and gave me a heads-up," he said as Anna crossed to the traditional visitor's chair by his desk. "First thing she told me to do was to find out how bad hurt you really were and if you'd been sugarcoating it for her.

"So. How are you really?"

Instead of retreating behind his desk he perched on the corner looking down at her, the heel of his shoe knocking softly against the wood. Anna suspected, even in repose, there would be some small part of him that tapped, twitched or fidgeted. Before the years had gentled his energy, he must have filled rooms.

"I'm good," she said. "The ankle hurts, but it's braced. I can walk on it. The burns and frostbite are superficial."

"Good. Good. Let's get on with it then." He circled around his desk and sat down. The office chair with its high back looked as if it had been made for a child. Kastner chose not to be scary, and Anna was grateful. She expected intimidating people could be part of how he got things done. And she didn't doubt he was a man who got things done. Not a visionary, perhaps, or even a creative thinker, but the sort of sergeant-at-arms who keeps the great slothful beasts bureaucracies grow into from drowning in their own fat.

"Okay. Here's where we are. Leo's sent two rangers up the hill. They'll try to find the man who attacked you. Do you think this guy is dead, this Mark?"

Before she could answer, he'd flipped through a stack of Post-it notes stuck in an overlapping fan-shaped pattern near his left elbow. "Mark Bellman. At least Bellman's the name we got from the guy sharing Dix's tent with him. Without a date of birth or driver's license we haven't had much luck tracing him. By the time we got word of your incident on the Illilouette Creek Trail they'd cleared out of the park.

"You think you killed Bellman?"

Anna thought about it a moment, pictured the fire, suddenly voracious, leaping up from his fuel-soaked feet to snatch and lap at his face and hair. She recalled the screams trailing after her in the darkness as she fled. She waited a moment to see if an all-consuming grief or repentance would overwhelm her. Nothing. She shook her head. "I can't say for sure. The man was not a seasoned hiker. He was tired, probably dehydrated, badly injured"—she broke off this thought to tell Kastner about the eye-gouging part of the evening's entertainment. Describing the actual gore, the gush and the dangling, she braced herself for an onslaught of remorse. Nothing.

She resumed where she'd left off answering his original question. "He was bound to be suffering some shock before the burning. With another man I'd be pretty sure the cold had finished him off. With this guy I'm not betting on it. He was one of those cockroach kind of guys, quick, creepy and almost impossible to eradicate."

"Eradicate," Kastner echoed her last word. Before he'd had a chance to change the expression on his face, Anna thought she saw horror there—or revulsion—and wondered if it was of Mark, the incident or her.

"We'll get word back from the rangers soon." He glanced at his watch. "They left shortly after eight o'clock. It's nearly nine-thirty. They should be up the trail to where the incident occurred."

"Will they go all the way to the lake?" Anna asked. "There's no hurry. I'm pretty sure the guy I left up there is dead." As she uttered the words she was taken aback at how heartless they sounded, the ruminations of a sociopath.

Kastner wasn't deaf to nuance.

"Tell me about him." Kastner folded his hands together on the desk and looked at her from beneath bristling white eyebrows, giving the impression of a psychiatrist rather than a law enforcement ranger.

Anna didn't like it. Didn't like that she'd sounded so callous about Phil's being dead, so disappointed that Mark was not; she didn't like it that she felt precisely as callous and disappointed as she'd sounded.

In careful professional language she told him of hitting the man called Phil and of Mark's sinister assertion that Phil wasn't yet dead when he'd left him. Kastner asked her a lot more questions, but they were pertinent to the case rather than her mental stability. After Leo Johnson, Anna was relieved to at last be giving a proper report.

In closing she added her own conclusions: "I think you might want to get a helicopter up to Lower Merced. Even before I left there was buzz around Camp 4 that something was up, big money to be had. If I could figure out which lake this bonanza was at some of the climbers are bound to. If Mark . . . Bellman . . . is still alive back there or got out and his buddies are up the Illilouette, there could be trouble."

"More trouble," Kastner said.

"More trouble."

He took notes. When he'd satisfied himself she'd told him all she could, he sat strumming his fingers and jiggling his knee for a minute or more. Still and quiet in her chair, Anna waited.

Contemplations complete, he said: "Okay. I'll work with what you've given me. Here's what we've got. It's not much, but then we've not had much to work with."

Anna knew he blamed this on her, but since it was the sort of general ambient accusation superiors often threw out, she ignored it.

"We traced the license plate on the red Ford Excursion. I won't drag you through all the hoops, but we weren't able to tie it directly to Mark Bellman or whatever his real name is. The Excursion is owned by a subsidiary of a corporation. The pink slip must have frayed edges, it's filtered down through so many layers of obfuscation."

"So it told you nothing."

"On the contrary. It told us a good deal." Kastner responded with the verbal pouncing of a teacher who has elicited the response he wanted and is itching to make a point out of it. "Casual thugs or penny-ante drug dealers don't have the intelligence or the machinery in place to hide the ownership of a vehicle that completely. Your playmates on the Illilouette were, if not very big fish themselves, then in the employ of very big fish." Suddenly the joy of deduction and intellectual exercise drained out of Kastner's faded hazel eyes. Compassion replaced it. "You're lucky you are alive."

Anna had been more comfortable with intellectual joy. Compassion was an iffy thing. Had he compassion for all human life the look of horror and revulsion could return when he remembered at what costs she had managed this staying-alive business.

"Any results on the tox scan of the blood in the syringe?" she asked to stop Kastner's brotherly love before it could metastasize.

"Yup, as a matter of fact. Leo got that in pretty quickly. Hang on. No DNA of course. What's the point till you've got something to match it to? Besides the budget doesn't factor in the high tech unless its well warranted. Here we go." Kastner smoothed a multipage printout on the desk with the care of a master craftsman hanging wallpaper, then pushed his glasses up on his forehead the better to read the small print. "Nope to cocaine, barbiturates, some hallucinogens, though they don't test for a lot of them. Trace of THC—marijuana." He looked up. "Far as it goes, it doesn't look to be connected—at least materially—to our drug-dealing compatriots, but it was meant to kill you. The blood is not just HIV positive. The virus has matured into AIDS. There is little doubt that, had you injected the stuff, you would have gotten the disease."

A shudder went through Anna's insides, the kind that quakes the viscera and draws the blood from the skin. Dying in a fight, by a bullet to the brain, the crashing of a plane, a knife between the ribs, a Lexus between the shoulder blades—these held little terror for her. It had been a wondrous and glorious while since she'd looked forward to death as the antidote to a loneliness and grief that robbed life of its luster, but she'd lived so many years thinking of death as a friend that even now, when she wished to put off acquaintance with the grim reaper as long as possible, she still did not fear him.

AIDS she feared. Because Zach had been in the theater— or perhaps because they'd lived in New York—or maybe because both she and her husband had delighted in wit and irreverence, they'd known a lot of gays of both genders: the wild and the wonderful, the crazy, the coy. Then the eighties had come and people began to die. The sins of the sexual revolution coming to roost on just the one group while the rest had to watch, whisper, "There but for the grace of God," and live with the ragged holes left in the fabric of their lives.

Fearing hospitals, helplessness, sickness and pity, Anna doubted she could face such a death with any dignity or grace.

"Jesus Christ," she whispered. "Who'd do that to me? Who'd do that to anybody?"

Kastner was looking at her, that nasty debilitating compassion warming his gaze.

"Close call," she said, trying to brush away the heebie-jeebies. "Any fingerprints?"

"None."

"Could you trace the syringe?"

"Too common, and it didn't come from the clinic here. We use a different manufacturer. Lowest bidder of course."

"Of course."

"This doesn't strike me as a drug dealer's response," he said. Anna was pleased he'd once again become a man of business. "Guys who operate on a level where they can hide things in company-owned subsidiaries are usually more to the point. Giving someone AIDS might be a death sentence, but it's not quick-acting enough. If it was meant to shut you up, it wouldn't work. The walking dead have nothing to lose but their souls. Makes them too brave to be threatened much."

Anna said nothing. She was thinking.

"I've got to make some calls," he said. Assuming it was a dismissal, she rose to leave. He waved her back to her seat and reached for the phone.

While he dialed and talked, Anna sifted through her mind, picking out pieces of information. Blood. A used syringe. Her first thought should have been AIDS. Had she been thinking in her capacity as an emergency medical technician she would have. Because her mind was full of the drug connections, she'd overlooked the obvious.

The syringe had been meant to scare a nosey obstructionist waitress into quitting, not to shut up a law enforcement ranger. Scott had seemed—at least for a moment, till he recovered himself—to know something about the needle when she'd first shown it to him.

Scott had met Jim Wither in the penitentiary. Wither had been teaching there so he might be near a good friend of his, a friend who had died of pneumonia. AIDS victims died of opportunistic diseases that invaded their compromised immune systems. Many died of pneumonia. The blood in the syringe had come from an infected person. Jim Wither was an old bachelor, no sign of wives, ex-wives or girlfriends, ex or otherwise. Jim's pal in Soledad was most likely his lover. If that was true, the blood had probably come from the head chef. Scott Wooldrich roomed with Wither. Both men had access to her locker. Jim had been furious with her. Could he have believed she knew of his illness and would tell, thus getting him removed from his dearly loved position as chef?

She pondered that while George Kastner hung up, dialed again and began talking. Why would he use his own blood to kill, infect or frighten her? If he was trying to keep the knowledge of his disease under wraps, sticking a sample of his blood in a place it might be sent in for analysis was insane.

Accepting that Jim would use his own blood against her for whatever reason was mad, the next step in her reasoning had to be that someone else had used Wither's blood, planted it in her jacket, then said something to the chef that would make him behave inhospitably, thus making him the prime suspect, and, after a DNA match, the fall guy.

"Okay," Kastner said, dragging her thoughts back into the room. "The cavalry is on its way. The Navy is sending a helicopter and a SWAT team to help us out. I doubt we'll need anything like that kind of firepower but the Navy boys could use the practice and I love a good show. The helicopter should be here around eleven o'clock. Why don't you plan on going up there with us?"

"Sure." She'd not expected to be included. When high adventure called in the guise of a helicopter ride and a drug raid, the usually peaceful park rangers hated to miss out on it. There was nothing like arriving on scene in a big military aircraft to make one feel like Arnold Schwarzenegger. A lowly import like her could expect to be bumped down.

"Anything on the downed plane?" she asked.

"Nope. It's being looked into. Naturally enough, no flight plan was made and no one called to say it hadn't come in at the estimated time of arrival. Once we get the plane out of the lake we'll have more to go on, but that'll have to wait till spring thaw. We can get a couple divers down but won't be bringing anything up till April at the earliest."

The radio on a narrow table behind the acting chief ranger squawked out his call number. "That'll be my guys," he said, and answered, repeating his call number, then: "Go ahead."

In the terse language of radio protocol one of Kastner's rangers reported they had found the place where Anna left the trail and followed her track fifty or so yards into the trees. There they'd discovered the remains of the burned sleeping bag, the camp stove and the flashlight. A second set of what might be tracks paralleled those Anna had left.

"I forgot," Anna interrupted.

"Stand by," Kastner said into the radio. He nodded to her to finish.

"I forgot to tell you. Before I left their camp up at the lake, I burned their boots. Mark—the one who came after me— had his feet wrapped up in sweaters or whatever."

"You burned their boots," he repeated, blank of face and voice.

"Yes."

"Roger that." Into the mike he repeated the part about the clothbound feet.

"Could be those tracks then," the ranger replied. "They led to the burn but not away. Not unless they came back to the trail. There were a mess of tracks. We couldn't sort them all out."

"No 1144?" Kastner said. "Corpse," he said, for Anna's edification.

"Nobody living or dead. Should Kenny and I go on up to Lower Merced?"

"No," he told her. "Head on out. Stay at the trailhead. Don't let anybody go up it, and stop and detain anyone hiking out.

"Is there anything else you forgot to tell me?" the acting chief asked Anna when his radio conversation was done.

She thought back over her report. "Well, I pretty much burned everything at their camp that I could get my hands on but, other than that, no, I don't think so."

"Did you burn that other man—what did you call him? Phil—before you left?"

"No!" Anna was shocked he would think her capable of such a thing. "He was out cold but breathing when I left."

"Did you maybe accidentally catch the tent on fire where the other man was sleeping? You know, when you were burning everything? A spark get away? An accident?"

Anna looked hard into Kastner's eyes. The compassion was lurking in the depths, but she saw something else too. Fear maybe.

The acting chief ranger was wondering if she was a homicidal pyromaniac who burned unconscious felons and drug dealers curled up snug in their sleeping bags.

Denying one was a lunatic tended to sound insane. Anna didn't know why that was true, but it was. Rather than risk it she simply restated the truth.

"I knocked out Phil with the blunt side of an ax blade. I burned what I could of their gear to keep them from pursuing me."

Kastner said nothing. For a moment he studied her. She sat quietly, dreading that he would see what it was he was looking for. Finally he said: "Lorraine tells me you intend to stay on at the Ahwahnee."

"That's right."

"If your theory about the missing kids is correct, if they got wind of this thing and were killed for claim jumping, it seems to me your work is done."

"There are loose ends."

"Like the bloody syringe."

"Yeah." There were other things too, but she wasn't sure what they were; mostly they were just stirrings in her gut. She didn't elaborate.

"Eleven o'clock, then."

This time he was dismissing her.

Anna decided to put off her crow-eating session with Tiny Bigalo a few more hours. With a bad ankle, Tiny would likely stick her at the receptionist's desk. Because Tiny was angry at her for missing a shift, she might very well put her on for today's lunch rush, and Anna had a helicopter to catch before noon.

At eleven o'clock Anna, Kastner and a half-dozen rangers waited on Crane Flat, a snowy meadow above the valley's rim. A cruel wind cut down from the northeast, stinging the tips of Anna's frostbitten fingers through the quilting of her gloves. Other than that it was ideal flying weather. The sky was the translucent blue of winter. The sun, painfully bright and cold, reflected off a burnished crust of snow. Grasses, usually hidden beneath a thick blanket of white this time of year, pushed through the shabby covering, each blade separate, frosted and glittering like the blades of a new-honed scythe.

Hunched against the cold, back to the wind, Anna shut out the bass chatter of the men and drank in the vast and impossible distances. Light and space, a horizon so far away the eye had to reach; everything she loved about the mountains poured into her. The sightless nights on the Illilouette Creek Trail were just a vague memory of one of Dante's seven levels, read about in high school then forgotten.

The thump of helicopter blades reached them long before the aircraft came into view. When it did, Anna was suitably impressed. They'd sent the heavy artillery.

Yosemite's fire cache provided the rangers and Anna with fire-retardant flight suits, helmets and ear protection. She was accustomed to aircraft of various kinds and always looked forward to flying. From the air she got a true sense of how the land lay, the rivers flowed. From ten thousand feet the world spread out with all the detail and intricacy of a living map.

Mostly she'd flown in small planes—Cessna 182s, Aztec twin engines, Comanches, Piper Cubs—the planes flown by local airport operators who contracted out to the parks to help with drug interdiction, fire fighting or search and rescue. The helicopters she'd had occasion to fly in had also been small and brightly colored, with bulging Plexiglas windows that made her think of dragonflies.

The Navy's Sea Ranger, painted in bright red and white, looked to be the mother of all dragonflies. The pilot never shut down but waved to Kastner, and he, Anna and several other rangers climbed aboard. There was the sudden feeling

of weightlessness, then the machine was airborne and hatch-
eting its way to Lower Merced Pass Lake.

It was offensive how quickly and easily the Sea Ranger
covered the miles that had cost her so dearly three nights before. Under perfect skies, illuminated by a glittering sun of
ice and fire, mirror-bright granite and snow-clad evergreens
unfolded beneath them like a Christmas card. Anna allowed
herself to be transported by the beauty. Instead of engendering
the deep calm she'd come to expect when immersing herself
in the majesty of wild country, the purity below, untouched
by the grisly events she'd been part of, made her feel sordid
by contrast. Little and mean and dirty, as if she'd committed
unspeakable acts in the sanctuary of a church. The feelings
she'd worried about not having—horror, guilt, fear—began
to rise within her.

Not now, she thought, and the last paragraph of *Gone
With the Wind,* a piece she'd memorized for a freshman
drama class, rose complete in her mind . . . *"tomorrow, at
Tara. I can stand it then."*

"Holy smoke, will you look at that!" Kastner's voice in
the earphones snatched her back to the present. Craning to
see out the side window, she looked down. They'd come over
a small shoulder of the mountain, and the lake lay suddenly
beneath.

"Holy smoke," she echoed on a breath. Where she had expected an unpeopled expanse of ice, a busy excavation was
taking place. Ten, maybe fifteen people, in bright-colored
winter parkas, were out on the ice worrying at as many holes.
Equipment lay scattered about: backpacks, shovels, axes,
even a chainsaw.

As one the miners looked up, faces blank and white turned
toward the sun. Arms began to wave, then they scattered like

cockroaches when the light is turned on. Leaving their finds, their packs and their tools, they ran for the woods.

The Sea Ranger hovered. The last man vanished into the trees. The pilot set down gently and switched off the rotors. Doors opened. Rangers poured out. Not wanting her bad ankle to slow the others, Anna went last. Rangers were shouting. Rotors chuffed to a stop. Then nothing. It was as if time had been arrested, there was no forward movement, no tick of the clock, no beat of a heart.

Silence came down like a blessing.

Into this a ranger said: "Should we go after them?"

"No," Kastner replied. "I don't think they are our guys. They're probably just opportunists. Guys looking to make a quick buck off an unexpected windfall. Radio Diane at the trailhead that she might expect company in a few hours. Tell her to get some backup."

They spread out then, Anna going with George Kastner. There was little to be done but photograph the depredations of the miners and the debris left by the crash in hopes of finding something with which to identify it.

That and look for bodies.

Phil was where Anna had left him, slumped over in the ruin she'd made of their camp. His throat was cut and she wondered if it was wrong to feel glad at the sight of the wound. Not glad he was dead—she didn't care one way or another about the man's continuing existence—she was glad it wasn't she who had killed him. At least not directly.

More photos were taken. Phil was put in a body bag, a chore that was never pleasant but was made even more macabre because he'd frozen in position. As they forced the corpse into alignment for packaging, there were the nauseating cracks of bones breaking, joints coming unglued. Phil dispatched, two rangers stayed behind to sift through what remained of the camp site. Anna and the others went in search of the backpack she had stumbled over on her night walk down the creek flowing out of Upper Merced Pass Lake.

With the water as a guide they found it easily. As she'd expected from her original Braille investigation, the pack was filled with fuel-soaked weed. Identification wasn't a problem. "T. Cauliff Spencer" was written on the nylon closure flap with black Magic Marker.

More photographs. Clean-up would be a big job—much bigger than a handful of rangers could hope to accomplish in an afternoon. With the exception of corpses, everything was to be left as they found it. Until the detritus could be cleared away, a guard would be posted at the lake to keep away scavengers of the two-legged variety.

Working in pairs lest some of the human cockroaches remained in the area, they began the search for Trish's body, Dixon's, Caitlin's, Patrick's. The ground in the high country had been frozen for a month or more. Anna doubted her buddies from Camp 4 would have exerted themselves to bury the corpses.

They found Caitlin first. Kastner's radio coughed up the news: "We've got an 1144."

"Why don't they just say 'dead body,'" Anna complained mostly to have an irritation to enjoy rather than the empty feeling searches ending in a body recovery always engendered. "I thought we didn't use ten codes these days." Even knowing the missing persons were dead, until the bodies were found, Anna, like most search and rescue veterans, was unable to extinguish that tiny hope for a miracle.

"I don't know. Maybe movies," Kastner said tersely. "I wish Hollywood would go back to westerns for a few decades. I got rangers wanting to hold their service weapons sideways like TV hoods. Ever try to aim a weapon like that?" He, too, wanted distraction. Anna felt less like a wimp for having company.

The rangers who'd found the body had touched nothing, whether from fear of contaminating the crime scene or because they didn't want to be alone when they did it, Anna wasn't sure. In as remote an area as Lower Merced Pass Lake there would be no special crime scene investigators to call in. The crime scene was short, brutal and contaminated by scavengers.

From beneath the overhang of a boulder the size of a small house trailer, a tangle of curly blond hair trailed through a mess of frozen leaves and duff.

"Caitlin," Anna said though no part of the face showed. "The hair. Hers was bleached and permed."

"Okay," Kastner said. In their brief acquaintance Anna had come to learn that "okay" was the acting chief's launch word, the word he used as an attention-getter before he made his point. This time there was no point and the word stood alone.

The photographs were taken and the rangers began clearing away the forest litter raked over what the rock failed to conceal.

Despite exposure to the black humor of wisecracking TV cops, no one made any grim jokes. Anna might have welcomed one; a little bad taste to distract her from the bad taste in her mouth. Rangers were too politically correct or too sensitive. And they may have known Caitlin. A death close to home has a way of stripping the mind's natural defenses against grief, fear and helplessness.

Though there were three other bodies to be found, three more young people the deaths of whom would shatter families, leave mothers, fathers, sisters and brothers with a wound in their lives that would never completely heal, when the other rangers came, George Kastner gave no immediate orders to continue the search. They stood huddled in a lonely little group, a de facto tribe deriving comfort from their numbers, as the two who'd found the body carefully scraped leaves away, then eased the little corpse from its crevice.

Anna's assumption had been that the girl was killed, then shoved beneath the nearest rock to hide the body. As the hands were dragged free she saw it hadn't been as she'd imagined it. Finger ends were bloodied, nails torn. The back of Caitlin's sky-blue coat was black with blood where two bullets had ripped into her, one probably severing her spine. Judging by the amount of blood spilled, she'd lived a while after she'd been shot.

This patchy information painted a new picture in Anna's head. Caitlin had not been killed and then hidden. Caitlin had run. Her pack would turn up somewhere in the woods, dropped so she could move more quickly. Panicked, she'd tried to hide, crawling beneath the overhang of rock. At some point, possibly when she heard her murderers coming, maybe after she'd been shot, she'd mutilated her hands trying to claw her way to safety through solid granite.

Leaves and duff had been kicked over her and she'd been left to die.

"Damn," Anna said. The violent horrors she had visited upon Mark and Phil suddenly seemed almost benign. A small part of her wished she'd stayed to make certain Mark burned to death.

When Caitlin's remains had been hammered from their curled and clawing shape into one the body bag could accommodate and the plastic zipped closed, George said: "Back to your search patterns. There'll likely be three more. Everybody okay?"

The rangers, including Anna, said yes, but in no case was it true. Anna had worked homicides in her career with the NPS, but she'd never had to work a mass slaughter of young people. As she and Kastner walked away, leaving the original locators to carry Caitlin to the helicopter, her mind choked on a single image. When the body bag had been closed a wisp of Caitlin's permed blond frizz got caught in the zipper. This pathetic and childish fluff of hair was ground between the metal teeth, pulled and tearing. It would tug and pull till it was yanked free of the scalp.

"Wait," she said to Kastner and limped back to where the body was being lifted. At her request they lowered it to the ground. Anna freed the tress and rezipped the bag. Nobody asked what she was doing. No one mocked her.

Finished, she turned back to the acting chief ranger.

"Sorry," she said.

"No problem. You want to wait in the helicopter?"

Anna did. She was cold in body and spirit and her ankle was aching. Like most good law enforcement rangers, she said, "No." It would be a weakness and a betrayal of sorts not to share in this grim duty.

By three o'clock they had located all of the packs and one more body, that of Dixon Crofter. Long limbed and strong, he'd made it almost to the top of the broken granite slabs at the lake's end before a bullet took him in the knee. A blood trail showed where he'd crawled on despite the wound. They found him wedged between two stone blocks, his skull crushed by a rock.

Dixon Crofter was lean, but he was six-foot-three and all muscle. It took four rangers to get him down the slope. Because of the difficulty of the carry-out, they chose not to bag him till they reached the lake, his arms and legs providing a better grip than the slick plastic of his waiting shroud. The pallbearers slipped and stumbled. Once they dropped him, and the corpse rolled down a sloping chunk of granite, the arms they'd broken at the joints to straighten them flopping in sickening angles, making sad cracking sounds as dead flesh flailed at granite.

It was funny. It looked funny. Grotesque. Macabre. *A Weekend at Bernie's* acted out on the gray and black stage of frozen stone. Someone laughed and was immediately hushed by their own sense of shame. Anna was relieved it wasn't her.

Time came for the helicopter and the pilot to go back to base. The corpses took the place of two of Kastner's rangers, who remained behind with food and gear. Till the dope could be cleaned up and hauled out, rangers would stand watch by the lake. From the look of it, the downed plane had vomited between two and five thousand pounds of weed onto the ice before it sank. They would probably never know how much had been packed out.

The park ambulance met them at the helipad to take the bodies and the returning rangers to the valley. As the rear door closed, the sound of subdued yet excited chatter began. The tragedy was being turned into a story. Before much time passed the story would be worked and reworked by subsequent tellings until it became legend. Storytelling was the way humans assimilated tragedy, made of it a thing that, instead of defeating, became strengthening: a cautionary tale, a teaching story, a rallying cry for the troops, a builder of pride and a sense of brotherhood.

Anna knew these things, understood them, yet when she and Kastner were alone in his patrol vehicle headed down the twisting two-lane road into The Ditch, she found herself unable to speak of it. Almost unable to speak at all.

Kastner, too, was quiet. After a quarter of an hour, time Anna spent not thinking but letting the strobe of dark timber and white snow hypnotize her, he said: "This finishes it. It's finished."

Anna let the words trickle gently through her idling mind. She could go home, fly out of Merced tomorrow, be in Jackson by evening. Paul would pick her up at the airport. Taco would probably be with him to cover all exposed parts of her anatomy with saliva in a doggie welcome. Piedmont would be waiting full of complaints about his abandonment. She could sleep in her own bed with her lover and her cat, her faithful dog sprawled on the floor by her side to keep boogeymen from molesting her dreams.

Unaware she did so, she sighed so deeply Kastner asked: "What is it? What's the matter?"

"It's not finished," she said. "Not by a long shot."

CHAPTER

18

Nicky was putting on her makeup, getting ready to work the dinner shift, when Anna arrived back at the dorm. Her ankle was killing her, and all the other bones of her body ached from being manipulated into unfamiliar duties to take the pressure off their cracked sister. Not in the mood for her roommate's high-intensity chatter, Anna slunk unseen from the open door and went down the hall toward the room Mary Bates shared with two other maids.

Not only did Anna need a shot of beauty and innocence to counteract the corpses dancing in her head, she wanted to make sure the girl had come to no harm during her absence.

Mary was in, lounging on her bed in pink sweats, playing Tetris on a handheld Game Boy. When Anna appeared in her doorway she squeaked, dropped the game and leapt up to give her a hug.

Unaccustomed to such affectionate welcomes, Anna was at a loss and patted the girl's back awkwardly. Though embarrassed, she was surprised at the comfort she derived from the girlish hug. For the first time in her life it crossed her mind that her decision not to have children might have been a costly one.

"Oh Anna, I've been so worried," Mary said, leading her back to sit on the bed. Still holding her hand, Mary went on: "When I couldn't find you this morning I got scared."

Given Mary knew who she was and that the gossip of the day's flight and the sad provocative cargo they had brought home would be all over the park within hours, Anna told her that Dixon Crofter had been found.

Mary was quiet for a moment and Anna watched a chunk of the girl's childhood break away and disintegrate. "I figured he was dead, but knowing is different."

"It is."

"I went to his cabin—I thought that might be where you were—you know, trying to find things out," Mary said and Anna got a clutch in her stomach.

"You must not do it anymore." Anna made her voice harsh.

Hurt showed in Mary's sweet blue eyes. Anna wanted to soften her words, but didn't. Should anything happen to this lovely child, the nightmares collected over a lifetime would pale in comparison to those she'd carry to the grave.

"I was careful," Mary said defensively. "And I didn't learn anything. I tried to get Scott to talk, and Jim and even Tiny, but all they'd do is tease. When you look like I do everybody wants to pat you on the head or watch you chase bits of string. It's a pain in the ass."

Anna laughed because it was true. Lest her merriment be considered condescending, she said: "I know what you mean. If I didn't already have a cat and a dog I'd be tempted to take you home and make a pet of you."

Perhaps hearing the genuine affection, Mary didn't take offense.

"I was serious about doing nothing," Anna pressed her point. "This is nearly over—maybe it is over—but if it's not, this is when people get desperate; when they feel cornered. It's the dangerous time. George Kastner's going to see if prints can be lifted from Dix's cabin and whatever was left at the camp those guys had at Lower Merced. Chances are at least one of them has a criminal record. We'll find out who they are."

"That means you're done here," Mary said. Anna was flattered at the disappointment in her tone.

"Pretty much." There were pesky loose ends—more than loose ends. Mark and Phil were not the big fish. Big fish didn't schlep dope on their backs down mountainsides. They didn't put bullets in the backs of people's heads. They ordered it done. These things Anna didn't share with Mary. The last thing she wanted, though it was she who had entangled Mary in the first place, was to have her back in the game.

"I'll hang around a few more days," Anna said. "Just to tidy up. At least I will if I've still got a job. Tiny must have been fit to be tied when I didn't show up for my last shift."

The conversation back on her turf, Mary brightened. "You've still got a job. At least I think you do. If there's a patron saint of waitresses you owe her big-time. A box of candles at least. You got bailed out again. Tiny had some family emergency and was out of the park for a couple days. She only got back today. Far as I know she doesn't even know you went AWOL. Somebody'll let the cat out of the bag eventually, but by then you'll have been back and it'll seem like yesterday's news."

Anna was relieved. After her adventures with Mark and Phil, facing the wrath of one small woman should have been a little thing, but when that woman was Tiny Bigalo, Anna,

like every other waitperson on staff and even the formidable
Jim Wither, quaked in her sensible shoes.

The clock on the bed stand read quarter till four. "I'd better suit up then." Anna rose reluctantly, hoping a long very
hot shower would entice her aching parts into working together long enough to get her through a four-hour stint carrying dishes and taking orders. She'd reached the door before
the exact wording of the reprieve struck her. "Bailed out
again," she repeated. "What was the first time?"

"That night Cricket got sick and you and Nicky flew the
coop. I got called in to help. The wedding party, remember?"

"Yeah. They were late?"

"They never showed. We cleared the plates and came
home, so the fact you'd taken off was no biggy."

"Ah."

S hampooed, showered and wearing a borrowed uniform,
Anna reported for duty at 5:45 P.M. Mentally, she'd
geared up to ignore Jim Wither's unaccountable animosity
and make her excuses to Tiny.

Expected battles have a way of disappointing. The chef,
who had been unable to speak a civil word or even look at her
when last they'd met, greeted her with something close to
kindness. For Wither the nod and "hey" she received was com-
parable to a ticker-tape parade from anyone else.

The cold hatred was not gone, however. Tiny Bigalo had
it. "You're damn lucky I'm not running the show or you'd be
out on your ass," she said as Anna walked in. The threat wasn't
casually given. The woman's eyes narrowed and the words
hissed from a mouth drawn so tight saliva collected in the
corners where her lips met.

"You'll be at reception. Don't expect a cut of the tips. Everybody else here works for a living."

Anna received. She handed out menus. She escorted parties to their tables and tried not to limp. She endured vicious looks from Tiny, apologetic looks from Scott. Apparently he'd forgiven her for her prying ways and was back to his desirable self. Anna was grateful. The dining room had grown cold. The spark of affection in his eyes was the only place she could warm herself. Nobody else spoke to her unless they had to. Tiny's hatred was the emotional equivalent of Agent Orange. The ground it was sprayed over was incapable of supporting the growth of collateral friendships.

Thus isolated in the midst of the many, Anna had time to think. Her social interactions had run the gamut from tedious to disastrous of late, but she found being an outcast restful and refreshing.

The men, the deaths, the incidents on the mountain, had fallen into a pattern she was glad to hand over to the greater machinery of Yosemite Park's law enforcement operation. They, in turn, would hand over parts of it to the Federal Aviation Agency and, because the plane had crossed state and probably national borders carrying thousands of pounds of illegal substances, the Drug Enforcement Agency, and possibly the ATF or the FBI. Eventually they would find out who the men in Dixon's cabin were. From there they'd move up the line to the bigger fish. At least that's the way it was supposed to work.

The National Park Service didn't have the manpower or equipment to pursue crime into the cities, up to the cartels or rings or godfathers. A ranger's jurisdiction, except under special circumstances, ended at park boundaries.

Rangers were sworn to protect the natural and historic resources entrusted to their care and see to the safety of those in the park. It was that safety that concerned Anna. The wreckage of the airplane would be cleaned out of the lake come spring. The bodies of the other two missing kids—Trish and Patrick—would be found and carried out, or eaten, or returned to the soil. The park would heal itself.

The people mightn't have such powers of regeneration. The evil she'd sensed—owned for a time—on the Illilouette Creek Trail was connected in some way to the life of the park. Regardless of how many arrests were made of urban and pastoral drug dealers, if that connection wasn't severed, sickness within the park would fester and grow.

As Anna's aching body went through the prescribed paces of an Ahwahnee hostess, her mind, purposely put in neutral and helped to remain there by the mindless repetition of her tasks, floated free. Ideas came to the surface.

Trish: a dealer who worked at the hotel. She—probably tipped off by Patrick, who'd stumbled across it while working trail crew—knew about the downed drug plane before the thugs squatting in Dixon's cabin had.

A last-minute reservation had been made for a wedding party. Anna and both roommates were called in to work. Cricket and Nicky, busgirls at the bottom of the dining hall's pecking order, were elevated to servers.

Cricket collapsed.

Nicky was assaulted. Their room was searched.

The wedding party canceled.

Anna began asking questions. Jim Wither was inexplicably angry with her. A syringe of infected blood was rigged in her jacket sleeve. Scott Wooldrich seemed to remember, recognize or connect to it in a way he wouldn't talk about. Scott had spent a number of years in prison. He'd met Jim Wither there. Tiny Bigalo had gotten Jim the teaching gig.

Jim's friend died of pneumonia but he didn't quit teaching cons to cook.

Anna spent two nights in the high country: Phil killed, Anna injured, Mark burned and his eye gouged out.

Tiny Bigalo had a family emergency. Anna returned. Tiny Bigalo hated her and Jim Wither was, in his aloof way, positively heartwarming.

For four hours information, memory and images came and went in. By the end of her shift, Anna's ankle was aching in fierce protest and she was more tired than she would ordinarily have been, but the pieces had begun to connect and interconnect. She had the rudiments of a story. Till she tested it out she wouldn't be able to sleep. And, too, late night was a time for lowered defenses and confidences that one might rue the next day. If she was right, there would be little risk to her already battered and assaulted person.

If she was wrong . . .

But she wasn't wrong. That snug solid feeling that comes when the bats are out of the belfry, the marbles are found and answers become sane was upon her. After two nights of literally and figuratively wandering around in the dark, it felt good.

Because lightning quite frequently strikes twice in the same place, Anna inspected her jacket before slipping it on, then clocked out and left the hotel.

The night was as rich and glittering as the previous nights had been blind. The river of sky visible over the valley was thick with stars, and the edge of a three-quarter moon showed above the cliffs to the west. Granite, glazed with ice where the sun had melted snow in the high places and the water had made it nearly to the Merced River before night stopped its run, reflected each small spark from the sky till the cliff faces glowed as if lights of their own burned within.

Deeper cold came with the clearing skies. Anna didn't mind. Breathing in the icy air she cleansed hours of re-breathed air and cooking odors from her lungs.

The pines beyond the parking lot showed black. Boulders amid and beneath them were drowned in shadow. Though the trail ran that way, Anna had had enough of darkness; she walked along the edge of the meadow between the Ahwahnee and the main road.

Grass was gilded silver with moonlight. Crushed places showed where deer made their beds. Two does, out late doing whatever does do on Wednesday nights, trotted across the road fifty yards in front of her.

On the opposite side of the meadow from the hotel was a row of old houses. Each fronted on the meadow, their "street" was a footpath. Built on the flat as they were, it was a wonder they'd not been destroyed by the flood in the late nineties. The homes were small—beyond small, tiny almost, like the shops on Main Street in Disneyland, built to three-quarter scale the better to charm the hearts of children. Once these wee dwellings had been less varied, simple housing built for workers. Over the years the residents, a proud lot, Anna guessed from the loving care the miniature porches and narrow brick walks received, had individualized them: a stained glass window, an ornate garden gate, gingerbread under the eaves. Walking in the quiet with the crystal of the night stilling the valley in a silver embrace, she could almost believe she'd stumbled onto a fairy village, one that would disappear with the morning mists burning off the meadow.

She wished her errand were more benevolent, her heart more pure and her motives less sullied. Turning in at the gate of the seventh house, gray with darker gray trim and careful plantings—bedded now for the winter—to either side of a

brick path, she shook off the milk of nature's kindness and
made ready for human interaction.

These delightful little homes housed the concessions'
elite: managers, chiefs of maintenance. Four-star chefs. The
front yard of Wither's house was no bigger than a badminton
court. Anna stopped beneath the one tree. Lights were on.
The window to the side of the chimney glowed behind a
gauzy curtain. Scott wouldn't be back for another half hour.
Probably Jim waited up.

For longer than she intended, she stood in the storybook
yard, beneath a storybook sky. It wasn't that she was afraid of
knocking on the door; at least not afraid she'd be met by a
shotgun blast or anything so sinister. Jim Wither was dying.
The walking dead posed social problems for the living.
Anna, soaked in the luminescent life of a winter night, wanted
to put off knocking on Death's door a few minutes longer.

Before too much time passed, cold soaked through her
clothes and the ache in her ankle cut through her mind's repose. She stepped onto the miniature porch with its tidy
wreath announcing the Yuletide season and knocked.

Wither opened the door. He had changed from his chef's
whites to striped flannel pajamas and a fine floor-length
fleece bathrobe in bright red. Stripped of his badges of office
he looked small and old and sick.

"Hey, Jim. Sorry to bother you so late but I need to talk
with you."

"Could it wait till morning?"

The question was weary, pleading, unlike the Jim Wither
who terrified waitpersons at the Ahwahnee. Anna wasn't the
only one who wanted to postpone the inevitable for one more
minute, one more day. The talk could wait till morning but
she wanted to get it over with. Having no better argument
than selfishness, she said nothing.

"Come in, then." He turned to walk back into the house, trusting Anna to close the door and follow.

He preceded her into a living room as small and well appointed as the outside of his house intimated. A fire burned low in the grate. Two leather chairs arranged before the hearth were warmed by a reading lamp of old brass and alabaster. A book of psalms lay facedown on the ottoman.

Nothing like disturbing a condemned man at his prayers to get a conversation off on the right foot.

Wither resumed his seat. Uninvited, Anna sat in the other chair. A coal-black cat, fat from four-star leftovers, laboriously leaped into Wither's lap. "Stinker," he said by way of introduction.

Before she could actually begin to like the man, Anna launched into the reason for her late-night visit.

"You're gay," she said without preamble.

"Yes," he said, and: "You're a prying female."

"Yes. Did Scott tell you about the syringe of blood taped in my jacket?"

Wither said nothing. He stroked Stinker. Anna could hear the cat's rumbling purr from where she sat and wished he'd come to her lap instead of Jim's.

"The blood tested positive for AIDS," she said.

Still Jim said nothing. The skin of his face, already drawn tight across the bones, twitched, a spasm around the mouth.

"What do you know about the needle?"

"I didn't put it in your coat."

"But you know who did."

Wither was not indifferent to Anna's words. Though silent, his attention apparently on the cat filling his bony lap, there was nothing relaxed or insolent about him. He almost seemed to be collapsing in on himself, the thick red robe swallowing his gaunt frame.

"I'll tell you what I think," Anna said when it was clear he wasn't going to chime in anytime soon. "I think you had a lover who was arrested for some reason and sent to Soledad. You finagled your way into the prison system as a teacher of the culinary arts because you wanted to be with him during the last months of his life. He had the AIDS virus and eventually succumbed to pneumonia."

Anna was alarmed to see a fat tear leak from the corner of his eye to begin a perilous journey down the cliffs and planes of his face. "He was twenty-seven when he died."

The tears irritated Anna. She'd come prepared for raging, verbal abuse, even self-pity. Wither's obvious grief was unnerving. To counteract these unsettling feelings of compassion, she was unnecessarily harsh. "So the guy kicks the bucket and you take up with Scott Wooldrich and stay on at Soledad."

"You're a stupid bitch," Wither said with a hint of his customary fierceness. "Scott's not gay. Gay men, believe it or not, are capable of having friends they don't fuck."

That was better. Anna felt less sorry for him.

"The night the needle was put in the sleeve of my jacket you were mad at me. Why?"

The fierceness left him as quickly as it had manifest. Without it he looked even smaller, frailer than before. Seeing this crumpled, ailing man, his cat in his lap, his fluffy bathrobe dwarfing him, cowering under her tongue-lashing sickened Anna. She didn't like who she was or what she was doing. The greater good of truth and law seemed far away, irrelevant in the face of breaking a human spirit even further.

Jim kindly rallied and attacked, relieving her of some of her guilt.

"How dare you come flouncing in here and grill me? You're nothing but a damn waitress."

Anna was offended. She never flounced. Still, she was glad to see his customary arrogance. After she had tiptoed around in fear of his wrath for two weeks, it had been disconcerting to see him shrunken, old and pathetic.

"You come in at the top of the food chain even though you're a lousy waitress and start poking around in things that are none of your business. You'll get a thick finger stirring in this pot, I can tell you that."

Anna was stung. "I'm not a lousy waitress," she said before she could remind herself not to engage in peripheral matters.

Jim sniffed. "If the pasta primavera isn't served hot you might as well leave it out for the coyotes."

One little visitor complaint and a girl's reputation was ruined. Anna took a moment to mourn the tarnishing of her new career, then began again.

"There's more going on at the Ahwahnee than food," she said in exasperation. "Talk to me. You're making me crazy here. There are four dead kids and one—maybe two—dead thugs on the mountain. Something is going on in this valley. I think you know about it."

The blast of words scorched over and around him. Anna watched decisions made and unmade and made again on his face. For a moment she believed he would tell her what he knew, then that he would say nothing. Then:

"I was mad because I thought you knew I was sick and were going to noise it about. Cooking is what I do."

"Why did you think I'd do that?"

Silence.

"Somebody told you, didn't they?"

Silence.

"They were setting you up, so when the syringe was found you'd be the number-one fall guy."

Nothing.

"Don't you care, for Chrissake?"

Nothing.

"Who told you I was trying to get you fired?"

Exasperated, Anna decided to try another tack. "Tiny got you the job in the prison. Tell me about that."

For a moment she didn't think he was going to respond to this either, but he pulled himself up from the depths of his bathrobe and began.

"Tiny's brother has some pull in the criminal justice system. Tiny and I had been friends for a long time. She knew about Lonnie. When I started researching ways I might be with him, she got her brother to call in some favors. At least that's what she said. Maybe my proposal would have been accepted anyway. I don't know. At the time I thought she was helping me and I was . . . grateful."

"Tiny knows you have AIDS?"

"She knows."

"Are you afraid she'll tell?"

"It doesn't matter now. I told the general manager—Dane Trapper—tonight."

"Why now?" Anna asked.

In lieu of answering he pulled back the lank dark hair that fell forward over his face. On his temple near the hair line two lesions marred the skin. In the gentle firelight they appeared black and deadly, the harbingers of death.

"Ah," was all she could think to say.

The sound of the front door opening caught their attention. "Hey Jim, you still up?" Scott's voice.

"In here," Jim replied like a drowning man calling for help.

Scott came in, dwarfing the small room. With him came the smell of cold, of pine, cologne and the faint odor of food. When he saw Anna he stopped and the smile of greeting left his face. No other expression replaced it. He looked at her with a countenance so carefully blank she couldn't but wonder what he was hiding.

"A little late for social calls, don't you think?" he said neutrally. Without taking his eyes off of her, he let his jacket slide to the floor and sat on the low hearth, his knees up around his broad shoulders. "To what do we owe this honor?" The boyish smile was back but Anna didn't trust it. She was distracted by the biceps pushing out of the thin sleeves of his black T-shirt, of the broad blunt hands that could snap a small woman's neck in a heartbeat.

"I had some things I wanted to ask Jim about," she said.

"She figured out I've got AIDS," Jim said. "She came to see if I'd put my poisoned blood into a needle to infect her." The way he said "poisoned" carried such a world of hurt and bitterness it made Anna ashamed to have come quizzing him. To dispel it she said:

"Do you know anything about that, Scott?"

Before answering he looked at his roommate. Jim looked back. It was as if each challenged rather than accused the other. "I was there when you found it," Scott said noncommittally.

"You recognized the syringe."

"All of them look alike."

"The blood."

"It crossed my mind it could've been Jim's, but he's got no reason to want to hurt you," Scott said.

"Except you're a lousy waitress," the chef put in.

"I am not," Anna snapped before she thought. Jim smiled. A point for him.

"I know Jim," Scott said. "He would never give anyone the

virus knowingly. He's phobic about it. Won't let me use the same coffeepot as him. I'm surprised he lets me keep my tuna cans next to his in the cupboard."

"Screw you," Jim said.

"Don't you wish you could."

"Everybody else has."

"Don't believe everything you read in the papers," Scott finished and smiled.

There was no rancor between the men and Anna got the idea it was a private joke, that the lines had been said many times. Lines: it was from a play. "*Love Letters,*" Anna said.

"A lover of theater," Jim mocked her. "I knew you couldn't be a real waitress, too many complaints."

This time Anna did not rise to the bait. Needing to regain control, she changed the subject. "He was telling me about Lonnie, the guy in Soledad prison who gave him AIDS."

Jim suddenly took fire. Rising out of his chair he pointed a bony finger at Anna. "Lonnie did not give me AIDS. Goddamn you. Damn you. Get out," he yelled. "Get out of here before I . . . Get her out of here, Scott." He was shaking so bad he fell back, remaining standing only because he supported himself on the back of the chair. Spittle flecked his lips and his eyes had gone wild.

Anna stood and gathered her coat from where she'd dropped it beside the chair. "Sorry." She'd hit a nerve squarely and hard. Now was the time to press the issue. Wishing she knew what the issue was, which nerve she'd triggered, she watched Jim. He was as a flame around a dying wick, all shimmer and heat, no substance.

"Jim," she said. "If—"

"I'll walk you out." Scott took her arm in a firm grip.

"I can find my own way," she said, but didn't try and pull away.

Ignoring the rebuff, Scott went with her to the door, catching up his own coat as he did.

"Want me to walk you back?" he asked as Anna stepped onto the little porch.

"No thanks." Scott lived with Jim. He knew the man had AIDS. Very possibly he helped his old friend and mentor with medications. Scott would have been in a prime position to withdraw blood after giving a shot and keep the syringe for later use. For the first time since she'd met the man, Anna had no desire to be alone with him in the dark.

"Let me walk you. It's late," he insisted.

"No," Anna said, too tired to bother with amenities or kind excuses.

"Be careful."

She left not knowing whether Scott's parting words were a warning, a banality or good wishes.

CHAPTER

19

Again Anna eschewed the darkness of the forest path and walked the less prosaic road edging the meadow. Late on a winter night so close to Christmas the park was stunningly quiet. The stillness was so deep Anna sank into it, sank into herself. Blind with a thousand thoughts, she walked, head down, trusting her feet to find their own way.

Jim's fury at the suggestion Lonnie had given him the virus, Scott's insistence that the chef was careful—overcareful, to the point of obsession—not to spread his disease had rung true. Jim had not been the one to booby-trap her coat sleeve, but there was little doubt that his blood had been used. Both he and Scott had seemed to accept that. That left only Scott, the man who lived with him, helped him with his medications, gave him shots.

Anna took her time with that thought, making sure she wasn't fooling herself because she was attracted to him. Crushes, lust, pheromones—whatever the mechanics that kicked in to ensure the continuation of the species—clouded judgment. Since she had known Scott, she had spent too much time with him in her mind. It was hard to know how many gray cells had been rearranged.

Regardless of how stern she was with herself, the sense of his innocence, at least of trying to kill her, remained strong. Scott as perpetrator of this awful attempt on her life didn't feel right. Scott was a bookkeeper. He looked the part of an enforcer from the neck down, but everything else—personality, smile, attitude—denied he'd lived a life of violence.

The muted roar of coming wind tickled through the layers of external silence and internal noise. Idly, Anna wondered if a storm was brewing. The roar deepened, came closer until it pulled her out of her brown study. Not a storm; the meadow grasses lay as still as a painting, their frost-rimmed tips bent in sleep or seasonal death.

A car engine then. Or a truck. Anna turned and looked back down the road. At first she saw nothing, then movement, metal caught by faint silvery light. A pickup truck with its headlights off was headed toward the hotel. Because the truck was without lights, Anna watched it.

Whoever was driving pressed down the accelerator. The engine whined and wheels sang on the asphalt.

"Holy shit," Anna breathed. Without taking time for further thought, she threw herself into the meadow grass, regained her feet and began to run. Behind her she could hear the truck leaving the roadway, engine loud, frozen earth and grasses crunching beneath the tires.

The winter-dead growth, waist high in summer, pushed down by cold and snow in winter, tangled, caught her ankles, bound round her knees. Anna fell. The bone cracked in the high country cracked again, the sprain twisted. Pain so intense it threatened consciousness screamed up her leg.

Not trusting it to carry her further, she began to roll. Like a log. Like she and Molly had done down grassy slopes as children. Roll till they could scarcely stand, then stagger about laughing.

The truck smashed by, the tires so close Anna could smell the hot rubber, and the sky was lost in racket and bulk. Then it was gone. A red flare of taillights. It began backing toward her at a reckless speed. On hands and feet, Anna loped, a Navajo skin walker changing to a wolf, a crippled animal being hunted. The images flashed. The truck came on.

Suddenly grass went flat, frozen stalks no longer cutting across her face. Warmth struck her, and an earthy, milky smell. Flesh pounded into her shoulder, scrabbling and bleating. She went down. A sharp hoof grazed her cheek.

The deer she'd frightened leaped over her and ran. There came a sickening *thunk* as it collided with the oncoming truck and the sound of glass breaking, then the high horrible cry of an animal in pain.

Fighting the need to go to the deer, Anna crawled across the fragrant bed it had made for itself to burrow into the grass on the far side, working herself as deeply under the cover as she could. For a brief time the only thing she heard was the scuffling crackle of her own passage. When the last of the sky was crosshatched with an impromptu thatch roof, she stopped. In daylight she'd be easily found. At night, by a lazy son-of-a-bitch in a truck, she might get run over accidentally, but she doubted he'd even know it till her body went *thump thump* under his wheels.

The rustle and snap of frozen stalks ceased. The laboring of her heart and lungs continued to deafen her as she strained past this internal cacophony, listening for the scream of an engine. Stephen King's *Christine* came to mind. A psychotic car with a grinning grill and staring headlights. Anna laughed. It crashed in her ears with the force of a sonic boom. Every whisper was a shout, every mote a beam. There was so much adrenaline coursing through her veins, nerves were frayed, each breath a hurricane. The upside was she felt no pain. She half believed she could lift the truck off of her with one mighty shove, should it come to that.

Thudding and wheezing subsided. Pain returned. The super-reality of nature's altered state ebbed. She could see, touch and hear in real time. No hum of an idling engine bent on homicide sullied the night. Anna didn't move. She'd run toward the middle of the meadow. Once she showed herself, there was no cover for a hundred yards in any direction. Her adrenal glands were pumped dry; the chemically induced strength of ten men wouldn't recur to save her.

Time passed. Anna let it, Stephen King's nightmare only one careless move away.

The soft pop of grasses beginning to recover resounded comfortingly in the new quiet. Cold seeped through the seat of her pants and the knit of her gloves.

A thin mewling cry cut into this speckled stillness. Anna stiffened. It went on, long and low and incredibly lonely, a sound to break the heart—or of a heart breaking. She put her fingers in her ears. The cry came through her bones, the roots of her hair.

Finally she could stand it no longer. Gingerly, she poked her head above the protective covering of grass. The truck was gone. From her vantage point, the meadow appeared as perfect and unmarked beneath the silvering light as it had when she'd first walked to Jim Wither's house. It was as if the truck had never been. For an unsettling moment she wondered if the whole thing had been a hallucination, the fevered workings of a mind unstable from trauma and lack of sleep.

The crying was real. All that was good and clean leaking out of the world on a single note.

She stood. Dark cuts where the truck had smashed through the meadow, black gouges where it powered back up onto the road reassured her she was not paranoid; someone really was out to get her.

Following the sound of the pitiful cry, she limped to where the deer had fallen. It was a young doe. Both forelegs were smashed, bent in nauseating angles nature never intended. The animal lay unmoving, trying to limit the pain.

When Anna neared, the doe lifted her head. Faint light glittered like tears in her dark eyes.

"Oh, sweetie," Anna whispered. There was no saving her. Anna could drag herself back to the dorm and call the rangers to come put her down, but in her present shape the trip would not be short.

Perhaps because she was tired, perhaps because the deer had accidentally saved her life, dying in her stead, Anna couldn't bring herself to leave. Ignoring the pain from her reinjured ankle, she lowered herself to the frozen turf and took the doe's head onto her lap. The deer almost seemed to welcome her touch.

Whispering "Shh, shh" and "It's all right" as one would to a suffering child, Anna put her gloved hands over the doe's nose and mouth and held tightly. As her oxygen supply was cut off the deer flinched once but didn't fight. Anna went on holding for several more minutes not wishing to add to the trauma by botching the death.

The dark eye never left Anna's. She watched as that ineffable spark dimmed and went out. Where once there had been a graceful woodland creature, there was only carrion. Anna loosened her grip and sat for a while, her hands on the still-warm corpse of her inadvertent savior. She was crying.

She'd been crying a lot of late. Whether the tears were for the deer, herself or the condition of mankind, she wasn't sure.

It was too cold to mourn for long. Anna had no desire to have her frozen carcass added to the carnage the rangers would have to clean up the following morning. Because this was a national park, not only would the deer's body have to be moved, but the scars left by the truck would be rehabilitated, the meadow made new—or at least to look like new.

Her days of leaping up and trotting off being behind and—gods willing—ahead of her, Anna moved like an old and crippled woman. The ankle brace permitted forward motion, but the bone exacted a high price. Had crawling been less painful, she might have thrown dignity to the winds and gone back to the dorm on all fours. Since it wasn't, she walked. After a fashion. Three or four steps then she'd stop, rest, let the level of pain drop. She'd been injured before but didn't remember pain being so exhausting. Fighting it left her breathless and sweating. Maybe it was age. As she got older she found she had less patience with her own stupidity. It was why she rarely drank, if at all, and scarcely ever got sunburned. The hangover and tender skin hurt no worse than when she was twenty, but the self-recriminations were hell.

Scott had warned her not to walk home alone.

Or threatened her.

Either way she should have paid attention. Instead she'd let herself wander along the road deaf, dumb and blind to the world around her. She'd been had as neatly as a rube on a street full of city pickpockets. And she'd be dead if the deer hadn't startled the driver, busted the taillights, loosened the bumper or whatever. Having worked the Natchez Trace Parkway in Mississippi for coming on two years, Anna knew the damage a deer-car collision could do to the car.

She'd covered half the distance from where she'd gone

into the meadow to the hotel when a set of headlights flashed, a car coming toward the Ahwahnee from Yosemite Village.

Several yards ahead of her a line of trees began. Clenching teeth against the pain, she hurried her steps till she reached the first protective pine. The trunk was two feet or more in diameter and the bark fragrant, smelling slightly of vanilla. Tucking herself behind this bulwark, she watched the vehicle approach. She doubted it would be Christine in her truck persona. For one thing it was a smallish sedan. For another, it had its headlights on. If the driver of the truck had any sense, he'd be out of the park by now, before a phone call to the rangers could trap him in The Ditch.

The car slowed. Anna tensed. It stopped. She could not run and resisted the urge to hide. The national parks were jampacked with good Samaritans. Cell phones had cut down on most actual hands-on assistance from kindly strangers. Dialing 911 from the comfort of one's car and reporting a citizen in need apparently soothed consciences enough their owners no longer felt the need to lend a hand personally. Still, it happened often enough not to be a rarity. Especially to middle-aged limping white ladies with torn and muddied clothes.

Anna braced herself for an assault of either deadly force or gooey sympathy demanding too many explanations.

She got neither.

The car, a late-model Mercury sedan, pulled over to the side of the road. A faint whirring and change of light on the glass indicated the passenger window's descent. Out of the darkness inside came the sharps and flats of Tiny Bigalo's imperious tones.

"You're not fit to work," was the greeting. "You're lame as a duck. First I thought you were drunk, hitching along the way you been. Get in. I'll give you a ride to the dorm.

Tomorrow you resign. I don't give a damn that Dane Trapper's got a hard-on for you."

As knights in shining armor went, Tiny Bigalo was a bit of a disappointment. It occurred to Anna to sniff disdainfully and walk on, but it was too late, she was too cold and her ankle hurt too much.

"You're all heart, Tiny," she said and levered herself awkwardly into the car. Anna hadn't suddenly decided to trust her Napoleonic boss. Tiny was tied into the web that spun out through Yosemite Valley, maybe from the Ahwahnee itself. But Tiny was tiny and older than Anna by a good ten years. The dome light had shown her clad in turtleneck and slacks, her coat thrown in back. Beneath the snug clothes there was no sign of a weapon. Even crippled and brain-dead, Anna figured she could handle the headwaitress. Besides, she wanted to ask her a few questions. A car was the next best thing to a confessional for privacy.

"What're you doing gimping around in the middle of the night?" Tiny demanded as Anna buckled her seat belt. She sounded so much like Mrs. Kay, Anna's dorm-mother in high school, Anna nearly confessed all out of knee-jerk reaction.

"I went calling," she said mildly. "Your old buddy, Jim Wither."

Tiny grunted, the sound of a satisfied piglet. "He must've been thrilled. Jim is such a social butterfly." The car was running, doors closed, engine idling, but Tiny made no move to pull out.

"He was moderately chatty," Anna said. "At least till Scott came home and rescued him."

"Scott." The hatred in Tiny's voice startled Anna. She'd seen Tiny appear charmed by the big blond felon more than once.

"You have something against Scott?" The car still was not

moving, but Anna didn't much mind. She was warm, the weight was off her ankle and Tiny was in a mood to talk. This confluence of serendipitous events might not happen again for a hundred years.

"He's a pain in the patootie," Tiny said. "A handsome pain but still a pain. Beefcake's never been my favorite dish."

Anna didn't know whether Tiny was stating a preference for women or just being spiteful. Since her gender preference had no bearing on the case, Anna didn't pursue it.

"How so?"

"With Scott around, Jim thinks he can do as he damn well pleases."

The car pulled ahead slowly, and despite the fact that Anna had thought she was happy the way things were, she felt a small rush of relief. Tiny wasn't acting true to form. For one thing she'd done a good deed in stopping for a pedestrian in need. And she was talking, being personable almost. Over the years Anna had learned not to trust people when they were acting out of character. It usually meant they were sick or they wanted something.

Tiny didn't look sick.

"Up till he and Scott got all buddy-buddy, Jim and I were real close. He'd told me he'd got AIDS and I helped him with his meds and all. When Lonnie—his lover boy—got it from him he cried on my shoulder for weeks. Jim's got a thing for guilt."

"Jim gave Lonnie the disease?"

"Anal injection," Tiny said maliciously.

Anna scarcely heard her; her mind was working overtime, things falling into place, small things. Had Jim inadvertently killed his lover, his anger at her saying it was the other way around made sense, as did his bone-deep terror of infecting anyone else. It was no wonder he had moved heaven and earth to find a way to spend time with his sweetheart. Love was a great motivator, but it paled in comparison to guilt. Guilt could move mountains one painful shovelful at a time.

They reached the parking lot. Tiny didn't stop to let Anna off in front of the dormitory but continued, circling around looking for a parking place.

"You helped Jim with his meds," Anna said. She should have kept her mouth shut, but she was so tired the guard between thought and speech had gone to sleep.

"Oh hey, Nancy Drew's just figured out who put the bloody syringe in her sleeve."

The change in Tiny's voice as well as the words jolted Anna into hyperawareness. They were just cruising past the last of the parking places. Tiny was not slowing down.

"You can let me out here. I'll walk to the dorm," Anna said.

"I don't think so," Tiny replied and accelerated.

CHAPTER
20

It crossed Anna's mind to jump from the car, but they were already moving at thirty or forty miles per hour. A lot of damage could be done hitting frozen earth at those speeds. Anna was scared, but not that scared. Still, she couldn't afford to wait. If bad guys wanted to move one from point A to point B, odds were B was going to be a whole hell of a lot worse than A.

"Don't do it, Tiny," Anna said and reached for the wheel. Going into the ditch or a tree at forty miles an hour wouldn't be a picnic, but with seat belt and airbags Anna figured she'd survive.

A snaky slithering sound came from the down coat behind the seat. A cold hard circle of iron pressed into Anna's skull. "Don't you do it." A woman's voice.

"Trish." In the split second before Anna uttered the name, two more ragged pieces of information fit themselves together. Cricket's terror at the hospital. Her insistence that Dickie

Cauliff hadn't come to see her though the ID-checking receptionist had a scrawled D. Cauliff in the visitor's register. Not *D.* Cauliff but *T.* Cauliff. Trish had gotten in by flashing an old ID, one still bearing her maiden name. And Cricket had said to Nicky, "If you see her, tell her I couldn't find it." Her. Trish.

"You're not dead." Anna let go of the steering wheel. "What a pity."

"Nope. Alive and intend to stay that way. You've got something of mine."

"You were in your brother's truck," Anna guessed. "You tried to run me down. What then? Search the body?"

"Trish is a fool," Tiny snapped. "She would have got us all killed."

"Yeah, well, I didn't," Trish said. Probably to regain face she tapped Anna hard with the barrel of the gun.

Tiny turned left at the main road, heading away from the village. Anna's mind should have been spinning with plots and plans, schemes to save herself, but it was oddly quiet; not the centered place from whence come the deepest thoughts but the weary blank one feels when, in the midst of going from one room to another, the reason for the trek is momentarily forgotten. Anna's mind locked down in that becalmed state, and for the life of her she couldn't kick it loose.

For the life of her.

Just to do something, to change enough outer variables so that inner gears might start to turn, she talked.

"So you draw off blood while helping Jim with his shots and rig that booby trap in my coat. What was your point? That in ten years I'd be dead and out of your hair?"

"The point was to get you the hell out of my dining room," Tiny said. Because she was so small, she drove like Anna's grandmother—a four-foot-ten fighting Quaker Democrat—

hunched forward clutching the wheel, peering over its top. Anna was pleased to note her brain had thawed sufficiently to dredge up the image but wished it had snagged something more useful.

"Dane Trapper'd put you in and you were nosing around. I pegged you for a company spy from day one," Tiny gloated. "Besides, you're a lousy waitress."

Anna wasn't tempted to defend herself. Over the last couple of hours she'd become resigned to the fact that she didn't have much of a future in the food-services industry.

"Clever you," she said. "What were you afraid I'd sniff out, your little drug-dealing operation?"

Tiny said nothing. Trish gave Anna's skull another rap with the gun barrel. The crack rattled Anna's brain. Several more pieces fell in place: Tiny was childless. Tiny sent money to her beloved nephews. Tiny had left the valley for a family emergency the day Anna had come down from the high country. This was a family business.

"How's Mark?" Anna asked. She needed to keep them engaged. Why, she wasn't sure; as long as they believed she had whatever it was they so desperately needed they would keep her alive. She just felt better talking. Words covered the blank spot in her brain that refused to come up with any heroic measure faster than a speeding bullet. That Trish would pull the trigger, Anna had no doubt. Though she couldn't see the woman's face, she could feel the sick excitement of a thrill-seeker lusting after the ultimate high, the murder of a fellow human being. "Your nephew," Anna said when Tiny didn't take the bait. "Last I saw him he had a bit of a hotfoot."

"You'll wish that's all you got," Tiny hissed.

"You take him to the hospital?" Anna pushed. "What did he do? Hike out?"

"When Mark didn't come out I told those bozos he was with to clear out and went looking."

"There it is," Trish said.

"I know where it is," Tiny snapped. "I'm not blind."

"Unlike Mark," Anna said.

"Shut up." The pistol barrel cracked against her head again, this time hard enough to set her ears ringing.

"How did you know where the plane went down?" Anna asked and flinched, but Trish didn't hit her again.

"Ever hear of cell phones?" Tiny sneered. "My nephew Luther called me before they crashed. When Trish showed up with the dope she'd 'found,' I knew exactly where they'd gone down."

Luther. Anna's paralyzed brain began to creak to life, thoughts coming slowly, laboriously. The name Luther was ringing bells. For a moment she was quiet, listening to this internal clamor. When it died away the memory was there. She'd heard the name from Scott the night they'd gone out, he for bourbon, she for tea. Luther had been his cell mate in Soledad penitentiary. Luther had shared in the joy of cooking, been a recipient of the "treats" Jim smuggled in along with the food for his classes.

Nephew Luther had been dealing dope in prison. Jim Wither served as a mule getting him product. Anna guessed that was the price Jim paid for the privilege of being with Lonnie the last months of his life.

A hefty price tag. Tiny had power over him until the statute of limitations on his crime ran out. No wonder he'd turned a blind eye and asked no questions when she'd taken his blood.

Tiny was not a small-time dealer, she was a franchise. Her brother, who Scott said had connections in the field of corrections, must run a family business, one that had taken the life of one son, Luther, and the eye of the other, Mark.

Tiny turned and drove into a campground at the end of the valley, a lovely spot on the banks of the Merced River away from the bustle of the village. It had been empty since a spring flooding had damaged the campsites and facilities.

Tiny neatly negotiated the car around the sawhorses bearing the "Closed for Rehabilitation" sign and pulled deep into the trees where they wouldn't be seen by a passing patrol ranger. She turned the lights off but left the motor running. It was too cold to sit long without heat and, Anna noted, the car had automatic door locks, the kind that locked without human interference and stayed locked till the ignition was turned off or a magic button pushed. Anna had no idea where the magic button was. Anticipating a future need for this information, her right hand crept to the door and began exploring.

"Hands in your lap," Trish ordered. The gun barrel struck. Momentarily Anna forgot where her hands were.

"Where is it?" Tiny demanded.

At first Anna thought she spoke of the door-lock button.

"I don't know what you're talking about." She was mortified to hear the whine in her voice. She had grown terribly afraid, the kind of fear that smothers thought and unravels courage. In the ice and ink of the high country with a psychotic drug dealer hounding her, there had always been something she could do: a place to run, a face to strike at, a burrow to hide in. In this warm and comfortable sedan, a gun to her head, seat belt safely fastened and no idea in hell what was wanted of her, she was crippled with helplessness.

To stave off that unacceptable sensation, she breathed deeply through her nose and pressed the foot with the bad ankle into the floorboards. Pain dispelled incipient hysteria.

"Before you hit me with that damn gun again and addle what brains I have left, tell me what you're after," she said as reasonably as the situation permitted. "Honest to God, I don't know what you think I've got."

"Bullshit," Tiny said.

"My apron," Trish snapped. "My fucking apron. Where is it?"

The surreal swept away the real and with it Anna's fear. "Your *apron*?" she cried. "This is about your *apron,* for Chrissake?" The absurdity brought her up against her shoulder restraint as she turned in the seat to face Trish. By the dim green light from the dashboard she saw the gun, looking as big as a cannon. A silencer was affixed to the end of the pistol. These women were well connected with the underworld. The shot would never be heard. The gun was probably stolen and certainly unregistered. Anna would be found dead in an abandoned campground and the murder weapon would never be traced.

Fear returned. "Your brother came and got it with the rest of your things," she said.

"That was my spare apron. The other apron. You kept it. Where is it?" Trish punctuated her words with another vicious blow to Anna's temple. Had she not been sitting she would have fallen.

"You hit her too hard," she heard Tiny say as if from a distance. "We need her conscious."

Anna took that as a cue and went limp.

"If you've killed her I'll wring your neck," Tiny fumed. "That stunt with the truck used up your stupid quotient and my patience for one day."

"She's faking." This was said in Anna's left ear. Trish was leaning close. "Watch."

A rustle. A move. A sharp object was jammed in Anna's upper arm and twisted. Anna cried out.

"See?"

"Let's cut the crap, Anna," Tiny said. "Where's the apron? Tell us and we'll let you go."

They wouldn't let her go. During the short drive from the hotel to the deserted campground Tiny had told her secrets. Nobody puts all their secrets in one basket, then lets that basket live. Besides, Anna had gouged and torched a favorite nephew. That was bound to go against her in the final reckoning.

For a long and frightful moment, she couldn't remember where the apron was. Just as she thought she had really and truly lost it, it came back to her. The night she and Scott went to Yosemite Lodge for drinks she'd been wearing it. Scott had noticed. She'd taken it off and thrown it in the backseat of his Mustang along with her day pack. She'd never retrieved it.

"I hid it," Anna said.

"Where?"

"You can't get to it without me." Reflexively, she threw her hand up to protect the side of her face. True to form, Trish struck. This time the barrel rapped across Anna's knuckles. Pain in the small bones of her hand was worse than the pain in her skull, but at least it didn't scramble her brain.

"You tell us," Trish said. "We'll worry about getting it."

"I tell you. You shoot me. What's in that for me?"

Trish whacked and prodded for several more minutes, but Anna held her ground. It wasn't hard. The moment they no longer needed her she was dead. A halfhearted beating was nothing compared to that.

She had no plan, no deep reason for leading them to the apron. She only knew that where she was—point B—was

hopeless. The variables had to change before she could man-
ufacture a chance to better her odds.

Tiny put a stop to Trish's redundant and stupefying brand
of torture. "All right, Miss Smarty-pants, we'll play it your
way one time."

The "Miss Smarty-pants" coming so close on the heels of
being bludgeoned about the head struck Anna as terrifically
funny. She was going to be killed by a Sunday-school teacher.

Hilarity and battering dizzying her, her mind spun through
Tiny's next words.

"We'll go one place. One. You'll give us the apron or we
shoot you where you stand."

The need to laugh evaporated. Anna didn't doubt for a
moment that Tiny spoke the truth.

"Go toward Ahwahnee," she said and was relieved to feel
the car begin to move. During the short drive no one spoke.
Anna's mind turned on the coveted apron. She'd liked it because it was stiffer, had more body than the other one. Something must have been sewn into the back panels. Something
light and supple, like the interfacing used in cloth belts and
collars. Cash was the first thing that came to mind, the cash
from the pilot's satchel she'd found among Trish's things.
But unless the denominations of the bills were greater than
any the U.S. Treasury printed, the apron couldn't hold
enough to tempt a businesswoman such as Tiny Bigalo into
risking kidnapping and murder to get it back.

Besides, Tiny and Trish didn't feel as if they were moti-
vated by greed. Not at the moment anyway. They were
scared. Fear boiled off of them in palpable waves that, when
inhaled, left a bitter taste at the back of Anna's throat.

Therefore the lining of the apron must contain papers
which, if not retrieved, threatened their lives.

These fragmented ideas banged around in her aching head

as they drove through the sleeping valley, the moon casting a perfect light on frosted trees and the glittering shingles of the marvelous old buildings. Blind to the beauty, Anna remained in her own skull.

The pilot's satchel: maps, maybe cash, a change of underwear, a toothbrush. What else would be deemed necessary to the personal health and hygiene of a man flying a plane loaded with weed?

Names and addresses of contacts. The thought illuminated Anna's dark contemplations so suddenly she glimpsed the cartoon lightbulb above her. The apron contained the pilot's little black book with the names of the drug dealers he bought from and/or sold to. Trish must have taken it along with whatever else the satchel contained.

"You tried a bit of blackmail, did you?" Anna asked. "Thinking you could squeeze the big boys for some real money?"

"Trish is a fool," Tiny said. "Where to? Don't mess with me. I'm old and it's past my bedtime and I never liked you anyway."

They'd passed the village. Anna was taking them to the employee housing where Scott's Mustang would be parked. She'd not thought much further than that. No brilliant idea came to her now. "Turn left," she said. "I'll tell you when to stop."

Tiny did and they drove down the quiet lane behind the row of homes facing onto the meadow. Scott's Mustang was parked behind the house he shared with Jim Wither.

"Stop," Anna said as they drew level with it. "Park here."

"Where's the apron?" Trish demanded as if she'd expected to see it hanging on a tree marked with a big red X.

"I'm taking you to it," Anna said irritably and cringed, but the expected blow didn't come. "We get out," she said.

Tiny turned off the ignition and Anna heard a satisfying *thunk* as the automatic locks popped open.

"Me first," Trish said.

For a woman so young Trish Spencer was well versed in controlling prisoners. Fortunately, Tiny didn't take well to orders from underlings. She took off her seat belt, opened the driver door and turned her back on Anna.

Quicker than she would have believed possible given the slings and arrows which had abused her body over an impossibly long day, Anna grabbed the dash with her right hand, the back of her seat with the left, pivoted on her butt, lifted her feet above the console and with all the strength of desperation planted both boots in the small of Tiny's back.

The little woman shot out, smashed into the half-opened car door and fell face first onto the roadway. Anna released her seat belt and scrambled after her, hoping to win free of the car before Trish realized what was going on and made it around from the rear passenger door.

Anna's hands were on the door's kick-plate when whatever it was that hit her hit. A boot. A knee. Not the barrel of the handgun; Anna'd become intimate with the feel of its caress.

Had it been light the world would have grayed out. As it was dark, Anna merely lost her sense of up and down, time and place. The stunning was short-lived. When her knees and elbows banged into the frozen asphalt, "down" was firmly reestablished. A new ache tampered with her tender skull. Trish had a fistful of hair. Jerking Anna's head up, she rammed the silencer into her ear.

"Don't shoot her," Tiny hissed. She'd come to all fours and crouched nearly nose to nose with Anna, two dogs ready to fight. "One sound out of you and I rip your fucking tongue out with my fingernails. Got that?"

Anna nodded. Tiny's fingernails, undoubtedly acrylic, were an inch long and painted the color of old blood. From the faint spill of moonlight through the trees, Anna could just see the woman's face: black and white, all eyes and years. *Nosferatu*. The right side of her face, from cheekbone to jaw, glittered in black stripes where the ice and pavement had scraped away the skin.

Deliberately, Tiny raised one long-nailed hand and raked hard down the side of Anna's face.

"We'll be the Bobbsey Twins," she whispered and Anna wondered if the headwaitress was entirely sane or if she'd delivered one too many turkey quesadillas.

Using the door for assistance, Tiny pulled herself to her feet. "Get her up," she ordered as she retrieved her coat from the backseat and put it on. Anna felt herself being lifted by the hair and was surprised at the younger woman's strength. Trish did it one-armed; the other arm, with the hand holding the gun, never wavered. The cold metal of the silencer's tip pressed and banged into the cartilage of Anna's ear till she could have screamed with the constant invasion of pain and noise.

"Where?" Tiny demanded.

The Mustang was less than ten feet away, the apron probably still behind the front seat where she'd tossed it nearly a week before. Nothing in that ten feet would save her, would even change the world enough so she could save herself. Once they had the apron they would kill her. If Scott had seen it, taken it inside, they'd shoot her because it wasn't there.

"Scott and Jim's," Anna managed. Her throat had gone dry. Talking was difficult. She'd not meant to endanger anyone else. It was against law enforcement ethics and against her personal code of conduct. For a brief flicker of thought she was ashamed at how effortlessly she would sell others out when her life hung in the balance.

"Go." Tiny twitched her head, first at Anna then at Trish. Anna led the way up the concrete walk to the cottage's door, not a back door as she'd have expected from the ginger-breaded porch and tended garden on the meadowside, but a second "front" door complete with doorbell and miniature wooden porch.

Light showed around the edges of the blinds on one of the windows flanking the entrance. Jim and Scott had yet to turn in for the night.

As she weaved up the narrow walk, the last blow to the head having awakened the cumulative effects of the others, Anna wasted brain time with justifications: Tiny wouldn't let Trish kill Jim or Scott—too much history between them, even some affection at one time. And Jim and Scott might not take Anna's part. There was a very real possibility she was trading two problems for four and one of those as strong as nine years working out in Soledad's weight room could make a man.

She hadn't sold out, she told herself. She was just playing for time, fighting for one more roll of the dice in hopes her luck would change. Her life expectancy in Tiny's car had been short, in the deserted campground even shorter. Maybe Wither's living room would present new possibilities. Maybe an armed law enforcement ranger would drop by for a post-midnight snack. Maybe the phone would ring and cause a moment's distraction.

Maybe Santa would come down the chimney two weeks early and bring Anna a nice stocking full of hand grenades.

The toe of her shoe hit a raised paving stone. The shock with its echo of pain in head and ankle woke her from the trance she'd fallen into.

"If she so much as breathes funny, kill her," Tiny ordered.

"Will do." Trish dug the barrel of the gun into the small of Anna's back.

"Stop that, for Chrissake," Anna snapped. What with one thing and another, fear for her life was turning into massive irritation. One more poke and bullets be damned, she was going to punch somebody. An old, old memory flared up; when Molly was in her twenties she'd had a little butterball cat named Sophie. Sophie was the sweetest of God's creatures till she was crossed, then she turned into psycho cat, a buzz saw of teeth and claws animated by the unleashed power of steam-driven hissing. Though she weighed only seven pounds she could leave grown women cowering. Anna knew how Sophie felt.

Brain turned back on and wit sharpened by anger, she set about damage control in the exposure of Scott and Jim, presumably innocent bystanders.

"Scott and Jim are idiots," she said derisively. "They don't know they've got the apron and wouldn't know to do anything but throw it in the washing machine if they did. A faggot and an ex-con; not exactly the cream of the intelligentsia." Anna hadn't much of a feel for what the relationship was between Tiny and Wither or Wooldrich, and none at all as to what Trish thought of the men. She was just spewing toxins in hope of making somebody sick enough to get stupid.

"They're sure going to be surprised to see you, Trish," she went on. "It's almost going to be worth the price of admission to this farce to see their faces. Everybody thinks you're dead, your body frozen into a corpsicle up on Lower Merced Pass Lake. Once word gets out you are alive and well, stalking around pointing guns at cooks, California will become way too hot for you."

Trish stopped. Anna heard the whisk of her sneakered feet on the icy walk cease.

"Tiny," Trish said.

"Stop," Tiny ordered.

Anna did and stayed very still, not wishing to trigger any fingers.

"I'd rather stay dead," Trish said. "What do we do? Shoot the three of them?"

"Now there's a bright idea," Anna answered before Tiny could. "Like the Manson Family. Jesus. There'd be an army of federal agents for a body count like that. Bet you didn't know that. Murder goes to the FBI unless the superintendent says otherwise. Hair, prints, DNA, fiber—the whole Thursday-night lineup. How careful have you been tonight?"

"Bullshit," Trish breathed, but she believed. Anna could tell by the lack of conviction in her obscenity.

"Relax," Tiny ordered.

"Park rangers caught Manson," Anna said. "Nailed him in Death Valley. Who knows, maybe you'll get a cell near one of the gang, maybe Squeaky Fromme."

"Tiny—"

"Shut up."

"Maybe we should—"

"Shut up."

Trish said no more. Anna waited, an unpleasant tingling sensation on the back of her head as if her mind's eye watched the deadly red dot of a laser sight playing across her hair.

"Give me the gun," Tiny said at last. "Soon as we're in, I'll open the shade. You stay by the door and watch. If I holler, you come in."

"What about Scott and Jim?" Trish asked, belatedly showing concern for her partner in crime.

"A faggot and a bean counter. Not a spine between 'em," Tiny answered acidly. "I've been running the two of them for years. I can do it one more night."

One woman, one gun; Anna felt marginally more optimistic. Trish came across as a tad psycho with a cup of sadism thrown in for flavor. Still, Anna wished it had been Trish going in and Tiny waiting. Tiny was a businesswoman and the family business was drug dealing. She'd be almost impossible to rattle or bluff.

Gun concealed in pocket or sleeve, Tiny edged past Anna, walking on the frozen grass so she would not be within lunging distance. As she drew level with Anna, her hand slid up to protect the bloodied cheek. The body as well as the mind remembering from whence bad things flowed.

Noticing this sign of weakness the moment Anna did, Tiny used the offending hand to grab Anna's upper arm in a grip that would have done a snapping turtle proud. Years of schlepping loaded plates had given the woman fingers of titanium. The gun, the barrel of which Anna had become all too familiar with, prodded through the down of her jacket.

"We're a coupla girlfriends come to fetch an apron," Tiny said evenly. Out of the corner of her eye Anna saw Trish slip from moonlight to shadow, her shoes crunching faintly as frozen blades of grass broke beneath them.

"I have no reason to kill these fools. They've been useful and both can cook. You want them gunned down, all you have to do is wink or grimace or even just look at me funny and I'll kill the three of you. My brother will have me out of the country before the bodies are found. Am I making myself clear?"

"Yes ma'am," Anna said.

"Good girl. Now ring the bell and let's get this over with."

The doorbell was from an old door, the kind with a butterfly knob that clattered a metal clapper when turned. Anna gave it a vicious twist. Brassy clanging shimmered and shattered in the frozen air.

"This better be it," Tiny growled. "My patience with you ran out a minute after you broke your second plate."

The knob turned, the door opened, light poured from around Scott's substantial frame.

He's an accountant, Anna reminded herself. Accountants didn't customarily kill people.

"Hey, Anna," he said, and she was relieved to hear both pleasure and concern in his voice. "And Tiny. The honors just keep piling up. Come in. Come in. It's freezing out here."

"Hi, Scott," Tiny said and walked Anna through the doorway. "We won't keep you long. Anna here lost part of her uniform and needed to get it back before her next shift."

The excuse, though true, sounded impossibly lame, but Scott never blinked. Maybe he was used to acceding to absurd demands from the headwaitress.

"Come on into the kitchen," Scott said. "Jim's fixing us a bite to eat and there's coffee on. You look like you could use something hot."

Tiny knew the house. She led Anna down a short hall to a doorway on the left. Beyond it was a surprisingly large kitchen, the size of the old house's living room, and filled with the gleaming accoutrements of a gourmet cook. Jim was standing behind a central island, chopping scallions with practiced ferocity. Five eggs, white and perfect, waited in a bowl at his elbow. Cooking had warmed the kitchen and he'd left off his bathrobe. The gray-striped flannel pajamas hung from his gaunt frame, the flowing fabric accentuating the wasting flesh and pale skin. Anna was surprised she'd never noticed before how sick he was.

Tiny steered till the both of them were standing with their backs to the wall beside the hall doorway. Scott followed them in.

"Have we got enough coffee for a couple of half-frozen strays?" he was asking cheerfully.

Jim stopped chopping to stare at the two of them. Seeing his roommate's shocked countenance, Scott ceased bustling and looked at them as well, the first time he'd seen them in the light.

"My God, what happened to you two?"

What with one thing and another Anna'd not bothered to think about the visuals. Her clothes were streaked and dirty from playing tag with the truck. The murdered doe had left blood and saliva on the front of her jacket and pants. It was pretty much guaranteed her short thick hair was proclaiming its independence. She didn't even want to know what her face looked like. Trish had hit her so many times with the pistol even her hair was sore. The left side of her face was bound to be swollen and discolored.

Tiny'd suffered only one indignity, a swift kick in the pants delivered by Anna as she was getting out of the car, but for a solitary event the fall had done considerable damage. Cheek and temple were raw and bloody. Her trousers were wet. One knee was ripped and beneath the jacket her sweater was dark with water and speckled with gravel.

They looked as if they'd spent the evening brawling. In Anna's case that was true. Unfortunately, she'd been on a losing streak.

By the look on Tiny's face, Anna guessed she'd not given any thought to appearances either. Battered and bloodied as they were, the tale of seeking a mislaid apron was made even more laughable. In less time than it took to draw breath, the untenable nature of their position registered on the headwaitress's face, dissolved, and was replaced by a look as hard and black as obsidian.

The hand clamped on Anna's upper arm loosed. The gun with its silencer came out from under her coat.

"Do as I say and nobody has to get hurt," Tiny said in her dull flat voice. Not one of the three of them thought to laugh at the cliché or at the sight of the little old lady with the great big gun. Just so might Ma Barker have looked when the G-men came.

Anna had once seen a photograph of Ma Barker in a museum or maybe on the History Channel. The headwaitress shared the same small bones and grim expression, the same hard, lifeless eyes, eyes that had seen it all and really didn't give a damn.

"We've just come to get something Anna shouldn't ever have had in the first place. Where's her apron?"

If Anna's earlier protestations hadn't convinced Tiny of the men's ignorance of what was becoming a thick plot, the looks of vacuous incomprehension on their faces should have done the trick.

"How the hell should we know?" Scott demanded. He'd recovered first. The muscles in his neck and shoulders bunched for a fight.

"Don't get lippy with me," Tiny said. Again the Sunday school teacher, but without the taint of heaven.

"They don't know," Anna said. "They don't know they have it."

"Fine," Tiny said. She leveled the gun at Jim's head. "You tell me where it is or I'll add his brains to the omelet."

"It's in Scott's car. We went out a week or so ago. I threw it in the backseat and forgot it. Unless Scott brought it in, it's still there."

"I never saw it," Scott said.

A tense waiting silence as cold as the frosty night outside

settled over the kitchen. Tiny was thinking. Anna wondered if the woman weighed the truth of her words. If they sounded hollow, would a bullet drop Jim?

Tiny believed her. She had just been reworking the criminal version of the fourth-grade story problem, how to get the fox, the hen and the bag of grain across the river in a rowboat built for two without anybody devouring anybody. Tiny couldn't leave, couldn't send Anna or either of the men and couldn't reveal that Trish Spencer was still of this world.

"Open the window," she said finally, addressing Scott.

"It's below freezing out there."

"Open the doggone window." *Doggone. Lippy. Smartypants.* None of these gentle expletives softened the orders they accompanied. Tiny's voice was an edged weapon.

Scott stepped to the window, one of two flanking the door they'd entered through, and banged the sash up about six inches. "That's as far as it goes," he said. "The wood's swollen with the damp."

"That's enough. Now you put your rosy little lips down there and say: 'It's in the backseat.' That's all you say and you say it, not yell it."

Scott did as he was told.

A rustling of feet across the grass let them know Trish had heard.

"Don't look out," Tiny snapped.

Scott dropped the curtain. "What now?" he asked.

"Now we wait. If Anna is telling the truth, we leave. No harm done. You ever mention we were here and Jim goes to jail for a long time. Men who smuggle narcotics into prisons are not dealt with kindly. Especially pathetic old faggots who do it so they can screw a little whore everybody else does for cigarettes and spare change."

Jim, who till this point had rendered himself relatively invisible by remaining immobile with his eyes cast down as if mesmerized by the pattern of scallions on his cutting board, looked up.

"You've no right to talk about Lonnie like that. Lonnie was the best thing that ever happened to me."

"Hah!" Tiny sneered and for the first time Anna saw her taking enjoyment in her work. "Your precious Lonnie killed you. The boy was a walking mattress. He was one of Soledad's 'girls.' Every hairy, tattooed, sweating pig in there had a piece of old Lonnie. You go prancing after him like Julia Child in boxers and think you gave the little virgin choirboy AIDS."

What color there was in Jim's face drained away. For a second Anna thought he was going to faint and readied herself to move should his collapse present her with an opportunity.

Wither managed to keep his feet by pressing his hands flat on the kitchen island. "That's not true," he said when he could speak. "Lonnie loved me."

"Lonnie 'loved' anything that moved. Do you know why Lonnie wrote you from the clink? Not because he wanted to recapture that long-lost love. My nephew, Luther, told him to. They wanted drugs. My lad to peddle, yours to take. God, they must've gotten a laugh out of you simpering around in your apron—"

"That's enough," Scott said.

"Making cow eyes and measuring out salt."

Jim's hands clenched into fists on the countertop. When he raised them, one clutched the heavy chopping knife. Training and experience told Anna not to watch eyes but hands. Jim's, one still holding the knife, disappeared behind the cooking island.

"Not true," he said again. He was shaking now but whether from sickness, shock or rage, Anna couldn't tell.

"Ask Scott," Tiny taunted him. "Ask Scott if Lonnie wasn't a two-bit whore. He was there. Watching you beat yourself up these last years would have been funny if it wasn't so pathetic."

Jim looked at his roommate. A fraction too late, Scott said, "It's not true," but the truth had been in his face.

Jim looked back to his torturer. Now Anna was sure; it was rage.

"Don't do it," Anna said.

"Knife," Tiny barked. "Put it back where I can see it."

Jim's arm came up. He set the knife carefully down by the cutting board. His face never changed. The knife hand, empty now, vanished again behind the counter.

"Hands where I can see them," Tiny ordered.

The hands came up again pressed tightly together, palm to palm in an attitude of prayer. Jim moved from behind the counter, oddly dignified in his rumpled pajamas, fingers steepled like a penitent approaching the altar for absolution.

"You praying for my soul?" Tiny laughed.

"Yes."

Still watching the hands, Anna saw the blood seeping from between Jim's palms to run down his thin wrist.

"Well, cut it out," Tiny said.

Jim kept coming. One more step and he spread his hands as if to take Tiny's injured face in them. His palms were scarlet, blood pulsing from a deep gash on his left palm.

Time, which had slowed for Anna, delineating each moment in the drama, speeded up with a vengeance. Tiny's face froze in horror. Scott began to move.

"No," Tiny screamed.

"Don't do it," Anna yelled.

"Jim," Scott cried.

Pounding came on the window glass.

Jim lunged.

The shushed *whump* of a silenced gun sounded twice, maybe three times. Anna threw herself at Tiny. Jim kept coming. The gun sounded again. Then the three of them were on the floor, Jim still, Tiny thrashing with the strength and violence of a furious bobcat. Anna was indifferent to shrieks and blows; every ounce of her attention was on getting control of the gun. Her body across Tiny's writhing form, she grabbed the scrawny arm in both hands and smashed it down on the tile floor till the fingers let go of the weapon.

Scott was around the island, bending over them. "Trish Spencer," Anna gasped. "Alive. Outside. Get her."

Scott dithered, hating to leave the carnage.

"Go," Anna yelled. She slid the gun away from Tiny and herself. That done, she loosed Tiny's arm and grabbed a fistful of the orange-blond overpermed hair and cracked the smaller woman's head against the floor. Tiny went still.

Crawling because she wasn't sure she could stand, Anna retrieved the gun. Back against the island, pistol in hand, she waited. In moments Tiny regained consciousness. For a heartbeat she was disoriented, and in that heartbeat Anna saw a different woman, not the heartless drug dealer with family connections who ran the Ahwahnee dining room with an iron hand, but a small lonely woman past sixty who'd lost those she loved most in life.

Anna was unmoved.

The momentary innocence of forgetfulness cleared from Tiny Bigalo's brain. Her eyes again became hard and dark as she sat up.

"You won't shoot me," she said to Anna.

"I'm a federal law enforcement officer working undercover. I will shoot you," Anna replied.

Tiny didn't afford her the pleasure of looking surprised or chagrined. "Bitch," Tiny said.

"You're under arrest for the murder of Jim Wither, among other things."

Tiny looked at the chef lying in a pool of his own blood, the slashed hand flung out still reaching even in death. "At least I killed the stupid fuck. He's better off," Tiny said coldly.

"Maybe he returned the favor." On Tiny's raw scraped cheek was a single bloody handprint. Jim had reached her before he'd died.

The rangers came. The body was taken away in the ambulance. Trish and Tiny would spend the night in Yosemite's jail, Jim in the morgue. Sealed neatly in an evidence envelope, the apron went with the rangers. Anna didn't even get the dubious pleasure of ripping the back out to see if she was right, if it contained names and addresses of drug contacts.

Though it was late, well into the still dead hours between midnight and sunrise, she stayed after the rangers, EMTs, murderers, suspects and victims had gone. Having lost his friend and mentor as well as his midnight snack in an unexpected bloodbath, Scott shouldn't be alone. And she was too tired to move. Sitting on the kitchen floor more or less where she'd sat holding the gun on Tiny, she kept the big man company while, armored in latex gloves, he cleaned up Jim's blood. There seemed a sea of it, too much for so wasted a body to contain. Perhaps it was an illusion created by the beastly brightness against the cool gray tiles.

They'd spoken little since the noise and clutter left them, but Anna was sure Scott was glad she was there. "Was Lonnie a whore?" she asked after a long silence.

Scott, on his hands and knees like a scrubwoman, left his

soap and water to sit across from Anna, his back against the
wall. He closed his eyes. Enough time passed that Anna
thought he had dozed off, his body shutting down after too
much horror.

"Yeah," he said finally. "Like Tiny said. All of it."

"Why didn't you tell him?"

Silence grew between them again. Anna hoped Scott
hadn't been offended by the question, but she was too tired to
ask or apologize.

"I thought about it," Scott replied after a while. "A lot. Especially after Lonnie died and Jim tore himself up. It was
Tiny who told him he'd given Lonnie AIDS, and Lonnie
thought it a great joke to play along. The whole thing made
me want to wring somebody's neck. But Jim had such a fantasy going. He'd known Lonnie way back when Lonnie was
just a teenager—and Lonnie was an NBW, a natural beauty
wonder—curly blond hair, big blue eyes . . . and the ethics of
a sewer rat. Jim never saw the rat part. To him Lonnie was a
gift from the gods. I thought the guilt he carried would be
less of a burden to him than the truth."

"Death of a lover instead of death of a dream?"

"Something like that. I knew he'd go ballistic if he found
out Tiny'd been using him the way she had. He smuggled
drugs for her as repayment for helping him be near Lonnie.
If he'd known the whole thing was a setup he'd have spilled
the beans just to get back at her. You know how that would
end, with Jim dying in a cell while Tiny got off. She's too
slippery. I doubt they could have proved the drugs Jim carried originated with her."

"What now?" he asked, opening his eyes. "What's the
whole story? I got some of it when Trish began to spew."

"Spew" was an apt description. After Scott had dragged
her in and the rangers arrived, Trish wouldn't shut up. She'd

put Anna in mind of a hippopotamus relieving itself, the tail windmilling, shit flying in all directions. According to Trish, when Mark and his minions had found her, Dix, Caitlin and Patrick jumping their claim, they'd started shooting. Trish said she'd dumped her pack and managed to get away. The others hadn't been so lucky. The spin she tried to put on it was that she'd sought the apron and the little black book to avenge her fallen comrades and help uphold the law by producing the incriminating list. The story was full of holes, but Anna didn't doubt a good defense attorney could polish it up nicely before trial.

She told Scott of the downed plane, Tiny's nephew Mark's burning, Phil's death, the mining operation—all that she'd seen and much of what she'd pieced together.

"I'm guessing things will move quickly," she said. "With the names that are in the apron, Mark Bigalo, a.k.a. Bellman's name and whatever comes back on the prints from Dix's cabin, it should be fairly easy to find at least some of these guys. Some will roll on others. The plane might answer a few questions, but it won't be recovered till the lake thaws. What a mess that's going to be."

They sat a while longer, Anna's rear end growing numb from the hard flooring. Her eyes closed. She drifted. Into that halfway house between the real and the dreaming, Scott's voice penetrated.

"Hey," he said. A deliciously warm hand cradled Anna's cheek. Had she been the size of Thumbelina, she would have curled up in its palm and slept for a week.

She opened her eyes to find Scott's face close to her own. He smelled faintly of talc, an innocent and reassuring smell. He smiled, tired and kind. The warmth and strength and sheer maleness of him wrapped around her.

"I want to sleep with you" he said. "No strings, just comfort. It's been one hell of a day."

It had. Scott was young and strong and handsome. And so very alive.

Anna needed an infusion of life. With an effortlessness that took her breath away he lifted her in his arms and stood. Anna was a small woman. Men had lifted her, carried her before, but its charm never palled. A part of the body or soul remembered childhood when, in her father's arms, she was safe and loved. No harm could come to her. The vicissitudes of the world would break harmlessly against the rock of his hard-muscled arms.

Memories of another life beat against the windowpanes of her mind, gray flutterings of fragile wings against darkened glass. She turned her face to the fragrant hollow of Scott's shoulder and shut them out. The warmth of his lips on her forehead put them to sleep.

Scott laid her gently on his bed and pulled away. The spread smelled of sunlight and cologne. Anna let the softness and perfume blanket her mind. Scott switched on a lamp shaded with rose-colored glass, then pulled off his shirt.

Unmoving but not unmoved, Anna watched the dark fabric slide up his back.

"Well, hey!" Scott said, injecting a dose of the mundane into Anna's shush of sensation. "What with the mayhem and all, I forgot. I haven't worn this shirt in a while." From the breast pocket he produced a square of pink paper, the kind offices keep for recording phone messages. "This came for you a few days back. I figured I'd better take it up and keep it for you. You were in such bad odor with everybody in the dining hall, I could see it 'accidentally' ending up in the trash. It came from registration." He handed her the note.

Anna didn't want to read it. The loose ends were tied. It would be old news. She rolled onto one elbow and reached to set it on the nightstand.

"It must be one of your drug buddies. It's from a 'Tico.' No honest man calls himself Tico."

Trousers still on, Scott sat on the bed next to her. "Let me know if I hurt you," he said and began loosening the Velcro on her ankle brace.

Anna didn't know any Tico. Her so-called drug buddies were either burned, dead or under arrest. The note became more interesting. Tilting it toward the rosy light, she unfolded it.

"Piedmont got lonely. We brought him home with us. Love, Taco."

The windows of her mind flew open. Life, her life, real life, rushed in.

"Wait."

"Did I hurt you?"

Anna didn't answer. She was looking at the date on the message. The call had come the night she'd spent in the high country, the night death had beckoned with the promise of golden shores and diamond waters. It was then, she'd seen it then: seen Paul lift the big orange tiger cat to his shoulder and carry him from her house in Rocky Springs.

Her heart remembered who she was.

The pretense and lies begun at the Ahwahnee and cemented in place by the horror in the high country broke and fell away. Her mind cleared. Into it came the warmth of a home and hearth waiting for her in Port Gibson, Mississippi; a man who was more than just comfort for a night, a man who, with luck and grace, would be comfort for a lifetime.

She laughed. It caught in her throat and became a sob. So

close, she had come so close to losing one of the few chances at purity remaining to hands so recently bloodied.

"What is it?" Scott asked.

Anna looked at him. Saw him. A nice guy. Not a hero or a soul mate or even a roll in the hay, but a good man deserving better than a woman's passing insanity. He deserved love.

And so did she.

"What's wrong?" he pressed.

"Nothing. Nothing a little fried okra and a visit with my priest won't fix." She punched him gently in the shoulder and laughed, without tears this time.

"Take me home," she said. "And count your blessings."

NOW AVAILABLE IN HARDCOVER

HARD TRUTH

Nevada Barr

PUTNAM

The *New York Times* bestseller
FLASHBACK
by
Nevada Barr

Fleeing personal problems, Park Ranger
Anna Pigeon takes a temporary assignment in
Dry Tortugas National Park, a grouping of tiny
islands seventy miles off Key West—where
threats from the distant past collide with
dangers in the here and now.

"TAUT AND TENSE...A SLAM-BANG DENOUMENT...
ONE OF BARR'S FINEST."
—*MILWAUKEE JOURNAL-SENTINEL*

"A TRULY THRILLING CLIMAX."
—*DENVER POST*

0-425-17895-1

Available wherever books are sold or at
www.penguin.com

From the *New York Times* bestselling author

NEVADA BARR

"Park Ranger Anna Pigeon is back."
—*Rocky Mountain News*

HUNTING
SEASON

An Anna Pigeon mystery

"An engrossing and deftly written thriller."
—*San Diego Union-Tribune*

"Genuinely thrilling."
—*Los Angeles Times*

0-425-18878-7

Available wherever books are sold or at
www.penguin.com